A
Shroud
in the
Family

Lionel G. García

Arte Publico Press
Houston
1987

The publication of this volume is made possible through grants from the Texas Commission on the Arts and the National Endowment for the Arts, a federal agency.

Arte Público Press
University of Houston
Houston, Texas 77004

ISBN 0-934770-71-9
LC 87-070271

This work is dedicated to the beautiful memory of all my ancestral family, with special appreciation to my children, Rose, Carlos and Paul, whom I love very much.

May their honeysuckle never bloom in December. May their locusts emerge singing beautiful songs heard throughout the countryside.

A SHROUD IN THE FAMILY

Lionel G. García

BOOK ONE

CHAPTER 1

Don Andres Garcia died on the last night of the year that he was supposed to, when his father, Captain Agustin Garcia, had predicted that the locust would emerge but would not sing and in the year when the honeysuckle would bloom in December.

"No one will take me until that happens," Don Andres said confidently, giving out his youthful laugh as he drank with his friends at the creek.

"Then the two events must coincide, Don Andres?" Amandito, the fat one, had inquired many years ago as they worked at the creek.

Don Andres had stopped digging on the creek bed, had rested his head on the shovel handle, and had rubbed his chin in contemplation of the obscure odds that the two events would coincide. "That's true, Amandito," he said, smiling at the improbability of his death.

But coincide they did. He died in 1940 at the age of 105 on the last day that it was possible to fulfill his father's prediction, the 31st of December, a hot day in San Diego, Texas, when the small locusts prematurely came out of their transparent hibernating shells, their legs still immature and soft, and the locusts were not able to sing. Several days before, the honeysuckle that he had planted and watered faithfully bloomed in the oppressive heat of the early morning of that December. The disoriented bees had come to feast on its nectar, but by the time the word was passed to the lazy wintering hive, the errant blossoms had fallen to the ground.

He was to find out later that the two improbable events were finally taking place in the same year. But first he had wondered to himself, as he lay in bed, about the many bees stinging at his morning window.

Our Aunt Victoria had been outside the morning of the unexpected blossoms, counting the chickens and watering down the yard, when she noticed the profusion of bees and the sickening sweet smell of the honeysuckle. She had dropped the water hose and grasped her head and squeezed it gently to avoid the throbbing in her head that the smell was beginning to cause. She ran to the front of the house and noticed that the honeysuckle had bloomed in error and that the embarrassed blossoms had fallen off almost immediately. The confused bees swarmed around her hair as she wondered if this was the day that her father was to die. So far today the locust had not emerged. She held her breath, mildly hoping that if they did leave their empty shells in this oppressive heat, that she would hear the noise of their spindly legs.

She had come to our house to inform our mother of what she had found.

"Clementina, this might be the day," she told our mother, removing her bonnet as several bees trapped in her hair flitted away and out through the window seeking the unfullfilled pleasure of the nectar.

"What does he say, Victoria?" our mother asked.

"Clementina, he doesn't know."

"Will you tell him?"

"No," she answered and then thought for a few moments about her predicament. "It would be very cruel for him to know. After all, today is the twenty-sixth and we still have several days for the locust to sing . . . If he is to die, let him die in peace. And you know what he would do if he knew . . . he would drive everyone crazy. Let him die in peace. He has been in agony for such a long time."

"Agony?" our mother asked. "Victoria, he's not in agony. Not the way he acts."

Victoria scratched her head at the spot where a bee was resting. She said, "He is in agony, Clementina. He may not show it, but he is in agony. I know Andres Garcia and he is in agony. I've lived with him for so long that no one knows what is in that man's heart except my God and me."

"Then he is ten times stronger than anyone else in the family," our mother said.

"Sure he is," Victoria responded. "Small but feisty, like the rooster. Doesn't he say that he pulled the plow when one of the mules broke her leg?"

Mother gave Victoria an unbelieving stare and said, "If that is to be believed."

"Clementina," Victoria scolded her, "my brothers, his sons, swear by the story."

"Be careful with the bee in your hair," mother said, shooing the lone bee away from Victoria's head.

Victoria, by this time had walked to the window and had put her head out to allow any more bees to escape toward the smell of the fallen nectar in the next yard. "Clementina, do I have anymore bees?" she asked with her head still outside.

"Get one of the children to check you out, Victoria," mother replied. "My eyesight is getting worse . . . . Concepcion," she said, "check your Aunt Victoria's head for bees."

Connie ran over and inspected Victoria's head intently, rummaging through the long strands of grey hair. "There are none, Mama," she said and Victoria pulled her head back into the kitchen and replaced the bonnet.

"Anyway," Victoria told us, "all of us are in for trouble if he finds out about the honeysuckle. You know he's been bothering the town for a long time with his diatribe. It will get worse. Mayor Lothario might make good on his threat to silence him."

Mother looked worriedly at Victoria. "How can he do that?"

"Silly, by keeping him at home," Victoria explained. "Lothario told me so. You know how much Lothario and Don Andres hate each other. Lothario can sign a decree."

"Decree or no decree, heaven help us if he finds out about the honeysuckle," Mother said.

"Heaven and hell help us, you mean," Victoria said. "We'll need the Devil's help also."

Mother sat down and studied her dusty shoes. "I hate to think what he'll do. Heaven help us. I hate to wonder what unnatural things will come about before his death. You know that his death will not be a natural event. It is predicted that people will do strange things. The earth will move, and the wind will howl."

"That is what has been said, Clementina. I would try to keep the children away from him as much as possible. God only knows what is going to happen."

"Things that no one has ever seen before will occur. You just mark my words," Clementina said and she reached into her apron and brought out her worn rosary and crossed herself many times with the crucifix.

Victoria looked all around and adjusted her bonnet as if to leave. She said, "Except for one thing that will always remain true."

"And what is that, Victoria?" Clementina asked her.

Victoria explained, "The spider will never pee."

"That's so true," Clementina agreed. "And," our mother added another proverb, "that is why God did not give wings to the cow."

"Can you imagine the droppings that would fall on our head?" Victoria asked seriously.

Mother shook her head at the thought, as we laughed. She collected her thoughts and asked, "Clementina, what did the doctor say this morning?"

"He said that father's doing fine . . . . What else can he say? There's nothing he can do about agony of the heart . . . that agony that comes when no one takes you seriously anymore. And you know the doctor, he's thinking of other things . . . about all his women and the score of illegitimate children."

Our mother blushed. "Don Andres shouldn't take things so hard. Like I told him the other day. I said, 'Don Andres, you're lucky to have lived such a full life. Forget about this so-called agony.' "

"And what did he say?" Victoria inquired. "Did he say he would behave himself?"

"Oh no. He'd never do that. You know him. If he ever behaved himself, I would surely think that he was going to die."

Victoria looked out through the door at her chickens, the old red and black rooster trying to mate a younger bird. "He's going to die, Clementina," she said. "I can feel it."

"*Ave Maria Purisima*," Clementina prayed as she kissed her crucifix. "If you are right, we are going to see things that have never before been seen in San Diego, Texas."

"He came in very late last night and he is still in bed," Victoria continued, shaking her head, "but I don't expect him to stay there for long. You know what his trouble is? He wants to do all the things he used to do. He's hard headed."

"I know," our mother agreed, "he's a Garcia, like a mule that does not want to be bridled. What can one do? I pray to God."

Victoria shrugged with her disappointment. "You pray to God . . . and you're not even related by blood. How do you think I feel? How do you think your husband, his grandson, feels? Andres is impossible."

"Now that we have him in bed, we ought to keep him there," our mother said.

Victoria laughed mildly. "I don't know if we can," she whispered. "Oh, how much better if we could. If we could get Mayor Lothario to scare him."

Our mother shook her head and said, "Andres Garcia is not scared of the devil himself, much less the puny mayor."

"I don't think he's puny," Victoria replied, defending somewhat her secret lover. "I think that he's handsome and domineering. Lothario has come a long way from the shy youth he was when he tried to court me."

"Shy? Tried to court you?" Mother asked. "You call that a try? He practically stole you away from Don Andres. Almost forced you to marry him. If Don Andres had not taken the strap and publicly flogged him, he would never have stopped his advances."

Victoria tied her bonnet around her chin and said, "To my father, no one was ever good enough for me. That's what he thought. He overwhelmed Lothario."

Mother made a small grunting noise and said, "He overwhelmed everyone else."

Victoria looked wistfuly at her past and said, "That's true."

"Well, you can't blame your father, Victoria. He always wanted the best for you . . . what every parent wants. You remember that in those days

Lothario was very poor. He only had one change of clothes, one pair of shoes. Your father would have never allowed him to court you."

Victoria lowered her head and said, a mildness in her voice, "I don't think it would have made any difference. Andres is so possessive. He never wants to give anything up. Look at the little grocery store. How long has it been since he closed it? How many people have asked Don Andres if they can open it and work it? But he won't let anyone have it, Clementina. What's his is his and he will never part with it."

Clementina, noticing the forlorn look on Victoria, ushered her toward the door. "Everything we're saying is water under the bridge, Victoria. Don Andres, the store, another love that could have been but never was . . . But if you notice, Don Andres has a part in all of that."

"That's what I'm saying," Victoria told her. "And we won't be able to handle him if he ever finds out that he's going to die. If only the mayor would scare him a little."

"You may be right about that and about Lothario. Now that he's the mayor, he carries a big stick."

"It's worth a try. At least," Victoria replied.

"What can we do?" mother asked in desperation.

Victoria was standing by the door, reluctant to leave, afraid that she might not find her father in the house. "We must do something. He's dying. He's in agony over not being understood."

"He's spoiled," Clementina told her. "He doesn't know what being in real agony is. Wait until he's dying. Then he'll be in agony."

"He says that he cannot live any more among what he calls diverging people . . . ignorance is what he's talking about. And yet he does not want to die. I know him and he will move heaven and hell before he dies."

"He's the talk of the town . . . running about in his old age, telling everyone that will listen about his father's escapades." Our mother wiped her face with her apron. "He's an embarrassment. That's what he is."

"Well," Aunt Victoria replied, "the reason is that he's become so insistent with everyone he meets. I sense that it has become a matter of life or death with him and that scares the people that don't know him. He is so desperate. And furthermore, he is telling the truth, Clementina."

Mother laughed. "Like the story of pulling the plow after the mule broke her leg? Did you know that yesterday he accosted the old widow that lives by the creek?"

Victoria sighed at the recycling of old news. "Yes. Her daughter came to complain about him when you were gone."

Our mother shook her head and looked at us innocently. "I don't know. I just don't know what to say or what to do. You, Victoria, are the one that

13

is stronger when it comes to situations like these."

"I'm not going to do anything yet, Clementina," Victoria responded. "I think that's the best plan."

"Victoria, what if he finds out what's happening?"

"That is when I have to make up my mind," Victoria replied. "He went to bed on his own late last night and he has not gotten up. God only knows what he was up to. I prayed to God last night that he would get ill, very ill, so that he might stay in bed."

"*Ave Maria Purisima!*" our mother shouted, imploring the Virgin Mary to intercede before God struck with his punishment. "If God hears you, he will surely take you at your word."

Victoria looked at her calmly and said, "Well, let's hope God was asleep and he didn't hear me."

"Don't make light of God and his powers, Victoria . . . . But you say that Andres was still in bed when you came over?" our Mother asked, bewildered. "Isn't that unusual for him?"

"Yes," Victoria replied. "It is very unusual. As if God had decreed it."

Mother slapped her hand to her mouth to stifle a gasp. "As if," she stumbled in her words, "as if God had heard you and has placed an illness in his body. God does those things, you know."

"I'm more inclined to believe that he is feeling bad over his agony or some premonition. You know how he is about premonitions," Victoria added.

"Yes . . . as if he knows," Mother said. "As if he knows that this might be the year of his death."

We had seen the doctor arrive early in the morning, getting out and then taking a long time to admire his new red car. We knew that he had spent the night at his mistress' house, the house that he had bought for her, because he was wearing his favorite blue suit and the very white shirt that his mistress had painstakingly bleached and ironed. The taps on his shoes that the shoemaker had ordered especially for him made a clicking metallic sound as he walked up the sidewalk leading to the house. He carried his small doctor's bag, swinging it wildly as he whistled in the happiness of his new-found affair. He was small and feminine, with small hands and a thin moustache that he had grown only the year before, the year that he had left his second mistress for the new one, the one that took pains to bleach and iron better than his wife. He looked at us as we played in the front yard. He smiled apologetically and we laughed at him because we had known him without his moustache.

Then Willie was crowing like a rooster and prancing about the dirt, intimidating Louie. Louie was running around Becky and Connie. Frankie was tired for the day already and was sitting under the hackberrys and the saltcedars, spitting between his legs. I was trying to keep Willie from catching Louie.

When the doctor walked into the house, our Aunt Victoria came out and ran us off for making too much noise. At that early hour she had not noticed that the honeysuckle had bloomed and neither had we and neither had the bees.

"Get . . . Get . . . Get out of here," she demanded. "You're making too much noise. The doctor needs quiet."

And now the doctor had left, hurrying on his way as he escaped the onslaught of bees at the front of the house. He had seen the honeysuckle for the first time, but he did not want to return to tell Victoria. He saw no reason to alarm the family. "We still have the locusts to go," he said to himself.

And now Victoria had discovered the honeysuckle blossoms on the ground and had come to tell us. "You children might as well know that this might be his last day on this earth," Victoria said, cocking a gray parrot-like eye toward us for effect. She was still at the door.

Rebecca let out a scared moan and our mother hit her on the head with her knuckle. "Don't be disrespectful," she cautioned her.

"But I'm afraid of dead people," Rebecca cried.

"He's not dead yet," Victoria said. "He's only half way there."

"Victoria," Mother said, wiping the perspiration from her hands on her apron, "I was just thinking. Do you think that it would be a good idea for the children to go and clean up the honeysuckle blossoms from the ground before Andres sees them?"

Victoria looked at us in an inspecting sort of way, making sure we were up to the task, and she said, "It would be good. Give them the broom and some paper sacks. Let's hope we can clean up the mess before Andres sees it. In the meantime, Clementina, you have to come with me. I have a feeling I may need your help."

And with that, Victoria and our mother left, but only after giving us the broom and the paper sacks for the cleaning up that we were supposed to do. On our way next door we began to play as the chickens would play, with Willie always being the large red and black rooster that ran off Louie and Louie the little white rooster that wanted to stay with Rebecca and Concepcion. Frankie went under his saltcedar and I was made to try to keep Willie from catching Louie as Concepcion and Rebecca cackled and screamed. Once in a while Louie would squat down and squawk, acting as if he was trying to lay an imaginary egg.

As we fought the irritated bees for each blossom, our mother burst out through the front door running. Our Aunt Victoria was right behind her shouting angrily about her father. "Stop!," our mother screamed at us. "It's no use cleaning up. He's seen the blossoms and he's gone!"

"The fool is gone!" Victoria shouted as she ran down the street towards town.

CHAPTER 2

Victoria threw the front door to the small City Hall open and stumbled through the debris of boxes and Spanish moss on the floor. Angelina, the city clerk, looked at her through her half-glasses as she kneeled among the debris, packing the town's Christmas decorations, the decorations that the priest had started and the mayor had continued, the ones that they were so ignorantly proud of, the old Spanish moss that the city workers threw over the street lamps and electric wires that crossed the streets, that gave the town the unmistakable impression of having been recently submerged under water.

"The mayor is not in," Angelina informed Victoria, showing her jealousy by trying to rip a piece of moss from under Victoria's foot. "And I don't know when he'll be in." She kept on with the unpleasantly demeaning task of trying to fit the moss into the boxes. "He tells me to do this. He tells me to do that. As if I was two or three persons," she said to herself. "You would think, Victoria, that he would allow us to leave the decorations up for at least a few days after Christmas."

"His arrogance is unforgivable, Angelina" Victoria exaggerated, trying to make Angelina uncomfortable. "You know that and I know that and the whole town knows that."

"Well, he's not that bad, Victoria. I'm faithful to him, you know that. But I've been faithful to every mayor we've ever had. . . even Father Procopio had to resign because your father said there was some conflict with church and municipal law. But you think . . . but who would run against him?"

"No one, Angelina. No one else wants the job."

"That's true," Angelina reflected. "It takes someone ignorant like him to think that the job is of any significance. Only he would think of taking the election by fraud."

Victoria leaned against the desk. "That's how ignorant he is."

"He enjoys it. He feels important."

"And coming from a poor family he needs that."

Angelina approached Victoria on her knees and when she could almost touch her waist she whispered, "If only you would have married him, Victoria. He wouldn't be the way he is. He was ruined when you turned down his proposal. Every advance he made was greeted by a retreat on your part. Every sign of love was answered with a show of disdain. Why didn't you both legitimize your love. Why, Victoria?"

Victoria eased back away from Angelina, as if she would not tolerate Angelina being so close. "I never liked him," she lied.

"Like . . . Like . . . Like . . . . What is like? You should have seized the opportunity. I would have. Victoria, so many opportunities are lost in this life. That is why one should never be a beggar with a club."

"It was always out of my hands, Angelina. You know that. My father Andres would not allow me to marry him."

Angelina smiled wickedly and said, "I suppose that's stopped you from seeing him all these years?"

Victoria drew her mouth tight and clamped her teeth. The vein running down the middle of her forehead engorged. "Has the mayor been in today?" she asked.

"Does the dog have teats?" Angelina responded.

"The man is unbelievable. He believes his own importance."

"He's like every politician. It's the people's fault for electing him."

"But it was nothing to be taken seriously."

"Victoria, he takes it seriously. He comes in every day. Saturday and Sunday. After church on Sunday he crosses the park and sits at his desk and looks out through the window at the town to make sure everything is running smoothly."

"This town? With one policeman. This horrible town?"

"He loves the town. You know that he believes the old saying that once a man has drunk water in San Diego, he will always return."

"He's more a fool than I thought . . ." Victoria said as her voice trailed off in her despair. "I've learned a lot just talking to you, Angelina. I'm glad I came."

"Well, Victoria, we've never talked before. You and your family have always been a step or two above my kind . . . . You had the grocery store. The ranch."

"I never had occasion to talk to you, Angelina. We're not rich. The store has been closed for many years. The ranch is abandoned. But I'm not here to talk about those things. I'm here because I'm worried."

Angelina noticed Victoria's preoccupation with her problem and said, "If you're worried about the decree, he has not signed it."

"I'm not worried about that right now," Victoria responded. "My father Andres is gone. I thought that the mayor would be the first one to know where he is."

"He did not say a word to me Victoria. You know that he only speaks to me in an official sense, nothing of a personal nature."

"It's come to that?"

Angelina was down on her knees throwing large portions of moss into the boxes. She looked sadly at Victoria. "It's come to that. He is the ultimate bureaucrat. Oh, he will sign the decree. When? That is the question. I think he's making your father suffer before he signs it. Don't you think?"

"He doesn't have enough signatures yet," Victoria said and hurried into the mayor's small office. She took a pencil and wrote on the pad on top of the desk and sealed the note. As she came out, Angelina was standing up, twisting her old spine from side to side.

"He's never forgotten what your father did to him, Victoria," she said.

"As far as I'm concerned he had it coming to him," Victoria replied.

"He's just paying back. The signatures will be collected. The decree will be signed."

"I hope not, Angelina, for the mayor's sake," Victoria replied.

"He'll do it to make him out a fool before the whole town, just as Don Andres did to him. He may have him flogged on New Year's day, just as your father flogged him when your father was younger and powerful."

"That's going too far. My father Andres is over one hundred years old."

"To a desperate man that wouldn't matter," Angelina replied.

Angelina threw moss into the cardboard box. She wiped her brow in the oppressive heat of that December morning. "That's the problem with poor people. They carry grudges for a long time."

"That's why God did not give wings to the cow," Victoria responded.

"Very true," Angelina told her. "And that is why elections are dangerous. One never knows who's going to win."

Victoria had reached the door and opened it. "It makes me shudder," she said.

Angelina did not look up from her job as she asked, "Shall I tell him that you were in?"

"No," Victoria told her in a trembling voice, "he'll know I've been here. He'll read my note."

After Victoria had left, when the Spanish moss had been placed securely in the city boxes for another year, Angelina went into the mayor's small office and sat at the desk. She made a tube of the note and took a peep inside. "Lothario," it read, "the honeysuckle has bloomed this morning in this oppressive heat. We may still have a chance. Please do not sign the decree. Victoria."

Angelina replaced the note on the desk, murmuring to herself. She said, "Everyone in town knows what they do in the dark in her room after old Don Andres goes to sleep. If only the poor man knew that the mayor sneaks in through Victoria's window at night. Well, honeysuckle or not, locusts singing or not, he would surely die."

The word came to the house by way of Faustino, the drunk, that Andres Garcia was to be found sitting at the creek bank watching for the locusts to emerge. On his way there Don Andres had caused a fight among two men while discoursing on his views of Texas history and the origin of the Shroud of Tamaulipas. "The shroud is a sacred cloth that belongs in a museum," he informed the men before they had started to fight.

"And how did it come about?" Tobias asked, nurturing Don Andres, as if he had not heard the story one hundred times before.

"It came about when my father, the *aide de camp* to General Santa Anna, covered the great general with a sheet during the battle of the Alamo. Santa Anna had become chilled while watching the battle. The great general and my father were up on a windy hill. Remember that it was very early in the morning. It was a simple act on my father's part to take the clean sheet from his saddle bag and drape the general with it. The horse too. Santa Anna threw the sheet off as he rode toward the Alamo when the battle was ending. My father got off his horse, picked up the sheet and folded it neatly and replaced it in his saddle bag. The image appeared sometime later. When? No one is sure. My father discovered it at the Battle of Tamaulipas."

"That's bullshit!" Manuel cried out as the three men stood at a street corner in town.

Tobias raised his fist in anger and Manuel did not back down. "Let the man speak his mind," Tobias said.

"I'll show you the shroud one day," Andres said, trying to separate the two men.

"You little old fart," Manuel said, "you've never seen the shroud, much less owned it."

"Leave the old man alone," Tobias said, reaching over Andres for Manuel's head.

"Leave Manuel alone," Andres told Tobias. "He's ignorant."

"Who are you calling ignorant, old man," said Manuel, stepping off the curb. "You're the one who's ignorant. Look at what's going on in your own house, under your very long nose. Things you don't know about."

Tobias raised his fist at Manuel. "One more word out of you and I'll hit you," he shouted.

Manuel, standing in the deserted street, laughed at Tobias. "You and the old man couldn't beat an egg," he said.

And with that the fight started.

From there Don Andres had walked toward the creek and had met the widow who lived by the creek, the widow Andrea. He had accosted her and had made her take him to the spot where the locusts would emerge. The widow, who knew nothing, had run away and had gone to the sheriff and the sheriff had sent the fat Amandito to threaten Andres Garcia with the decree. That, according to the drunkard Faustino, had quieted Don Andres down. Now Andres could be found reflecting on his fate at the creek bed.

"What a horrible thing it is for a father to do to his favorite child," Andres Garcia spoke to Amandito while they both sat at the bank of the creek. "He loved me so much that he thought he was giving me eternal life."

"That can't be," Amandito said, innocently. Then he changed his mind and asked, "Or can it?"

"No. Sadly enough, no one lives forever. My father, although a military man, was also a very religous man. Almost a priest. He could have been a priest for all that matters, as much as priests respect the church nowadays."

"That's the truth," Amandito whispered.

"He taunted fate. He asked God for two special events to occur before I could die."

"Everyone in town knows that, Don Andres."

"Who would ever think that the two events are taking place right now? I had a premonition. Amandito, I've had a premonition for a long time that this would be the year."

Amandito looked at Andres and very mildly said, "You've been with us for such a long time. I'm sorry its got to be, Don Andres."

"I am too," Andres said. "I am angry also. No one listens."

Amandito looked down at the creek bed for signs of the locusts. "Well, Don Andres," he said, "everyone is so busy just making a living . . . making ends meet."

"I know I may be rude at times. I may cause people to fight among themselves. I may be a troublemaker. But goddammit, someone has got to tell the truth."

"Yes," Amandito replied. "It looks like God has chosen you for that job."

"He has cursed me, you mean. Look at what's happening to me now. I should be enjoying my last days on earth."

"It's still too early, Don Andres. Maybe you'll get another year."

"I hope God hears you. I don't want to die, if you must know. I have so many things yet to do."

"Well, the mayor doesn't want you to do anything else. He wants you to stay at home. Your disturbances in town have given him the excuse he needed to make a fool of you."

"What disturbances? The fights? The arguments?"

Amandito looked away from Andres Garcia, not wanting to confront the gentleman. "Don Andres," he whispered mysteriously, "don't act as if you have been the innocent one."

"What's a disturbance, anyway? How is it classified? One man's disturbance can be another man's party."

Amandito said, "All right. Do you want me to list the whole thing? Didn't you cause Father Procopio to resign, causing the last election, opening the door for Lothario to get elected?"

"Yes. But Father Procopio was the priest and the Church should not be involved in politics."

"Didn't you petition for a recall referendum on the city council?"

"I got the signatures. It was all within the law."

"Didn't the city council resign?"

"They were incompetent."

"I thought you said that they were crooked."

"No. I said they were incompetent. I wouldn't have said anything if they had been thieves. All the referendum would have done would be to trade one thief for another. Like one Sam Houston for another."

"Didn't you threaten to close the church down? Didn't you assault Father Procopio?"

"I did not assault Father Procopio. I ran into him accidently and the good father fell down."

"And the church?"

"Sure I wanted to close it down. All their income was from the Wheel of Fortune, a game of chance. What kind of religion is that?"

"You're crazy, Don Andres."

Andres added a twinkle to his eyes and said, "Maybe. Maybe not."

Amandito laughed. "You don't seem very sad," he said to Andres.

Andres took a small stone and threw it at the creek bed below, causing some of the imbedded locusts to shake the earth slowly. "I am sad though," he answered. "I have been in agony all this year. You know how bad I am about premonitions." He threw another rock into the middle of the swelling ground. "I don't want to die," he cried. "There is so much I need to tell."

Amandito wiped a tear from his eye and took out his bottle of whiskey and drank from it. He offered the bottle to Don Andres and Don Andres refused politely. Any other day he would have told Amandito that he only drank from a glass, like a gentleman.

"Well, Don Andres, you've told us a lot through the years. I would think that by now all your knowledge would have been known to the whole town."

Andres Garcia shook his head in disagreement. "I was just now beginning to tell what I know about the history of Texas."

"That's been told and retold so many times, Don Andres."

"Not the real history. The true history. How Sam Houston tricked General Santa Anna into coming to Texas, knowing full well that anything that Houston wanted the General would do. Had Santa Anna not been a Mason he would never have been trapped. What a cheap friend Houston was to use his Masonic ties to lure Santa Anna to Texas."

"That wasn't a very good friend. You've been a good friend no matter what you've been," Amandito said.

Andres could not help but laugh. "You're talking like the doctor now," Don Andres responded. He thought for a few moments as Amandito attacked his bottle. "Right now, Amandito, I am in my altered state," Andres said, "I can feel the ghosts of all my antecedents around me."

Father Procopio stroked his chin with the same left hand that he used to twirl the Wheel of Fortune. Self-consciously he lowered his hand and placed it in his pocket. Then he ran the fingers of his right hand through his sparse hair. With this movement the hollow crucifix that hung at his chest swung from the center to cover his right breast. He felt for the crucifix instinctively and centered it, as though that slight change in his habit had bothered and disoriented him. "If you really want me to go get him, I will," he told Victoria and our mother.

"*Ave Maria Purisima!*" our mother shouted joyfully inside the sacristy, looking through the door toward the side altar at the Virgin Mary dressed in blue and holding the pink baby Jesus. She crossed herself in appreciation, kissing her thumb when she ended.

"Thank you, Father," Victoria said. "You don't know how much it means to me. We, Clementina and I, could go get him, but that would set him up for ridicule. Just imagine, two women leading an ancient man down the streets of town as one would an errant child. He would be furious."

23

Father Procopio, who had the habit of moving his eyebrows up and down, did so, moving the whole head of hair at the same time, like an automated wig. "I understand," he said. "I understand completely how he feels. Don't be surprised. I know Don Andres. I know exactly how he thinks. You're absolutely right. We don't want to embarrass him."

"Isn't Father Procopio wonderful?" our mother asked Victoria. "He's so forgiving."

Victoria shrugged her shoulders at the futility of apologizing for her father and looked at the priest and explained, "He has nothing against you, Father."

Father Procopio moved his eyebrows rapidly. "I know," he said, "but still he scares me somewhat."

"He only objected to the Wheel of Fortune. That was all. He didn't mean to knock you down when you were struggling for the Wheel of Fortune."

"I understand how he felt," Father Procopio said, sadly wondering at the things he had to do to keep his religion going. "It wasn't like I loved the idea myself. I would rather do it like the Methodists. It's just that now we're broke all the time."

"And about the referendum," our mother tried to explain, but the priest was way ahead of her. He had known it was coming.

"Forget about that," he said. "Don Andres did me a great favor getting me recalled from the mayorship. The people were becoming too demanding."

"He said it was the mixing of religion and politics . . . something he could never go for," Victoria explained.

"Oh yes," Father Procopio informed them. "How many times did he tell me that in front of all the city councilmen."

Victoria interjected, "But not to embarrass you, Father."

Father Procopio, still not convinced himself, said, "I don't think he meant it that way either."

"You will go anyway?" the worried Victoria asked.

"To get him?"

"Yes."

Father Procopio sighed the sigh of the chosen man. "Yes, of course," he replied.

Victoria waited for just the right moment and said, "You realize that today the honeysuckle has bloomed?"

"Yes, I heard it being murmured during mass," the father replied.

"That means, Father Procopio," Victoria told him as she kissed his hand, "that we may be seeing you very often for the next few days."

"Whatever I can do to help," the good Father assured them.

Late in the afternoon the note from the mayor to Victoria arrived. The mayor had seen us playing at the park in front of the church and had run out of his small office, yelling at Willie to meet him at the street. "Take this note immediately to your Aunt Victoria under penalty of a fine," he ordered. Willie grabbed the sealed note and took off running with us running after him.

Victoria went into her bedroom to read the note written in block letters. It read: VIKOTRORIA I WIL MOV AL OFF HEBEN AN ERT TOO HAV DEKRE SINED AGANS YOU ARE FATER. He signed his "Lothario" in the cursive that he had learned in order to become elected.

Victoria took the note, ripped it apart, and set it on fire. "How bitter. After all these years it has come to this," she said to herself.

"What smells?" our mother asked as Victoria opened the door.

Victoria closed the door loudly. "The note," she answered. "The mayor's note. I burned it, resin and all."

"Good news, I hope?"

Victoria went over and began to boil the water for the dinner tea.

Clementina asked again. "It's good news, Victoria?"

"No," Victoria sighed in anguish, "Lothario will sign the decree."

"God in heaven above," our mother prayed. "And you can't get him to change his mind?"

"Apparently not."

Mother hesitated and blushed, feeling that she was about to go into a part of Victoria's secret life. "As . . . as . . . friendly as you two have been for so many years."

Victoria blushed also. "You knew about that?"

The question flustered our mother. "Yes," she answered turning away from Victoria and looking out the window at the few persistent bees that were demanding their nectar. "Sure I knew. The secret meetings at the house after Don Andres has gone to sleep . . . I've seen them. I've seen the mayor climbing through the bedroom window. Everyone except your father knows."

"I'm curious. For how long, Clementina? How long have you known?"

"We've known for many years. It's just that I never said anything. I enjoyed playing the innocent. And now that it's out in the open, it bothers me. I felt better when you didn't know that I knew. If you know what I mean?"

"I understand exactly, Clementina. You're the perfect sister-in-law. You're so nice."

"I thought that it was none of our business. Like I told the children and their father, your brother Pablo, we just wanted you to be happy."

"Well," Victoria said, pouring the tea leaves into the angrily boiling water, "I guess I knew that everyone knew. I was just fooling myself if I thought differently. You can't hide anything in this town." Victoria gave a desperate sigh toward the flaming stove. "We haven't been together for a long time. We're getting too old for him to be climbing windows. He still sends me notes now and then. And now," she whispered, "the affair will finally end if he signs the decree."

"As you wish," our mother said. "You know Victoria that we will support you in any decision that you make."

Victoria set her jaw as the brown water boiled over onto the stove top. "I have made the decision," she said. "Now it's up to him to come begging me."

Our Mother lifted her eyes to heaven and the exposed kitchen beams overhead covered with spider webs and she said, "*Ave Maria*, and God and Jesus and all the angels and archangels help the innocent Victoria. Elevated be God."

"Now we'll know how much love there is between us," Victoria said, cleaning the steaming water off the stove top.

Father Procopio, early into the night, arrived with Andres Garcia and with the four other gentlemen that had been helping Andres Garcia at the creek. They were: Faustino, the drunkard, who had noticed Andres Garcia at the creek in the first place; Amandito, the fat one, who had already been there helping Andres Garcia placate the disturbed locusts; Bernabe, the crazy one, who was helping at the creek when the Priest had arrived; and Fecundo, the prolific, the man with many children, who had also joined the other three in helping Andres Garcia. Andres Garcia walked erectly in the center of the group as they neared the house. "This reminds me," he said making a circle with his arms to signify the group, "of the death of James Bowie after the battle of the Alamo. Just as you are surrounding me, so did General Santa Anna's men surround the hated Bowie. Do you know that Bowie had the nerve to spit on my father's boots, while my father was trying to convince Travis that Santa Anna did not want a battle at the Alamo? What ignorance! There you had Captain Agustin Garcia, right hand man to the great General Santa Anna, educated in Spain at the most prestigious academies . . . . And then the ignorant Bowie, whose claim to fame was that he made a knife."

"What happened to the man?" Faustino asked him, as they walked.

"What man?"

"Bowie."

"Bowie was found alive after the Alamo. So was Crockett. Crockett hated Sam Houston for what Houston had done to General Santa Anna at the Alamo. Hated him so much that he joined Santa Anna's troups at San Jacinto." Andres Garcia adjusted his collar with both hands and tried to walk even more erect. "By that time Crockett had changed his name officially to David Cruz."

"This man knows everything," Bernabe said in awe. "Didn't I tell you that he knows everything?"

"Goddam right I know everything," Don Andres replied. And then when he remembered that Father Procopio was at his right side he said, "I apologize for taking the name of God in vain, good Father."

"I don't have time to confess and forgive you," Father Procopio told him as he tried to hurry the group through the darkness. He was feeling drowsy, having missed his nap. "I can only do one thing at a time. Just remember that if you die right now, even as we walk, that you will go to hell. There is no purgatory for you."

"The way I feel," Andres replied, solemnly, "in the agony that I'm in, purgatory and hell will be the same."

Amandito put his abundantly fat arm around Don Andres Garcia. "Be more cheerful, Don Andres," he said. "You're just tired from all the work we've done. After all, you are over one hundred years old."

"No, Amandito, that's not it," Andres said. "At my age I'm still used to working like a mule. But don't think I don't appreciate what you men have done . . . the work you put in today with me. I don't care what the town and the mayor say about you. You men are my friends."

"The mayor says bad things about everyone," Fecundo said.

"Yes," Andres agreed, "especially me."

"He's never forgotten what you did to him, Don Andres."

"What was a father to do? Lothario is illiterate. He's poor. He had no chance of success at anything. How could I give my consent for him to marry my daughter?"

"Yes," Bernabe said, "but you flogged him at the park."

"But only," Andres replied, "when he persisted in his silly dream."

"How things have changed," Fecundo said.

"Yes," Andres thought, "and now here I am digging for my life at the damn creek."

"What were you doing at the creek?" Father Procopio asked.

"Lots of work, Father," Don Andres responded. "All five of us, from the Fat One to the Crazy One to the Prolific to the Drunk. We worked hard, but to no avail."

"What happened to Bowie?" Fecundo asked. "You never said."

Don Andres Garcia stopped abruptly to gather his thoughts. He had been thinking of what Father Procopio had said about purgatory. Everyone stopped with him. At the same time he thought that he could still smell the honeysuckle blossoms from the front of his house. "My father killed James Bowie with his trusty derringer," he said. "Shot him in the head after he tied him to a horse ring on the wall of the Alamo. General Santa Anna asked him to. My father had been very pleased that Bowie had begged for his life . . . that Bowie had lied and said that his mother was a Mexican and he should be allowed to live. Bowie's death was the highlight of my father's life up to that point. Of course, he did not know that he had accidently formed the perfect figure of the great general and the general's horse on his sheet . . . the illusion known as the Shroud of Tamaulipas. That was his greatest accomplishment. That and dying for his country at the Battle of Chapultepec."

Victoria and our mother greeted them at the front door, ignoring the bees that were still trying to decipher the events of the morning. They had earlier gathered the chickens and counted them and put them to sleep. "Only Father Procopio can come in," Victoria informed them, she and our mother guarding the front door. She knew the reputation of the other four men that had helped her father at the creek and she was not going to allow them into the house.

"Pay them something for their troubles," Andres told Victoria as he embraced the men and walked tiredly into the house. "They are good and faithful friends."

Victoria took some money from her apron and passed it out to the four men. When she confronted the priest she bent over and kissed his hollow crucifix.

"Don Andres, we'll see you tomorrow," Faustino yelled at Andres Garcia.

Andres was already inside. "If God wills it," Victoria told them.

"Getting your father away from the creek was like trying to remove a tick from a starving dog," Father Procopio told Victoria as they settled in the kitchen. Victoria was up getting tea.

"Father Procopio, how easy would it have been for you to leave under the same circumstances?" Don Andres asked the priest. "It's one thing to be talking about death in church. It's another thing to be living through the experience."

"Don't be disrespectful with Father Procopio," Victoria scolded her father. "Be grateful that he consented to go get you."

"So it was you who put him up to it?"

Victoria, holding the stack of saucers in her hands, raised her full body to tower over him. "Yes," she said. "Or would you rather that Clementina and I go get you and embarrass you in front of the whole town?"

"Victoria, I wouldn't have let you," Don Andres insisted to his daughter. "You could not have brought me back."

"That's why I begged Father Procopio to go get you."

Our mother said, "Don Andres, it was the best thing that we could do to preserve your dignity."

Father Procopio refused a cup of tea, wishing instead to go home to take his nap before the nightly rosary and said, "Andres Garcia, I forgive you for what you said. Now you can die and go to heaven."

"Thank you," Don Andres told him. "I was truly afraid after all these years."

And as Father Procopio left, the determined bees, attracted to his white habit, made him run off the porch and across the sidewalk and cross the street immediately.

That night, slipped under her screened window, Victoria received another sealed note from the mayor. It read: I HAV AL EVADANCE I NED DON TAK HARD I HAV WATED MENI YERS FUR THEES THU DEKRE WIL BEE SINGD TOMORO. And then again his "Lothario" in flourished cursive.

As Father Procopio raised his gold ciborium to expose the Blessed Sacrament to the few that attended the nightly rosary, he felt the first slight tremors under the church from the agitated locusts at the creek that were ready to emerge.

CHAPTER 3

A disgusted Victoria threw her bonnet on the table as she slammed Clementina's kitchen door. She had tried to run to Clementina's house, but the hungry chickens, expecting to be counted and fed early in the morning, had gotten intentionally underfoot and had slowed her down. "The rooster almost attacked me," she complained. "What is this world coming to?"

Our mother was already pouring the boiling coffee into Victoria's cup. "You didn't try to run over here to tell me that, did you?"

"No. It's worse than that. I don't know what to do," she told our mother. Then with a solemness that hurt her she said, "Father has gone again."

Our mother sat down under the weight of the seriousness of the situation. "*Ave Maria Purisima*," she prayed. "He's gone again? Is he insane or what?"

"I think so," Victoria replied. "There must be something in his fate that is making him lose his mind. He has not eaten in three days."

Clementina served the coffee on the table for the both of them. "That's not good. Not for a man that's one hundred and five years old. Did the doctor get to see him?"

"Oh, no. He was gone even before I got up. The doctor came, knocked on the door and left when I told him what had happened."

"What did the doctor say? Does he think Don Andres is coming back?"

"He doesn't know. He just shook his head. He's like us. He thinks my father's crazy. Everyone, from the Mayor on down believes he should accept his fate."

"I'm sure the mayor is very happy about that. He's in his heaven thinking that Andres is going to die."

"He's carried a grudge a long time. But he's cunning. He has the threat of the decree hanging over my father's head. That's just in case my father doesn't die."

"Oh, Victoria, that's ridiculous," Clementina replied. "How much longer do you think the old man is going to live?"

"You never know. With Andres Garcia one never knows."

"He's gone to the creek, I'm sure," Clementina assured her, blowing on the coffee in front of her. Victoria had taken a chair across the table.

"Yes, I'm sure that's where he's gone. I don't know what he and his companions are doing."

"The same thing they do every year, Victoria. They spread their quick-lime on the creek-bed and pound it into the ground with their shovels. They beat the poor locusts down . . . ."

"Yes, but this year is different," Victoria reminded her. "He has the problem of the blossoms. He has his premonition. It's driving him harder than ever before. In other years they would go to the creek and go through the motions of fighting for his life. They would take food and drink."

"They're not doing anything different today than they did the years before, Victoria. They are condemned to repeat themselves."

"I just hope he takes care of himself . . . that he knows what he's doing."

"Victoria, Don Andres knows what he's doing, but in truth, what can he do?"

Clementina blew on the steaming coffee that she had poured on the saucer and said, "Nothing, I suppose. May God in heaven help us," Clementina prayed, "but that is the tragedy of the situation. He can't help himself and no one can help him."

"Did Pablo say anything about helping him?"

"No. And you know Pablo. He gets up in the morning and goes to work without as much as a word."

"He's such a good nephew and for you, Clementina, he has been a good husband."

"Yes, he's been good. He's good with the children. He's a hard worker. Nothing keeps him from his work. He goes from work to the beer joints, comes home drunk, eats, goes to bed."

Victoria looked through the window at the man carrying a lantern and a shovel approaching through the back yard and said, "A perfect husband."

Our mother looked to see what Victoria was so interested in and replied without thinking, "Almost . . ." Then she saw the man and asked Victoria, "Who is it?"

"I think it's one of my father's so-called friends, but with the dust on the window I can't tell exactly who." Victoria put down the saucer and walked to the window. "The closer he gets the more it looks like Bernabe . . . or maybe it's Faustino."

"It looks like Bernabe," our mother said from the table. "What is he carrying?"

"It's Faustino. I can see him now," Victoria answered as she rubbed the window with her forearm.

"You've always had such good eyesight," Clementina praised her. "I've always been very proud of you for that."

"I thank God I was born with good eyesight," Victoria replied. "It's Faustino and he's carrying a shovel and a lantern."

"Just think," Clementina laughed, "I was seeing Bernabe carrying a long stick and lunch bucket."

"Maybe he has news of Don Andres," Victoria said, hopefully, walking to the kitchen door.

Faustino rested his shovel and lantern by the kitchen door, knocked, and repeated his diatribe to anyone that would listen: "Attention please. This is Faustino, the drunkard. Do not be afraid of me and about the way I look and speak. This is normal for me. I have never harmed anyone in my life. If someone answers the door, I promise that I will be the perfect gentleman, as Don Andres Garcia has instructed me."

Victoria was at the door looking for the latch. "What do you want?" she asked brusquely.

"Can I come in?" Faustino pleaded. "Just a drink of coffee to get my circulation going?"

Victoria latched the screen door just in case Faustino would try to get in. "No," she scolded him, "you can't come in."

"Is this Victoria I'm talking to behind the screen door?"

"Yes, this is Victoria."

"Victoria, I come from your house. I looked for you everywhere inside. You weren't there, so I thought that you would be over here."

"How dare you go inside my house!" Victoria screamed.

"Don't be angry, Victoria. Don Andres gave me permission," Faustino explained.

Victoria felt the anger toward her father surge through her body and come to rest like a ball of fire in her heart. "You tell Don Andres that he has no right to give you permission to go into our house. If I'm living in it, it's our house . . . ." And to Clementina she turned and said, "He's gone crazy."

Faustino took off his wrinkled grey hat and reshaped it, studied it, and then replaced it on his head. "I'm afraid I have to agree with you, Victoria. He's not well. He says he's going to die."

Victoria leaned into the door, the cup of boiling coffee in her hand. "What does my insane father want, Faustino? Where is he? When did he leave?"

Faustino shook his bowed head so that Victoria could only see the top of his sweated hat. He solemnly studied the door steps. "He left very early this morning, Victoria. He was at my house at four. Can you imagine what a scare he gave me and my wife? You know my wife has been ill with heart trouble. The doctor has her on dynamite."

Clementina gasped and placed her delicate hand to her mouth. "*Ave Maria Purisima*," she cried. "Dynamite? Are you giving her dynamite?"

"Yes, Clementina, the doctor put her on dynamite," Faustino replied, trying to peer through the door at Clementina. "The same one that explodes and knocks down mountains."

"May God have mercy on her soul," Clementina prayed. "That's the worst thing I've ever heard of in my life. That doctor should not be allowed to practice medicine."

"That's what I said to some of my friends," Faustino replied dejectedly, "but they say that half the old people in town are on dynamite."

"He'll be the end of us, for sure," our mother said, shaking her head. "One day this town is going to explode."

"I hope Don Andres didn't scare Gloria," Victoria said to Faustino.

"Just a little," Faustino replied, holding his thumb and forefinger to where they almost touched. "Just a little. She didn't know who it was and that scared her. If she had known it was Don Andres, she would not have minded it at all. Gloria loves Don Andres as does everyone else that is honest. Everyone knows what a forgiving man Don Andres is. Every wrong that has been done to him he has forgiven. The mayor is the only one that doesn't love him. And yet Don Andres does not hate him. What do you think Victoria? You're close to the mayor, or so they say."

"Shut up!" Victoria shouted to him through the door. "How dare you." Victoria looked at our mother, stomped her foot, and said in disgust, "Clementina, even the lowest of the low dares to talk about me."

"That's the trouble with living the life you've lived, Victoria," our mother responded.

"Don't get so angry, Victoria. I was just saying, that's all," spoke Faustino.

"Where is Don Andres? At the creek, I suppose," Victoria scolded him.

"He is at the creek with me and Amandito and Bernabe and Fecundo. He says for me to tell you that he is not crazy and that he intends to spend his days at the creek. He is not coming home."

"He's crazy."

Faustino replied, "That's what we told him," agreeing with Victoria. "But he wanted me to come and get his clothes and food and something to cover himself with in case it should get cold."

"He can't have anything," Victoria told him, "and that's final. Tell him to come home. He's making a fool of himself."

"It makes me sad to see him like that, Victoria," Faustino said. "But what can a friend do?"

Victoria said, "You can begin by telling him to come home."

Angelina arrived with the signed decree a few hours after Faustino had left. In her hurried pace to get to Don Andres' house, the hem of her skirt had caused a small puff of dust to follow her all the way from City Hall. The decree was an official looking document that she had copied at the mayor's insistence from a book on municipal laws for the State of Texas. After the mayor had signed it, she had taken it to the meat market for Don Sebastian to sign.

Don Sebastian had had his red flag out to alert the citizens that he had butchered an animal. He had interrupted his sawing on the carcass of the goat and had wiped his bloody hands on his apron and read the decree as best he could and had laughed. It had taken him some time to find a clean place to rest the document and it had taken him longer to write his signature. Then Angelina had returned to City Hall for the mayor to verify the signature and as he did so, she gathered the small amounts of Spanish moss that still clung to the corners of the floor. With Don Sebastian's signature the decree became official. Don Sebastian's had been the fourth signature, the one he withheld until he was sure the mayor had signed.

"Here it is," Angelina said as she handed the document to Victoria. "This is the decree. Signed by the mayor and three councilmen. Do you want to read it?"

"No," Victoria said, angrily bored, "just tell us what it says."

Angelina placed her hand over her heart and tried to catch her breath. "I almost ran over here," she explained.

"In your glee?" Victoria asked sarcastically.

"Oh, no," Angelina answered, "heaven forbid. I feel for Don Andres. I agree with the whole town. He is such a courageous man."

"Just tell us about the decree," our mother said.

"In essence it means that Don Andres must be confined to his home for a period of one year."

"Don't make me laugh," Victoria informed her. "Andres Garcia is going to die in four days."

"The mayor doesn't believe it. You know how superstitious the poor and ignorant people are. He believes this is all a scheme to embarrass him once more. He is prepared for Don Andres this time."

Victoria took the decree and sat at the sofa in the living room of her house. Clementina sat by her. "This is ridiculous," Victoria said. "I've never heard of such a thing."

"It's a menace-to-society thing that is written in Texas law. Any creature that is a menace to society can be quarantined by any municipality."

"And how does the mayor figure that Don Andres is a menace to society?" our mother asked Angelina, who had not been invited to sit.

"You haven't heard?" Angelina asked them.

"No," Victoria replied. "What happened now?"

"The charges are posted at City Hall. The daughter of the widow Andrea that lives by the creek has charged that Don Andres attempted to sexually molest her mother yesterday as Don Andres accosted her mother and took her to the creek."

Victoria laughed as did Clementina. "And what is it my father is supposed to have done?"

Angelina blushed for a second. "It's embarrassing, but the charges explain it all."

"We're all adult women, Angelina," Clementina told her. "You can tell us."

"If you are sure I won't offend anyone," Angelina spoke softly.

Victoria said, "You have our permission to speak."

"Well," Angelina started and hesitated, "the specific charges are tacked up on the bulletin board, but what they say is that Don Andres tried to touch the old widow lady in the you-know-what."

"What you-know-what?" Victoria jumped up and demanded to know.

Angelina retreated toward the hallway. She could barely get her words out. "I'm scared of you Victoria. I've never seen you angry before."

"This is mild compared to how she can get," our mother cautioned the retreating Angelina.

"Answer the question!" Victoria shouted.

Angelina swallowed and cried out, "You know . . . the you-know-what."

"No I don't," Victoria said. "Tell us. Tell us right now!"

"The part," Angelina said almost in secret, "the part that looks like the Spanish moss that the workers throw over the electric wires every year for Christmas."

Victoria looked at our mother and said, disgustedly, "The cunt, Clementina."

Our mother had long since blushed. She said, very concerned, "Yes, I had gathered. May God in heaven help us!"

Victoria ushered Angelina out through the front door and as the disappointed bees were gone, she was able to walk slowly down the sidewalk and across the street. She was wiping the nervous perspiration from her brow as she hurried on her way, the puff of dust still following the hem of her skirt like a faithful ghost.

Victoria, standing at the front door, shouted in anger, "You tell the mayor that Andres Garcia has not seen a cunt in fifty years and that he is one hundred and five years old and wouldn't know what to do with one, even if it was presented to him on a silver platter."

"I will," Angelina yelled nervously as she sped up even more, raising more than her little cloud of dust behind her, fearing someone would hear them.

"On second thought," Victoria yelled at her, "don't say anything. The mayor knows better than I do."

Once inside, Victoria said to our mother, "To think that Lothario would post the charges of sexual molestation on the bulletin board. What ingratitude." She opened the decree and studied it. It had been signed by two X's and Don Sebastian's signature in a twitching primitive cursive and the mayor's signature which he had practiced at home for hours on end when the results of the fraudulent election were announced. The mayor had mastered his own name in cursive for the first time in his life, the name appearing with lines seeming to flow like porcupine hairs from every direction in and out of his letters. The two X's were for Don Jorge, the postal employee that could read but could not write, and for Don Pluto, the owner of the tortilla factory who only knew how to count in twelves. The wording came exactly out of the State Municipal Law book. Andres Garcia was to spend one year, not under house arrest, but under house quarantine. If for any reason he was found outside his house, he was subject to arrest and a fine of up to one thousand dollars and six months in jail.

Victoria felt like crying. "Don't feel bad yet," Clementina said as Victoria collapsed onto the sofa. "We still have several days to go."

"I can't help but feel bad. What a predicament for a daughter to be in."

"Don't think like that," Clementina said. "Your affair with the mayor is over, Victoria."

"I still can't believe it. Why did he sign the decree? He never gave me any indication in twenty-three years that he would."

"Did he ever talk to you, Victoria?"

"Not very much, Clementina. He was like an animal making love. The most things he would say to me were abusive things as he finished his business. It was all physical. You would think that he would have said something about his hatred for my father, but he never did. I only heard it from other mouths."

"Be careful how you decide," Clementina told her.

"Oh, Clementina, don't be foolish," Victoria said. "There's only one choice to make." Victoria stood up and walked around the living room. "We both know that, Clementina. I will fight for my father. I know he can't last forever, but I don't want him to die like this, even if it means having to put up with him for one more year."

"Oh, Victoria," our mother said, happily relieved, "I knew that I could trust you to stick by your father."

"What do you take me for? Clementina, I'm surprised that you would even think I would not be on my father's side. He is my flesh and blood. Isn't he? The mayor will know that I am not to be made a goat. This is going to be a battle with many violent surprises."

"May God in heaven help us all, then," Clementina prayed.

"Take out your rosary and keep it close to you, Clementina. I have a feeling you are going to need it."

"I will, Victoria. My rosary from now on will be in the pocket of my apron. You know I can't be violent. But I can pray."

"That's going to be violent enough," Victoria said.

Clementina took the rosary from the pocket on her skirt and placed it in the pocket of her apron. She said to Victoria, "You won't mind it if he survives for another year. A year goes by so fast. It'll be over before you know it. There will even be new elections by then. We may even run you for mayor." Clementina put her arm around Victoria and squeezed her tightly. "I'm glad you have this attitude. I'm glad you're changing."

Victoria straightened her long torso and set her jaw and said. "You know, Clementina, I've been a fool. For the small pleasure that Lothario gave me I sold my soul. It wasn't worth it. How do you think I have felt all these years that I have made a fool of my father? I felt like I had a knot in my throat all this time. It was never enjoyable . . . thinking that one night we might get caught. It looked bad even to me to see Lothario climb in through the window. Like a common thief. And for what? That wasn't even love."

"But you wouldn't have listened to anyone at the time, would you?"

"No, I wouldn't have, Clementina."

"Women do foolish things for love."

"I can't believe that after all I gave Lothario, that he would pay me back like this . . . sign a decree on a trumped up morals charge against my father."

"Men have no respect for women, Victoria. Especially when you give them what they want."

Victoria allowed Clementina to squeeze her once more and they held hands. Victoria said, weeping into her shawl, "And Clementina, I gave him everything. You know what I mean?"

Clementina patted Victoria's hand. "Yes, I know what you mean. No grown man is going to climb a window at night just for a kiss. Even I know better than that."

Victoria smiled and looked at the opened decree on the sofa. "And to think that he used me for so many years and didn't love me."

"Don't feel bad, Victoria," Clementina advised her, "maybe he did at first. Men don't love any woman for long."

"No, I don't think he ever loved me at all. He was using me to hurt my father. And like a fool I helped him. My only concern now is that my father never find out, Clementina. Do you understand? You must help me. He is not to ever find out."

"*Ave Maria Purisima*," Clementina murmured quickly, making the sign of the cross over and over again, using the crucifix of her rosary. "If he ever finds out he will surely die of a broken heart. Who would have a heart so black as to tell him?"

Victoria ran her finger on the floral pattern on the cushion. "You never know. There are some people that would do it. That would, in effect, be a harsher punishment than the decree . . ."

Clementina stared at Victoria with a sense of despair slowly filling her body. She whispered through the crucifix on her rosary, "Worse than the honeysuckle and the locusts, Victoria. It would be worse."

"I agree . . . It's ironic, Clementina, that I have the potential for hurting him more than anyone. What a fool I have been."

Clementina trying to raise Victoria's spirits said, "Just pray to God, that's all you can do. Maybe confess to Father Procopio."

Victoria shook her head. "I could never do that," she replied. "I'm too embarrassed."

"Now you know from personal experience, Victoria," our mother told her, "why the spider never pees."

Victoria looked at our mother and cried into her shawl. "Yes, I realize that now. And if anyone ever tells my father my darkest secret, I will kill that person. I promise you that on my mother's grave. You can pass the word around town about that."

Our mother fell on her knees on the hard wooden floor and crossed herself numerous times, going faster with the sign of the cross than with her prayers. "May God in heaven not hear what the faithful Victoria has said," she prayed. "Amen. Victoria, repeat the prayers after me, please."

"No," Victoria replied sternly. "I am very angry and very hurt. I meant every word I said."

At the same time that Victoria made her vow, Father Procopio felt the ground under the church sway as he kneeled at the altar praying for the salvation of all the nuns of the Order of the Sisters of Charity after having argued with the Mother Superior at the nunnery. When he felt the slight tremor he thought with brief tenderness of Andres Garcia and how Andres would be at the creek at this hour with his shovel, fighting for his life, trying to keep the unsinging locusts from emerging on this hot December day. He included Don Andres in his prayers, hoping that the struggling man would survive at least one more year. Had he known of the decree and the sexual molestation charge, Father Procopio would not have been so generous. As to his visit with the Mother Superior, the visit he was praying about, she had become even more domineering and had not listened to him and she had refused to allow anyone but the parochial school children to use the catholic swings.

"Be more generous, Mother," Father Procopio had implored. "This is the Christmas season, the time for giving, for sharing, for loving one's fellow man. Especially the children. If we don't start with the children, where can we start?"

"No, Father," she answered curtly. "A rule is a rule. Christmas or no Christmas."

"But, Mother," he pleaded, "it's Christmas. All the children from the public school are out for the holidays. How can you let them just stand and watch the parochial school children swing?"

"If I allow the rule to be broken, then we will never be able to enforce our rules again," she replied. "First it's the swings, then it's the bathrooms. Before you know it, the riff-raff will take over."

For the job of watching over the swings, a job that involved sitting by the window and rapping on it all day long to prevent the swings' misuse, the Mother Superior had chosen poor Sister Carmela, the ugliest one of the bunch, the one most likely to scare the children away.

Father Procopio prayed for guidance and restraint, but in the presence of the Mother Superior, his gall boiling, he had threatened to send all of them packing, to return to San Antonio from where they came, even though he had not invited them. At that time, had he not been praying, he could have cursed the Bishop at Corpus Christi for sending them to San Diego without his consent. Little did he know that there was no room for the nuns in San Antonio, that if he ran them off they would have no place to go.

Andres Garcia looked at the blistering sun of the oppressive heat of that

December and wiped his brow with his arm. He replaced his felt hat and raised the shovel high over his head. His small frame grunted as he gave the last blow of the shovel at the trembling creek bed from which the unsinging locusts were trying to emerge. Neither he nor Amandito, nor Faustino, nor Bernabe, nor Fecundo noticed that high on the creek bank stood the mayor and the sheriff. In the mayor's right hand he carried the folded replica of the decree.

"Don Andres Garcia," the Mayor shouted to the man below.

Don Andres, fatigued and disoriented for a moment, thinking that the locusts had called out his name, fell to his knees in prayer. He had thought that if the locusts could talk, then they could sing and his life would be spared. He trembled as he prayed in joy and thought that his great father had saved him for one more year. The other men with him fell to their knees at seeing Don Andres pray.

"What is happening?" the crazy Bernabe asked, unsure of what it was they were doing.

"Don Andres Garcia," the Mayor shouted again, this time cupping his hand over his mouth to form the bell of a trumpet.

Andres realized that the voice was coming from above. He stood up slowly, disappointed and dejected and looked up into the sun. He could see that it was the mayor and the sheriff. "What do you men want?" he asked, irritated that he had been at first fooled and now interrupted. "I can't afford to stop. Can't you see that I'm working to save my life?"

"We have a decree," Mayor Lothario informed him, "properly signed and duly executed, saying that you are a menace to society."

Don Andres Garcia laughed and his friends laughed with him. "You're crazy," Don Andres said. He had placed his shovel on the ground and was on his way to the top of the creek bank. "Let me see the decree," he demanded.

"Old man, I'll be glad to show it to you. We're not crazy," Lothario corrected him. "You are the one that's crazy. Look at what you're doing right now. This marks you as being insane."

"I do this every year," Don Andres replied as he climbed up the embankment. "Why would I be marked as being insane now?"

"Because, old man," yelled Lothario, his eyes askew with hatred for the old man, "this year I am the mayor and I say who is crazy and who is not."

"And under what law do you give yourself this authority?" Don Andres asked.

"I don't need a law," Lothario informed him. "Do I, Gonzalo?" he asked the sheriff.

"If he says he doesn't, he doesn't," Gonzalo told Don Andres.

Lothario tried to grab for the old man as he reached the top of the embankment. "This time you lose and I win. The Sheriff and I came to take you home."

"Take me home? Why? What have I done?"

The Mayor spewed out his wicked laugh. "You know what you've done, you filthy minded old man. You ought to be glad you're not going to jail. The charges are posted at City Hall."

"What charges?" Andres asked.

"What charges, he asks?" The mayor grabbed the frail unsuspecting Don Andres by the neck and held him stooped over as Gonzalo tied Don Andres' hands behind him. "The charges that you grabbed the widow Andrea by her most intimate of parts. Her daughter heard the story from her mother and has brought charges against you. The poor widow is beside herself. The daughter says no one will ever marry her mother again. She is ruined for life. She cannot show her face in public from now on."

CHAPTER 4

Father Procopio slapped at the persistent gnat that had been interrupting his third novena, the novena dedicated to the immutable Mother Superior. The grey gnat flew toward the altar and then returned to harangue the priest's ear with its constant humming sound. Father Procopio swatted at it again and missed, the vortex of air created from his own hand moving the gnat from harm's way. Earlier, by the end of the second novena, he had gotten it into his head that he would ask the nuns to leave the convent, close the parochial school, and return to San Antonio. He had enough problems to contend with without having to put up with the self-serving Mother Superior and her three nuns. Feeling badly about his decision, he had agreed to pray one last novena for the troublesome nuns.

At the end of the novena, when the drone of his internal voice had mastered and overcome the disconcerting gnat, Father Procopio sat back on the pew and took out the Bishop's old letter. In it the Bishop had described San Diego as a beautiful small town with lovely, caring people. But that had been years ago. Now he knew that the Bishop had been right about the people, but not about the town, a dusty shack-filled place with only a few refined families. And what the Bishop had also meant and Father Procopio realized now was that Father Procopio would be on his own. There were times like today that he felt so lonely and desperate that he wanted to quit, become a baptist, and leave everything to the Mother Superior. And ever since Don Andres had brought up during mass the moral question of using the Wheel of Fortune as a money making religious device, the church had been in poor financial shape. That was compounding his problem. If only Don Andres had kept his mouth shut and had allowed Father Procopio to shoulder the guilt of using a device of chance to fund the Holy Mother Church.

He raised and lowered his eyebrows in his typical way and clamped his jaw and felt the pain from the many years of grinding his teeth. He thought it out carefully, for he was an educated and reasonable man. Tomorrow he would go talk to the Mother Superior and, with the detached emotion of a bishop, would calmly tell her to get all of their possessions together and leave for San Antonio. If she happened to ask for a reason, he would not list all the improprieties and inconveniences that they had committed toward the town, instead he would reply, "Because I say so, goddammit!"

He was practicing saying the words to himself when he heard the church door open. He turned as he swatted at his companion gnat and tried to make out who it was. He was looking into the bright open door. "Who is it?" he asked. Before the two women could answer, the church moved gently with the events taking place at the creek.

"It is Victoria and Clementina," Victoria replied from the open door.

Father Procopio arose and went to them. "Come in . . . come in," he invited them. "Come and sit. How is you father, Victoria?"

"He is gone," Victoria replied. "He is at the creek struggling for his life."

Father Procopio stroked his chin. "He's a courageous old man. May I live to be that courageous. Right now I feel like I'm faltering. I, like Don Andres, have a premonition about myself."

"Nothing bad can come to a priest, Father Procopio," Clementina said.

"Oh, that it were so, Clementina," Father Procopio sighed and filled the church with despair.

Victoria said, "I don't know about his courage good Father. Some of us think he has gone insane."

"Nonsense," Father Procopio answered. "A man has got to fight for his life." He looked suspiciously at the two women, wondering what had brought them there. "And you Clementina? How are you?" he asked.

"Fine," our mother replied.

Victoria said, "She's always fine. She has a good husband. I know. Pablo's my nephew."

Father Procopio jiggled his eyebrows. "You're right. Pablo's a good man. I just wish he'd come to church. Sit . . . sit," Father Procopio said. "Sit right here on the pew behind me."

Victoria and Clementina sat on the pew. Victoria said, removing her bonnet, "You know Mexican men don't go to church unless they see death's door." Father Procopio smiled at the irony of his fate. He recalled that early in his career the only men he had been able to gather close to the church were the older men in an association called the Mutualists, old men that still wanted to talk and drink beer, the men that the wives and sons and daughters would have to bring to the meetings, cataractic men that could not find their way home at night. It surprised him at how soon he became disenchanted waiting for the last old man to be picked up and after many years he failed to convince them that religion and not story-telling was the original intent of the association. Finally, when they persisted, he had had to let them go, just as he had had to let go of the town's most powerful group, the Ladies of the Altar Society. He had grown tired of the old men's constant unreligious ramblings about the dreaded whip snake and the evil eye and the *empacho*, that constipational intestinal bolus that does not allow food to pass through the digestive tract (perhaps an uncooked tortilla) and much, much more—time consuming diatribes. His head reeled after the meetings and he mildly cursed Don Andres Garcia, as he felt the heaviness of his soul, for having destroyed the concept of the Wheel of Fortune. Furthermore, these old men had expected the beer to be free and to be served and none of them was well enough to spin the Wheel of Fortune, now resting in faded majesty against the corner by the parochial school stage.

"It's tragic but true," Father Procopio joined in about Mexican men attending church. He looked at Victoria for the longest time and finally Victoria fell forward, toward him, on her knees. Clementina took out her rosary and made the sign of the cross with its crucifix. Clementina began the droneful praying of the Sorrowful Mysteries.

Victoria whispered, "The decree has been signed. My father is to be quarantined."

Father Procopio shook his head gently as he disapproved of what the mayor had done. "After all these years, he still can't forgive the man. I can't believe it," was all that he could say.

"Believe it, Father, because I have it right here in my pocket." Victoria took the folded sheet out of her dress and handed it to the Father.

Father Procopio took the decree and, giving his back to the front of the church, read it by the purple light coming from the windows on both sides of the altar. When he was through he asked, "And what are the specific charges that are referred to?"

Victoria hesitated. "Tell him," our mother said. "What good is it going to do us not to tell him?"

Victoria said, "For once, Father, I am embarrassed to speak."

Father Procopio seeing another way out of the problem said, "Maybe you want to go into the confessional? Would that make it easier, Victoria?"

In the confessional Victoria was able to tell the priest what had happened, not that she used the vulgar term for the female part. Instead she covered the poor priest with euphemisms until he was able to understand what it was that Andres Garcia had done.

"In the Spanish moss, you say?" he asked Victoria in a whisper.

"That is how Angelina described it," Victoria whispered her reply, sitting behind the shielding black cloth in the confessional that separated her from Father Procopio.

"And that's all?"

"That was all Lotario needed. That was enough for him to get the quarantine signed."

"And you, Victoria?" Father Procopio asked. "What do you have to say about yourself? Now that you're here, isn't there anything that you would like to confess?"

Victoria hesitated behind the cloth and, if Father Procopio could have seen her, he would have noticed how much pain she was in.

"Victoria, are you there?" he asked when Victoria did not reply. "You're not gone, are you?"

Victoria swallowed her bitterness. "I'm here," she answered.

Father Procopio waited a few seconds to see if Victoria would continue on her own. "Then?" he asked. "At least, Victoria, for your father's sake."

"I told Clementina that I would never confess," Victoria said.

Father Procopio moved the black cloth out of the way. He looked first at Victoria and then at the praying Clementina, who was giving them her back and was sitting in one of the middle pews so as not to be able to hear Clementina's confession. Father Procopio whispered, "Clementina will never know unless you tell her."

"It's not so much Clementina, Father Procopio. Clementina knows what I've done. It's my father I worry about. I don't know what he would do if he ever found out. I know that it would break his heart. And then . . ."

"He would never find out, Victoria. Not from me."

"It would kill him."

"Yes, that's true, Victoria."

"But now that he's dying, Father . . . I just don't want him to die with a broken heart because of what I did."

"I understand," Father Procopio said. "It's just that everybody knows about it but him."

Victoria took the cloth gently in her hands and spread it across the opening between her and the priest. When she no longer could see him she said, "Forgive, me Father, for I have sinned. It is twenty three years since my last confession."

Father Procopio reared back in solitary disbelief at the length of time that it had taken Victoria to confess and re-kissed his stole several times and implored God to provide him with the vestment of immortality, for he knew that this would be a long and trying confession.

As Victoria began to confess about her affair with Lothario, Father Procopio could hear the many sighs of the ever repentant Clementina as she shifted gears within the Sorrowful Mysteries.

Lionel G. Garcia

As the Mother Superior was imploring Sister Carmela to rap harder on the window to scare away the public school children from the playgrounds, the bound Don Andres Garcia, the decree in his tied hands, was being led from the creek by Mayor Lothario and Sheriff Gonzalo past the widow Andrea's house. When the mayor shouted for her, the widow stuck her wrapped and embarrassed head out of the window and nodded with a grave countenance that Andres Garcia was the man that had touched her most intimate of parts while trying to get her to show him where the locusts were ready to emerge.

"Don't worry Andrea," the Mayor said to the widow as she quickly jerked her head back inside the window, "he won't bother you again."

"I never bothered her to begin with," Don Andres replied. "The lady is insane. Why would I want to touch her? Of all people. And you know how shameless some women are. They are the ones that would like to be touched. They are the ones that would like to start an affair. I come from a family that married beautiful people. The women in my family have always been true beauties. The men in my family never messed around with old hags or old widow ladies. We never needed to."

"Like your father, I suppose," the mayor said. "You're always saying that he was better than anyone else."

"Not true, my dear ignorant man," Don Andres replied. "My father was no better than any man. But no one was better than him. Why would General Santa Anna chose him to be his aide? Because he was a great soldier and a diplomat, that's why. Educated in all the military and social graces. He was multilingual. Do you know what that means?"

The mayor looked at the sheriff and replied, "No, I don't. But that doesn't make any difference. I'm still the mayor."

"You're an asshole, Lothario. You're the mayor in title only. No one runs San Diego. The people here are not governable. I've lived among them most of my life. I know. You are still considered the town idiot."

The mayor grabbed Andres by his frail arms and shook him violently. "Listen you crazy sonofabitch," he screamed, "if you call me an asshole or an idiot one more time, I'll whip you. I don't care if you are one hundred years old."

"Don Andres, he's right," the sheriff advised him. "God only knows what Lothario will do when he's provoked. I've seen him beat up some good men."

Don Andres Garcia stopped to catch his breath. "Lothario, in my younger days you wouldn't have done that," he said. "I would have killed you on the spot with a sword or a pistol. You name your weapons."

The mayor, now leading the group, turned back and said, "Old man, you had your chance to kill me and you didn't do it."

"And for that I'm sorry," Andres answered as he staggered behind.

"Come on, Don Andres," the sheriff said, "let's get going. You may die before the day is over, just from what the Mayor has in mind for you."

"And what does this scoundrel have in mind for me? Is he going to kill me? You couldn't do that. As much as you want to, you can't kill me. The town will hang both of you."

The mayor turned back and waited for Andres. "Don Andres," he smiled crookedly, "I thought the town didn't care for anyone. Isn't that what you just said?"

"No," Andres replied in his tired voice, "They love me. They don't love you."

"Then why am I the mayor?"

"You know, Lothario, that that was a fraudulent election. All your votes were counted five times. You can't have more votes than there are people."

"Don Andres is right," the sheriff agreed, nodding his head. "He has a perfect right to say what he is saying."

Lothario grabbed the sheriff by the collar and said, "Shut up you dumb fool. Someone might hear you. If it wasn't for me, you wouldn't be sheriff."

The sheriff tore away from Lothario. "I never wanted to be sheriff," he said, rearranging his collar. "It was all your idea. Just to make a fool of Don Andres and to show him up. As if what you had been doing all this time hadn't been enough."

Innocently, Don Andres said, "Lothario hasn't been doing anything to me."

The sheriff walked away without a word. He felt he had already said too much.

"Gonzalo, if one is honest about things," Andres said to the sheriff as he walked next to the mayor, "Lothario has not given me any trouble until now with his decree. And I appreciate that. Sure, we had our differences a long time ago. But this is now." He looked at the mayor, stopped and cocked his head and said, "Lothario, for many years now I have secretly wished that I had never flogged you at the kiosk at the park in the middle of town. You were so persistent, though. I didn't want you for Victoria. Surely you understand, even though you don't have any children, that one wants the best for them. I didn't want Victoria to have your children. I had other men in mind, the priest's cousin who came to visit from Spain. How educated he was. I could sit and talk to him for hours without being bored. He understood the history of Texas as I explained it to him. The treachery of Sam Houston. The integrity and honor that dominated General Santa Anna's life. I could explain to him the battles of the Alamo and Goliad and San Jacinto. Logically, as my father had lived them. He knew that the Texas Rangers were men that were not to be trusted. He knew how the Mexican people had been exploited by Anglo justice. I could make him understand the destruction of culture that took place when the ignorant Anglo came to Texas. How they made everyone into an animal of greed and avarice. This is mine, the Anglo would say to the Mexican. Give it to me or I'll kill you. How much is that? Sell it to me or I'll kill you or I'll steal it. Through hook or crook, I'll get it. With or without the law. And if the law is against me, why I'll change the law. That's what a gentleman of breeding understands. That no one of culture ever came to save Texas from Mexico. They were castoffs of other states, dumb enough to come here just to die . . . . The priest's cousin was a true gentleman. And he was not the only one, if you remember, Lothario. You didn't stand a chance with me or Victoria. Victoria had many suitors that you didn't know about. But I think her trouble was that she couldn't make up her mind. Remember that there was the engineer for the highway. A recent graduate from the University of Texas. He was equally intelligent. He understood everything about Texas history also. He was able to understand the ambush at San Jacinto better than any other man I had told the story to. Too bad he had to leave. He cried at the doorsteps on the night that he said his farewell. And there was the young doctor that came and left in a matter of months. He wasn't as good a prospect, but still he was educated."

The mayor said, "I don't care about them. That's water under the bridge."

Don Andres looked away from him and began to walk again. "I just wanted you to know why you never could have made it with Victoria," he said.

"And I just want you to know that you are a fool," Lothario responded. "And that now you are under quarantine. That now the decree has been signed and is legal."

Don Andres pleaded, "Why, Lothario? Why are you doing this to me? I'm at death's door. Can't you see that in a few days I will probably be dead?"

The mayor took Don Andres by the arm to hurry him up. "I can't be sure. What if you don't die? What if the goddam locusts emerge and start singing like mockingbirds?"

Don Andres looked to the heavens. "Lothario, if only God could hear you . . . Is it that important that you make a fool of me?"

The mayor stopped and shook the frail Andres Garcia. "Yes, goddam-mit," he shouted. "It's that important to me. The whole town must know that I have turned the tables on you, after all these years."

"Don Andres, Lothario carries a grudge a long time," the sheriff said as he walked in front.

"That he does, Gonzalo," Don Andres replied. "But not me. Thank almighty God. I am a forgiving man, just as my father before me and his father, et cetera."

"Do you two think," the mayor informed them angrily, "that I've en-joyed being the butt of all these jokes for so many years, that every time someone gets a shave and the blade is stropped, everyone thinks of me and the beating I took from Don Andres?"

Andres stopped to get his breath. "You're being too sensitive, Lothario. Your ignorance is showing. No one cares that much about you. Anyway, the flogging wasn't that bad, was it?"

"As far as I'm concerned it was."

"Lothario, you're exaggerating. Idiots have a habit of doing that. I only hit you three times."

The mayor grabbed Andres once more and shook him. "That's a god-dam lie, Don Andres. It was thirty times. Thirty times. My mother counted the red marks on my body."

Gonzalo came back to where the two men were standing and separated the mayor from Don Andres. "Let him go, Lothario," he said. "You can't treat an old man like that."

Lothario took Andres Gracia and shoved him to the ground and Don Andres fell in a pile of old flesh and bones. "I'll treat him worse than that!" he yelled. "Gonzalo, get Don Ramon and meet me at the park."

Father Procopio read the bishop's letter for the tenth time while Victoria tried with all her might to remember all the details of her affair. "Victo-ria," he implored her, "you don't have to tell me everything. We all know the details. All I ask for is a confession in general terms. I can forgive you in a general way. I want you in a state of grace for your father's funeral."

"Do you know about how he came in through the window?" Victoria asked.

Father Procopio clenched his aching teeth. "Yes," he whispered back. "Everyone knows that. What's more important is when did you do it last with him?"

Victoria tried to lie. "It's been two or three years," she said.

"Is that the truth, Victoria?"

"Well," she replied, "it's . . . I can't tell you, Father Proccopio. I'm so ashamed."

"Victoria, we're here for confession," Father Procopio whispered in desperation. "To clean your soul. To put you in the state of grace for your father's funeral."

"Well, then," Victoria said, persuading herself to tell the truth, "it's been between six months to a year."

"Did you know of the decree at the time?"

"Heavens no!" she responded "What do you take me for?"

"I'm glad to hear that, Victoria. I'm glad that you remained faithful to your father."

"Father Procopio," Victoria cried softly, "if you only knew the shame that is in my heart. Please don't tell Clementina."

"I understand," Father Procopio replied in a forgiving voice. "I'm bound to secrecy. Poor woman, you must feel like the Mary Magdalene of the town." Father Procopio scratched his head thoughtfully and jiggled his eyebrows. "I forgive you all your sins, Victoria. Go and sin no more. And for your penance . . ."

"Yes?"

"For your penance . . . ten rosaries a day for ten years."

Victoria stood up and said, "Very well, Father. I had it coming. I'll do whatever you say. I feel better already. About how long do you think it will take to say all those rosaries?"

The good Father made a quick mental calculation and replied, "About one year of your life."

"So be it," Victoria responded.

"I hate to say this, Victoria," Father Procopio was nice enough to inform her, "but now you know why the spider never pees."

And with that he flung open the black transparent cloth that separated them and exposed a Victoria now in the state of grace and hugged her.

As the three left the church arm in arm they could hear the muffled cries coming from the park across the street. There against the bright sunlight of that December day, on the floor of the kiosk, was the figure of Andres Garcia bent over and being held down by the sheriff and being flogged by the mayor, using the same strop that Don Ramon the barber had lent Andres Garcia so many years ago.

CHAPTER 5

Andres Garcia was carried home in the arms of Faustino the drunkard, Amandito the fat one, Bernabe the crazy one, and Fecundo the father of many children.

Victoria and Clementina and Father Procopio had had difficulty getting Don Andres away from the mayor. Once the flogging had started and once Don Andres had started to bleed, the mayor had been reluctant to stop. He had gone way beyond the obligatory thirty lashes that he owed the old gentleman. Victoria had been the first one to run from the church to the kiosk and jump on the mayor's back, knocking both herself and the mayor down from the kiosk and onto the freshly pruned ligustrums below. The two were locked in a fight like cats in mid-air as Victoria tried to take Don Ramon's strop away from him. The sheriff had been more lenient. He had let go of Andres once he saw that Father Procopio was right behind Victoria. Don Andres, once free of the grasp of the sheriff, had staggered and crawled down the concrete steps and had fallen, exhausted with an uncontrollable cough, by the side of the pomegranate hedges. Several of the townspeople that had been crossing the park at the time had stopped to take in the flogging, promising that they would never vote for the mayor again.

Victoria and the mayor had rolled on the ground for several minutes before Father Procopio could run to pry them apart. At the same time Clementina had come down from the kiosk and was attending to Don Andres and cursing Sheriff Gonzalo, her first cousin. Gonzalo, remembering that an angry Clementina and Victoria were not to be dealt with, ran off toward City Hall, across the street where the astonished Angelina was standing at the side-walk looking across to the park.

The mayor was able to get away from Victoria with the help of Father Procopio, but he did manage to attempt one swing with his strop at his former lover. Victoria dodged the leather strop by jumping behind the priest and Father Procopio took the blow of the strop across his jiggling eyebrows. Lothario, astonished at what he had done, stared paralyzed toward the church, waiting for immediate retribution and then ran to City Hall almost catching up with Gonzalo. The ever faithful Angelina ran and opened the door for them and made sure to lock it behind them. There they would be forced to stay, locked in by the Ladies of the Altar Society, until the day that Andres Garcia would die.

51

At that moment, Don Andres' companions arrived from the creek and took him home, but not before they paraded the flogged old man through the dusty main street—in and through the C.O.D. Bar, the pool hall, the drug store and Don Ramon's barber shop—as Father Procopio, Victoria and Clementina followed in the processional closely behind.

Now that he had been given an injection of morphine by the doctor and had been soaked in epsom salt and water by Victoria and Clementina, Andres Garcia felt better, more relaxed, warmer, sleepy. He felt a slight pain in his back-side and tried to lay on his side. With one hazy eye open he could see through the window at the crazy Bernabe as Bernabe, worried for the old man's health, pressed his nose against the window pane.

Andres Garcia closed his eyes and he immediately felt the familiar presence of the ghosts of all his antecedents. Heading the crowd that he imagined around his bed was the wounded but ever jovial Colonel Fernandez, the Artillery Commander at the Alamo, holding the Shroud of Tamaulipas on high, the exact replica of the beloved General Santa Anna and his horse perfectly clear on the face of the sheet. To the side of Colonel Fernandez stood Captain Agustin Garcia, his father, dead now so many years from a knife buried in his heart. He had been killed at the Battle of Chapultepec by General Zachary Taylor, the same Zachary Taylor that had been defeated by Santa Anna at the Battle of Buena Vista. Standing erect on his father's left shoulder, in his bright red and green plummage and constantly kneading his father's uniform with his eight claws, was Jorge the parrot, General Santa Anna's personal messenger, who had tried valiantly to warn the great general of the cowardly ambush at San Jacinto and who had died at the infamous battle, the same faithful parrot that had brought news of the death of Santa Anna's son, flying from Mexico City to San Antonio to inform the general of his tragic loss. The parrot bounced around on his father's shoulder and tried to speak, but he had long ago lost his voice. Andres Garcia had not heard anything coherent from the parrot for over fifty years. To his father's left stood his mother, who had given so much love to her husband and her children. It warmed Andres Garcia's heart to see her so often. Behind her were Don Andres' brothers and sisters, laughing and poking each other in the ribs.

General Urrea, the Cavalry Commander at the Alamo was there, as were Colonel Sesma, who had secretly sealed the back door of the Alamo the night before the fight, and Colonel Almonte, the Infantry Commander for General Santa Anna whose infantry had spearheaded the attack at the Alamo. Behind them stood the other commanders, General Filisola and General Amat. Behind Filisola and Amat stood the members of General Santa Anna's staff: the adjutant, Colonel Susto-Arrendondo; in charge of

Intelligence, Colonel Arriola; operations officer, General Trevino-Sanchez; supply officer, Colonel Garcia-Perez. And behind them he could see the hundreds and hundreds of Indians and *mestizos* that had faithfully come across into Texas, following their great leader only to lose their lives because Sam Houston had wanted to be King of Tejas.

Off to one side by the door and grinning widely was David Crockett, now David Cruz, having changed his name after the battle of the Alamo, not so much for his hatred of Sam Houston, but out of respect for Santa Anna. By him were his wife, Rosa Veronica and his children Fernando, Gumercindo and Agustin, the latter named in honor of Don Andres' father.

"Forty-seven lashes you say?" Father Procopio asked as he sat by the bed and watched as Andres slept.

Victoria sighed and shook her head. "Forty-seven," she repeated. "Isn't that right, Clementina?"

Clementina was sitting behind the chiffonnier, her chin in her hand, wondering what it was that she had said to her first cousin Gonzalo in the heat of the afternoon. "What?" she replied, not knowing what it was she was being asked.

"How many lashes did we count on Don Andres? That's what I'm asking. Father Procopio wants to know."

"I don't remember," Clementina said.

"It was forty-seven," Victoria assured her. "And don't be so preoccupied with your first cousin. If you cursed him out, you cursed him out."

"That's all right, Clementina," Father Procopio said, "I just asked. I don't need to know."

Clementina stuck her head out from behind the chest-of-drawers. "I'm so embarrassed. I've never done that before. What did I say?"

Father Procopio felt Andres' forehead and without looking to Clementina said, "Don't be ashamed Clementina. I've heard worse before. I've been known to curse once in while."

"*Ave Maria Purisima*," Clementina cried, "who would have thought. But no . . . I'm sure you're just saying that, just to make me feel better."

Father Procopio got up and walked around the bed. "No," he said, "I curse very frequently. Especially when I read and re-read the Bishop's letters."

"If only the Bishop would come to visit us," Clementina cried.

"What for?" Victoria replied.

"For him to see in what conditions we live," Clementina said.

"I'd rather he wouldn't," Victoria answered. "I'm ashamed. I'm really ashamed . . . and angry. If Father Procopio were not here, I would be a different person. I'm not showing my anger out of respect, good Father."

Clementina showed her face to them once more. "Heaven forbid that we see Victoria fully angered, Father Procopio."

"I wouldn't blame her one bit," the priest informed them as he walked back and forth.

"I wish that you would let me take care of the wound on your forehead," Victoria told him.

Father Procopio felt softly of his jiggling eyebrows and then studied his hand. "There's no blood," he said to himself. "It's swollen, but I'm not bleeding."

Victoria walked to the priest and studied the blow of the strop that had fallen across the eyebrows and had turned Father Procopio into an unrecognizable beetle-browed stranger. "The man has no shame," she informed the priest. "He has lost all of his senses. Not that he had any to begin with. My father was right about the man, as usual. I can't believe he was trying to hit me when he accidently hit Father Procopio."

"He's lost his senses," Clementina agreed.

"I wish I had been a man so that I would have taken the strop and beaten him with it . . . . Thank God I didn't have a gun at the time. I would have shot him on the spot," Victoria said.

Father Procopio was letting Victoria apply epsom salt and water to his brow. "Would you have killed him?" he asked, almost certain that she would have.

Victoria pushed the solution gently into the skin. "Father, I would have killed the sonofabitch twice . . . three times . . . if I had had the chance this afternoon."

"*Ave Maria Purisima*," Clementina said and crossed herself many times. "But Victoria's right. I have seen her angry and she's capable, Father Procopio, of many things."

"What good would it do you to kill him? Just think of that," Father Procopio said.

"It's not a matter of doing me any good, Father," Victoria said, "it's the matter of killing him. He needs killing."

"That's enough of the epsom salt," Father Procopio informed Victoria. "I'm beginning to taste it and I'm not due for my purgative until next month."

"No one ever got hurt with a good purgative," Victoria said, taking her basin full of solution and placing it by the bed where Andres Garcia slept. "Poor man," she said, looking at her sleeping father. "What's to become of him?"

"Well, Victoria," Father Procopio replied with a sigh that hurt his brow, "you are already in a state of grace and prepared for his death. What a wonderful way to be. You have helped prepare a path of glory for the old man. In the meantime he's going to be awfully sore in the morning."

"If, Father Procopio, he's not dead from the beating he took," Victoria warned the priest.

Father Procopio looked to Don Andres as he slept on his side. "That's true," he whispered. "He did take quite a beating. But he is a very strong man for being one-hundred and-five-years old."

Clementina showed her embarrassed face once more. "That he is," she agreed.

"What was it he was saying as they took him through town?" Father Procopio asked.

"He was whispering, but I think he was saying that he would kill the mayor in the morning," Victoria answered.

"And the men at the barber shop laughed," Clementina said.

Victoria looked at the sleeping man and said, "We'll see who has the last laugh," as Andres Garcia smiled in his dreams at how strong he had been when the mule went down and he had had to pull the plow.

"Victoria, what did the doctor say about him?" Father Procopio asked.

"Not much," Victoria replied. "You know how he is. He said it might affect his liver or his kidneys or his brain. He couldn't tell which one at the moment. He tapped his foot to the beat of the Don Andres' heart and said that his foot was in good rhythm, whatever that meant."

Clementina got up to go to the kitchen. "The only thing is that we don't want the doctor to give him dynamite like he's given half the town. God only knows what that's going to do. He'll blow us up one day. Mark my word. There won't be enough novena's and stations of the cross to put us back together."

"Clementina, where are you going?" Victoria asked.

"To the kitchen," she answered. "You know that when the Ladies of the Altar Society hear about this, all four of them will be here in force. I'm going to make some lemonade for them."

Father Procopio winced when he heard the news. He turned from the old man to the two women and said, "Be careful that they don't over-pray for Don Andres. You know how they can over-do some things."

Victoria shook her head and said, "Like the flood."

"Yes, like the flood and other things," Father Procopio warned as he gathered the alb and the stole that he had been wearing when he ran out of the church and which he had taken off at Don Andres' house and wrapped around his fore-arm and then, having made a ball out of them, tucked them inside his shirt. "I've got to leave," he said, nervously. "You know that the Ladies of the Altar Society and I don't get along."

"Yes, Father," Victoria said to him. "We know. You don't have to explain it to us. We understand."

"It's just that they cannot meet at the church anymore. As much as I want to, I can't allow it."

Victoria looked at him and tried to smile. "You can't afford it, you mean, good Father."

Father Procopio walked hurriedly toward the door and said, "Precisely."

"If only my father Andres had not campaigned against the Wheel of Fortune," Victoria said wistfully. "He's been so hard-headed all his life."

"You can't change life," Father Procopio said, feeling of his swollen forehead before putting on his hat.

"That is why . . .," Victoria said.

Father Procopio, familiar with the proverb, finished it by saying, "the spider never pees."

Clementina, cutting lemons for the lemonade said, "Precisely, Father Procopio. You've learned a lot since you came here."

"More than I care to admit," the good priest said, opening the front door and letting himself out and at the same time being watchful that the honeysuckle was not full of bees. "I'll see both of you tomorrow," he said. "In the meantime, if you have any problems with Don Andres or the mayor or the sheriff, or anyone, let me know. I will be at the rectory."

Father Procopio walked briskly through Main Street looking down at his feet, acting worried and preoccupied so that no one would stop him to talk. At the barber shop the men came out to the door and asked about Andres Garcia and he told them in short, curt words that Don Andres was injured, but seemed to be holding his own. Time would tell the extent of his injuries. The men went back inside, shaking their heads and wondering why the priest was in such a hurry.

He went into the rectory and wrote out his own decree. From there he went directly to the Parochial Hall to where the Mother Superior and her nuns were cleaning the stage for the annual New Years Eve play. There he handed the decree to the Mother Superior and told her and her nuns that they would have to leave for San Antonio. He had arrived at his decision while watching over Don Andres and thinking about the playground swings, the Wheel of Fortune, and the decree that the nuns had issued that no young girl could wear patent leather shoes.

The Mother Superior objected and left running, her habit flowing behind her like a single black wing. She was yelling back to Father Procopio that she was going to call the Bishop. Father Procopio yelled back at her that if the Bishop did not back him up this time against the nuns, that he was going to become a Baptist minister, whereupon the two youngest nuns fainted.

The Ladies of the Altar Society, the four that still persisted, arrived in an orderly group, two by two, each distinguished by the large gold Virgin Mary medallion that hung from a red, white and blue ribbon around their necks, a medallion so large that it covered at least half of the largest one's, Olivia's, breasts. They had heard of the large population of bees that had infested the front of the house around the honey-suckle, so they very carefully entered the house through the back door and into the kitchen where Clementina had already set the glasses of lemonade for them.

"Clementina, are the bees still around?" Olivia asked as she sought help to climb the steps, her medallion beating between her breasts.

"No, come in," Clementina said by the open door. "We haven't had bees for two days."

"Thank God for that," Carmen said. "We had heard that the bees were covering the house. Was that right?"

"No," Clementina answered. "You know how people exaggerate."

"Well, we prayed . . . . Where's Victoria?" Sylvia asked as she climbed the steps behind Carmen. "Is she around?"

Clementina looked toward the door where Andres Garcia was resting. "She's in with her father right now," she said to them. "In the meantime, drink your lemonade. Enjoy it."

"How can one enjoy anything nowadays with the things that are going on," Olivia said as they all sat down. "Decrees. Floggings. Insults. How degrading. You know how we feel about the priest, but one should never raise a hand against a man of God."

Clementina sat down with them with a glass of lemonade. "Father Procopio, may God bless him, took the blow intended for Victoria. Right on the eyebrows. It was Don Ramon's strop."

Sixta, the youngest and prettiest one of the ladies, whose husband had been killed by a dairy bull, ran her finger on the rim of the glass. She said, "There's no respect nowadays. Not with Lothario as the mayor."

Olivia looked all around. "And how is Victoria taking all of this? You know what we mean?"

Clementina looked away, out through the back door at the chickens as they waited patiently to be counted. "Yes," she whispered, as ashamed as if she had been the one having the affair with the mayor. "Victoria is very angry. You know how she is. She's been made a fool of. And now this. But you know she's slow to anger. As the day wears on she'll get angrier and angrier. And angrier."

"You don't think she'll do anything foolish?" Carmen asked. She had always wanted to be a nun, but she had gotten married instead.

Clementina was still looking outside. She noticed that she had not seen the red and black rooster among the flock. She sighed and drank her lemonade. "No, not right now. But you know their blood lines. Heaven help us if they get angry."

"I meant something else," Carmen said. "Like, is she dangerous to herself?"

"Like taking her own life," Olivia said. "That's what we were worried about . . . what we've been praying about for these few days."

Clementina shook her head and smiled at them. "You don't know the family," she answered. "Victoria would never do anything like that. The one that's got to be careful is the mayor. Victoria had already made up her mind. She'll back her father one hundred percent."

"We're here because we want to help Victoria and Don Andres," Sylvia remarked. "We needed to be sure they were together."

"They've always been together, Sylvia," Clementina informed her. "They've never been apart. Today she even went to confession."

Sylvia shuddered at hearing what Victoria had done. "Oh, how horrible," she said. "She went to confession with the horrible priest? The whole town will know about it now."

"Sylvia, Father Procopio has never betrayed his trust. And now, with the long confession out of the way, Victoria's in a state of grace," Clementina argued. "Prepared for her father's death. Father Procopio told her that she would help pave the way for his glory."

"Father Procopio," Olivia said, "doesn't even have enough money to pave the way to pay the light bill. That's why he's been using the candles. It's not that it creates a better effect on the stained glass, as he claims."

"He's struggling with the church. Anyway, we're all poor," Clementina said.

"You can say that again," Sixta replied.

"Let's not talk about Father Procopio anymore. That's not why we're here," Carmen said.

Olivia took a swallow of lemonade and focused on Clementina. "Clementina," she said, "I still can't believe that the mayor would flog Don Andres. What did Don Andres do?"

"Nothing," Clementina answered. "It's just the same old grudge that has been going on for many years."

"That was like thirty years ago," Olivia thought out loud.

"That's exactly right," Clementina said. "But you know how the ignorant carry a grudge."

"And now," Olivia said, "everyone is prepared for Don Andres to die. We've been praying for him and for the doctor."

Clementina said, "The prayers haven't helped the doctor. He says that he can't figure out what it is that will kill the old man. One day he says it's the heart. Another day he says it's the kidneys. Then the lungs. Then the brain."

Sixta took a drink of lemonade and said, "Well, that way eventually he'll be right."

Sylvia arranged the medallion in order to distrubute the pain from one breast to the other. "A lot of good that will do, Victoria," she said.

"When is Victoria coming out?" Sixta wanted to know.

"Clementina," Olivia said, "would it be too much trouble to go get Victoria? She needs to hear this."

Clementina got up and said, "I'll go. She's been talking to her father. I hate to interrupt. You know what I mean. This might be the last conversation that they have together."

Carmen raised the large medallion and kissed the Virgin Mary and said, "We understand. Do you want us to leave then?"

"Oh no," Clementina told them. "Please don't go. Let me see if Victoria is ready to come out."

Victoria was stroking her father's forehead when Clementina walked in. "You're hot," she said to the old man. "It looks like you have a fever."

"From the beating, I'm sure," Don Andres moaned.

"It could be," Victoria told him. "Then again it might be something else. At your age any little thing upsets your body. Anyway, that's what the doctor says every time he comes over."

"But this is from the beating," Don Andres insisted. "I feel it. If you only knew the pain that I'm in."

"The best thing for you to do, father, is to rest," Victoria said, wiping the perspiration from her father's brow. "Forget about vengeance, father. You're much too old for that. Besides, look at the predicament that you're in."

Andres Garcia sat up with a lot of difficulty. "Victoria, you ought to know by now that our family's honor comes first. And Andres Garcia is never too old to protect his family's honor."

Victoria stood back and shook her head. "You're too old, father. Those days are gone forever. You're at an age where nothing in your life goes right."

"Excuse me, Victoria," Clementina said, "but the Ladies of the Altar Society are here to see you."

Victoria finished cleaning Andres' face and said, "Father, do you want them to come in?"

Don Andres thought for a moment and wiped his own brow with the long sleeve of his nightgown and said, "Yes. By all means. Let them in."

Clementina came back with the four women that comprised the most powerful group in town, the only four that were united for one good cause.

Don Andres could see the reflection of the whole room, even himself as a small white dot with a grotesquely pink face, in each of the ladies medallions as they circled his bed. He was comforted, though, by the good intentions that he felt that they represented. He had not been against the rosary. He had been against the imposition of the Wheel of Fortune in the rosary's place. But, he had to admit, as Father Procopio had tried to explain, no rosary had ever made money for the church.

"How do you feel, Don Andres?" Olivia, the chief instigator, asked him.

"Not very well, Olivia," Don Andres replied. "I was flogged early this afternoon."

"That's what we heard," Olivia responded.

"Forty-seven lashes they counted," he said.

"Like I always say, Don Andres, there is no respect left in this world," Carmen said.

"That's true, Carmen," he answered. "At your age you're so wise to realize that."

"At my age?" Carmen smiled. "Don Andres, I'm sixty-five."

"A spring chicken," Don Andres replied and all in the room managed to laugh.

"He still has his sense of humor," Clementina said. "That's one thing that no one can take away from him."

Don Andres saw his reflection in all the medallions and remarked, "That's so true. I've always had a sense of humor, like my Father Agustin, and I've always had a forgiving nature. Isn't that true, Victoria?"

Victoria moved about in the darkness of the room beyond the Ladies of the Altar Society. "That's true," she agreed with her father.

"We all know that," Olivia said. "We all know what a good person you have been all your life. When we heard about your first predicament we began to pray for you, Don Andres. And so far the locusts have not emerged. And now when we heard about the flogging, well . . . ."

"It was too much," Sixta interrupted. Her medallion was almost touching the bed.

Victoria approached the group. "What do you propose to do?" she asked.

Sylvia took the medal and nervously swung it between her breasts. "We heard that the mayor and the sheriff ran and locked themselves in the City Hall. Is that right?"

"I couldn't see anything at the time," Don Andres said.

Clementina stepped up from the shadows of the room and said, "It's true. I know Don Andres couldn't see anything because he was dying by the side of the pomegranate bushes. And Victoria was locked in battle for Don Ramon's strop with Mayor Lothario. At the same time Father Procopio was trying to separate Victoria from Lothario. The sheriff was running to City Hall. I could see Angelina waiting for them so that she could open the door. The mayor was right behind the sheriff. Angelina let them in and they locked the door."

"They're still locked in City Hall," Olivia said. "They're waiting for just the right moment to come out."

"And what is the Altar Society going to do?" Victoria asked.

"Well," Olivia said, "simply put, we're not going to let them out."

"Until when?" Don Andres asked.

"Until the mayor agrees to come here and apologizes to you, Don Andres," Olivia said, moving her medallion from the pain of one breast to the other. Don Andres glared at his ridiculous reflection on the medal as it went from one side of the Virgin Mary to the other.

"*Ave Maria Purisima,*" Clementina said, crossing herself many times with the crucifix. "What is this going to lead us to?"

Don Andres laid back slowly and smiled for the first time in many days, his physical pain not as bothersome as before. "Tell him, Olivia," he said to the woman, "that I am willing to forgive him this one time if he comes to me and apologizes. The whole town knows that I have always been a forgiving man." He looked to the window and saw the ever faithful crazy Bernabe staring through the window to make sure that his old friend was still alive.

"Tell that crazy Bernabe to go away," Victoria said to Clementina and Clementina came out from the shadows of the room to shoo Bernabe away.

"Wait Clementina," Andres pleaded, his heart suddenly heavy from the thoughts of his imminent death, "ask the poor man about the creek. What is my fate?"

Clementina went to the window and tried to stop the fleeing Bernabe, but Bernabe, thinking that he had done something wrong, refused to stop.

"Leave him alone, poor man," Victoria said. "He's crazy. He doesn't know what's going on."

"Poor man has been like that since the day he was born," Andres Garcia said. "People said that he was born following the month when there was no moon. He also needs the prayers of the Ladies of the Altar Society."

"Right now we've been concentrating on you," Sixta informed him.

"We've been praying for you, Don Andres," Carmen comforted him. "Every day we've prayed. Your fate is now in God's hands."

Not to be outdone, Olivia said, "We've all prayed for you, Don Andres. Not only us but the whole town. As always, everyone is praying that you live one more year."

Don Andres wiped tears of gratitude from his eyes. "You don't know how much mental and physical pain I'm in," he said. "I appreciate what the town has done for me. But it's been hard to live from year to year all my life."

Victoria and Clementina accompanied the four ladies out through the kitchen door and they alternately hugged each other, past the difficulty of the medallions, as they said their fare-wells. They were on their way, two by two, to block the door at City Hall until the mayor apologized. As they walked across the yard Olivia said, "It is so good that Don Andres chose to forgive the mayor. This way we are sure that there is no blood-shed."

Victoria yelled her reply. "I'm so relieved also," she said to the women as they crossed the yard and then the street, looking back to be sure that the bees that had attacked the honey-suckle and the doctor were gone.

Then Victoria and Clementina counted the patient chickens and found the missing red and black rooster making love to a strange white hen in the pomegranate bushes. "You're just like all men," Victoria scolded the fleeing rooster as she threw a stick at him. "Making love at a time like this."

CHAPTER 6

The same gnat that had been there the morning before was bothering Father Procopio again as he tried in vain to pray his morning novena. He knew that it was useless to shoo the persistent drone-maker away and, once he gave in to the inevitability of the hovering insect, he was quickly mesmerized by its sound. In this altered state he wondered if God in his own way was trying to tell him something. So he sat back on the creaky pew and jiggled his eyebrows in spite of the pain in his forehead. He felt the spot for the hundredth time where the strop had hit him and the thought came to him that God wanted him to pray the Stations of the Cross in order to release some poor soul from Purgatory.

He was at the eighth station, where Jesus speaks to the women, when in through the door came the tiptoeing widow Andrea, dressed in black, the lower half of her disgraced long face covered with a black shawl like a muslim. She went in quietly, creaking only a few of the floor-boards and fell to her knees at the back of the church where the pews began. She took out an enormous rosary, its beads as large as lemons, and crossed herself with its heavy wooden crucifix repeatedly and then let out such a mournful sigh that she filled the church and Father Procopio with sadness. From there she proceeded in her hunched way to walk on her knees toward the altar. Father Procopio watched her from the side pews from where the Stations of the Cross were located. He thought better about disturbing the widow and he waited patiently until she reached the altar and touched the railing around it, the railing that protected the Holy Sacrament from the all-conniving women in the church. It was at that precise moment when Father Procopio, fearing that the woman would blurt out her pain without knowing that he was there, cleared his throat and acted as though he was gagging. The widow, awakened from her trance, jumped up from her knees and, thinking that Father Procopio was Jesus Christ, jumped one more time clearing the railing and running to the sacristy from where she screamed as she ran outside. Father Procopio went to the window and saw her as she hobbled through the playground and through the area of the swings where the ever watchful Sister Carmela was on guard. Father Procopio saw the nun rap on the window pane and then noticed how much faster the poor widow had to run in order to get out of the nun's domain.

"My God," he said to himself, "I would love to see them gone."

Lionel G. Garcia

Early in the morning before sunrise, before anyone had counted the chickens, Andres Garcia, one-hundred-and-five years old, felt the accumulated pain not only of his beating the day before, but the pain of the beatings of all his antecedents as well. At his age he felt the soreness not only along his back-side but in front as well. God only knew how many times he had fallen and how much of the soreness was due to Clementina beating on his chest as he lay by the pomegranates, the latter a medical tidbit demonstrated by the doctor to both Victoria and Clementina in case the old man's heart should ever stop. In that respect and in his propensity to keep mistresses, the whole town had to admit that the doctor was a little ahead of his time, medically speaking.

Andres Garcia swung his thin frail legs one at a time until they were touching the floor. Then he sat up on the edge of the bed. He stood up stooped, without being able to straighten out his back. "This sonofabitch has done me in," Andres whispered to himself, referring to the mayor, as he grabbed his back with both hands. Now that he walked he could feel the ache in his liver and his kidneys. He was being very careful to be quiet. He did not want Victoria to know that he was looking for his father's heavy revolver inside the clothes closet. He found the heavy revolver in the pocket of the overcoat, checked it in the light and made sure it was loaded. In the pocket on the other side he found his trusty backup, the small powerful derringer once fired at the scoundrel, James Bowie. He shuffled back to bed and placed both guns in the bottom drawer of the nightstand by his bed and covered them with newspapers. By this time he had forgotten that he had agreed with the Ladies of the Altar Society that he would pardon the mayor if the mayor would only come to the house and apologize. His darkest thoughts were of how he would get up and kill the mayor sometime during the day, but when he tried to get back in bed he was struck as though by lightning with the extremely painful urge to relieve himself, a pain that quickly became so much more intense and deep that he felt as though both his kidneys were locked in a burning vise and he had to cry out for help.

In the other bedroom Victoria was sitting by the window where she had been praying Father Procopio's penance since four in the morning. Between Hail Marys she had considered what a fool she had been for so many years and she reached her own conclusion about the mayor as she finished the Five Joyful Mysteries: If she had to, she would kill him in order to keep him from telling her father about the love affair. She vowed that Andres Garcia, her father, would die an honorable man.

She was on the Agony in the Garden, the first of the Sorrowful Mysteries, when she heard her father scream. Immediately she threw off the rosary and the missal that was guiding her through her penance and she ran to his room. She found Andres floundering inside his sheets, trying to get up. "I need to go to the bathroom, but I can't get up," he cried to her. "The pain is so great. If only you could feel it."

"Hold on to me, father," she said as she picked him up and rushed him away.

She lowered his pajamas exposing his frail body and causing him a pained embarrassment. He tried to object, holding on to the pajama strings, but Victoria insisted. "Don't be foolish," she admonished him, trying to get him to hurry up. "I'm your daughter. You need help."

"It's just that . . . that," he cried, trying to hide from Victoria.

"What? . . . Come over here and urinate," she demanded of him.

"That you've never seen a naked man before," Don Andres said and proceeded to urinate blood.

Victoria stared horrified at the red stream coming from the old withered penis. "My God!" she cried. "The doctor needs to see you right away."

All through the night the mayor and the sheriff had not been able to sleep in the cramped space that was City Hall. Angelina in her faithfulness had created another problem for them. She refused to leave them alone, insisting on sticking out the hostage situation with the two men. Three people in the two small offices was too much, especially when one of them was a woman. The sheriff was particularly stressed because he was one of those big men that enjoyed eating offal and tripe and lungs and the vulva of the cow and he was prone to belch and pass a lot of gas. For the last twelve hours he could feel the gas ricochetting inside his gut without ever having the opportunity to let it go. Everytime he thought he had a chance to sneak some gas, Angelina came in from the outer office to inform them of what was going on outside.

The Ladies of the Altar Society had arrived late in the afternoon of the previous day and had set up their prayerful watch outside the door. Olivia was big enough so that her sitting on the sidewalk by the door prevented anyone from going in or out.

"Anyone having anything to do with the mayor or the sheriff must go over me," she had said as she lowered her large body in definite stages in front of the outside door, her large medallion swinging wildly like the pendulum of a large clock. Her other sisters-in-prayer sat at the edge of the sidewalk. They were all taking their turn at being the priest, leading the group in praying the rosary.

"This is going to be hard on all of us," the mayor informed the sheriff and Angelina. "We must figure out a way to get out of here."

"You're the one that sealed the back door," Angelina reminded the mayor.

"She's right," the sheriff said. "I remember you wanted to seal the door."

"Oh, shut up," the mayor said.

"It's true," Angelina reminded him. "You're the one that had the men seal the back door. You were afraid someone would come in and shoot you."

"Angelina, that's not true," the mayor replied. "Why would anyone want to kill me?"

Angelina said without hesitation, for she had the memory of an elephant, "The Christmas decorations. Remember?"

"Oh, that," the mayor remembered.

"Mayor, you had the door sealed and now we can't get out," the sheriff said.

"Well, it was for all our benefit," the mayor said. "I admit that there were some people angry with us that year . . . . The important question is what to do now?"

Angelina, seeming to enjoy the camaraderie, took a chair by the sheriff and sat down to contemplate. The sheriff had at that time expected her to leave the room and had prepared himself to vent some gas, but when Angelina unexpectedly grabbed the chair, he once again tightened his resolve and felt the pain similar to a heart attack course from the middle of his chest down to the belly button and back up to the left arm, his left hand paralyzed in the shape of a claw.

"Mayor, I've talked to them and talked to them. You know what they want," Angelina begged. "Give in to them."

The mayor stroked his chin wondering why the Priest had not had the city build a restroom in City Hall. Father Procopio, if he had been there, would have had a simple explanation: People should never see a priest go to the restroom. It detracted from his ability to convey to the people a state of grace. "And you insist that Father Procopio never once needed to go to the bathroom, Angelina?" the mayor asked, his thoughts carrying him away from the conversation.

"Mayor, what is it?" Angelina asked, surprised. "What did you say about Father Procopio?"

"Nothing," the mayor answered. "I was just thinking out loud."

"Father Procopio never once needed to go to the bathroom," Angelina said. "If that was what you were asking."

"No . . ." the mayor mumbled. "That was not what I was asking. Everyone knows that Father Procopio does not go to the bathroom. Forget about that. Our problem is how to get the Ladies of the Altar Society off our doorsteps."

Angelina raised up in her chair as if she were leaving to the outer office, but then she sat down and moved her chair closer to the mayor. "You know what they want, Lothario. All you have to do is go to Don Andres and apologize for the beating that you gave him."

"I don't want to do that," the mayor shouted, slamming his fist on the desk. "Don Andres never apologized for the beating he gave me. Why should I have to apologize?"

"Because that's what they want," the sheriff said, moving his weight from one buttock to the other. "And if I were you, I'd apologize. What harm would it do. It would even make you look like a better man, Lothario. Just look at what the city would do. There would be a fiesta. People would love you."

"I don't want to do it. I will not apologize. My bladder will break before I apologize."

Angelina whispered, "Then, Lothario, you will never leave here. The Ladies of the Altar Society is the most powerful group in town. Once they attack something or someone they will never leave it alone until they win."

"We'll see," the Mayor said and took out a piece of paper and his pencil and began to write in block letters. "Angelina," he said, "when I finish this note I want you to take it and go talk to the women, talk of anything, but get outside. Once outside give this note to the first person you see and tell them quickly, before the Ladies of the Altar Society can stop you, to deliver this message to Victoria's window. We'll see who is going to win this little war."

Amandito, the fat one, was at Don Andres' window by daybreak. He rapped on the pane several times before Andres Garcia heard him. Andres Garcia feeling the pain of a thousand needles pricking his kidneys, rolled over very slowly and again felt the urge to urinate blood. Amandito, noticing the pain that the old man was in, opened the window from the outside and asked the dying man how he was.

"Terrible, Amandito," Don Andres replied. "The doctor is coming this morning, if Victoria can find him. No one knows where he spent the night. I'm passing blood from the kidneys. I can feel it. I can feel my kidneys bleeding."

"May God have mercy on your soul, Don Andres," Amandito prayed for him. "It was the beating you took."

"Yes," Andres replied. "I believe you're right. It all comes from the beating. I was good as new before that. Don't you remember?"

"Don Andres," Amandito said, "you were better than new. Look at how hard you were working at the creek. And you've always been a hard worker. Remember the story that you love to tell about you pulling the plow?"

"I don't like to talk of those things anymore, Amandito. I'm too weak."

"You don't look weak, Don Andres," Amandito said, trying to cheer up the old man. "You have tremendous powers. My God, by tomorrow this time you'll be up and about and working at the creek."

"Amandito, even if I could, I couldn't go. Remember the decree."

"Forget about that, Don Andres. I just came from the barber shop and everyone there says that they will not allow you to be confined to your house. Everyone in town says that you can come and go as you please. Everyone is against the mayor. This time he has gone too far. The decree cannot be enforced."

"That's good to know," Andres said. "It's good to know that the town is behind me."

"The Ladies of the Altar Society are not letting the mayor or the sheriff out of City Hall. Did you know that?"

"I remember that they came by, but I don't remember when."

"Yesterday, Don Andres. They visited you yesterday."

"I don't know the days that I live," Andres said, shaking his head at his predicament.

"You've been in too much pain, Don Andres. Once you get out of pain you'll remember everything. You'll be as good as new. We still have to fight the locusts. Remember that, Don Andres. Don't give up."

"Amandito, if you only knew the pain that I'm in. My kidneys are on fire. I'm urinating blood. I feel pain inside of me. Like my kidneys and my liver had been flogged. I can't walk very well. I feel like I have one good effort left in me and I don't know how to use it. I don't want to spend it on something that is beyond hope."

"You've got to go to the creek, Don Andres."

"I can't make it today, Amandito. What day is today?"

"Don Andres, today is the twenty-eighth of December. You've got three more days to go."

"For a man my age . . . three days is an eternity."

"No it's not, Don Andres. In three days you'll be as good as new. We'll hitch you to the plow on the first day of the new year."

"Don't make me laugh, Amandito. It hurts too much. I can't help you. I'm sorry. You know that I've never quit on anything in my life, but today I can't get up."

"Don't worry, Don Andres. We'll be at the creek for you. And then tomorrow you can join us."

"I'll try, Amandito. I'll try very hard to get up tomorrow. I won't fail you. I promise. And when Andres Garcia makes a promise, he keeps it."

"Always a man of his word. That is the reputation that you've always had. This is precisely why the town loves you and not the mayor. Who ever heard of an election where there were more votes than people?"

"He's an ignorant scoundrel," Andres Garcia said. "What else can you say? But that is what some people like. I don't doubt it that there are some that love him."

"Don Andres, the town is saying that he's a bastard."

"In more ways than one, Amandito."

"He's not stopping us from working on the creek, Don Andres."

"He better not."

"Is it true that you promised to forgive him if he apologizes in person to you?"

"I don't remember saying that."

"That's what the Ladies of the Altar Society are saying. If he comes out of City Hall and apologizes to you, you will forgive him."

"Well, if I said it, I said it. And I stand by my word. You know, Amandito, that I am a forgiving man. I have always been a forgiving man. It's in the nature of all the men in my family. Why if you go back in history . . ."

"To the Alamo, right Don Andres?"

"Precisely, Amandito. Bowie would have been forgiven and so would have Travis, even as arrogant and treacherous as they were. My father had already spoken on their behalf. Be careful with arrogance, though. That's what got them killed."

"Arrogant, like the mayor," Amandito said and he stepped back from the window. "I better be going, then," he said.

"I wish I could go," Don Andres told him, "but it's impossible. I know now that I'm dying for sure."

"Oh hush, Don Andres," Amandito scolded him. "You're not dying. This is temporary. I know you. In the mean time we'll be at the creek helping you out."

"You don't know how much this means to me, Amandito. Is everyone going?"

"Yes, Don Andres, we'll all be there."

"You know how much I think of all of you. Right now Victoria is asleep, but when she gets up I'll tell her to go to the creek and take some money to you. You'll need it to buy your supplies and some food and drink."

"No need to send Victoria," Amandito told him. "I'll just send the crazy Bernabe over later on."

Two hours later the mayor was still hard at work finishing his note, writing in his block letters.

"That's the longest note or the slowest writing I've ever seen," Angelina said.

The sheriff had gone to the front office to vent his gas and had left Angelina and the mayor together.

"This is the last note I'll have to write to ugly Victoria and damn glad of it," the Mayor said. He had his face down by the paper, sticking his tongue out as he wrote slowly.

"That's the fifth pencil you've used," Angelina informed him.

"Don't you ever shut up, Angelina?" the mayor said, trying to dissolve her with an angry stare.

When the mayor raised his head from the paper and signed his name with his usual flourish, Angelina said, "You're finished?"

And the mayor, proud of his signature, looked over the short note and said, "I'm finished." He sealed the note and handed it to Angelina. "Get outside and hand it to the first person you see. Tell them to take it to Victoria's window. That is the second window from the end of Don Andres' house on the west side. The west side. Remember. Don't forget."

"I know perfectly well where Victoria's window is," Angelina replied, taking the note and walking away with it.

Angelina managed to get outside to talk to the Ladies of the Altar Society. They had no animosity toward her, they told her. She was free to come and go as she pleased. They asked Angelina how the mayor was holding out and she was able to tell them truthfully that the mayor was doing fine, that it was the sheriff and his gas that she was worried about.

The first person that came across the park, around the kiosk where Andres Garcia had been flogged, was the crazy Bernabe, who was running to Victoria to get the money that Andres Garcia had promised them. Angelina yelled at him and when he came over, she handed him the note and gave him instructions quickly as to where to deliver the note.

Bernabe, not being of normal mind, thought he understood the directions perfectly and promised Angelina that he would deliver the note. Angelina ran inside and locked the door before the Ladies of the Altar Society could realize what she had done.

The crazy Bernabe delivered the note to Andres Garcia's widow, slipped it under the window frame, where it stayed overnight.

CHAPTER 7

Andres Garcia felt the agonized pain of all his antecedents through his liver, his lungs, his kidneys and his spleen. Only his heart had been spared for the time being. He moved slightly in bed and oddly enough seemed to feel a little better than yesterday. Yesterday had been a day that he would not want to repeat. The only good news was that he had heard from Victoria that the locusts had not emerged. And whatever the doctor had given him in the injection yesterday had eased the pain somewhat today. The pain notwithstanding, he had been able to get up and urinate on his own all during the night. Only a faint streak of red was visible in his copious urine. The doctor had ordered that he stay in bed for fear the bleeding would start all over again. Along with the injection he was to take one drop of mercury every hour on the hour, like a water clock.

He had reached his altered state, the Shroud of Tamaulipas held high by Colonel Fernandez, and he could see the throng of people surrounding his bed, when he heard the scratching on the window. It was Amandito making his early morning visit.

The first thing Amandito noticed was the note that the crazy Bernabe had left sticking between the window and the window frame. He took the folded note and looked at it and noticed that there was no name on the outside. Never having had occasion to do business with the mayor, he did not recognize the imprinted mayoral ring on the wax seal. He opened the window and whispered, "How are you doing this morning, Don Andres?" at the small bulk wrapped in sheets, not knowing if the old man was alive or dead.

Andres rolled over at hearing the familiar voice and raised his head up slowly and with difficulty, like an old upside-down turtle, and saw the fat Amandito through the window. "I'm feeling a little better," he shrugged.

"What does the doctor say, Don Andres?"

"He hasn't been here this morning yet. I expect him in a few minutes. Victoria has gone to see where he slept last night. You know the man is impossible to find when you need him."

"All he cares about are his women, Don Andres."

"Precisely," Andres replied. "That's what his trouble is. That and the fact that he doesn't know too much medicine."

"He's good enough for us, don't you think, Don Andres?"

Don Andres sighed weakly, expiring a small pain-filled wisp of air, "That's the trouble with us Mexicans . . . ever since the Anglo came we've been getting the dregs."

"Ever since the battle of San Jacinto, as you correctly point out, every chance you get, Don Andres."

"That is precisely why I say it, Amandito. It has been our destiny. Just think, to be ambushed at San Jacinto where no Mexican army intended to fight and to allow Santa Anna to dine the night before with Sam Houston. How was my father to know that it was all a trap? Luckily, most of the Mexican army had stayed behind at the Brazos River . . . It all adds up to this."

"The doctor, Don Andres?" Amandito asked innocently. These were the times when he couldn't keep up with the old man.

Andres said, "Yes, the doctor and all this other mess. Just remember that when they ruined our culture, they ruined our people, and now you have the mayor that cannot read or write, the merchant that still kills his goats on a wooden floor, and the ones that have to count in twelves. Our children ruined. And It's not going to get better, Amandito."

Amandito shook his head slowly, trying to imagine the future. "You're right, Don Andres. Not even the shroud which you possess will encourage the children."

"Amandito, not even if the shroud develops an aura . . . . The only redeeming thing is that they ruined themselves in destroying us. Consequently, Texas has never and will never produce a great Anglo mind."

"You know, Don Andres, that I believe you're right all the time."

"Of course I'm right, Amandito. I can think. I can see these things . . . . Like the doctor, one of these times he's going to get a case of the clap so bad that not even God and Father Procopio and all his prayers can cure him. And what's worse, he's going to give it to all his mistresses and they're going to pass it on."

"They said yesterday at the barber shop that he gave you mercury. Could that be true?"

Andres propped himself on his pillows, almost making a cave for his torso. "Yes, that's true. One drop an hour."

"Like a drip," Amandito said.

"Like a drip is right, Amandito. No one realizes how fast an hour goes until he has to take mercury by the drop."

"But you're feeling better. That makes me happy, Don Andres."

"I feel better. Not much but better, but better. My kidneys cry to go a lot. If only I could rid myself of my misfortunes, I'm sure my health would improve."

"Oh, you know the old saying. There is no misfortune that does not have some good in it."

"Amandito, I've never believed that proverb. It was thought up by God to keep the Mexicans hoping for better times."

"I believe in it, Don Andres. I see it happen all the time. With all due respects, take the widow Andrea. When her husband died in a fight some forty years ago, everyone said it was such a tragedy. Compared to the married women in town, I've never seen a happier woman in my life . . . up until now. Now she's sad over everything that's happened. Forgive me if I wink, Don Andres, but if you could have approached her more gently, maybe she would not have objected."

Andres replied with defined resignation, "Amandito, you know that the men in my family have never attached much importance to being gentle . . . and we've never touched women that are ugly like the widow Andrea."

"Whatever was done is done. I think that she imagined it, Don Andres . . . . Believe me, these misfortunes will make you a better person. And no need to worry about the creek, Don Andres. We have that under control now that we bought more quicklime. But still . . . don't get me wrong. We'd like to see you there, as hard a worker as you are."

"Amandito, nothing would make me happier than to see you and Faustino and Bernabe and Fecundo at the creek. I've always loved to work there with you. You may not believe it, but those days were some of the happiest I've ever spent."

Amandito was overwhelmed at Andres' generosity. "Do you really mean that?" he said as he brushed a tear from his eye, and using nothing but his fingers, blew his nose like a horn. "You are a very good man, Don Andres. It's very kind of you to say that. We . . . we also thought that those days, year after year, were some of the happiest we have ever spent. We've done a lot of drinking and eating through the years."

"But always under some apprehension, Amandito. I may have laughed, but inside I was always worried for my life."

"We knew that, Don Andres. We were just trying to make you feel better. And yesterday we sat down at the bank of the creek and we thought what promises we could make for you. Faustino said that if you would get well and not die, that he would never drink again. Fecundo then said that if that were the case, he would never father another child. Bernabe said that he would learn to read and write and learn how to follow directions. I myself promised before God that I would not eat for a year."

Andres looked out through the open window at Amandito's globular head framed by the window and sighed heavily, filling the room with nostalgia. "I'm indebted for your kindness. But it looks like the end is coming soon," he said.

"Oh, Don Andres," Amandito scolded him gently, "how many years is it that you have been saying that. And every year . . . why look at you now. Your color is back. You're not bleeding like yesterday. Your strength looks like it's coming back and look at how you can sit up. Yesterday you couldn't do that, could you?"

"You may be right, Amandito. It's too early to give up."

"Andres Garcia never gives up. Right Don Andres?"

"Precisely, Amandito. Andres Garcia never lets his friends down and he never gives up. What day is today?"

Victoria entered the room with the doctor and said, "Today is the twenty-ninth and the doctor is here."

"Good morning, Victoria . . . Doctor," Amandito said from the window. "Don Andres says he's feeling better. I myself can see the change in him from yesterday. It looks to me like he will weather this storm and live to fight again."

"If only God could hear you," Victoria told him as she prepared her father for the doctor's examination.

"Oh, we've already made our promises, Victoria . . . . What do you think, Doctor?" Amandito asked.

The doctor wiped the eternal sleep from his eyes and yawned. "I won't know until I examine him," he said.

"If you can tell me," Amandito said, "I can pass the word to the men at the barber shop and the pool hall, the C.O.D. Bar and the drug-store."

The doctor took out his stethoscope and listened to Andres' heart and lungs as Victoria and Amandito remained silent out of respect for the process that was taking place. When the doctor lifted the stethoscope from Andres' chest, Victoria asked, "How does he sound?"

The doctor waved his hand at Victoria with more or less of a rocking gesture, indicating an undecided state of mind and said, "Eh . . . maybe yes, maybe no."

"They'll be glad to hear that in town," Amandito volunteered.

The doctor felt the abdomen, tapping his well-placed hand with his finger, creating the familiar percussive sounds from the organs below. "The liver extends to here," he said, making a line from one side of Andres' rib cage through the belly button and around to the other side. "Very enlarged." He listened intently as he continued to tap-tap. "The spleen has a small hole in it that should heal on its own. The kidneys would like nothing better than to start bleeding again. All in all, the man is in good shape for the shape he's in . . . . If he stays in bed."

"For how long, Doctor?" Victoria asked, worried.

"For as long as it takes," the doctor replied.

"That could or could not be good news," Amandito said to himself.

"It depends on whether he gets well or not," the doctor answered to the man at the window and gathered his equipment and placed it inside his bag. "Be sure, Victoria, that he takes the mercury every hour. One drop every hour."

Victoria said, helping him out of the room, "He'll get his drop every hour, Doctor. You can be sure."

Outside she followed closely behind the doctor, her arms crossed in disappointment, aggravated by the clicking sounds of his heels on the sidewalk. "At least the damn bees are gone," he said to her.

She grabbed him by the arm as he was about to get in his car. "We're very worried about him," she said. "What do you think?"

The doctor bit his lip and threw his bag on the front seat. Then he shook his head. "In this situation, Victoria, maybe the locusts know more than I do," he said.

When she went back inside to her father's room, Amandito was resting both his arms inside the window and she noticed that he held a folded piece of paper in his hands. He was passing the note from one hand to the other. "This is a piece of paper, a note, I found on the window sill," Amandito said handing it over to Victoria.

Victoria took the note from Amandito. If she had taken the time to inspect the seal, she would have immediately recognized it as coming from the ring on the mayor's finger and would have known it was a note intended for her and not for her father. But she didn't notice the seal and she placed the note on the night stand. "It's for my father," she said, smiling. "From one of his admirers."

"Probably from the widow Andrea," Amandito laughed.

"Oh, go away," Victoria scolded him.

"Amandito," Andres said, waving feebly at him, "tell them at the barber shop that I'm doing better. That I haven't given up yet. Tell them I'm even getting notes from admirers."

"I'll tell them everything," Amandito said, closing the window and running away.

In the oppressive solitude of his room, with Victoria gone, Andres Garcia broke the seal on the note and read it. After he was through he felt in his heart, the only intact organ he had left, the weight of all his lifetime of misfortunes multiplying in heated waves to an insuperable degree.

After he was sure that his heart had not stopped, he re-read the note, hid it with the revolver and the derringer, and then proceeded to stare at the ceiling, trying to find some order in this world. Finally, after several hours of contemplating Victoria's infidelity, he screamed for her.

Victoria and Clementina were outside counting the chickens when they heard the scream and, thinking that the old man had died, they dropped the hot red and black rooster that they had been checking and ran into the house.

"What happened?" Victoria asked when she and Clementina saw Andres, his face as red as the sunset. "What's wrong? Why did you scream?"

Andres stared at Victoria intently, full of hate for his daughter.

"Father," Victoria said tenderly, trying to reach for him. "Why do you look at me like that? What's the matter?"

"How does it feel to be a whore?" Andres asked her and Victoria pulled back away from him.

"What do you mean?" she asked. "Are you going crazy? Why would I know how a whore feels?"

Clementina had been crossing herself with her rosary since entering the room and seeing the transformation that had occurred within the old man. "*Ave Maria Purisima*," she prayed. "What has happened now to Don Andres? Why are his eyes looking like that. Why is he in a rage? Is he destined to lose his mind now, Victoria?"

"Whores, all of you!" Andres screamed. "Get out of my room!"

"Father, let me touch you," Victoria pleaded with her father. "Let me soothe your forehead."

"If you touch me, I'll kill you," Andres Garcia screamed, wild-eyed, at his daughter.

"Was it something in the note?" Victoria said. "Was it the widow Andrea wanting to marry you?"

"The note is none of your goddam business," Andres told her. "Now get out of my room and never come in here again."

"Oh my God," Clementina cried out, "another decree!"

At the nunnery the Mother Superior had gathered her three nuns and was complaining about Father Procopio. Their edict on the proper washing of the female part had been challenged by the priest and the doctor. Their edict on the wearing of patent leather shoes had gone unenforced by the priest. He had told the parents of the young girls that had already bought the shoes that their children could properly wear them to the first communion and all the masses and to graduation if they so desired. The public school children were trying more and more to use the parochial school swings. And this morning she had caught two unknown children masturbating in the restroom by the swings. All the playgrounds were in chaos since the beginning of the Christmas season and it was Father Procopio's fault. For all she knew, she told the younger sisters, Father Procopio was now a Baptist, as he had threatened.

Father Procopio was in the confessional while all these things were being said about him. He had begun to read the latest letter that the Bishop had sent him. All things in the Catholic church must remain the same, the Bishop of Corpus Christi wrote. The church in San Diego needed to raise more money and not less, the Bishop having never been told that his favorite, San Diego's Wheel of Fortune, was now long gone and collecting spider webs, its large round useless face pointing toward the wall by the parochial school stage, where the workmen had set it after the fight with Andres Garcia. The nuns must be given their lead, the Bishop said in the second paragraph. They had a job to do, to stir up the town. Father Procopio was to leave them alone. It would be useless to run them off. If he did, they would not go back to San Antonio from where they came. San Antonio could not absorb one more nun.

Father Procopio folded the letter in fourths and felt the trembling ground under the church. At the same time he realized that the widow Andrea, who had run into the confessional, had stopped talking. "Go on," he said, trying to act irritated. "I'm listening."

The widow said through the sheer black curtain, "I thought I could see you reading a letter."

"I can do both things at once," the priest answered. "Didn't you realize that?"

"No, Father," she replied. "Now do you want me to confess?"

"Absolutely," the father said.

"Well, Father, it's hard for me to begin . . . it's hard for me to tell you the truth."

"Andrea, you must. And if this concerns Don Andres, you must tell the truth and do it right now. The poor man is dying and he must die in a state of grace."

"Well, Father, you see . . ."

"No, I don't see anything. Tell the truth and no harm will come to you."

"Well, Father, what I told the mayor and the sheriff was not true."

"Tell me some more."

"I've been a widow for forty years, Father. I've been happy. I haven't had a man to bother me constantly like the married women do. I look younger than my age from lack of worrying and I do mostly light work, meaning that I haven't had all my life to take care of a Mexican man. I only had one child and she was very easy to raise. Now she's having her problems. She's not working, father. She lost her job. She used to work in Alice, but they closed the store. I always wanted her to work at the court-house here in San Diego. But who are we? We are not that deep into politics. One day I thought that if I could do something for someone, she might get a job. The perfect opportunity presented itself when I met Don Andres by my house. He was very disoriented and I knew that if I accused him of something everybody would believe me and not him. The rumors were out all over town that the mayor wanted something on Don Andres so that he could get the councilmen to sign the decree. I figured the mayor had a lot of friends at the courthouse. If I helped him, maybe my daughter could get a job."

"So you accused him of violating you sexually," Father Procopio said.

"Yes," the widow Andrea whispered through the curtain.

Father Procopio jiggled his eyebrows and cleared his throat and shoved the curtain to one side. "Listen, Andrea, you must tell the mayor what you told me. It could save us all a lot of trouble."

The widow Andrea rose as quickly as she had entered when Father Procopio had been hiding in the confessional reading the Bishop's letter. She started running out of the church. Father Procopio ran after her and caught up with her outside at the park.

"Your penance, Andrea," he told her. "You didn't wait for your penance."

"I'm so repentant," she said, "and I've been crying so much that I forgot."

Father Procopio turned the widow Andrea around and faced her toward City Hall. "Do you see the Ladies of the Altar Society at City Hall?" he said.

The trembling widow said, "Yes, Father."

"Well, Andrea, inside City Hall should be the mayor being held as a hostage. I want you to go tell the mayor what you told me. That is your penance. Do you understand?"

"I can't do it, Father," Andrea cried. "I'm much too ashamed."

"Well, then you'll have to carry the curse of your sin for all eternity. You'll never get to heaven, Andrea," Father Procopio warned her.

"I guess it was never meant to be, then, Father Procopio," she said to him as she walked away crying. "I may have had my heaven here on earth, so perfect has my life been up until now."

Father Procopio rubbed his painful forehead and looked at his fingers.

"Still no blood," he said and walked back to the rectory.

Andres Garcia, after thinking it over like a rational man, had decided to kill the mayor for what the mayor had been doing for the last twenty-three years. He got up and dressed quietly and with much difficulty. He took the revolver out of the drawer and tucked it in the front inside his belt. He put the note in his pants pocket. He would confront the mayor with the note, question him about it, before killing him. When he stepped out of the room, dressed in his khakis with his felt hat lowered over his eyes, Victoria and Clementina had tried to force him back in. But Andres Garcia had pulled the revolver on them and had threatened to shoot them. Victoria and Clementina, knowing the hate-filled condition he was in, did not take any chances. They let him go. Victoria ran to the church for help while Clementina ran for her husband, Pablo.

They didn't have very much to fear. In his very weakened condition, Andres Garcia did not get beyond the barber shop, much less reach City Hall. As he approached the barber shop he created a major disturbance when the men there saw him staggering down the street, the trail of fresh blood streaming out from inside his pants leg. The men ran to him to see what he was doing but before they could ask him he turned around as if spinning, as though he were a top, and he fell to the ground. The men quickly picked him up and took him by the barber shop, through the C.O.D. Bar, the pool hall, the drug-store and back to the house.

At home, with the bleeding having stopped, the doctor proclaimed that Andres Garcia was one of a kind. "His liver is gone," he told the throng of people that had gathered in the room. "His lungs are gone. The hole in the spleen is larger instead of smaller. His kidneys no longer filter the poisons from his body. They just bleed. His urinary bladder is too small. His brain is failing him and he speaks of nothing but being surrounded by prostitutes. The man needs to be put on nitroglycerine."

Clementina crossed herself with the crucifix on her rosary. "Heaven be kind," she said. "That's the dynamite that everyone in town hates!"

"Nitroglycerine, my good Clementina, is not dynamite," the doctor corrected her. He turned to the throng of people in the room and said, "Goddammit, I wish you people would understand that. I'm tired of having to explain to everyone that the patient is not going to explode."

"First mercury and now dynamite?" Victoria asked the doctor.

"Definitely," the doctor said. "Nitroglycerine. This man is barely alive. I don't see what keeps him going."

"He is Andres Garcia," Amandito said from the open window. "He never gives up. He will never quit."

Don Ramon, the barber, wiped a tear from his eye and said, "He looks bad, but I think I have seen him worse. I've never known him to quit. Amandito is right."

"You haven't seen him worse," Don Sebastian, the goat killer, said. "This is the worst I have ever seen him."

Don Jorge, the postman that could read but could not write, said, "We should have never signed the decree. This is what started it all."

Don Pluto, the tortilla man that only counted by the dozen, looked down at the floor and said, "I will never sign another decree again."

"It's not anyone's fault," Victoria told them. "Father Propio will attest to that."

Father Procopio raised his hand and blessed everyone and said, "It's time for all of you to go and leave Victoria and Clementina alone with Don Andres. We all know that he needs to be cleaned up."

"He whispered to me that he was on his way to kill the mayor," Don Ramon told the crowd.

"Who would blame him?" Amandito said.

"What we need to do is save Don Andres," Don Sebastian said and everyone agreed.

The doctor looked at Amandito out of desperation. "Well then," he said stroking his chin, "if that's the case, he needs to be re-started." And with that he put his instruments in his bag and walked through the crowd of people that were in the room and to the door. "What he needs more than anything right now is a special prostitute from Laredo. Someone to flush him out."

CHAPTER 8

The oppressive heat of the morning of that December 30th made Andres Garcia certain that the locusts would emerge and would not sing. His feeble mind had crossed back and forth all night long between his altered state and the certainty of his death. All night long he had felt the slight tremors shake his bed, the same tremors that Father Procopio could feel at the church and the rectory.

There was so much energy emanating from the creek that Amandito and Fecundo and Bernabe and Faustino could not work. They had had to quit when the trembling ground prevented them from wielding their shovels. Amandito, the most cowardly of the group, had been the first one to realize the futility of their work. He had thrown his shovel away and he had run up the creek bank and had not turned around to warn anyone as he ran off. The other three, realizing what Amandito had done, also threw their shovels to the ground, accepted the inevitability of their defeat and ran off also. They caught up with the fat puffing Amandito at the barber shop, where the men there asked them what the problem was. Without stopping, Fecundo, running as if demons were yapping at his feet, yelled to the men that the locusts were ready to emerge and definitely would not sing.

"Goddammit," said Don Ramon the barber, snipping the air with his scissors, "this means the premature death of Don Andres."

"What a horrible way to die," said the wrapped-in-white hair-cut customer in the chair as he uncrossed his legs and leaned forward. "To know that you're going to die."

"Death is bad enough," Don Ramon replied, having put his scissors away and now stropping his razor, "without having to stare it in the face . . . . But I've known Don Andres for many years. In his younger days he was the bravest man I have ever known. He will not go willingly. Death is going to have to rip him away from this earth."

"I thought I felt the earth move," the customer said. "Is the earth trembling?" the customer wanted to know, nervously holding on to the chair.

"Yes," Don Ramon responded. "Can you imagine what it will be like on the last day of the year?"

After having counted the chickens, Victoria and Clementina had gathered wood to start a fire to burn Andres Garcia's clothes. Victoria was lighting a match when the red and black rooster ran by them chasing a hen. They followed the rooster's persistent zigzagging as he tried to catch and jump the uncooperative hen. "It must hurt a lot to lay an egg," Victoria said, "as much as she's objecting. But then again, she's old."

"Victoria, if you would have married and had had children you would know that laying an egg is child's play. I'd rather lay a thousand eggs than have a child," Clementina answered. "But there you have it. There is a certain order to nature."

Victoria said, looking up the road at the cloud of dust, "That is precisely why the spider never pees."

And down the road the two chickens went, toward the four men that were running wildly inside the cloud of dust and fast approaching the house. Victoria had started the fire and blew on the match and said, "That looks like my father's friends."

Clementina shielded her eyes from the sun. "It's them," she said.

"Something must have happened," Victoria whispered to herself, holding on to Clementina when she felt the slight tremor.

"Victoria, hold on while I throw the clothes on the fire," Clementina told her.

Victoria, still watching the men running toward the house said, "Go ahead. Burn everything." And with that the note in the pants pocket was destroyed.

Father Procopio felt the tremors in the rectory and steadied himself in his chair by grabbing the edge of his desk. He looked at Andres Garcia's revolver on the desk, the one Don Ramon had handed him the day before for safe-keeping as they carried the unconscious Andres Garcia home. The Bishop had called from Corpus Christi earlier in the morning and he had told Father Procopio that the Mother Superior had written to him and had a list two pages long on how Father Procopio had managed to get all the people to evade the Mother Superior's decrees. The Mother Superior had written that she could not govern the town under those circumstances. The Bishop wanted Father Procopio to leave the nuns alone. They would be their own downfall, he advised. Never have nuns been able to stay in one place for more than five years, he begged the Priest to remember. Father Procopio made the calculations and he had three more years to go. Afterwards, Father Procopio had wanted to go to the small Baptist church to pray, but he had turned back half-way there. He would bend, he decided, but he would not break. Now with the revolver before him, he wondered if he had the guts of an Andres Garcia. Could he take the revolver and kill the Mother Superior? "Of course not," he said out loud and he took out the ledger and studied the figures that the Bishop had cited. The Bishop was right. Without Father Procopio realizing it, enrollment at the Parochial School had almost doubled for the spring semester. "It's the swings," the Bishop had told him in all earnestness. "The Mother Superior understands human nature . . . . And now, if you could get more turns to the Wheel of Fortune, then you'd have this thing turned around and be the talk of the diocese," which was not the priest's idea of being famous.

He took the revolver and spun it around his finger like a movie cowboy and then placed it in the pocket of his coat which was hanging on the back of his chair. He would be sure to give it to Victoria for safe-keeping today.

"Pimena, I'm on my way to City Hall," he yelled at the housekeeper.

"Are you going to talk to the mayor?" she yelled back.

"Yes," he replied, feeling inside his coat for the revolver. "Where are you?"

"I'm in the kitchen . . . . Do you think you can convince him to apologize to Don Andres?"

"Yes, I think so," Father Procopio spoke. "If you would have asked me yesterday, I would have said no. But now the City Council is against him. There will be a recall election if he does not apologize."

"The whole town is against him," the housekeeper shouted from inside the kitchen.

"That too," Father Procopio said. "All the combination of forces should be enough to convince the mayor. And then the widow Andrea . . . ."

"She confessed, Father. I know she did. I saw her go into the church running and come out running with you running behind her. She admitted she lied."

"You know very well I can't talk about what is said in the confessional, Pimena. Let it be said that Don Andres Garcia is being falsely accused."

"I thought so," Pimena shouted.

"And now I must go to convince these crazy people to do what is right."

"I don't know why you take on the problems of the world," said Pimena.

"That's my job."

"Do you have your handkerchief?" she asked.

85

"Yes, ma'am," the good Father replied.

"Then go, Father. You know a priest without a handkerchief is not a priest . . . . I'll have lunch ready by twelve."

"What are we having?" he asked as he put on his coat, heavy with the revolver.

"Soup. Mexican soup."

"I'll try to be back."

"May God be with you," she said and he could tell from her voice that she was standing in front of the stove cooking something good for breakfast for herself.

"God is always with me," a hungry Father Procopio whispered as he let himself out the door. "If not, today I would have become a Baptist and killed the Mother Superior."

Never could Father Procopio imagine that at home by the creek, in the damp solitary room full of dark ominous corners, the widow Andrea sat on the bed with the mattress stuffed with Spanish moss and prayed that she would at least be accepted into purgatory as she prepared to hang herself. She felt the tremors coming from the creek, reminding her of the agony of Andres Garcia, intensifying her will to die, and she steadied herself with her hand on the iron headboard as she kneaded the heavy beads of her rosary, convinced that not having been married for long had been her heaven on earth.

By the time the four men had gotten to Don Andres' house where Victoria and Clementina were burning the old man's bloody clothes, Amandito was bringing up the rear. He arrived huffing and puffing after the thin Bernabe and then Faustino and then Fecundo had arrived.

"You women should have waited until tomorrow to light the fire," Fecundo said to Victoria and Clementina. "There will be a lot more belonging to Don Andres to burn then. The locusts are emerging."

"Fecundo is right," agreed Amandito, catching his breath as he leaned against the salt-cedar. "I stood as much as I could. When a man cannot raise a shovel over his head because the very ground he stands on is shaking so much . . . well . . . I'm ashamed to say it. I couldn't help it. I ran away."

An excited and exhausted Faustino said, "I saw you running, Amandito. I was trying with all my might to persuade them not to come out. I was beating them with a shovel, but there are too many. And then I look back over my shoulder and I see Bernabe crying as he tries to beat them back into the ground. Fecundo was crying . . . . Why were you crying?"

Fecundo shook his head as he tried to catch his breath. "I was scared. I had to cry."

"And then what happened?" Victoria asked as she watched Clementina stoke the fire. She could taste the smell of the blood on fire.

Faustino answered, "I look back and Amandito's gone! Then is when I look up and see him running away. So I dropped the shovel and ran too."

"We all did," Fecundo apologized to the women. "And that's the truth. We can't deny that we ran, Victoria. So we ran here to tell Don Andres. At least we could be faithful to him and do that."

"He's asleep. But I'm sure he understands that you men tried. He knows that there are certain limitations to friendship."

"No . . . no . . ." Amandito said. "Not when it comes to us and Don Andres. We love the man, but we have failed him in his last days."

"Amandito, you're the one that started running," Fecundo said.

"I don't deny that, Fecundo," Amandito told him as he looked intently at the burning clothes. He too, as could everyone else, smell the blood on fire. "I just ran. I wasn't the man Don Andres would have been. In the end I have failed him."

"Amandito is not alone," Bernabe said. "We all failed him. If he had been there, he would not have run and we would not have run."

Victoria tried to get out of the way of the smoke as Clementina further stoked the fire. Clementina picked up the burning pair of pants with her stick and turned them over on the flames. Clementina said, "You don't have to apologize for anything. You men went beyond what any friend would have done. He would be very proud of you."

"You four men," Victoria told them as she followed Clementina around the fire, "have honored yourself for what you have done. Don't feel bad. It's not your fault.This time had to come."

Amandito scratched his head and said, "I wish I could accept your generosity, Clementina, and yours, Victoria, but I can't. I know in my heart that what I did was wrong. And now there is no way to return."

"The tremors are being felt all the way in town to the barber shop," Fecundo said. "Don Ramon said that after the last haircut he was closing down for the day out of respect."

"We felt the tremors here a short while ago," Victoria said. "I had to hold on to Clementina."

"Don Ramon says that on the last day of the year the tremors will be unbearable."

"Let's hope not," Clementina said. "For the good of the town . . . ."

"There must be something else going on," Victoria said, shielding her eyes and looking toward town at yet another cloud of dust that followed the street. "I wonder what it is?" she asked. "I'm curious. It looks like a cloud of dust."

"It's the people," Bernabe told them. "I've seen them like this before in a dream when they took me away."

The widow Andrea sought to make some meaning out of her life as she kneaded her large beads, her meager thoughts interrupted by the tremors that had become more and more violent. Soon her bed was shaking out of control. She heard a terrifying crash and her daughter scream and run out of the house. Through the dusty window the widow Andrea could see her daughter running away from the creek and toward town. She prayed that Andres Garcia forgive her. As the whole house shook, she threw the rope over the rafters, tied one end to the foot of the iron bed and made a noose at the opposite end while she stood on the bed. She climbed to the top of the headboard and slipped the noose over her head. Then she jumped off the headboard and hanged herself at the same time as the throng of people arrived at Andres Garcia's house.

In the lead were the four proud Ladies of the Altar Society, their medallions around their neck shining bright and reflecting more sunlight than the sun itself. Behind them was Father Procopio, jiggling his eyebrows, the weight of the heavy revolver in his coat pocket listing him to the right. With him was the mayor, who had been convinced by the priest to apologize to Andres Garcia. He did not show a single thread of remorse, his decision to apologize to Don Andres being strictly a political one. Behind them were the gas-filled Sheriff Gonzalo and Angelina. Behind them were the city council and Don Ramon the barber. And lastly, behind them was a collection of ne'er-do-wells who infected the town with their lazy presence and who had all voted twice for Lothario to be mayor and had now turned against him.

Father Procopio faced the mumbling crowd and asked for silence and was well received. To Victoria he said, "No one takes full credit for what is about to take place here. Surely God knows that the Ladies of the Altar Society played a large role in getting us to where we are. I also, in my own humble way, talked to Lothario. I reasoned with him. He is a man that can be reasoned with. I know that some of us here have turned against him. But he is willing to forgive and forget as our Lord does with everyone here every single day of our lives. The Scriptures say that for every thing there is a season . . . a time to be born . . . a time to die. Let us all pray for Don Andres . . . that he die in a state of grace . . . . Victoria, we are about to witness our fine mayor apologizing to your father."

"I don't trust the mayor," Victoria said to the crowd. "He has never shown himself to be trustworthy. How can a man in good conscious win an election in which there are more votes than people? How can a man that is honorable issue a decree that does not allow my father to go out of the house, a decree based on the word of a crazy widow lady? How can anyone trust a man that flogged an old man, a beating that is causing the old man to die?"

"Victoria, what do you know how I really felt all these years?" the mayor said. "I have tried so many times to explain . . . ."

Father Procopio held up his hand for silence once more. "Wait . . . wait . . . wait. No more talking," he said. "We all know that there is a relationship here that has a potential for violence. We all know why, too. We are all adults. Arguing is not going to solve anything. Don't you agree, Victoria?"

"Yes, Father Procopio. Like always, you're right." Then, glaring at the mayor, she said, "Some things are better left unsaid. There is too much hurt already."

"Precisely . . . as Don Andres would say," the priest told the crowd. "Now, Victoria, if you would be so kind as to allow us in your home, we have work to do." And to the crowd he turned around and said, "Listen up! We are not all going to fit in the room, so don't be pushing and shoving. Some of you must stay out in the hall . . . some in the kitchen. Some of you might want to look through the window where Amandito and Faustino and Fecundo and Bernabe will surely be. Remember to be respectful of the Ladies of the Altar Society and the City Council."

As they walked into the house, Father Procopio, without anyone seeing him, sneaked Don Andres' revolver into Victoria's apron pocket. "Here," he whispered to her, "this is your father's gun that I've had since yesterday. Keep it away from him. No telling what he'll do if he ever can get up and use it."

Victoria felt the heavy revolver hit the bottom of the apron pocket and said, "Don't worry, Father, I'll hide it from him. He'll never use it again. I'll make sure of that."

Andres Garcia was in a perfect stupor, trying in vain for his altered state, not awake, not asleep, feeling the pain of groaning kidneys and all the bruises that he had accumulated the past two days. And unbelievingly, since yesterday, his heart ached more than any organ he had. The errant note from the mayor to his daughter in its heavy block letters kept interfering with his dreams. He could not rid its imprint from his mind.

"DER VIKOTARAI," it read. "IF YU DOO NO CALL OF DE BICHES OF THE ALTR SOCATY I WIL TEL YOU ARE FATHER OF

HOW I MAK LUV YU FOR TENTY TREE YEERS DOO IT TOO YU IN YOU ARE ROM TOO DORS FROM HIM SLEP SOM TAMES SVEN DA A WEK HOW YU LAK IT AL TIM LIK DOG . . . ." And then his "Lothario" in his inimitable flourished cursive.

Andres Garcia cried silently for relief from the agony of the note. He knew now how minor his physical pain had been before he had found out what his daughter and Lothario had been doing in the room two doors down, mating, tied like dogs, while he lay in his bed in his altered state, the ghosts of all his antecedents surrounding him, the light-blooded Colonel Fernandez holding the Shroud of Tamaulipas on high. No, his physical agony was nothing compared to what he was going through. He tried again and again to reach his altered state, for the relief that that would give him. He was awakened from this entropic plane—weak and almost blind from the heavy loss of blood, aching from the flogging with Don Ramon's strop, emotionally destitute from uncovering his daughter's infidelity—when he heard the strange noise of voices outside his bedroom. He welcomed with relief and anticipation the presence of the ghosts of his antecedents and, as the throng burst through the door, he smiled at the thought that he would at last be comforted by his people and the revered shroud. You can imagine his confused state when into the room exploded a collection of unexpected women and men, the women unrecognizable, flashing bursts of blinding sunlight from heavy metal objects hung around their necks, the strange men shouting for someone to ask forgiveness or face the consequences of another flogging. He thought that he had finally been attacked, an ambush was more like it, as had his beloved father at San Jacinto. Instead of the familiar shroud, he saw the ghost-like figure of the mayor, an aura completely surrounding his body. Wildly, before he could be engulfed by this cloud of humanity, he reached into the bottom drawer of the night-stand and he pulled out his father's trusty derringer and closed his eyes and fired twice at the mayor that he thought was an evil apparition.

Luckily for the mayor, both shots went over his head as well as the heads of all that were present. One shot hit the light-bulb. The other one, if anyone had taken the trouble to look for it, hit the darkened far corner of the room two inches from where the ceiling met the wall.

The mayor, scared beyond belief, was running out through the crowd by the time the second shot hit the wall. He pushed and weaved his way out of the room, almost beating everyone there to the hallway. Father Procopio, without fear for his life, ran to Andres Garcia's bedside after the two shots were fired and struggled with Don Andres for the gun, finally taking the derringer away from the confused old man. Most everyone had tried to run out through the door at the same time, causing such a forceful crush that the wall leading to the hallway buckled at first with the weight of the screaming mob and then slowly gave way until it was knocked down against the opposite wall. Seeing the wall coming down, some of them chose to jump through the window, long ago abandoned by Amandito and Fecundo and Faustino and Bernabe. These four were running home in full stride by this time. The Ladies of the Altar Society all fainted on top of each other, forming a pyramid covered with gold medallions, the large Olivia at the bottom. Of the three City Council members, two had helped break down the wall and one of them, Don Pluto, the tortilla man that could only count by the dozen, had jumped out through the window. The ne'er-do-wells that had jammed into the room were the ones that broke down the wall. Their friends that had not fit inside the bedroom, with a feeling of relief at their good fortune, had run out of the house through the kitchen, tearing the screen door off the hinges. The whole throng, with the exception of Father Procopio and the fainted Ladies of the Altar Society, had created the largest dust cloud ever seen in the small town of San Diego, Texas.

Victoria, who had not been allowed inside the bedroom because of her father's decree, had been saying her penitential rosaries when she heard the shots. Not knowing what had gone on in the bedroom, she instinctively took the heavy revolver out of her apron pocket and ran down the hall. The first person she saw running out of the room was Lothario. She ran after him, mixing in the crowd, as the falling wall narrowly missed crushing her. In the kitchen, Victoria ran by the praying Clementina. Clementina shouted at her to stop and crossed herself with the crucifix of her rosary, having seen the revolver in Victoria's hands. Outside, with Victoria in ominous pursuit, the mayor ran to his left, stepping on the flock of cackling chickens. His speed made him think that he could jump over the pomegranate bushes. Victoria, thinking the worst, that the mayor had shot her beloved father and was now running away, aimed the heavy revolver at the mayor as he reached the apex of his flight. She closed her eyes and pressed the trigger. Unlike her father, her shot hit its mark. She shot the mayor in the rectum, just as he was coming down over the pomegranates. The impact of the shot was enough to send the wounded man over the bushes. Had it not been for that impetus, the mayor would have been impaled on the pomegranates. As it was, he landed on his feet and ran home covering his bloody rear-end with both hands.

CHAPTER 9

In the morning Don Andres Garcia remembered faintly that at some point in his agony he had shot his father's trusty derringer at the evil vision of Lothario the mayor. He had seen the hated Lothario leading the collection of ghosts of his antecedents. He had noticed immediately the absence of the shroud. All this had been too much for a man of his pride to take. Now as he opened his fogged eyes and took in the scene before him he wondered what had happened in his room that the wall had been knocked down and was leaning on the opposite wall. He felt the second tremor, more powerful than the first one that had reached his house this morning.

Amandito and Faustino and Fecundo and Bernabe were at the window fighting for space, watching for Don Andres to wake up.

"Don Andres, are you alive?" Amandito whispered from the window.

Andres Garcia felt his dull aching heart beat steady and strong before he would answer. "I'm alive," he said from under the covers. He uncovered himself and slowly sat up in bed, alternately pushing himself up with one hand and then the other. "I smell bad, but I'm alive."

"Like the most intimate part of the female," Fecundo said.

"Precisely," Don Andres replied, looking around the room wondering what had happened. "What evil force invaded my room? Do you men know?"

"People, Don Andres," Amandito informed him.

Don Andres looked to the window at the faces of the four men and asked, "People?"

Faustino said, "The people that were here yesterday to witness the mayor's apology."

"And how did the people do this? How did the wall fall down?"

"They shoved it down, Don Andres," said Fecundo. "They were fighting to get out. Everyone was screaming for their lives. The Ladies of the Altar Society were fainting. The mayor, scoundrel that he is, was trying to save his hide and to hell with everyone else. People were jumping through the window, this window here, Don Andres."

"Why?" Don Andres asked them, innocently.

"Why?" Amandito asked him. "Because, Don Andres, you were shooting at the mayor . . . trying to kill him, and everyone was trying to run for their lives, trying to get out of the line of fire."

Andres Garcia rubbed his chin and felt his heart ache once more. "Then it wasn't a dream."

"No, Don Andres. You shot at the mayor," Fecundo replied.

Don Andres stroked his lower lip. "Answer me this. Did I kill him?"

"No," the four said at once.

"Bull shit! " Don Andres said. "In my younger days, in my sixties and eighties I could shoot the legs off a gnat with the heavy revolver . . . . But I didn't use the heavy revolver, did I?"

"No, Don Andres," the four said as one.

Don Andres thought for a moment as the third and then the fourth tremor shook the house. The four men at the window took hold of the window sill and steadied themselves.

"I used the trusty derringer," Don Andres remembered not showing fear of the tremors. "My father's pistol. The one he used to kill James Bowie after the battle of the Alamo. James Bowie, there was a sorry sonofabitch. He spit on my father's boots the day before the battle when my father had been sent to reason with Colonel Travis. But Travis was crazy. He wanted to fight Santa Anna. So they gave him a fight. When they found Bowie after the battle, he was hiding in the wash-house with the two women—de Zavala's beautiful daughter, Maria del Jesus, and her maid, a Mrs. Dickenson. To my father went the honor of executing James Bowie . . . using the same derringer that I used on the mayor. It shames me to think that I missed."

"You were delirious, Don Andres," Amandito said. "Didn't I say that Don Andres looked delirious?"

"That was what Amandito was saying," agreed Bernabe.

Faustino said, "He must have said it one hundred times, Don Andres."

"I was delirious . . . I still am a little bit," Don Andres said. "You know that as the day wears on I feel weaker and weaker."

"Victoria shot the mayor," Bernabe blurted out to Don Andres.

"She did?" he asked, concerned. "How did she do that?"

Amandito began to explain. "Father Procopio had your revolver, Don Andres. Don Ramon took it away from you when you went into town to kill the mayor. He gave it to Father Procopio. Yesterday, when Father Procopio came inside the house, he gave the revolver to Victoria. Victoria had it in her apron pocket. What the people in the barber shop are betting will come out at the trial is that Victoria thought that the mayor had shot you and she ran the mayor down and shot him in the you-know-where."

Don Andres thought about what Victoria had done. "She ran him down and shot him in the you-know-where?"

Bernabe said, "Yes, Don Andres, right in the hole."

"Well," Andres Garcia said, "I guess the proper question is, is he alive?"

"Yes, but barely," Fecundo answered. "The doctor sewed him up, but you know the doctor. He says that if he lives, it will be days before he dies. The men at the barber shop say that the doctor has sewed him shut and he will never be able to go to the bathroom again."

"I don't doubt that the doctor messed him up," Don Andres said. "I've known him to do those things."

"Regardless," Faustino told him, "now that he's been through the surgery, he woke up being able to read and write."

"A lot of good that will do him," Amandito said. "He is being re-called by the people."

"In a way I feel sorry for the man," Don Andres said. "On top of being heavy-blooded, he was always trying to get out of his element. And one can't do that."

"That is why the spider never pees," Amandito said.

"Precisely," Don Andres said.

"Don Andres," Bernabe said, "do you think there will be a trial?"

"God only knows those things, Bernabe," he answered. "I don't think so, if you ask me. Lothario could not find twelve people to find Victoria guilty."

Amandito cleared his throat and said, "Don Andres, not wanting to change the conversation but . . ."

Bernabe interrupted Amandito, "Don Andres, Amandito ran from the creek bed yesterday. He's the one that started us running."

"I admit it," Amandito told them. "I admit I got scared. Any mere mortal would have done what I did. Only a man of Don Andres' courage could have stood there and fought the trembling ground and the locusts as they are trying to emerge."

"Don Andres," Fecundo spoke, "I don't know how you will judge us, but I hope you still have the old compassion that you are famous for. The truth is that we all ran. Amandito running first had nothing to do with it. We were all ready to abandon the creek. We feel that we have failed you."

Don Andres said, "It makes me want to cry, Fecundo, when I hear your words. If I wasn't a man, I would be crying with joy at the faithfulness that you men have shown . . . . Clementina!" he shouted. "You men wait and see what I have in store for you. Don't go away."

Clementina walked in and said, "Yes, Don Andres."

"Clementina, take a sheet of paper and a pencil from the night-stand and write what I'm going to tell you."

Clementina took the paper and pencil from the night-stand and sat down on the chair by the bed.

"Clementina, I want you to write that this is my last will and testament. Write that on the top. Fine . . . I leave the following to my best of friends. To Amandito: I leave my dog, if he ever comes back from the latest mating binge that he is on. I have not seen him in one month, Amandito, but you know what he looks like. Black and white. A fine dog. You can have him castrated by the doctor and my estate will pay for that. To Bernabe: I leave my pigeons that I released in nineteen thirty-five and have never returned. Bernabe will look for them. He has the sensibilities and the caring hand of a pigeon raiser. Be careful, Bernabe, that you don't breed too many. They have a tendency to attack each other. To Fecundo: I leave all the clothes in the house, Victoria's included, so that he will be able for once to clothe all his children. Don't wash them too much, Fecundo, they last longer if you don't. To Faustino, my drinking partner of fifty years: I leave a bottle of dark tequila that I have had for many years, so that he can think of me every time he takes a drink, which should be for one day, because that is how long the bottle is going to last. And lastly, to Victoria: I leave nothing."

Clementina dropped the paper and the pencil and fell to her knees crying. "Oh no, Don Andres. You can't throw Victoria out of the house. It wouldn't be fair. She is your only living daughter. Have compassion for the poor women. Hasn't she suffered enough?"

Don Andres said, "I have suffered, Clementina. How do you think I felt when I read the note and found out about her infidelity? How do you think I feel when I know that for twenty-three years the people of this town have been laughing behind my back?"

"*Ave Maria Purisima*," Clementina cried and then muffled her voice with her shawl. "Don Andres . . . you know," she whispered desperately at him. "My God, you know."

"Yes . . . I know. The note explained it all," the old man said, tasting the bitter gall that had invaded his mouth for the last three days. He took out a small handkerchief from inside the pillow case and wiped the tears from his eyes. "I loved her so much at one time."

"A woman needs to be loved by someone else besides her father," Amandito said.

Andres Garcia tried to shout, but his voice trailed off into the darkness that was the room. He said, "What Andres Garcia has said is what he means!"

"But Don Andres," Amandito said, "it wouldn't be right for anyone else to inherit everything that you have worked so hard to accumulate."

"You know the old Mexican proverb, Amandito? It says: No one knows who he works for . . . . All my life I worked and worked and for what?

For the disappointments that have come up the last few days? Was that it?"

"You can't feel that way, Don Andres," Bernabe argued. "Just look at me. If you feel bad, how am I supposed to feel? I've never had anything."

"Bernabe is right," Faustino said. "You can't leave Victoria out of your inheritance."

Clementina crossed herself with her crucifix and cried, "Don Andres, be forgiving. We all knew what she was doing and we never condemned her. She hasn't changed. She is still the loving person that she's always been. She loves you more than she does her own life. She is committed to pray the rosary more than any nun for the rest of her life so that you can die in a state of grace."

"She sacrificed her life for you, Don Andres," Fecundo said.

Amandito shook his head at what Don Andres was doing. "You can't do this, Don Andres. If that's the way you're going to be, I don't want your dog."

"And I don't want your pigeons," Bernabe said.

"Nor I your clothes," Fecundo said.

"Nor I your bottle of tequila," said Faustino.

Andres Garcia, his body weaker by the minute and in more pain than the day before, his aching heart stopping after every other beat, said, "Then all of you go, you ungrateful sonofabitches!"

At the rectory Father Procopio absentmindedly placed his hand in his coat pocket and felt the trusty derringer as the continuous tremors shook his small house. He took the derringer out of his pocket and placed it on top of his desk. As he did so, he stopped to recall the events that had led the small pistol to be in his pocket, the struggle with the surprisingly strong Don Andres. He knew he would have to go visit the family to see how Don Andres was doing this morning. He knew that he would also have to visit Lothario to check on his wound. At the same time he was opening a letter that had arrived by special delivery from the Bishop. When he cut open the envelope, he peered inside at the small slip of paper that would not come out. He reached in and with two fingers was able to extract the paper. He opened the slip in anticipation, with a premonition that something was going to go against him.

As usual he was right. Inside was a decree signed by the Bishop making his conclusions official. The Bishop had determined that, according to his interpretation of canon law, the nuns were classified as secular and not parochial, which in the Bishop's further explanation put the nuns in the position of being non-religious and just outside of the reach of the parish priest. Any priest that did not obey the Bishop's findings would have his church closed down, or would lose his church.

Father Procopio threw the decree into the waste-basket and cursed below his breath so that God would not hear him. He took the trusty derringer and checked to see that it was loaded. He aligned the loaded chamber with the barrel and placed the small gun to his head and pulled the trigger. He heard the snap and then thought himself dead. His aching heart, like the aching heart of Andres Garcia, was beating rhythmically and forcefully. There was no blood. The gun had misfired.

He got up slowly, his whole body shaking in fear of what he had tried to do. Quickly, trying to press out of his mind his evil thoughts, he threw the gun on the desk and he yelled at Pimena that he was on his way to the nunnery to talk with the Mother Superior. When he arrived there, still shaking at the thought that he could be dead, he knocked on the door and had no one answer. He finally opened the unlocked door and went inside only to find that the nuns had packed during the night and had left and that the children had taken over the swings.

He could think of nothing except that he would lose his church, a failure that he would not accept. He had no time to lose. Like a wild man, he ran back to the rectory, put his coat on, took the derringer and slipped it in his coat pocket and ran off toward the train station. On his way he could feel and hear the thunder that was now in every tremor. The train would be arriving and he had to hurry.

Victoria and Clementina were outside having difficulty standing on the shaking ground while they counted the chickens, when they noticed that one of the older hens had an immature locust in its beak. Clementina, our mother, crossing herself with her crucifix, ran to the house to see if we could pick up the emerging insects so that Andres Garcia could not see them. "Hurry! Hurry!," she cried, as Willie and Louie and Frankie and Connie and Becky and I ran around the yard picking up the bugs and placing them in paper sacks.

"It's no use," Victoria shouted to our mother. "Send the children home. The ground is shaking too much. It's not safe for the children. Something might fall on them."

"Children," our mother yelled above the swelling thunder that was coming from the creek. "Go on home. Forget about it. Connie and Becky, both of you cook something for your brothers. Be sure and stay away from the windows."

"The wind is starting to blow," Victoria said. "Maybe we ought to go in . . . . Is that the train?" she asked. "Is that the train whistle?"

Our mother cocked an ear and waited to hear the sounds of the train. "Yes," she said. "It's the train. And it's already leaving."

"Even the train is very early today," Victoria said to Clementina, absentmindedly reaching for the kitchen door that wasn't there.

"What does my father say this morning?" Victoria asked Clementina when they sat down at the kitchen table.

"Victoria," Clementina said, "he knows about you. He feels you are unclean."

Victoria bowed her head and shook it. "I was afraid of that," she answered. "He was just acting so strange and for no reason. It was the note, wasn't it."

Clementina took off her bonnet and said, "Yes . . . . It was the note."

"Who could have been so cruel as to write him a note?" Victoria asked.

"Only one man, Victoria," sighed Clementina. "And that would be Lothario."

Victoria shook her head. "I curse the day that I gave in to his advances. It would have to be him . . . . I should have shot him in the head."

"You're in enough trouble as it is," Clementina warned her.

"No jury will ever convict me, Clementina. You know that."

Clementina thought a while and said, "You may be right. In San Diego you might not even stand trial."

Victoria, looking forlornly toward the chickens as they began to gather under the pomegranates outside, said, "I won't stand trial. I know it. Even if he dies."

A loud cry came from Don Andres' room. He was calling for Clementina. Clementina got up and went into the room through the tilted door of the fallen wall. Victoria could hear the old man pleading with Clementina. Clementina kept saying, "No . . . no . . . no . . . no,no,no,no. ."

When she returned to the kitchen, she sat down and cried into her shawl and said, "Victoria, you ought to go see him. He needs your help. He was not in his right senses when he ran you out of his room."

"He doesn't want my help, Clementina. I don't blame him. This is the hardest of blows for a man of his pride."

Clementina looked at the skittish chickens that were hiding from the tremors and the wind under the pomegranates. "He wanted the revolver so that he could kill himself," she said.

In the early afternoon in the heat of the last day of December, Don Andres Garcia recycled his body for the last time. The pains which had before been insuperably intense had become dull. His enlarged liver felt to him as though it weighed more than his entire body. The hole in his spleen, now a large tear, was no longer painful, but more of an itch. His kidneys had quit bleeding and crying and now longed to pass sparkling clear urine. His lungs, once the best organs of his youth, were trying to return to their former glory when Don Andres could pull the two-mule plow by himself. The only remaining piercing ache that remained to occupy his entire mind was in his heart. He tried to understand why it was that he felt better physically and he came to the conclusion that this was the unreasonable feeling of death.

Finally, not being able to stand the lonely agony that was in his heart and not being able to stand the separation, he screamed for his beloved daughter, Victoria.

Victoria and Clementina were praying the Sorrowful Mysteries of the Rosary in Victoria's room when they heard his cry. Clementina shot up from her knees and ran to Don Andres' room. "He's dead," she shouted, running down the narrowed hallway. Victoria jumped up also and ran behind Clementina but stopped at the angled door, unsure of whether to attend to her father or not. She leaned against the fallen wall and wept at her father's death.

"Victoria!" she heard Don Andres' cry in agony. "Where is my Victoria?"

Victoria heard the familiar voice, strong as it had been in his youth at eighty. She ran into the room and saw him sitting up, propped by the fluffy pillows that he had made into a cave, his face still ashen from the loss of blood.

"Victoria," he said, gently, "come over here."

Victoria, relieved that the old man had not died but still her defiant self, walked half-way to the bed and said, "Father, I didn't hear you say please," she reminded him.

"Please, Victoria. Please."

"Yes, father," Victoria responded as she went to his bed-side and sat at the chair.

"Victoria," Don Andres told her, "I forgive you. What a fool I have been all my life. Can you ever forgive me?"

"Father," she replied, "I forgive you."

Andres Garcia smiled for the first time in many days, as he felt the house shake. The pain that had clutched his heart surged out into the darkness of the room before it floated out through the window where

Amandito, Faustino, Bernabe and Fecundo were standing, clutching the window sill to steady themselves against the trembling ground and the wind.

In the heat of that December, they had seen the locusts emerging prematurely, not only from the creek but from every place that could be imagined. Even the chickens found the circumstances intolerable and were running away from the army of bugs. The men had run to Don Andres' house, regardless of what Don Andres had said to them this morning. They knew the painful agony that he had been in and they had forgiven him. And being faithful companions, they had come to pay what they thought would be their last respects.

Looking through the window at Don Andres and Victoria embracing, Faustino the drunk said, "Glory be to God in heaven. Don Andres has recovered his senses. Now I can drink in peace."

"I feel like making a promise!" Amandito cried out. "But I won't."

"Don't say anything, Victoria," Don Andres cried, holding her as tight as he could. "Don't say anything. I don't want to know anything. I forgive you. The more I tried to hate you the more I loved you."

"*Ave Maria Purisima*," Clementina rejoiced. "We are all going to die in a state of grace."

"Except for the widow Andrea," Fecundo informed them.

"What happened to her?" Victoria asked.

"They found her dead, Victoria. She had hanged herself," Amandito replied.

"Poor woman," Don Andres remarked. "I had forgiven her."

"The mayor is in good shape for the shape he's in, or so says the doctor," Fecundo said.

"He won't live two more weeks," Faustino informed them. "Not if he can't eat. The doctor sewed him up wrong."

"The doctor gives him a few days. And now you should see him, Don Andres, sitting in bed as he reads and writes," Amandito said.

"The bullet unlocked his brain," Don Andres said. "It can happen."

"He's got gangrene, Don Andres," Bernabe volunteered.

"Good. Serves him right," Clementina replied, bitterly.

"No, Clementina, don't say that. Andres Garcia is a forgiving man, like my father and all the men in my family. I can find it in my heart to forgive him also," Don Andres said.

Clementina fell to her knees and raised the rosary to the ceiling, to the broken light bulb. "Did all of you hear that? Don Andres has forgiven everyone. Don Andres is going to die in a state of total grace."

"And then . . . well . . . we haven't told you all there is," Bernabe said in a totally solemn voice.

Amandito looked at Don Andres in bed, at Victoria sitting in her familiar chair and then at Clementina, kneeling on the floor. "You people don't know, but the word from Pimena at the rectory is that Father Procopio has left the church and is carrying the derringer in his coat pocket. He has gone crazy."

Father Procopio had arrived too late. The train had arrived early for once and the four nuns had left for Laredo. His church was lost. Everything else at that moment had not mattered to him. He had run to the Rectory and had tried to call the Bishop, but the tremors had affected the phone lines. He took the derringer out of his pocket and tried to shoot himself once more and the gun had refused to fire. Seeing that Pimena had almost witnessed what he was doing, he had run in disgrace to the creek to see if he could find his death, as Don Andres had, among the locusts.

It was very dark now and Father Procopio had been sitting at the creek bank for hours, holding on to the root of a saltcedar to steady himself from the swaying and the rocking that the tremors were causing. The wind at the church had been terrifying, but at the creek bank it was unsupportable. He held on with one hand firmly to keep from falling down the embankment to the erupting ground below. He could barely see, as if in a nightmare, the emerging locusts in their immature state trying to sing, rubbing their legs constantly until they died of exhaustion. He had found a sack of quick-lime that Don Andres and his friends had left behind and he was using his free hand to throw the white dust at the locusts as they cleared their soft bodies of the mud from the creek. He had screamed many times in terror at the thought that his death would come at the same time as this horrible episode. And still he would not die as he clung to the saltcedar, as he tried to concentrate in the harrowing wind on taking out the derringer and trying repeatedly to shoot himself.

He was about to jump to the bottom of the erupting ground to die among the dying locusts when he felt several mysterious hands holding him back. It was Amandito and Faustino and Fecundo and Bernabe and Pimena, the housekeeper.

"Father Procopio," they screamed above the noise of the wind, "we've been looking for you for hours. It's almost midnight. Thank God you're alive. We thought you might be dead. Don Andres is dying. He needs his last rites."

"I hate to pile more bad news on you, Father Procopio," Pimena yelled against the noise of the wind. "But the nuns are back."

Amandito screamed in Father Procopio's ear, "The authorities would not let them off at Laredo."

"And the Mother Superior says that she is destined to die in San Diego and be buried under the swings," Pimena added. "That is what she says."

"Thank God," Father Procopio, his prayers answered, said to himself, wondering as he jiggled his eyebrows at how he would have the time to fulfill his promise of praying one hundred rosaries a day for one hundred years.

The doctor took his stethoscope and left it on one area of Don Andres' tired heart. Erratically he tapped his small foot with the small shoe with the taps to the beat of the heart. Everyone in the room followed the rhythm of the foot.

"To Amandito the fat one," Don Andres, now very weak, said, "I leave my black and white dog."

"Thank you, Don Andres," Amandito replied from the window.

"And you know, Amandito, what I said about the castration. Clementina has it all in writing. To Bernabe the crazy one: I leave the pigeons that I released in nineteen thirty-five and never returned. To Fecundo the prolific: I leave all the clothes in the house, except for any that Victoria would want to keep. To Faustino the drunk: I leave the bottle of tequila that I told you about, so that he may think of the good times we had together at the creek. To the church and Father Procopio I leave ten dollars so long as the Wheel of Fortune is not turned for profit. To Victoria I leave everything else, including the little grocery store that has been closed for years."

"And the shroud, Don Andres?" Amandito asked him. "Do you want us to wrap you in it when you die?"

Don Andres shook his head. "No, you can't. I don't know where it is," he replied, his strength visibly escaping from his body. "But friends, I do know that there is always a shroud in every family."

The house shook with the full weight of all the tremors that had accumulated for the one hundred and five years of Don Andres' life. Father Procopio, his hair on end from the episode at the creek and exhausted at having had to run to the rectory for his vestments and tools, walked around the bed sprinkling holy water on Don Andres, murmuring in Latin.

Clementina, our mother, and Pablo, our father, were there as were

Willie and Louie and Frankie and Becky and Connie and I. We were all kneeling as a family, each with a rosary in our hands.

Victoria was kneeling by the bed, the closest one to Don Andres.

Don Andres sighed heavily filling the room with the eternal solitude of his death, his small feet shaking underneath his white sheet.

Father Procopio had lit the four candles at each corner of Don Andres' bed. He was trying to get in between the dying man and the doctor. He anointed the old man's withered hands with sacred oil. Then he rubbed the oil into the forehead, all the time praying for the eternal rest of the soul of Don Andres. Lastly he rubbed the sign of the cross in oil over Andres Garcia's heart.

The doctor's foot tapped more arrhythmically now, only occasionally, as everyone watched intently at what Father Procopio was doing and what the doctor's foot was telling them.

The doctor's foot gradually stopped tapping and he took the stethoscope and placed it in his bag and left. "There is nothing I can do," he said at the fallen door as the wind howled outside.

Father Procopio asked all the family to witness the final agony as Don Andres Garcia, our great grand-father, took his last breaths amidst the tremors and the wind that shook the house around us.

Don Andres Garcia, in the strangeness of his death, saw for the first time the real presence of the shroud and of all his antecedents as they surrounded his death bed. His father and his mother welcomed him with open arms as soon as his brave heart stopped.

BOOK TWO
1986

CHAPTER 1

My friends call me Andy. My parents still call me Andres. Half the time I don't know who I am. I look through the clouded window at an old man in grey baggy pants and a heavy woolen coat with a torn shopping bag, trying to cross the street into the cold gusts of wind, and he reminds me of my grandfather carrying his sack from the meat-market and, strangely, behind him, marching in single file, I see the faint outlines of the drooping ghosts of my antecedents marching silently. One man stands out: Colonel Fernandez, limping and happily carrying a shining white banner, a sheet really, the revered Shroud of Tamaulipas.

As I see the spectacle in the street I remind myself that I am not to tell anyone of what I'm seeing, just as I never told anyone of the night that Father Procopio purposely burned the back of my hand with a cigarette while sitting on the park bench when he was angry with me for dropping the large pontifical-sized missal during the funeral mass. The missal fell with such a ponderous noise as I tripped over my home-made red cassock that the startled widow, along with the priest and my brother Frankie, the other altar boy, and everyone else that heard it, riveted their eyes on the coffin wondering if Mr. Torremolinos was pounding from the inside, complaining that he was being buried alive. The widow gave an almost melodic half-scream of restrained wonderment that made the priest shoot up in his spindle-legged chair as he sat trance-like wondering what he would order for supper. The choir sang the Angelus.

Later that night when I saw him as an eerie smoking apparition dressed in shiny black sitting on the park bench across from the church he asked me to come over to him and he murmured that I was to say the Rosary nightly until told otherwise as punishment for disturbing the funeral and for losing his place in the missal and I was to pray only the intercessory pleadings of the Sorrowful Mysteries because I would never be deserving of the better part of the Rosary, the Joyful Mysteries. And as I said, Yes Father, he looked up to the starlit sky, as if to receive God's approval for my punishment. He diverted my attention, making me look up also to see if even unworthy I could see God as well as he could, for we all knew that he could, and as as I looked up, he put out his cigarette on the back of my hand. You know that from then on I held on to the huge missal with such trembling force that I could have fallen several times and rolled on the altar among the brightly painted statues forever and not once would I have allowed the missal to touch the sacred floor or allowed even one page to turn over.

I married my first wife, Dolores, in 1958, a year after graduating from college, not knowing at the time that she had been falsely saturated with rumors and wives-tales by the gull-like nuns of the Sisters of Charity, the ones in Houston, not the ones in San Diego. But nonetheless the same order, the ones who had come to San Diego to start up the unwanted parochial school. The same nuns that would line us up like docile Jews and whip our hands with our own shoe-laces before mass. The same nuns that would tell the girls that if anyone ever touched their most intimate of parts, that they should scream until it depolarized the attacker's hemi- spheres and the images of parrots were seen flying between the attacker's eyes. Consequently, ever since I chased Dolores screaming in front of the old people down the corridors of our Galveston hotel on our wedding night, we were forced to hide our nakedness and make occassional love in the dark and only then inside the blanket that was her cave. The marriage could not last.

I love my present wife Rene some of the time. Nothing that ever hap- pens to her makes me want to cry. She is what we call in Texas an Anglo, to distinguish her from the Hispanic, the term Anglo being all-inclusive for non-Hispanics, except Indians, Italians, French, Blacks, Orientals, Jews, Arabs, and on and on—anyone that has the slightest color or a good nose. And that in itself originally created a lot of problems with my family. My parents did not want me to marry Rene. Willie and Louie and all the rest wanted me to marry a Mexican like Dolores. They don't say it to me but I know that they feel that I was trying to distance myself from them by marrying Rene—which is not true at all, but I could never hope to convince them.

Rene's presence around my family causes a certain unspoken restraint. Everyone changes gears when she shows up. Languages change. Conver- sations change. Dietary rules change. We cannot eat the offal of the cow and the pig, the spleen and the lung and the head and the foot and the beloved milk-fed intestine. Aunt Victoria cannot suck on the eye of the goat and spoon out the brain from the skull and spread it evenly on her corn tortilla that she then enjoys rolling into a flute and then acts as though she is playing it. My mother cannot boil beef tripe inside anymore, so now my father must do it inside the old garage in his famous barbeque pit, away from everyone so that he is not seen, only smelled, holed up the entire day with the permeated smell of boiling cow shit into his hair and skin and clothes, alone in the eternally guilty solitude of his upbringing as if he were committing a crime.

Rene being divorced and having a child made it worse. The Mexicans feel that once a woman is used, that she is second-hand goods. They may not admit it, especially the women, but specifically they are referring to her cunt. It just isn't any good anymore, as if it wears down. Not so with the Mexican pecker. The pecker is an enigma, always new, self-cleansing, and never wears out. The family felt that I, the one considered the most successful of the group, was getting short-changed and should have deserved better, to wit: a beautiful Mexican virgin, a big wedding with all the relatives there, something more pleasing to everyone, like the first marriage where one thousand people attended and ate the offal and drank the beer that had stagnated over several days.

Earlier that afternoon Maybelline had brought in the phone messages. Many people had called. Sol had called and when I tried to return the call, the secretary slurred her words and said that Sol was busy, not to bother her. She was already drunk as were probably most of the lawyers in my old firm, drunk early to hide the bottomless monotony that comes from screwing with the truth. Louie called and when I called back Donna Marie, his current prostitute, answered and got him on the phone. He wanted to know what I thought about him moving to Florida somewhere around Disney World. I didn't know. I had never been to Florida. The question that came to my mind was if Florida was ready for Louie and Donna Marie? Donna Marie wanted to work for Disney to see if that would get her to Hollywood. What did I think? Why not go to Hollywood and forget about poor Disney World? He would think about it and promised he would not bother me with Donna Marie again. But I knew that he would. Donna Marie wanted to know what I thought. Did I think she was talented enough? They both sounded naked and very happy and said that they would see me soon, if not they would see me at the party on Sunday.

Willie called and when I finally got to talk to him he said that Angie was very depressed because it had been nineteen years since their son Chris had been needlessly killed in Viet Nam and she still missed him. He sounded all right. I could see him shrug his shoulders and weep at the whole thing. It had been that long ago and now he did not cry as much. But they would be at the party on Sunday and he would bring the charcoal and some ribs. He had not heard from Connie today but she had promised to be there for Aunt Victoria's one hundredth birthday and she was bringing ribs and bean salad.

"God only knows what man she's going to bring," Willie said of the five-times divorced Connie who was now selling her merchandise at neighborhood sex aids parties, selling fuckerware as Louie called it.

I spoke to Becky and she was angry that Connie had not called her to tell her what it was that Connie was bringing and I told her Connie was bringing ribs and bean salad. She had wanted to bring the bean salad because Connie did not know how to make good bean salad and she began to tell me how to make bean salad until I had to stop her. Besides, she insisted that Connie was dirty with all the fuckerware around the house and Connie went around with so many men and did so many ugly things with them that she knew that no one washed their hands. She talked herself into bringing potato salad as she always did because Connie insisted on bringing her dirty bean salad and since no one could get hold of Connie no one could change her mind. Al would bring ribs and a roast. He was all excited about the party, working whenever he could during the week to have time off on Saturday to help my father rig up the famous barbecue pit.

My father called as he always calls as a show of affection to say that he is having a hard time getting ready for the party because the barbecue pit has worked its way to the back of the garage and he can't get it out by himself. He sounds so worried as though the party were about to start without him. I calm him down and reassure him that he has plenty of time and that Al will be there Saturday to help him. He doesn't want Al to help him because Al is an Anglo and doesn't know the Mexican ways of cooking and eating ears and eyes and tongues and tendons. What does that have to do with getting the barbecue pit out of the garage? He doesn't want to reason with me. He doesn't like Al. But for some strange reason he has grown to like Rene. I tell him to relax that even if he can't get the barbecue pit out by himself that all of us together can get it out on Sunday but at his age that bothers him. He is getting old and preparing to die. He needs to have everything set at least one day ahead of time. Not that he's changed that much, only now it's worse. He senses what I'm thinking and he asks me if I remember that as a young father in San Diego he would go to take the morning train to Laredo the night before so that he wouldn't be left behind, that he slept under cover of the yellowing eaves along with the diurnal bats?

Frankie is dead, having shot his head off in the front bedroom of the old house because as he told me and I did not believe him during one night of drunkenness that he could not stand to live anymore among diverging people.

The phone rings. Maybelline has gone home and I answer it. It is Judge Masters office. First the lady wants to know why I'm answering my own phone and after I explain she asks if I would please hold for the Judge.

"Andy?" he asks with a lot of jurisprudence, "are you terribly busy?"
I don't think I have anything.

"Well, it could be a short trial or it could be longer. It's hard to say."

"What is it?" I ask.

"The District Attorney just called. Houston Police have arrested this man for killing his wife and his mother-in-law . . . and his father-in-law. He's an illegal. Doesn't speak English well. He's completely lost. Went beserk. I'm appointing you to defend him."

I was about to tell him that I did not want to do it, that I was tired, when he interrupted. "Don't say anything just now. Think about it. Call me Monday." Then he reminded me of where it was that I was supposed to be. He asked, "Weren't you supposed to be at the doctor's this afternoon? You better go see him. You haven't been yourself recently. You look horrible."

CHAPTER 2

It seemed to me that all the Jews were growing smaller. Sol had grown smaller and more stooped, as if he worked as his father had in the garment district cutting suits by dim lights six days a week. The doctor sitting before me, since I had seen him last, had grown smaller and beaked like a strange little stooped black bird. I had not remembered him so small and dark and his nose so huge and angular.

"How would you feel if someone walked in just at closing time?" he cried in his high Jewish voice, playing with his tongue against his dentures.

"I forgot the appointment, Doctor. I apologize. If you want me to I'll make another appointment. I can come back later. Listen, I know how you feel. I don't like it when someone comes barging in. I really don't need to see you. It's like everything else, like going to the dentist. I feel fine now."

He hadn't made up his mind whether to see me or not. I had caught him alone in his office just as he was leaving. He sat with his woolen overcoat on, the coat of the same color and style as the old man that I had seen earlier this afternoon trying to cross the street against the wind, leading my antecedents.

"What's your problem? Why did you need to . . .?"

"I was feeling odd," I jumped in hoping to confuse him. Why had I rushed over here? "Odd, that's all," I said.

"Tell me exactly how you feel?" he asked.

"Odd, like I say. That's all."

"Why did you want to see me? You make an appointment to see me and first you almost don't show up and then when you do, you don't want to tell me what is your problem?"

"I'm over my problem. I don't feel odd anymore."

"What do you mean by odd?"

"Oh . . . Just an odd feeling."

"Like a heart attack?"

"No . . . No . . . Nothing like that. It was just a fear, an odd fearful feeling." I resented that he would think that I would have a heart attack. I was too young and thin. But then I remembered my grandfather at that same age trying to rip the fat off his chest to ease the intolerable pain from his heart as he left the meat market, falling, dead before he hit the ground.

I could see myself doing the same. But please God, I prayed, not here, not in front of the angry doctor. I wanted to die alone like an unloved Mexican dog in the lonely wet darkness under a house far away from the crowd.

"Did you have an irrational fear? Was that it?" He was in the process of taking his coat off and getting down to his white smock with rust stains and at the same time taking his old black rubber stethoscope out of his pocket as he got up from his chair and walked to my side of the desk. He threw the coat on the floor. He was going to take my blood pressure. I remained quiet while he pumped up his bulb. He looked intently at the column of mercury and shook his head. "Your pressure is way high," he said. "I would be concerned about it. It's high. Do you eat a lot of grease and beans? Mexicans eat horrible. Is there any history of heart disease in your family?"

"No," I replied. How were we to know if my grandfather or my father had heart disease? And to admit it without proof seemed to add an unforgivable deficiency to my family. Physically speaking, wasn't being a Mexican bad enough? At this point I would have felt like a traitor to volunteer any information about my antecedent's health. Furthermore, I was not about to tell him that my grandfather had died instantaneously of a heart attack while buying red meat.

"Are you under a lot of stress? Your blood pressure was a little high the last time you were here, but I believe we decided that we would just watch it, keep track of it. That was . . ." He went back to his chair and checked his records. "In 1979," he whistled. "You don't come around often, do you? How's the law profession doing anyway?"

"Fine," I said in a high voice, almost answering as an entrapped child.

"Are you sure? I hear that there are a lot of lawyers out there in jungle-land. The competition for a buck must be . . . I'm just glad I'm not a lawyer. Anyway, what I'm getting at is this. Maybe you're working too hard. Worrying too much. It can get to you, you know. Blood pressure shoots way up. Lots of tension. That sort of thing. Before you know it you start feeling bad. I see it all the time among the Jews. Got too many payments to make. Not making enough money. Not as much as you used to. Bills piling up. That's very common right now. That's why the Mrs. and me live within our means."

"None of the above," I said.

"Well, it could be that you're getting older. Your arteries are not as stretchable. You're accumulating some plaque in there. The heart has to work harder and harder every day just to get circulation to itself and the brain and the kidneys and all the rest of the body. Pretty soon you're a candidate for a heart attack or a stroke. It happens all the time. Do you

Lionel G. Garcia

think that you should go into the hospital?"

"No," I answered. I was very definite with the answer, so that he could not interpret it as a sign of weakness.

He sighed and took out his pocket watch to look at it. "The Mrs. and I have supper about now," he informed me, replacing his watch. "Well, what about a psychiatrist?" he mumbled. "Do you want for me to recommend a good psychiatrist?"

"Are you serious?" I said. "Do you know what would happen to a Mexican if his family knew that he was spending good money on a psychiatrist? You couldn't live among them."

He said, "That's foolishness. We Jews are always going to psychiatrists. It's just a treatment for an illness, that's all. If you have liver problems, we treat the liver, don't we? Well, the brain is an organ just like the liver is an organ. We in the medical profession don't see any stigma attached to psychiatric treatment. Maybe he can calm you down. It may be nothing more than tension. You may be under a lot of tension and you may not even realize it. For example, how is your marriage going?" He did not give me time to answer. He was on a medical roll. "Sometimes you think that your marriage is going great but there are tensive undertones. Little things. Just those little things that are enough to drive you crazy but not enough to give them a second thought. Women are bad about that. They are different than you and me. They have little irritating habits that to them mean nothing. They don't even know they're irritating someone. That's part of being female. You add those up and you wind up with a rage that is being sublimated, placated, so to speak. You are like a walking volcano inside, especially being Latin . . . and outside, well, my God, you feel that you should be civil. After all it isn't anything to get into an argument over, is it? Pretty soon you're drinking too much. You're thinking that your wife is to blame for everything from skates in the driveway to the fucking Palestinians. Your stomach is upset. Heartburn . . . You develope heartburn all the time. That's it . . . heartburn."

He looked at me again with his large black Jewish-olive eyes over the half-moon glasses to see if he had hit a diagnostic nerve, to see if I concurred. He took his glasses off and I could see the indented imprint half-way down his long pointed nose. He raised his thick black eye-brows to relieve the tension that the glasses had caused on his nose, to smooth out the self-same imprint. He was disappointed and pouted when I shook my head in disagreement. It wasn't that I didn't completely agree with him. It did irritate the hell out of me to see Rene use my scissors and not put them back where they belonged. And the list goes on. The indelicate habit of passing gas the minute she got in the car after a party, saying,

114

"Thank God we left. I was ready to explode. I could feel my farts bouncing up and down inside of me. What was in that food anyway?"

He kept on when he noticed that I was not buying his theory, hoping, I suppose, that he would stumble onto something else that would give him his triumph: the medical nail being hit on the head. He was rounding up his covered-wagon train of thought and circling it around my problem. His intention, I knew, was to close the circle until I had no escape. Then he would exalt himself by saying: "I thought so. I knew it all the time." But why all these games? Was it because he knew and I knew that we could never get at the uncomfortable truth?

"Life has a way of being irritable all the time if you let it," he informed me seriously. He was opening and closing the temple pieces on his glasses as he spoke. He looked at me suspiciously and stopped talking. Had he seen something? "Maybe the children have been getting into trouble, no?" I sometimes wished that Andy would be the type to get into a little trouble. And Marie, Rene's daughter from her first marriage? What trouble could she get into? She had been on the pill since she was twelve. No, the kids were fine.

"Nookie?"

"What?"

He staightened up in his chair and I could barely see his embarrassed red dark face with his metallic sheen toupee on the top of his head. "Nookie?" he repeated, opening his mouth to be sure he pronounced it in a gentile way, so that I could understand it. "You know . . . nookie."

"You mean . . .?"

"Yes. Are you getting plenty of nookie?"

"But Dolores is such a fine woman, Andres. Why would you want to leave her?" My mother wiped the tears from her eyes. My speechless and depressed father was sitting next to her at the kitchen table. Aunt Victoria was racing away on her crocheting, her fingers moving like the webbing feet of a harried spider. It was not her position to say anything. I could hear the Mexican sounds of the locusts outside, their chirping, chirping, chirping, resolving into a long drawn out high pitched stacatto, hard-shelled mariachis rubbing their spiney legged violins and hugging trees, the same effort that they had failed to do for our great grand-father. One followed another one's mating call and I remembered how Willie and Louie would take the thin skeleton of chitin with its sticky legs that had once been the live insect and would attach it to their tongue and hide the dead animal inside their mouths, sticking their tongues to expose the skeletons to the screaming girls. Once my brother Louie made one of the skeletons cling to the tip of his nose all during supper and my father laughed throughout the meal. My mother, the same one that is crying next to me, had left the table to eat in the kitchen, scared that the little hard animal had died of some strange disease that would kill us all and render us hard and empty as the bug.

"But Dolores is such a fine, fine lady," she cried. "How could you think of doing something like that? How could you betray a fine and honorable woman?"

I knew exactly how my father felt. He loved Dolores. She was his favorite daughter-in-law. The only thing he could think of asking during the conversation was, "Will we never see her again?"

I could hear the monotonal Doctor talking in the background like the drone of a pestering horse fly. He sounded as though he was asking me more about the description of Rene's sexual parts, but I was not paying attention.

"What happened?" Willie asked me one night when we were trying to get drunk.

"I'm in love with Rene," I said. How could I tell him or anyone else that Dolores had been sexually brain-washed by the crow-like nuns, that she would undress only under the cover of darkness and that I would have to cover her mouth when I touched her to stifle the scream that depolarized the hemispheres and sent visions of parrots flying between the eyes and when she did, would make love only under the blanket that she made into a cave?

Later on Willie said, "Goddamit, why didn't you just fuck her real good, bang her around. You know what I mean? Fuck her real good and then leave her. Why did you have to mess up your life so much over a piece of ass? And look what you did to Mom and Dad and the rest of the family. You really hurt them. You brought an Anglo woman into the family, man. We can't even act right when she's around. Can't eat the things we like to eat. Can't bull-shit around. You know what I mean? She tries real hard, you know, to go along. She's a good gal. Nobody's saying she ain't, but goddam it man, you really fucked it up. Louie and me and Becky and Connie we don't have the fun we used to with you since you got married to her. We miss you. Old Frankie, he's so hurt he don't talk to anyone. Just stays in his room playing with his blanket."

"Frankie's sick. Leave him alone and I don't want you talking about Rene like that." He looked at me red-eyed and wept. I knew he was drunk if he was crying. "Why doesn't Al bother you? He's Anglo."

"Al don't mean shit to anyone. He's useless. We don't pay him no mind. I love you, bro," he said. "I'll do anything that makes you happy. If I hurt your feelings I'm a sonofabitch and I'm sorry."

"I'd appreciate it if you tell Louie the same thing."

"Bro, whatever you say. Louie and me love you. Shit, man, we raised you. Don't you remember? We raised you, Louie and me and Frankie. We just want what's best for you. That's all. Louie and me talk a lot about you and we worry about what's going on. You just aren't the same guy anymore. Oh, we know you're kind of important and a lawyer and all that, but you've got to remember that we, all of us, helped you when you needed help. Connie, Becky, Louie and me, we all helped you some . . . Even Frankie as sick as he's always been."

"I've said I was grateful many times. What else can I do? It just happened. I didn't set out to hurt anyone. Rene is a good woman and so is Dolores. I just out-grew Dolores. I didn't know it when I married her but I didn't have anything in common with her. But that's not why I got a divorce. I didn't realize any of this until afterward. Hell, I was satisfied with Dolores. We were settled down. We were planning on having children. But then this happens. Rene walks in my office and I knew something was going to happen. She made my skin crawl. I had never had that feeling before. Have you ever had that feeling? I never had it with Dolores."

Willie stroked his chin with the cigarette hand. "No," he said calmly.

"Well, don't condemn me until that happens to you. To know that you want someone's body so badly and that she wants you so badly is . . . Well, we were like dogs in heat. And it was over before we knew it. I thought that maybe when I saw her again that the feeling would be gone, but it wasn't. I did make one effort. I tried to send her to another attorney but she wouldn't go. Dolores didn't have a chance."

"Jeez, man. Why didn't you screw her a lot and let it go at that? You didn't have to marry her. Lot's of men do that. Fuck her good until you can't stand her and then tell her to get lost."

"Have you ever done that? I know you talk about it all the time, about how *macho* you are and all the women you've had, but really is that all a bunch of bull-shit or is it the truth? Have you ever had a woman really love you so much that she would throw herself at you like Rene did to me?"

"Sure I have," Willie lied. He had ordered another beer. The bartender had seen Willie raise his empty bottle and had the waitress bring him another beer. She also brought another round for me. "Like that waitress," Willie said, looking at her as she left. "You could just screw her and leave her. There's no sense getting serious about her. Hell, she ain't serious about you."

"There's a lot of difference between the waitress and my wife, shit ass," I informed him. He raised up slightly from his chair as if he were about to reach over the small table to choke me. "Relax, you ignorant sonofabitch," I said. He didn't know how to take it, whether to continue intimidating me as he had always done or leave me alone. When he realized that he had hurt my feelings, he settled down.

"I'm sorry," he apologized. "I didn't mean it like it sounded. It's just that we all love you so much and think so much of you. We were all hurt. That's all. I don't even know if we will ever get over it."

I couldn't believe what he was saying. "My God," I pleaded, "when are we going to put this thing to rest? When am I going to have some peace in this world? If it's not you it's Louie or Connie or Becky or mom or dad. Connie called me the other day and she was crying. She had just been to see Dolores and Dolores was crying. Everybody wanted me back but not with Rene. They would never forgive me. What kind of support is that to give to your brother? Willie, I need all the support I can get right now. I'm desperate. I'm afraid that maybe I made the biggest mistake of my life. I got married and it was like a dream that I couldn't get away from. I realized what I had done one afternoon during a trial. Can you imagine that? It hit me right in the middle of a trial. I had gotten a divorce and remarried. I had to think to remember Rene's name. I started sweating and had to ask for a recess. The judge thought I was having a heart attack. He sent me to the hospital and I stayed there over-night. I couldn't even tell my own doctor that I was in the hospital. He would've kept me there. You know how careful the Jews are. I've got high blood pressure. I'm under a lot of stress. The doctor wants me to take all these damn pills that keep me sleepy all the time. I've begun to have doubts about Rene. Now Connie telephones and starts this shit about how ungrateful I am not only to Dolores but to the whole family and the Mexican race. What does being Mexican have to do with it?"

Willie lifted the beer toward me and gave me a salute with it. "Everything," he said.

Connie's voice was shaking over the phone. "Think back to all Dolores did for you. She cooked and slaved and worked for you so that you could get ahead and this is how you pay her back. How ungrateful you are. Really, Andy, I can't believe you're doing this. Poor Dolores can't understand what it was she did to you that you would treat her so badly."

Poor Dolores? How could I tell them that when she made love, which was seldom, that she did it under the woolen blanket made into a cave?

And that I could not take her nun-like screams and flapping parrots anymore?

Now it was Willie's turn at the bar. "I didn't mean that Rene is like a waitress. What's a matter with you, you dumb shit. Whatever gave you that idea? What I was saying was that I could go out with the waitress and get it and leave it. That doesn't mean I'm going to throw my life away. I ain't getting a divorce and going through all that just for a woman. Let me give you an example, bro. This airline stewardess was the best I ever had the other night and . . ."

"Would you leave Angie for her?"

"Angie's my wife. That's the trouble with you, you never learned loyalty."

It was my turn to want to hit him.

Louie had found us. We had not seen him in a long time. He entered waving at some people that he knew. He walked over and sat down next to Willie. He shook our hand and bummed a cigarette and a light from Willie. "How long you guys been here?"

"Couple of hours," said Willie.

"You talk any sense into this shithead here?" he remarked, pointing his thumb across the table at me. He was talking to Willie. Willie shook his head. "Shit, he's beyond helping. He's married already."

"Married already! What the fuck you do that for? When did you get married? Tell me, sonofabitch. Tell me when you got married?"

Louie was always tougher than Willie. I started to say something when Louie interrupted. He poked Willie in the ribs. "How come you let this crazy sonofabitch get married?"

Willie wasn't going to take the blame for me. "Hell, I ain't my brother's keeper like the bible says. I didn't know he was going to do it."

I could see Louie's face tighten and his large neck grow before my very eyes. "What the fuck do you mean getting married without telling anyone? Who the shit do you think you are? Do you know what this is going to do to Dolores?"

"To hell with Dolores!" I screamed.

"To hell with Dolores he says," Louie was telling Willie. "That's not the idea, you dumb ass. You are supposed to be with Dolores and saying to hell with what's her name."

"I don't want to . . . Don't you dumb shits understand that I'm tired of begging Dolores, that I want Rene now?"

"We know that," Willie pleaded in a condescending voice. "We know that you want someone other than Dolores. We were here to tell you that we understand. No one wants to fuck his wife all the time. Shit, man, that's the most boring thing a man can do. What we're saying is that you don't have to leave Dolores to screw Rene, that's all. Was that so hard for you to understand? Aren't you a lawyer or what? Aren't you one of the best trial lawyers in all of Houston? A defender of the poor and all that shit. But you can't defend yourself. Don't you have the brains to understand what you did? Do you know that me and Louie are going to have to go tell the folks about what you did? Do you know that you'll break their hearts? As much as they loved Dolores."

Louie was getting as fat as Willie and I said so. "What the hell is it to you?" Willie said. "You leave Louie alone. You don't give a shit about this family anyway. You're just trying to change the conversation, just to save your ass."

"Well, if that's what you two want, let's talk some more," I explained. I was looking at Louie to see that he wasn't going to get up and take a swing at me. He had been known to do that. I kept on hoping that Louie would cool off. "It's not going to do anyone any good. All this arguing is good only to get our blood pressure up. No one is going to convince anyone about anything. You're just not going to change my mind. Can't you two fools see that I'm married already? Why can't you be civil about it? Accept Rene into the family and let's shake."

Louie said, laughing, "Hell, this is like trying to wipe your ass with a hoola hoop. You just go round and round and don't get much done."

The little doctor was shaking me rapidly by the shoulders. "Are you all right? What's come over you? You haven't been hearing what I've been saying. Get a hold of yourself."

The brown and yellow wave pattern on the walls bothered me. I could see the faint outlines of the receding ghosts of the parade I had been seeing and had seen this afternoon. The shroud was getting more distinct the longer I stared at the wall. The doctor looked even smaller as he shook me. He sensed my disorientation. "Maybe you'll feel better if you go to the hospital," he said. "I am the doctor, you know."

I was feeling better. I was not panicking. I had had these feelings before and knew that I would be back to normal in a short while. I had to answer. "I'll be all right in a few minutes," I said. "I've had this problem several times now. It's the first time that scares the hell out of you. Now I know that if I just try to relax and breathe normally I can get over the attack. At first I thought I was hyperventilating, but then I figured it out. When I get nervous, like tonight, I forget to breathe. And I see . . ."

"See what?"

"Nothing."

"If you don't want to go to the hospital, then I wash my hands off the whole mess," he complained, disgustedly throwing his mother-of-pearl fountain pen on the desk and bouncing it on one of the plastic Chinese dog book-ends. The hurled pen slid over the top of the head of the dog and hit me in the chest. Luckily it had not opened. "At least you should get psychiatric help. You're a man ready to explode."

I bit my lip and asked him where he wanted me to go.

"Why, Methodist Hospital," he said, giving me his winning smile, showing his bad European dark teeth. "Where else?" And he picked up his phone and had a room for me in five minutes. He was playing his role with relish, malicious God-likeness. He had finally defeated me, so now he loved me. All I had done was agree to go to the hospital, but he felt in his little head that I had become subservient. He handed me a piece of paper in which he had been writing with a cheap substitute pen when he had been on the phone. "This will get you VIP treatment," he said. "You'll be on the fourth floor. That's where the Duke was. Get on over there right now. They're waiting for you. I will see you tomorrow morning." Then he remembered my family. "What about your wife and children? Do you want me to call them?" I told him no very gently. It amazed me how well I was already feeling. Across from me the doctor was clearing his desk top. I could see and he could too his expensive pen, the one he had thrown in a childish fit, as it lay in the corner by the dying leafless rubber plant, its once green leaves now yellow and stacked neatly around the base of the trunk. Neither one of us seemed in a hurry to go pick it up.

I thought about Rene and I decided it would be better if I called her from there than wait till I got to the hospital.

Andy answered. Rene was at the store buying groceries for the weekend for the party because "You Mexicans eat a lot". Andy did not include himself and sounded embarrassed. Aunt Victoria would be one-hundred years old on Sunday, he said, as if I didn't know. I did not want to talk to Andy. I did not want to explain to him that I needed to go into the hospital and then have him explain it to his mother. I gave him the phone number. He said all right.

The doctor had lit a long cigarette, much longer than his face, and had his slippered little feet up on the desk. He appeared to be contemplating his pen on the floor and the juvenile act that he had performed to get it there. He was trying to be introspective as if that were what would endear me to him. He had the all-knowing smile. He wanted to know more about me while we waited for the call. He had seen my picture in the newspapers many times. He had seen me interviewed on television. Hadn't I been the defense attorney in some very sordid crime cases? Why didn't I just let them plead guilty? What was all the fuss about? Then he leaned over across the desk blowing smoke in my face and as confidentially as he could he asked, "Does being a Mexican bother you?"

"What do you mean by that?" I asked.

He jumped up and took out his watch, studied it and wound it and gave me a perturbed look. He had nothing more to say. He had already spent too much time on me. He had to leave to go eat with the Mrs. and then off to the Friday synagogue party. I wanted to try to call Rene one more time but the good doctor was putting on his ragged woolen coat and he showed me out. I would call from the hospital, he informed me.

"Do you drink at all?" my boss asked me when I refused a drink the first time I met him. He shifted his weight very gently from one thin anemic buttock to the other. "The reason I ask is that nowadays some of the young lawyers drink a little too much. I'm glad to see that you have sense enough to refuse a drink when you don't want one. It's too early to drink. It makes me less concerned about you . . . That doesn't meant that I'm not . . . concerned, I mean. I'm concerned for all the young attorneys that join our firm. You're one of five, I believe, that we hired. And if you will forgive me saying so, I especially wanted to put on a person of your . . . race. I'm glad that the other partners agreed. So here you are. You represent your race here, Andrew. Do they call you Andrew? Are you comfortable with Andrew? I don't like nicknames. Especially in the office. You should be called Andrew. That's a good name. Where did you get it? In honor of your father's employer?"

Sol was next to me urinating heavily without the hindrance of a foreskin and he said, "How are you enjoying it here?"

"Fine," I said, innocently.

"If you want some advice from someone who's been here for a while . . ." He stopped and looked at me seriously. I felt that he would mean every word that he was about to speak. I had already finished washing my hands. He was shaking his hoodless pecker-head at the urinal. "Don't speak Spanish around here. The people in power do not like it." I realize I had spoken to the cleaning people and one of the secretaries in Spanish, a sin in some places in Texas. It had been an exchange in Spanish about how things were going, nothing more. "They think that you're talking about them. Maybe making fun of them. I've overheard complaints. It's like that all over Texas, everyone here is paranoid. That's the way the powers like to keep us. Just a word to the wise."

Dolores agonized about the office Christmas party since early November when the invitations had gone out. She worried constantly about what to do, how to act. She was always so self-conscious because she was dark-skinned that she began to rinse with dilute hydrogen peroxide and rubbed her face and arms with pumice. Every day was a scrubbing ritual to lighten her color and gain acceptance. What would she do if the boss's wife talked to her? What about all the other wives? Would she be accepted? What to wear? Properly attired meant black tie for the men and the women in white formals. She felt she didn't look good in white. Maybe she could get by wearing light blue. More agony. Place? The Warwick in Houston, the hotel for royalty, ambassadors and celebrities. Our car would not look good there. Louie was recruited to get a nice looking car from a pimp friend. Not only that, he chauffeured us wearing a borrowed tuxedo and he bowed as he opened the door for us and called us Madam and Sir.

As the party progressed it became rowdier and the boss left, but before he was gone, his gin-filled wife staggered over to speak to me . Never once during the whole night had she thought I was an attorney with the firm. She assumed that I was working for the caterer. I did not have the heart to tell my wife.

Late at night, as the men began to chase and fondle the women throughout the porticos and the terrace, I heard the scream that depolarized the hemispheres and sent visions of parrots flying between the eyes, as some unsuspecting man grabbed Dolores' crotch. The whole scene became a wet still-photograph, polarized and frozen by the piercing sound. I saw the man run out from the crowd, screaming in pain, his eyes bulging and swollen, watery blood running from both ears, his wrinkled-armed wife running after him and yelling for him to stop before he could jump from the terrace. She grabbed him as he was about to kill himself and they both plunged, like attached twins, from the terrace to the floor below, falling among the recently pruned ligustrums unharmed but scratched, ruining the evergreen shrubs, his marriage and his hearing and courtroom career. I was not welcomed into the firm.

As the young lady at the hospital asked me for more information, I could see visions of Louie balling his large hairy fist, getting ready to hit me. I must have startled her when I reared back to keep away from the imagined blow. She looked at me in a panic and asked if everything was all right.

An old wrinkled black-pompadoured nurse with lots of facial hair came over to where I was seated and introduced herself. She loved my little Jewish doctor, she said, speaking of him as one would of an animated toy. He always called her nookie-head. "Whatever that means," she said proudly. He had phoned her personally and I was to be treated like a VIP, his words exactly.

"Doctor didn't tell me whether you are on high blood pressure medication. Are you?"

"No," I told her.

She wrote that down and had me walk by her side for a short distance down the hall and then she stopped in front of a wheel chair and she rolled it away from the wall and pushed it toward me.

Like a child begging his mother, I asked, "Do I have to?"

She nodded her large hairdo and smiled through her thin white beard. "Hospital policy," she explained.

It wasn't until after I had changed into hospital pajamas that I had a chance to call home. But first the nurse had taken my blood pressure and she had whistled in disbelief. She was still shaking her head and writing something down as she left. What did she expect, after making me ride in the wheel chair, making me angry?

Rene sounded scared when she answered. "Where in the world are you?" she asked. "Andy said you called. I hadn't had a chance to call the number Andy gave me. I just got in from the grocery store. I've never seen a family eat like this one. We were out of bacon, eggs, milk, cereal, popcorn and bread. I just went grocery shopping yesterday. Are you bringing people in to eat at night or what? And then I had to buy the stuff for the party. You know how your people eat. I couldn't find tripe or tongue or tendons or feet or your favorite intestines. . . . and the crotch of the poor cow . . . Uuuugggg. Why did you want that for?"

"To scare Willie," I said. I knew it was a silly trick. "Louie and I wanted to scare him. Serve it to him."

"It gives me the creeps. Can you imagine that staring at you at the meat counter? They don't sell stuff like that. Isn't it against the law? Why don't you people eat like human beings? I don't know   which is more embarrassing, to ask the butcher for all that stuff or to stand in line with it. People ask what that stuff is and it embarrasses me. It does Andy too. He turns red, especially when they ask how we fix it before we eat it. We're all denying that we eat it. It really grosses people out, you know. I'm not doing that anymore. We're not cooking that shit in my house again. It smells like the air at the ship channel. I was so embarrassed asking for all that stuff that I forgot to buy the Christmas tree."

"You're not going to believe this," I began, ignoring her usual diatribes on Mexican cuisine, "but I'm in the hospital."

I could feel that she had sat down. All she could do was ask, "Why?"

"Remember I had the doctor's appointment?"

"Yes, but that was just for a check-up. Or were you lying?"

"No, I wasn't lying. Why would I lie to you? It was just a check-up, like I said."

"Then what are you doing in the hospital?"

"The doctor says that I am under too much tension. My blood pressure is very high. He's afraid for me. He wants me to have a physical."

"And why didn't he do it in the office? Why the hospital?"

"I don't know. I'm assuming *he* knows. Anyway, I'm giving him the benefit of the doubt for once. I have been feeling kind of tired lately."

"Sure you have. You haven't had a good night's sleep in a long time, tossing and turning. You drink too much."

"Baby, if I didn't drink I couldn't sleep."

"Buuuullllllll-shit! You could sleep if you didn't drink."

Well, who knew better, her or me? That's what I loved about being married. All of a sudden we're arguing about something else. We have forgotten that I am in the hospital. "Baby, I know what I'm doing."

"For being so smart, you sure are dumb." she said. You're going to die young. Did you know that? One of these days you're going to have a heart attack . . . just keel over dead like you told me about your grandfather. You're going to die just like him."

"Oh, come on. Don't be ignorant. Who knows how someone is going to die? But the important thing is that I'm here, isn't it? Doesn't that show that I'm trying to be a good boy? That I'm changing my ways?"

"Does that mean that you're not going to drink?"

"Absolutely not. What that means is that I will watch what I drink more carefully. You can't expect me not to drink at all. That wouldn't be fair. What would my family think?"

"I hate you when you make fun of serious things like this. You're killing yourself. Don't you see?"

"No, I don't see! I hate you when you say you hate me! Don't *you* see?"

This time Willie was not able to stop the blow from Louie. Louie had been waiting for me to relax before he threw the punch. I was looking at a beautiful girl that had just arrived with a large bearded man, wondering what attracted her to him, and they took a table for two in front of us. Louie timed the punch perfectly. He hit me as I turned away from the girl to look at him. Willie was looking somewhere else. I had been relying on him to protect me from Louie. The punch hit me in the mouth and it felt like he had hit me with the large cast-iron skillet, like he had done when we were kids, the time when he had loosened my front teeth. I was numb. My whole mouth was numb. I was on the floor feeling for my mouth, trying to figure out what parts of me were missing. I had my fingers in my mouth feeling teeth. I checked for blood, but there wasn't any . . . not then anyway. It would take me a while before I started to bleed. Willie was trying to get me up on my chair. He placed a handkerchief on my mouth and told me to hold it there. Louie had sat back on his chair, stunned at what he had done.

Willie was yelling at Louie. "What the fuck did you do that for? Are you crazy?"

"Sonofabitch left Dolores for someone else. The little fucker married someone else. He pisses me off. Who the shit does he think he is?"

"But, you dumb fart, you don't have to hit him in the mouth when he isn't looking."

"I'll hit the fucker whenever I feel like it."

Willie was looking at my mouth. "Jesus Christ," he said "we're going to have to take him to the hospital. You really screwed up his lower lip. One of his teeth went right through it. I can see the tooth right through the hole."

It was better that we left before we could stop the bleeding. The manager had already called the police. We needed to get out of there. Louie was on probation.

The coiffed nurse had returned and walked in very confidently in the display of total superiority over me, just because she knew the little doctor that caller her "Nookie-head." Her uniform seemed whiter than before and better pressed, as if she had purposely changed just to intimidate me. I could hear the unnatural rustling of the starch that I had not heard before as she darted about the room. Had she shaved? She said that in thirty minutes someone would come for me and wheel me around, like it or not, and take me to begin the gathering of body samples so that they could run tests overnight. I was to give them blood and urine, and sputum, sputum because the doctor felt that being a Mexican I may have tuberculosis. X-rays. Many of those on my chest and abdomen and hips and colon and neck. It would take, she informed me, two to three hours. It was now ten-thirty at night.

As soon as she left I did what I should have done that afternoon. I knew that I needed companionship. So I phoned Louie and in fifteen minutes he and Donna Marie and Willie were in my room and I dressed as they stood guard and they helped sneak me out of the hospital and drove me to where my car was parked. I hugged them and told them that I would talk to them on Sunday when we were all together for our Aunt Victoria's birthday party. But I would see Louie and Donna Marie before then.

December in Houston: It had been very cold in the morning with early fog and ice on the roofs. The north wind had brought pollution from the ship channel that during the night had sneaked into our homes and lungs. The dog was huddled warmly in his bedding at the corner of the garage and did not even lift an eyelid to greet me as I drove off. By late morning we had all discarded our woolen coats and had rolled up our sleeves. Tonight it had started to rain in squalls throughout the city and the cold had settled in for its nightly visit. My own perspiration was giving me chills as I drove out of the parking garage.

God and the dog only knew whether the dog had moved during the day. He was still in the same bed and position that I left him in that morning. This time he got up, chore-like and with the look of someone that is being imposed upon, and he came over and asked me with his eyes how the day had gone. I grabbed the old guy by the ears and massaged them gently and I told him that my day had been hectic, that he probably would not believe me if I told him. He nudged my hand with his cold wet nose and I relented. "Well, old bud," I said putting on my coat to ease the chill, "I was in court all morning long. You see, this man got angry with another man over a pool game, but it was not the pool game really. This man was going out with this other guy's wife and the guy had just found out about it. He goes to the *cantina*. You know what the *cantina* is, don't you?" The dog nudged my hand again. He needed for me to continue massaging his ears, pay a price for making him listen to the story. He begged me to continue. "The husband pulls out a gun and shoots the man and kills him. The murderer does not have a lawyer. I take the case and I spend the day in court. Well, almost the whole day. In the afternoon I worked at my desk and then I realized I had a doctor's appointment. I ran to the doctor's and he told me awful things and he sent me to a hospital. In the hospital I was treated like a prisoner. I called Louie. You remember Louie, don't you?" And he and a lady of the night and your uncle Willie helped me escape and here I am."

Then I thought as I rubbed the top of his head at what a simple moral standard the dog has. I have seen male dogs fight over a female in heat, but only when she is in heat. And I have never seen a dog kill another dog over a bitch. Man, yes. Dogs, no. He does not get married. The dog does not complicate his own life. Man does that for him. Lost in my thought, I had stopped rubbing his head and he was nudging me on when I came to. Realizing I was not good for any more affection, he walked away dejectedly and laid down on his pallet and gave out a doleful sigh. My day had been too much for him. He was asleep before I could unlock the door.

"What the hell happened to you?" were the first words I heard from my bitch. She was sitting at the breakfast room table drinking coffee from a large mug without a handle. Everytime I saw the mug it reminded me of Korea. The sailors drank coffee in mugs like that.

"I had to go to the hospital. The doctor wanted me to take some tests."

"Why did you leave. The hospital just called. They're all looking for you. The doctor knows. You escaped or what?"

"You don't escape from a hospital, Rene. A hospital is not a prison."

"The hospital says you escaped! You fool!"

"Please don't call me a fool. You can call me a sonofabitch or something else, but don't call me as fool. Do you understand?"

"What else can I call what you did? It was foolish. That's what I meant. The doctor must be beside himself."

"Fuck the doctor. The doctor is a little ass-hole. I did not need to be in the hospital."

"He would not have put you in the hospital if you didn't need it."

"Is that what you think?"

"Yes."

"Well then, you're the fool . . . Where are the children?"

"Andy's asleep and Marie's gone out with Jack."

I walked over to the bar and got a glass and put some ice in it. "How about a drink?"

She gave me her favorite worried look, the "you're going to die young" look. "No," she snapped. "And you shouldn't either."

"Why not?" I asked as I poured bourbon in a glass of ice. I added a little water.

"Because you're going to kill yourself, that's why . . . Your drink looks awfully dark. Are you drinking straight whiskey?"

"Yes."

"To hell with you," she said and ran upstairs.

I was about to pour another drink when the phone rang. It was Sol. He was at the synagogue party and the doctor was there and had told Sol what had happened. Sol wanted to know if I was doing all right. When I told him that I was, he asked if I wanted to reassure the doctor. The doctor was standing right by him. I had suddenly gotten well, I said.

Sol whispered into the telephone. "The doctor just walked away. He says that you need a psychiatrist. I have a Jewish friend that's a psychiatrist. You want his name?" he laughed.

"No. I want a Mexican psychiatrist if I'm going to have to go to one."

"My friend will know one, I'm sure," Sol replied. He wanted to talk more. "How's it going?"

"The party must not be going good if the most interesting thing you can talk about is me."

"Well, it's, you know . . . boring. All Jewish parties are boring. Most of the mothers and mothers-in-law that are still alive are here and they don't get along. They're all competing. They're counting our money and our drinks. Seriously, how's it going?"

"Great. Just great. I hadn't heard from you in a long time. I returned you call today, but everyone was drunk."

"Yes, I figured. It's getting bad."

"You want to change."

"What for? I'm too old. Listen, I keep reading about you in the paper. You've handled some well publicized cases. I saw your picture in *Time* magazine."

"It was a very small picture."

"Yes, but it made *Time*. You got coverage nation-wide. I really envy you."

"You're pulling my leg, Sol. You're the one that has it made. Big law firm. Security. Good salary. Hell. Me, I don't know what I'll be doing next week."

"That's what I envy about you. Your freedom."

"How wrong you are. I wish it were true." I got up from the table and poured another drink. The first one had not had any effect on me. I doubled the amount and did not add water.

"The case was a land-mark decision. You went to the Supreme Court. You were instrumental in changing the law. Do you know how important that is?"

"Sol," I answered, "cut out the bull-shit. Thousands of lawyers go before the Supreme Court. It's not like I won the Nobel Prize or something. Are you sure your mother is there counting your drinks? How many have you had?"

"A lot. My mother can't see to count anymore." He laughed again.

"Why don't you come with me? We could practice together. See if it's as glamorous as you think it is."

"What a time to ask! Now that I'm drunk and old."

"I mean it, Sol. You and I could make a terrific team. Just think about it. You get the Jews and I get the Mexicans."

He did not laugh. "I feel sorry for your people," he said. "I feel sorry for you. They never gave you a chance."

"I thought you said you envied me. Make up your mind, you old fart."

"I do. I envy you. It's just that you were not treated fairly at the firm. And that wasn't right. Whatever else you may have wanted to do with your life, you should have been treated with dignity."

"Fuck dignity and the law firm. I was angry all the time. They did me a goddamn favor to get rid of me. Anyway, that's been so many years ago. I don't think about that anymore."

"I do," Sol whispered into the telephone. "That was one hell of a party, the last one we ever had too."

"What about you? Being a Jew hasn't been a piece of cake. You didn't get treated as well as the other guys your age."

"Well, that's right . . . You're right. Maybe I should be looking at myself more and not feeling sorry for other people."

"You're a hell of a guy, Sol. Look out for yourself and don't trust the mother-fuckers. Think about what I said."

"Are you sure you're all right?"

"Sure. I'm sure. You act like I escaped from a mental hospital."

"No. I didn't meant to imply that. If you need a psychiatrist, let me know. This guy I told you about is my cousin. A helluva guy. He's at the party tonight. He moved here from Brooklyn. He's been here a couple of years. Loves Houston."

"If he loves Houston, then he's crazier than me. I need a Mexican psychiatrist that will tell me that I'm normal. I know that in my family I'm the most normal one. If I need a psychiatrist, then I'm going to make an appointment for the whole family. And I won't be the first in line."

This time he laughed and said, "Take care. Mazel tov."

"Thanks," I said and took the rest of the drink.

I needed two more drinks before I relaxed. I was thinking that I would agree with Rene that I was drinking too much, except that she would have kept on and on. I did not want to listen to her tell me how she had been right, how I must always listen to her. I did not want what would come afterwards: the counting of drinks that we had been through before. I went upstairs and the bedroom door was locked. I went to sleep in the extra bed in Andy's room. Sometime during the night I was awakened by the noise of a car door slamming shut. Marie was coming in. I heard the front door close. I was cold and now that I was awake it would be hard to fall asleep again in the strange bed.

I got up and took a shower and went back to bed.

The sailor's coffee mug and the battles of Korea came to mind and gradually I fell asleep. Little Andy was snoring gently. I heard the first sergeant telling me again for the hundredth time to keep my little fucking head down if I wanted to live long enough to see my family again. Just then, for the hundredth time, I looked at his face and in an instant it exploded like a watermelon falling off a truck, as he took a tracer bullet through the eye. I had dreamed it so many times that I could slow the action. I could see the bullet as it gently penetrated and disappear into the eye. I could see the head expand slightly at first and enlarge, bigger, until it exploded into so many fragments of so many sizes. I had been blinded by the spray of the innumerable pieces of his head. So fast had the bullet hit him that I had not had time to blink and close my eyes. I was spitting his warm blood and flesh and brains and hair out of my mouth, not able to see. I could feel the lifeless weight of his plump headless body as he fell on my lap in the trench. Tonight as I fell asleep I was able to stifle a scream as I was not able to do in the trenches of Korea. Martinez and Garcia and Soliz and Benavidez crawled to me and wiped me off and told me to quiet down, that the gooks were there all around us and to forget Rodriguez, the top-kick with the large family from El Paso. He was dead. We were surrounded and about ready to be killed.

CHAPTER 3

It was at the time that Willie had come home from the war and Louie was working at the beer-joints with the many colorful prostitutes. Willie took me to see the fat naked lady with the small breasts of a dog that performed incredible feats, picking up dollar bills with her most intimate of parts, squatting down over the folding money on the bar and picking it up with her outer lips, letting the money dangle between her legs so that everyone could gape in amazement as she continued to slowly gather the bill up with seemingly hairy tentacles with a life of their own until the money was hidden in the deep greasy recesses of her cavernous part.

I was a child. "Why did you bring me here?" I yelled at Willie trying to be heard against the noise as we sat at the bar and watched the lady fold and refold the dollar and Louie hysterically striking the bar right behind her, gazing up between her short bluish fat legs. She did have eight breasts like the dog, four pairs of tiny brown nipples scattered in two rows in the many folds of her abdomen and chest. I was having fun.

"Why? . . . . . . So that you can see things," Willie answered above the din of the crowd. "You got to learn about the world. These things are happening all around you. Don't you want to know? This woman can nurse eight children at one time if you feed her enough. But just wait, you ain't seen nothing yet."

The lady's hairy lips released the dollar bill, allowing it to float like a wet green butterfly that landed gently between her large square bare feet and everyone screamed in their pleasure. Then she danced in unmeasured jerkiness across the bar, her eyes closed, her lips pursed—to the delight of the crowd—in a virginal mock. She moved gracelessly to the music of guitar and accordion making her way slowly over to an empty beer bottle that Louie had set up. He lit a cigarette as the men and prostitutes screamed. He showed the sweaty crowd the dirty toothpick and ran it crosswise through the cigarette. He placed the cigarette, lit end first, into the bottle dangling it by the toothpick across the opening. The lady had danced until the bottle was between her feet and she slowly squatted over the lit cigarette, her fatness trembling as she went down, and she grabbed the cigarette with her most intimate of parts, like a scurrying hairy crab grabbing a fingerling, and she began to smoke it, the ember glowing brightly on and off between her legs as she puffed on it more visible now, as Louie had dimmed the light to further show the increased brightness with each contraction that she made with her engorged abdomen.

I was seeing the remarkable lady trying to dance while Willie threw fifty cent pieces at her in my dreams.

"You look awful," Marie said, bringing the tomato juice to my bed. I had taken two aspirins when I took a shower, two aspirins at six and two at nine. I asked what time it was and Marie said ten. Then I suppose she felt sorry for having said that I looked awful. She made amends, or thought she did anyway. "Mom is sorry about last night," she confessed. "She feels real bad. You need to go down to forgive her."

The lady was not through dancing and puffing on the cigarette. Willie was not through throwing good money that he should have been giving to our mother to help with his keep. Louie was slapping the bar and screaming as he did night after night with his prostitute, never tiring of the spectacle.

"Quit thinking and get up," Marie interrupted. "You need to get something to eat. Mom's made a tremendous breakfast. Eggs. Yummy. Yummy. Pancakes. Yummmm. Bacon. Yummmmmy! Get up, sleepy head."

I sat up on the edge of the bed leaving my stomach behind, a slight wave of nausea coming over me. I felt my pulse. My heart was regular and barely moving. I didn't know what to say to the young woman in front of me. I needed to stand up and get dressed. "Do you mind if I get dressed?" I asked her and as she started to walk out I asked, "Are you working today?"

"Yep," she answered. "From twelve to six."

"Where are you spending the week-end?"

"With Dad," she replied.

"Does your mother know what time you came in?"

She thought she had sneaked in. Her face reddened. "No," came a guilty reply. "Are you going to tell her?"

"No," I said. "Now get out."

I went in my room and dressed and went down to eat. "How do you feel, Honeybun?" Rene asked, her back turned to me as she stood by the sink.

At first I thought she was asking someone else the question. I looked up from the plate and Andy and Marie were staring at me. "Okay, I guess," I said when I realized that she was talking to me.

"Did you talk to the doctor last night after you got in?"

"No," I answered.

"Who called?"

"Sol."

"Oh? . . . What did he call about?"

"Nothing."

"Are you angry?"

"No."

"Well, you sound angry. And I don't know what you could be angry about."

I got up and dialed Willie's number but he was still asleep. Angie answered and she wanted to know what had happened. Willie had come in drunk saying that I had been handcuffed and put in a psychiatric ward at Methodist Hospital against my will and that he and Louie had gotten me out, commando-style, just like World War Two, which meant Willie because Louie never left the states during the war and was dishonorably discharged in San Antonio for stealing the camp commander's car and driving it into a tree. I told Angie that some of what she had heard was true, but I was there of my own will. She seemed confused. "But Willie was saying . . ." I told her to forget it, that she ought to know by now when Willie is lying and have Willie call me. I needed to find out what to bring to the party on Sunday, since Rene had not been able to find tendons and guts and feet and the crotch of the cow.

"I'm glad Rene didn't buy the crotch," she said. "It's gross. When are you guys going to grow up?"

"Louie and me just wanted to scare Willie. That's all. No big deal."

"Why don't you all buy it? Why send poor Rene to get all embarrassed? Anyway, Willie doesn't get scared anymore with things like that."

"We know," I said. "It's all in fun."

But there was a time when he was scared, when the insistent Father Procopio who burned us with cigarettes had told him that to look at a crotch would cause him to lose his eye-sight.

She wanted to know if I was really up to going to the party. I was all right, I told her. Well, then she would have Willie call me later in the day. "If I'm not here," I said, "I'll be at Mom and Dad's." I had to make my regular Saturday visit and I had to take Andy with me, as much as he hated it.

Rene was cleaning the table over and over again unmindful of what she was doing. Andy and Marie had gone to their rooms to finish dressing. I was trying to ignore Rene's lack of concentration, this scene typical of the innumerable times when I wished that I could leave her. But for some reason I wouldn't. Not today, anyway. To occupy my time I dialed Louie's number and Donna Marie answered. Louie was asleep. I asked her not to wake him up, to just tell him that I had called to tell him that I had not found the crotch of the cow and to forget it, that I felt that everyone felt that we should not pull the trick on Willie. Donna Marie giggled and wanted to kow how I was doing. They had worried about me enough to stop at the liquor store to buy a half-gallon of scotch which they drank in my honor. She wanted to ask a personal question but was too shy to ask. I insisted and she finally asked me if I thought she could make it in Hollywood? Should she start at Hollywood rather than Disney World? I didn't know and she seemed crestfallen, as if I had been appointed the judge for such matters. Then she wanted to know if I had gotten in trouble with the hospital? "Of course not," I informed her. She blew a kiss to me over the telephone.

"You're not going to apologize to the doctor?" Rene asked as she carried a stack of dishes to the sink.

"No. Why should I?" I was in no mood to apologize to anyone.

The phone rang. Donna Marie had been prophetic. It was the hospital. I owed over three hundred dollars in admission fees and cancelled tests. Hospital policy, they said. They would send me a two page computerized list of everything that I had used in the room during the fifteen minutes I had been there. I told the young lady to sue me, knowing full well that I would eventually pay. I just wanted them to work a little harder for their money.

Rene started to yell to the children to come down and help her clean the kitchen. "This ain't a hotel," she yelled. To me she said, "They're going to sue you. You just watch."

I was sleepy again and I went to my room and laid down to think.

The voice on the office intercom startled me. I was sitting at my desk thinking of where I was supposed to go with a case. My hand holding a pencil was motionless over the legal pad. I heard Maybelline's thick voice say through the box, "It's Mrs. Winfield here for her appointment." I checked to see who she was. I did not have anything on her in my appointment book except her name and the word "Divorce" underlined. I told Maybelline to let her in. I got her file out and was looking into the empty manila folder when she opened the door and as she did I remembered who she was. She had talked to me on the phone.

She closed the door and walked toward me, slowly, each step a picture. She was smiling, as if the divorce suddenly didn't matter to both of us. Her face was not beautiful, but very sensuous. Her mouth was so full I had to stare at it to see if it distorted the rest of her features. Her eyes were set wide and she had a small nose. But then her body: She appeared devastating in her elegant suit. She sat down as I stood and watched her curl herself into the chair like an animal. She crossed a leg so perfect that my heart ached as I saw the inside of her leg way above the knee.

I cleared my throat to see if I could get my mind on the case. I grabbed the pencil and was ready to write. "Mrs. Winfield," I said, "I'm going to get some information from you before we talk about your problem. Just some stuff that we need for our files." I turned the page over on the pad and was ready to write. My thoughts were still on her. "Your legal name?" I asked looking up at her. She stared at me and she blushed. Sensuous and sensitive, I thought. What a beautiful combination! I was hoping that she was thinking what I was thinking.

"Maureen is my first name but everyone calls me Rene. Maiden name Jackson, married name Winfield."

After I wrote it I went around and showed her what I had written to make sure I had spelled everything correctly for the court records. As I got close to her I could smell her body. She was wearing expensive perfume. I didn't know what it was but I had smelled it in an elevator at an expensive store. But there was more than the perfume. There was a fleshy, healthy smell to her that made me ache for my childhood and the things we did under houses when the sentinel-nuns were out of town, precisely the smell of virginal parts that the priest had told us to avoid for fear of blindness. Blame it on the inciting priest and the whetting nuns, but she was the most desirable person I had ever met.

I sat down almost missing my chair, the thought of parrots singing throughout the room, and swallowed hard. "Address?" I had to clear my throat.

"Where I'm living now or where I lived with my husband?"

"Give me both."

"I'm living with a friend right now in an apartment at 17603 Westheimer. I lived at 26093 Southwest Freeway when I was living with my husband."

"Children?" I asked, wondering who the friend was she was living with.

"One. A daughter."

"Name?"

"Marie."

"Age?"

"Eighteen months."

"Marie's date of birth?"

"September thirteenth, 1965."

"Husband's name?"

"John Winfield."

"Do you happen to know his address?"

"No." She sounded relieved.

"What is your age? Nothing personal," I laughed nervously.

She looked at me and she almost blushed again. She lowered her head slightly, as if she were in the confessional, and she said, "Thirty-two."

Perfect. She was my age. "Date of birth?"

"August fifteenth, 1934." She moved her purse from her right thigh to her left thigh. I noticed that she was uncomfortable with the purse and I offered to take it and I did and I placed it on top of the chair by the door. She smiled and thanked me. "I didn't know what to do with the purse," she confessed. "I really don't know why I brought it with me. It's so small it's useless."

"Women feel better dressed with a purse," I said, repeating what Dolores had always told me.

"You're right. I know I do," she said. She uncrossed her leg and recrossed it. I saw the smooth inside of her thigh once more in a sneak glance. I could imagine her beautiful butt on the chair moving as she crossed her leg.

"When did you get married?"

"April first, 1965."

She didn't give me time to figure it out. She told me: "I was four months pregnant when I got married." And indeed she was. This had been more natural for her, I thought, since she didn't even give a hint of blushing.

"Any more children?"

"No. That's it."

"Tell me about your marriage and what happened so that I can have a better understanding of what you and I need to do."

She leaned forward and moved the chair, getting closer to the desk. She asked if I minded that she smoked and I said no. I wouldn't have minded if she had set fire to the office. She went over for her purse before I could get up to help her. She begged me to stay in my chair. I saw her from the rear for the first time and my heart stopped. She was as beautiful from the back as from the front. Her long legs ended in the most beautiful butt that I had ever seen. "I believe I've been too much of a bother already," she said lighting her cigarette. She offered me one and I took it. I hadn't smoked in a long time—Korea, to get rid of the mosquitoes, to be exact. She blew the smoke down at her precious thighs. I slid the ashtray toward her so that both of us could use it. I don't know why but without thinking, and thinking that she probably could use one, I asked if she wanted a drink. "I'd love one," she replied and with that she seemed to loosen up.

"I don't have anything but bourbon and water," I apologized.

"That's all I drink now," she said. "I love it."

I went to the little bar I had by the wall and poured two drinks. "Tell me about yourself," I said as I leaned back in my chair and admired her. She crossed her leg again but I couldn't see anything with the desk in front of me.

"Well, I married Jack. When I married him I thought I knew him. How wrong I was. I was already pregnant and he talked me into it. I regretted marrying him from the first day. I mean, he changed the day I married him. He was insanely jealous. I could never go out. I don't know how I managed to keep my job, as insane as he was. But I had an understanding boss, a lady who had never been married because she feared that something like I was going through would happen to her. You know what I mean?"

"Yes."

"I'm sorry. I'm nervous and I don't know if I made myself clear. She didn't want to lose her independence."

"I understood perfectly."

"I graduated from U of H with a degree in marketing and I've been working for the same dress shop for a long time. He'd follow me to work, but I didn't catch on until later. Or if he couldn't make it, he'd have one of his friends follow me to and from work. He was convinced I was seeing another man."

"Were you?"

"No. I wouldn't cheat on my husband." (That was music to my ears.) "I've never been that type of person." She took a drag from her cigarette and flicked the ashes into the ash tray. She took a sip from her drink and almost choked. "That's a strong drink," she managed to say as she held her throat.

"I'm afraid that was intentional," I confessed. She looked at me jokingly squinting, as if had poisoned her, and she cooed, "Are you trying to get me drunk or what?"

I laughed and said nothing. I changed back to what we had been talking about. Embarrassed, I said, "I apologize. I didn't want to imply that you had been seeing someone else. It's just that nowadays some of this goes on all the time."

"I know," she said. "That's what went wrong with the friend I live with. Her husband started to run around and then she started to run around and before they knew it, they wind up getting a divorce."

"It happens," was all I could add. "But didn't he act like this before you married him? Didn't he give you some indication that he had this type of problem?"

"If he did I didn't notice. But you know how love is. I may have seen it and ignored it just because he was the father of my child."

"Did he make love to you enough?"

This time she blushed and she hated herself for doing it. She tried to ignore it. "I suppose so," she said. "But why do you ask?"

"Oh. They may ask you all kinds of questions. It's hard to get a divorce just because your husband is the jealous type. We need to pile on more stuff. Sexual problems, things like that. Did he have sexual problems? They may never come out in the divorce, but then again they might. One thing I can tell you. The more I know about him, the more his lawyer is going to know that I know. That almost guarantees that we won't have to testify about things like that. I need all the dirt I can get on him, in other words."

"He did have certain things that he did."

"Like what?"

"I can't tell you," she blushed. She took a long drink this time and finished it off. I got up and got two more drinks.

"Well, let's go on to something else. Did he ever hit you?"

She turned red with anger. "Yes," she replied. "He hit me one time and that was it. I told him if he ever laid his hands on me again that I would kill him." She took another drink and her angry hands were shaking.

"And what did he say to that?"

"Nothing. He never hit me again."

"Did he ever threaten to hit you again?"

"Yes."

"Would you classify your life with him as bad, horrible? Enough to want to get out badly? I'm trying to see how badly you felt about the marriage. I'm trying to get some feel for your problem."

"I was damn glad to get out. We just could never get along. He was insanely jealous. He hit me that one time. He threatened to hit me many times after that. I was in fear of the man."

"You were actually scared of your husband?"

"Yes."

"And the safety of your baby? Were you ever scared for the safety of your baby?"

She thought about that one for a few seconds. "No," she answered. "I can truthfully say that he loved Marie a lot. He would have never done anything to Marie. He adored Marie."

"Was he mentally abusive?"

She did not hesitate on that one. She answered, "Yes," right away. She finished her drink.

I could not help myself. After the two drinks I was attracted to her as I had never been before to another woman. I had this urge to sit next to her. I got up and went to her side of the desk and placed a chair by her. She smiled as I gathered the chair from the wall, the one with her purse. We sat without talking for a few moments, taking in the feeling we were both getting. I got up and brought back two more drinks. On the way back I noticed how large and firm her breasts were, again how long her legs were, how firm and small her butt was. Her hair was combed professionally. She had obviously taken great pains to get ready for our first interview.

As I sat and gave her her drink, she looked me in the eye and she asked, "How about you? What kind of problems do you have?"

Just looking at her full mouth and the words coming from it, along with the thought of the question, was enough to make my hair stand on end and the cautioning screams from the nuns disappeared and no one was burning me with cigarettes as I rested comfortably to await the inevitable.

I had to wait for Andy to finish helping Marie clean the kitchen. Then Andy had to go upstairs to change again. He did not want to go see his grandparents in the clothes he was wearing. I thought he looked all right myself, but he always tried to delay his trip and, if it had not been that my parents loved him so much, I would have left him behind. I poured the last cup of coffee and unplugged the coffee pot. Rene had recovered her self-confidence and was back to her old screaming self. I could hear her upstairs screaming about Marie taking something from her closet. Marie was yelling back about something else. She would not stay quiet. The door bell rang and Rene yelled down that that must be Jack coming for Marie.

I went to the door and let Marie's father in. I forcefully resented this man standing in the doorway for having made love to Rene, no matter that they were married at the time. But I had to be Anglo-civil to keep from being called childishly prudish and there I was, smiling uncomfortably, shaking his hand, the same one that had played on Rene's most intimate parts at some time—no matter which hand, either one for I was sure he had used them both . . . . But used parts!

I would go on and on until my fading ghosts would laugh, mockingly. I sometimes wondered if he wondered if I was wondering . . . And whenever the three of us would gather, the grotesquely obscene images grew and the conversation became restrained, on my part at least, as I wondered how two people could talk to each other as if nothing had ever happened when you knew that they had seen each other's intimate parts as I had seen Dolores's under the blanket that was her cave? How forgivingly civil the Anglo culture is, I thought.

"Come in Jack," I said, trying to hide all that was going through my mind. I let go of his warm hand very shortly after he offered it. It had felt electrified to me.

"Thanks," he responded with smugness. I had noticed for many years that not being married to Rene had given him more of a sense of security and he had never married again.

He walked in front of me and I could see his ass, the exact same one that Rene had seen for two years. He stopped at the end of the foyer and asked if Marie was ready. "Almost," I said.

It amazed me the ease with which the sonofabitch walked into my house. Even his hands were warm. He looked at me and I must not have looked very good from last night. "You don't look very well," he commented.

"I had a rough night," I said, brushing my hair back with my fingers, hoping that that would help.

"Have you seen a doctor lately?" he asked.

"As a matter of fact, yes," I replied. "Just last night. Thank you for your concern."

We could hear Marie running down the stairs and she came around the den and into the foyer where we were standing. She kissed her father. He took the suitcase and started walking out when Rene yelled from upstairs that she wanted to say something to Jack. We stood in silence as we waited for her to make her entrance. She had gotten ready for Jack. She came down in a great show of beauty, enough to try to make Jack miserable for having behaved like an ass when they were married and enough to make me jealous and she kissed Marie good-bye and she shook Jack's hand, the same two hands coming together that had played on each other's most intimate of parts. Surely, I thought, there is a possibility that there remains in the microscopic folds in each one of their hands some unwashed cells of skin deposited there during their marriage, during their lovemaking, a cell of cunt, of pecker, of tit, of ass that is now being rubbed and exchanged right before my very eyes. And what was it he did to her that she never spoke about . . . . ? What were they really thinking?

"Don't let Marie stay out all night," Rene was telling him, probably thinking of some intimate part as she spoke. "She and Jackie can talk you into anything. Set a curfew for her. Well, why don't we set one right now so that we can agree on it?"

"Whatever you say, Rene," Jack said, being his gracious self. I thought he was puckering his lips unnecessarily. Jealous, wife-beating sonofabitch!

"She's got to come in at one. How's that? Is that agreeable?"

"Sounds good to me," Jack responded. And in his voice I could tell that he was not going to insist that Marie come in at that time. Marie was smiling, knowing well that she was not coming in at One.

Rene kissed Marie one more time and they hugged and the overly confident Jack picked up the suitcase trying to make it appear lighter than it was since he was now playing tennis and they left as the image of old cunts and dangling tits and fallen ass and orange peckers and yellow balls ran through my aching head.

Willie had said it to me the night that Louie beat me up at the bar. He said, "It's hard enough for a Mexican to marry a divorced woman. It's harder still when she's Anglo. God only knows what's been going on with her, man. It's enough to drive a man crazy!"

CHAPTER 4

Sometimes Willie, Louie, Frankie and I would go by the old leaning house by the edge of the creek, the one-room house with the cactus growing on the roof, where the man lived that we thought ate brown ants. At first we had been astounded to see the man laughingly throw the little brown insects into the back of his mouth without getting bit, but then one day he allowed us to get closer to him as he sat rocking on the porch and we found that the ants were really little pieces of brown chocolate in the shape of the ant. Willie laughed and so did Louie and Frankie and I when he opened his dry hand to show them to us. They were chocolate covered ants. He could buy them in Mexico, he said, just to impress ignorant people. After that we went just to watch him eat his ants and listen to him tell us about the unnatural things that happened at night in the creek. Long before that our mother had told us not to bother the man, that he was a *curandero* that had been touched by the hand of some spirit. And indeed, when Becky got sick one night, we had to go get him out of bed so that he could come to save Becky from the drenching fevers of the evil eye. He followed us silently in the dark as we ran in desperation. He swept the shivering Becky with his broom and then laid her in bed on her belly, reaching under her night gown to rub her body with both warm hands until Becky moaned, and when he turned her over Becky was flushed red, redder than she had ever been, and perspiring, her eyes looking up into her head. When the man reached under the gown and began to rub her legs, working his way up her thighs, my mother had us leave the room and only she and Aunt Victoria stayed to watch, but throughout the house we heard the excessive moans and later the depolarizing screams that the pontifical nuns had taught the girls, the screams that only Dolores had retained and that Becky and Connie had long since given up for the child's play that it was.

"I had an orgasm! My first one," Becky used to holler later when she had grown up and was married to Al and was drinking beer.

Connie screamed in laughter, throwing beer over her head. "That's . . . That's . . . That's why the little fart stayed sick so much!"

Becky laughed with her. "Damn right. I liked it!"

Connie said, "I wish to hell I had gotten the evil eye. I should have pretended."

"That was all that dirty old man was doing . . . Going around town fondling little girls and boys."

When I finally got to see the famous house in Arizona with all the cactus on the roof, it had saddened me for some reason. Neither Rene, nor Andy, nor Marie had cared about it. They had made me stay by the car as I looked at it from across the road while they stayed inside the car with the air-conditioner on. What the old man would have done with a house like that.

Now, today, this morning I was having trouble with little Andy in the car. "Are you all right?" I asked him.

"Yes," Andy responded sadly, resting his head on the window. I had only gone the six blocks that it took to get to Shepherd Street so I knew that he wasn't car sick. I stopped the car and asked him if he wanted to go back home and he said no.

"Are you sure? You don't have to go this time," I said. I knew that he did go just to make me feel good. But I had never been able to make him realize that it wasn't me, that it was my parent's tradition that needed to be satisfied. We would both feel ill at ease, but after a while, after we sat to eat, we would be comfortable. It just took time. One couldn't be expected to go from West University Place to Mexican Town without making some type of adjustment. I knew exactly how Andy felt. And furthermore, I was ready to concede that Andy had a little rougher time than me in adjusting. He had been raised in the Anglo culture. I had not. I hoped he wasn't really sick. He had always been a sickly boy, very white and thin and small, with little arms like a girl. He had the small delicate nature of Rene's father, who had been accused of being a homosexual all his life just because he had been born with one testicle that descended once a year. "Are you sure?" I asked him again and he said he was just tired.

"How are you doing in school?"

He barely opened his eyes to look at me and answered; "Not good. Didn't Mom tell you I got an F in math?"

"No, she didn't. But your mother likes to take care of those things. How are your other grades?"

He sighed effeminately with his eyes closed. "Oh, a little better . . . but not much."

"What's going on? You used to do good in school."

"That was grade school. I just can't do it anymore. I'm not smart like you. I wasn't born smart. I'm like mom.

"Your mom is smart."

"No she isn't. Mom and me aren't smart. Marie is smart, but she's crazy."

I sighed. "You shouldn't talk about yourself like that. Don't run yourself down. You could do it if you studied more. Look at me, I'm always studying."

"You enjoy studying. I don't. I don't learn anything from it." I turned left on Shepherd and drove north toward the Southwest Freeway. At the Freeway I took a glance toward him and he still had his eyes closed. I turned right on the feeder road and took the entrance ramp, got on the Freeway and sped the car. I couldn't leave him alone. "How are you feeling now?" I asked him. He opened one eye and gave me a soleful look.

"I'm okay, Dad. Just tired. I didn't get to sleep till late and I got up early."

"Rough night, huh?"

"Yeah. But from what I heard, not as rough as yours."

I felt like laughing. "Yep, podnuh. I had us a whale of a night. All I needed was to wind up at Gilley's and get into a fight with a shit-kicker."

I took the North 59 Freeway and after downtown got off on Quitman. I turned left on Quitman and went by the old high school. One block past the school I turned right, went two more blocks and turned left on Boundary. I didn't need to count houses. I had done this so many times before. I drove onto the old shell drive-way covered with grass and stopped the car. Andy woke up and yawned. "How long are we going to stay?" he asked.

"At least a couple of hours. You know how much they love you and how great they think you are."

He said, "Yeah. Sure." And he opend the door and got out.

It had taken us less than thirty minutes to get from West University Place to Mexican Town, but in terms of culture the difference was more like three hundred years. The air smelled different. Everyone was eternally cooking, no matter what time I came. The people were different, happy and open to all strangers, but heaven help you if you angered them. Across the street and beyond the open field was Moody Park and as I stood in the sodden drive-way I could see the care-free Mexican children playing. In the cool December morning everyone was yelling in Spanish, hitting a ball or kicking a ball or catching a ball or running around bases, or running after kites, the sounds of their childish laughter always filling the air with joy.

These are my people. I stand on the cold wet shell, crunching it under my feet and I seriously wonder what is to become of all these happy children. I know that they will go to school and that the system will destroy most of them. They will be told that they are not smart enough and they will no longer laugh and play. They will believe that they are igno-

Lionel G. Garcia

rant. Uncaring teachers who have been assigned to them—even though they hate the Mexican-American child—are underworked and overpaid and overindulged, prejudiced beyond belief, scheming forever to see how to get out of teaching the child, expecting the child to come to them educated already, so that they can sit in the smoking lounge to criticize and blame the child and the parent and the schools. The menaced children, raised in the beautiful Mexican tradition that the teacher is the respected master, will believe them as I believed them and as Willie and Louie and Frankie and Connie and Becky believed them and all the rest. Children ruined through the unforgivable prejudice of idiots who we give the privilege of shaping our children's lives! And these students will believe them when they are told not to think about going to college, that traditionally they do well in the menial labor work force, to expect a broom in your hand or a shovel or a trash can, to which I said fuck you Mr. Smith and Mrs. Jones, and these laughing children will live miserable lives, dropping out of school because there is no hope, no one caring enough to give them hope, when all it would take would be a kind word that no one wants to say . . . And then they wonder why the child drops out, and if that weren't enough, the parent takes them out of school because they don't do well and would be better off working at exactly the same job that the counselor and the teacher predicted that the child was suited for. "I told you so," the educators say. But how many of these children can open their mouths to say "Fuck you, I can do better than that, better than the teacher and the counselor and the principal?"

"Are you coming in?" Andy said. He was on the top step leading into the kitchen. My mother was standing at the door, all seventy-nine years of her.

I looked at the children playing, taking them in, they would remain happy forever, regardless. I saw myself playing as a child, not realizing that the world had already tried to make up its mind that I would follow in the footsteps of all my other friends, struck with the irreversible racial template.

Mother had made some flour tortillas for us and she sat us at the little table and we ate the tortillas with butter and honey. She served fresh coffee with an egg shell in it, as she had always brewed it since the days of my great-grandfather, because that was the only way that he would drink it because that was the way my great-great grandfather would drink . . . and that was the way the famous General would drink it. She sat down next to Andy and lovingly combed his hair back with her hand. "You look sick, Andy," she said softly, worried. She looked at me as if it were my fault. "Are you hungry? . . . What kind of question is that? Look at him eat tortillas. Home-made tortillas. Have you tasted the ones they sell at the super market? How horrible. My friend Juana buys them all the time. I hate them. I can't eat them. They give me heartburn. I don't see how they can eat those things. They taste like vinegar. But she likes them. She says that that is modern. That we should all be modern. Modern yes. But not that modern. Don't you agree, Andres?" She continued to brush his hair back as I ate my second breakfast of the day. Not to eat would be an insult. "Eat, little Andres." And to me she said the same thing. To little Andy: "How is your father treating you? Don't let him get away with anything. He was a bad boy when he was growing up. Oh, the things he and his brothers would do. Sometimes I laugh just thinking about it. I used to cry in those days. But in San Diego no one bothered them. In Houston no one gets away with anything, especially if you're poor. They took three little boys right from here to a juvenile home the other day. They were in grade school. And the police took them away from their parents because they had broken windows at the school. I can't begin to tell you how many windows your father and his brothers broke when they were that age. Those are the modern things I can't understand. They don't give a child room to grow and make mistakes." She looked toward the door leading into the hallway. My father had arrived at the door. "Look who's here already," she said about him.

My father stood at the door swaying gently, holding onto the door-jam. He was wearing khakis and a pajama top. He had not yet shaved. He walked slowly to the table and pulled out a chair and sat down. Andy had tried to help him, but he had brushed him off. "I don't need any help, but thank you. You're so kind, Son. Just like your father," he said. After he had moved the chair around to get comfortable he said, "When did you get here?" He raised his hand to let my mother know that he wanted coffee.

"We just got here about five or ten minutes ago," I replied.

"I already ate," he said as if anyone had asked. Mother brought the coffee to him and he took a sip. "I ate two eggs with tomato and onions . . . . Goddam doctors are trying to tell us not to eat eggs. I've eaten eggs all my life and I'm seventy-nine. What the hell do I have to live for? What am I taking good care of myself for? And I ate refried beans too. I always like to eat a good breakfast. Ever since I worked at the concrete plant all those years."

Mother asked, "Little Andres, do you want some eggs with tomato and onions and refried beans?" She had the skillet hot and ready.

"No," Andy said. "I already ate. But thanks anyway, Grandma."

My father grabbed a tortilla and poured some honey on it and folded it and began to eat it. He had to attack it from the side of his mouth, the honey dripping on the table as he chewed on the tortilla. He tried to talk as he ate and he had a small piece of tortilla with honey stuck to the corner of his mouth. I felt embarrassed for him. "I'm still hungry," he said, laughing and my mother laughed with him.

She said, "You know your father, always eating. He's just like his father and . . ."

My father couldn't talk. He had so much food in his mouth that all he could do was smile and nod his head. Honey was dripping from his chin and the piece of tortilla was still stuck to the corner of his mouth. I felt like telling him about it, but I knew that he would not appreciate it. I noticed that my mother finally got his attention and signaled to him to wipe his mouth and chin. He looked around for something to use and she gave him a paper towel. He was chewing on his meal and when he got through with the towel he still had the piece of tortilla stuck to his mouth. He apparently didn't feel it for he left it there during the course of most of our visit.

Mother threw another tortilla on the plate in the middle of the table and Andy grabbed it immediately and began to eat it with honey. My father laughed at how rapidly Andy had taken the tortilla away from him. "He'll get fat one of these days. You wait and see. You'd better be eating everything you can right now because one of these days everything you eat will make you fat."

"How come you're not fat?" Andy asked him.

Mother answered before my father could say a word. "That's because he's worked hard all his life. He never was fat. He worked like a mule."

"That's the goddam truth," said my father, the small piece of tortilla moving as if on a hinge as he talked.

"Did you bring anything for tomorrow that we need to unload?" my mother asked me.

I had.

"Let your father help you unload it."

It really wasn't that much. "All I brought today was what Rene packed in the trunk. I don't even know what it is, but it's just two small bags. I'll go get them." I got up and left them there talking about how thin Andy was and whether we were feeding him enough.

The problem with my parents was an age-old one. I realized that everyone as they got older arrived at an uneasy state with his parents. I felt very uncomfortable with them and, yes, some shame at the way they lived. But I was not the only one. I remember meeting Sol as he walked with a raggedy old man on Main Street one Friday noon. I had seen him a block off. When he saw me as I approached him he turned pale and tried to turn around among the lunch crowd. He rushed down the stairs to the underground, and not knowing what to do, I followed him, calling his name. I caught up with him easily. The old man couldn't walk very fast. Sol had to stop and acknowledge me. I could see the painful sadness in his eyes as he introduced me to the small tattered man next to him, his father that was so stooped, as Sol would be later on, from cutting patterns in the garment district of New York City. After he finished introducing us, I insisted that we eat together. I don't think Sol ever forgave me for that, for seeing the embarrassment from which he descended. His father ate and looked like a tramp. It was painful for Sol and he never, never spoke about it, as though it had never happened. When the old man died Sol did not tell anyone for several months and even then he announced his father's death, if the conversation required it, as one would mention the death of an unknown animal.

"I lika Houston," Sol's dad had said in thick English and I felt Sol cringe.

But still these were *my* parents and I wanted so much to be proud of them as I wanted to be proud of my son. I found myself feeling equally sorry for all of them, loving but yet not liking them.

Outside again in the coldness of the morning air and the dampness of the shell drive-way I could smell the smell of the Mexicanness of the area. I could smell *chorizo* frying somewhere and more tortillas being browned on the griddle and eggs being cracked and beaten into the cast iron skillets, with tomato and onions and refried beans bubbling in the fire. I could smell the fresh chili pepers in tomato sauce and the tripe being boiled for a whole day, a whole nauseous day, the smell of cow shit permeating the house because someone, probably someone that ate chocolate covered ants, at some time had said that you weren't supposed to use spices until the very end, the frying of spleen and the trying to eat it as one chewed and chewed and chewed to no end, finally swallowing it with the little remnant of tortilla that had remained through the ordeal, the rest of the tortilla mostly fallen to the plate, crushed into a doughy mush mixed with the fried blood of the spleen, the boiling of a kidney, the frying of a heart, the smell of the slow cooking of a beef-head somewhere in a hot-embered hole in the cold wet ground in someone's backyard, the little thin black and white dog waiting patiently, attentively all night long for his reward: the jaw bone.

The children were still at the grounds playing and screaming now in a jumbled Spanglish. A beat-up red and white car went by the house as I opened the trunk and its loud music of accordion and guitar made me turn to see who it was. I didn't know the family, just recently moved in probably, one of the thousands of Hispanic families moving in and out of Houston every year—nameless, faceless, forever lost in the great city, not knowing the language, the customs, running to their own kind and hiding there for some time until the safety of their numbers brought them out like little naked animals into the light of day—to work for their families, to send money home to their parents, to their wives, to their children: all illegals. I knew very few people from the old neighborhood. The song blaring out of the car radio was *no vale nada la vida*. It is uncanny how comically macabre the Mexican and his music can be. The man seemed satisfied with his lot, his wife next to him, a bundle of children jumping about in the back seat. I assumed they were on their way with his paycheck to buy groceries. When they would return, the children would try to open and eat everything in one day, as we had.

For some reason, as I gathered the two sacks that Rene had packed, I remembered the first time I had heard the song that was playing on the radio. Our mother, Willie, Louie, Frankie and I were taking a bus from San Diego to Alice. We were going to buy Willie a pair of shoes because he was joining the Army. We had heard the song at the bus station. On the bus was a fat oily lady with a tiny baby. She was wearing a Purple Heart Medal over her huge left breast. I sat on the bus with my mother and Frankie. Willie and Louie sat together. The fat lady was sitting across from us. As we left San Diego the baby began to cry and she moved it over to her right arm and unbuttoned her dress with her left hand and removed the dress and medal away from her left breast. She slid the hand under the breast and plopped the breast out, its immense volume making it appear as if there were something else beside it being forced out of the woman's body, as if the woman had been disemboweled. I gasped when I saw the sudden enormity of it falling away from the woman. She gently squeezed the nipple, which was bigger than my thumb is now, and brought a huge drop of purplish milk to its end. She forced the nipple into the baby's mouth and he sucked on it with great pleasure, making a slapping, gurgling sound, the Purple Heart Medal hitting the baby on the head as the bus rocked on its way. I remember that she smiled at me as I stared at her breast, a gentle smile to tell me that it was all right, that she understood that I had been frightened with the enormity of her breast. We bought Willie his shoes and took the bus back home. At the bus station the song was being played again. Someone said that the fat lady had lost a son in the war, the first one of our town to die. We felt so sad about the war that all of us started to cry as we walked back home. I remembered that she had taken the time to smile at me, to comfort me. What a great effort that must have been. Willie was scared about dying and our mother was worried. They were walking ahead of Louie and Frankie and me. Our mother had her arm around him.

"You be careful. Do you understand?" she said, crying, to Willie. "Don't do anything foolish. You know how you are. You're always trying to act the big man. You can't do that in a war. It's too dangerous. You're not in San Diego. Your corn is very green," which translated meant that he was very inexperienced.

All of us went to take Willie to the court-house where the other young men were gathered in the dark, early in the morning. We could hear the roar and smell the exhaust of the Army bus and we could hear the boys talking and laughing nervously as we approached the crowd, hidden in the fog. A lot of parents were there with their sons, trustingly giving them to the service of their country, the same country that did not allow them to get a hair-cut on main street in Alice, Texas. A lot of them never came back.

I slammed the trunk lid shut, and went back inside the house but not before the man in the car honked his horn at the corner and the horn played the "Eyes of Texas."

Victoria had joined the group and was sitting between Andy and my father. My mother was still rolling tortillas and cooking them on the griddle. My father had the piece of tortilla stuck to the corner of his mouth. Andy was eating slowly. Aunt Victoria looked at me as I walked in with the groceries and she smiled.

"Say Hello to your Aunt Victoria," mother said to me.

I went over and kissed her unwashed forehead and held her hand. "How are you?" I asked her and she smiled and nodded as if she understood perfectly what I was asking. "How have you been?"

She nodded her head and I saw in the vacuum of her eyes the shadowy figure of my great-grandfather and the house and the little grocery store which was stocked with everything except licorice, because to her licorice smelled of death. Both the house and the grocery store were never sold to anyone for fear that no one could take care of them as well as she. So she locked the house and store and came to live in Houston in 1952 while I was in Korea, intending to stay a while and then return, but she loved the new-found excitement of Houston and the neighborhood and she stayed. "People here are different," was the first thing she said as soon as she arrived. Once in a great while we would all go to San Diego to visit and we would stay at the spidered house, but gradually she moved what she needed to Houston and the house and the store remained locked and abandoned forevermore. I don't know when it was, but after one trip in which Aunt Victoria and my mother became very ill from eating left over canned food from the grocery store, we never returned to San Diego as a family. After a while there was no one there to go see.

"How are you?" Victoria said. "How . . . . .?" She had tears in her eyes. She looked at my father and she asked, "Isn't this a fine looking man? I've never seen him before in my life. He must be selling us something." To me: "Are you selling . . .?"

We were all smiling, trying not to laugh at her. I answered, "No, Aunt Victoria."

She smiled in the confusion of hearing me mention her name. I could see her wondering how I knew her and from where. "He knows my name," she murmured, surprised, under her hand to the others. Then she was flattered that I would know who she was. "Is there anyone else coming to . . .?"

"Tommorow?" I responded. "For the party?"

She seemed confused again. I had introduced something that she was not prepared to handle. I could see that in her mind's eye she was trying to imagine what party I was talking about. She looked at both my mother and my father for help.

My mother, the more astute, picked up on her discomfort. "He's talking about the party that we're having tomorrow for you on your birthday."

"Ohhhh," she said as if she understood, but one could tell that she was still not sure what we were talking about. She smiled and reached for the last tortilla on the plate. My father held her fragile hand with the tortilla in it and buttered it for her and asked if she wanted honey. She nodded that she did. I was standing by the table and decided to sit down between Andy and her. She took a very small bite from the folded tortilla and chewed very slowly, looking down at her thin spider-like bare feet. My father wiped the excess food from her mouth. My mother came over, having turned off the stove. She stood behind Victoria and started to comb her hair. Then she looked down on the floor and smiled. She reached down and gathered Aunt Victoria's panties that had fallen to the floor around her feet and put them in the pocket of her apron.

My mother laughed half-heartedly as we looked at Aunt Victoria. "I'm not making any more tortillas today. That's enough. If I made one hundred, your father would eat them all."

Andy said, "They're too fattening, anyway." And my parents laughed. They started counting and he had eaten six. "You would eat more if I would make them," my mother said. She had divided Victoria's long white hair into three strands and was beginning to braid it.

Victoria looked at Andy and me and spoke to my mother. "These sure are nice young men," she said.

My father winked at me, his little tortilla chip moving up and down as he wrinkled his face. "They sure are," he laughed.

Victoria was still chewing on the tortilla. "I wonder if they want to get married?" she asked and everyone started to laugh out loud.

She seemed hurt but she kept on. "Don't laugh," she told us seriously. "You never know about these things. I was almost married once. Isn't that right?" she said, looking for approval from my parents. "You may not believe it but I almost got . . ." She placed the tortilla on the table and she put her hand into her faded black skirt and she fumbled for something inside the pocket.

My mother, standing behind her noticed what she was doing. "What do you have in there?" she asked Victoria, teasing her.

"Something," she responded as she felt her way inside the pocket.

"What do you have?" my father asked.

We were all curious. She brought out an old post card that she handed to me. On the front was a couple. A chubby man wearing a tuxedo was bending from the waist kissing a young girl's hand. The young girl was sitting on a sofa. She was wearing a wedding dress and a large corsage on her wrist. In the background was a white wedding arch. The notation on the card said in Spanish, "Eternal Love. I promise that every day I will love you more and more." Having read that, I turned the card over and, in barely legible pencil, someone had written many years ago; "Dear Lady, I hope you do not think me too forward in writing you this way." The signature had been erased by time. That had been the proposal. I passed it on to Andy and he read it, not realizing the significance, the importance, of her memories. He passed it to my father and my father shook his head slowly. He knew what the card meant to Victoria and so did my mother when she read it. "Who was that?" she asked Victoria.

"Don't you remember?" she asked my parents. "Don't you both remember? Don't you remember that I almost got married to . . .?"

She could not remember his name.

"Ohhhh," my mother went, realizing who she was trying to remember. "Lothario. Was that Lothario writing to you?"

She blushed. "Yes . . . and," she said, still feeling guilty after all these years for having had her affair. She picked up the tortilla while my mother looked at the card and she continued eating.

My father was smiling, joining the charade, shaking his head. "And you never got married to him?" He looked at her wondering what she had thought about as a young lady. "You should have married him," he said.

Victoria shook her head. "No . . . It's . . . Like my father used to say, I wasn't born to be married. I was too mean," and she laughed at what she had said.

Everyone laughed with her. My mother had almost finished braiding Victoria's hair.

"It's time for us to go," I said as I got up from the table. Victoria pouted. She didn't want us to leave. But this wasn't anything new. She never wanted us to leave.

"It's just that I don't have too much time to talk to men during the day," she explained and both my parents laughed.

"Look at what a hussy she's become in her old age," my mother said in a mocking tone. She winked at all of us from behind Victoria's back.

"Hussy?" Victoria repeated, "I could have had many boy friends in my time. They were all falling in love with me. I could have had my pick . . . I could . . . ."

My father agreed with her. "You sure could have," he said as the piece of tortilla finally fell from the corner of his mouth to the floor.

My mother noticing it said, "Finally you look like a normal human being."

My father, not knowing what had happened, did not understand what she was talking about. "What do you mean normal?" he said, in his confusion. "She could have had all the normal men she wanted. She was beautiful. Weren't you, Victoria?"

She smiled at the mention of her name. She had forgotten what it was. "This is what I was trying to tell these strange men here," Victoria said and she pointed at Andy and myself. "It's all . . ."

I had to get up. I brought Andy with me from the table. My parents, realizing that we were leaving, followed us to the door. Victoria watched in silence, eating her tortilla. She made a noise as we got to the door. "Don't leave, yet," she pleaded. "We have so much to talk about. I want to show . . ."

My mother winked at me and she and my father led us out of the house.

"Don't forget to be here early," mother said as we got in the car. "You and Rene need to be here at around two or three. Everyone is going to be here."

"What else am I supposed to bring?"

"Rene knows. I talked to her yesterday. She's got everything."

My father stuck his head inside the window and said, "Tell Rene to be sure and come. We're expecting her."

My mother, hearing that, grabbed him by the back of the shirt and yanked him away from the car. "Rene knows that, you idiot. You don't have to be reminding her all the time. She know she's welcome here. You don't have to say anything to her. She's coming and she knows it. We've been talking on the phone. She's all excited about the party."

"You ought to get you a big car!" my father yelled as I backed the Mercedes 450 SLC out of the drive-way. "As much money as he makes," he complained to my mother.

The happy children were playing in the fields and among them were the mournful ghosts of my antecedents: my dead grandfather, the gash plainly on his chin when he had hit the wooden step that lead into the meat market, and next to him was my great-grandfather, thin as always and looking very somber as the children tried in vain to reach for the shroud carried by the cortege.

Andy was looking through the window at the traffic as I thought of what I had seen.

"Did you have a good time?" I asked him.

"Yes," he replied. "Did you?"

"Yes. They are wonderful people."

"Yes. I know."

"We always have a better time than we think we're going to have. Don't you think?"

"Yes."

CHAPTER 5

I had not told anyone that two months ago I had gone, despondent over my irreverence, to talk to the new young priest with the artificial left leg to ask him if I could be saved by using my old religion and he had told me quietly, as he rearranged the shiny stockinged leg under the desk, that it was not within the jurisdiction of the Catholic Church to interpret Mexican Catholicism. He would not allow any shenanigans in his church, although some indigent parishioners had sacrificed mightily to donate for his new polyvinyl jointed leg. It would be better if I talked to the old priest, the senile Father Rodriguez who smelled like freshly pressed garlic and who believed that in the end all of us were going to heaven, even the men without testicles.

"He's crazy . . . You know that, don't you?" the young Father Diaz said of his superior.

"Who knows?" I replied. "Nowadays, who knows who's crazy or not?"

"He's started to curse."

"He's always cursed. That's the way he is. I've known him for a long time."

"I know, but now he's . . . well, he's talking dirty . . . to the house-keeper . . . the parishioners. You know how tolerant these people are. And yet I don't understand why they haven't complained."

"Because he's the priest. It's that simple."

"Yeah . . . I realize that . . . but still . . ."

"Does the bishop know any of this?"

He gave a little laugh to tell me how naive I was. He said, "The bishop is only interested in the bingo. You know how much money this church makes? . . . Do you want me to ring Father?"

"No," I said, standing up. "Let him sleep. He won't know who I am anymore," I continued, even though he had buried my brother Frankie when no one else would because Frankie had taken his own life.

As we walked in, Andy and I could hear Rene cursing, as Father Rodriguez had cursed, over something that one of the children had done in our bathroom. Andy, realizing that he might be in trouble, went outside to be with the dog. I went over to the bar. Rene came running down the stairs, her hair wet, dressed in her house coat, naked underneath.

"It makes me so angry," she screamed, "when someone uses my expensive soap. And then they don't have the decency to put it in the soap dish. They just throw it on the bottom of the tub and it gets wet and soggy. Do you realize how much I pay for a bar of soap? I can't make these children understand. I pay five dollars for a bar of soap. I need that soap for my skin. No one else needs that soap. But someone is always using it. Goddamit! And no one will admit a thing. I can ask until I'm blue in the face and no one will ever admit that they've done it. Oh, it pisses me off! It's got to be Marie. Wait until she comes back." She turned around on one heel and quickly ran back upstairs, her house-coat flying in the turbulence that she had created. At the top she stopped and yelled back, "What did your mother say?"

"Nothing."

"What do you mean nothing? Did you give her the stuff I sent with you?"

"Yes. I sure did."

"Was that what she needed?"

"She didn't say. I left before she checked it out."

"Is she going to call me?"

"She will if she needs to."

"What time are we supposed to be there?"

"They want us there tomorrow at three."

"You know that tonight's party starts at eight."

"What are we supposed to wear?"

"They're all going formally casual . . . You know that you've got to buy the beer for tomorrow, don't you?"

"No, I didn't know, but I'll get it."

"Well, Willie called and then Louie called and they said that since you hadn't found any of the ugly things you were supposed to bring then you had to bring the beer."

"That's fine with me. I'd rather do that . . . take something simple."

"I told you, didn't I? I'm not buying any of that trash for you all."

"It's hard to find . . ."

"What?"

"I said it's hard to find all that stuff."

From the top of the stairs and yelling: "Are you teed off because I didn't buy you all that stuff?"

"No," I said.

"I'm glad," she said. "Not only me, but Andy too, we both hate it when you send us out to get stuff like that. No one I know believes me."

I had another drink and then washed it down with some water.

The phone rang and I picked it up right away. I had anticipated that it was either Louie or Willie, but it was Judge Masters. He wanted to know if I had made up my mind.

"I don't know," I answered. "I thought I had until Monday."

"Not any more," he said. "You'd better do it sooner. You would want to know what your client is up to, wouldn't you?"

"What do you mean?"

"He escaped this morning."

"What happened?"

"They were moving him to county jail this morning. You know how dumb the Houston Police can be. They left him alone out in the hallway while they were joking with each other and he just walked off. By now he's got his handcuffs off and is getting ready to kill someone."

"Do the police know where the rest of the family lives?"

"I don't know if he has anymore family. I think he's killed 'em all. What I want to know is do you want the case?"

"Give me until Monday will you?"

I could hear him sigh. "All right," he said, "but I need to know by then."

"Thanks," I said. "I promise."

"What did the doctor say?"

I could hear Rene calling me.

"He said I was in perfect health."

"That means you don't have to take any medicine or anything?"

"Right."

"You're not bull-shitting me, are you?"

"Nope."

"Then you're all right? What was the matter with you? Did he say?"

"He said I just needed rest. He said it looked like I had been burning the candle at both ends."

"I told you. Didn't I tell you?"

"Yep, you told me."

"Who did you go see?"

"Silverstein."

"The one who calls all the gals nookie-head?"

"Yeah . . . That's the one.

"He's a crazy . . ."

"I know . . . Jew."

"That's not what I was going to say. He's no good. He didn't even want to put you in for tests or anything like that?"

"Well, I didn't say that. As a matter of fact he did."

"And you were hard headed. I bet you didn't do it. Why are you Mexicans so hard-headed?"

"It doesn't look good for a Judge to be generalizing. It sounds prejudiced."

"You know what I mean. I'll bet you you didn't go to the hospital."

"How much do you want to bet?"

"I'll bet you one dinner."

"Where?"

"You name it."

"For how many people?"

"Just two. You and your wife."

"And you and your wife?"

"Yes."

"What a boring evening. Let's just make it us two."

"Are your betting or hedging?"

"I'm in."

"Okay. You didn't go to the hospital, did you? You bastard, you better tell me the truth. I can find out real easy."

"Well, suppose you find out. You aren't going to believe me anyway."

"So you're saying you went?"

"Yep. As they say in Texas."

"I don't believe you."

"I told you you wouldn't. Find out for yourself."

"And what did the test show?"

"I'm taking the fifth."

"Then you are sick."

"Nope. I didn't say that."

"Well, maybe I ought to appoint someone else to this case. It is getting kind of nasty. The DA is really on this case. He's all excited. You may not be able to handle it in your condition."

"If I say I can handle it, I can handle it. Understood?"

"You'll let me know on Monday?"

"Yep."

Rene was calling me again.

"It's just that I was worried about you Andy. Where do you want us to take you and your wife to eat?"

"You know us hard-headed Mexicans, take us out to the Taco House on Navigation Street."

I put the phone down and drank some more water, trying to get the lingering taste of the liquor out of my mouth. Rene was calling me again, saying something that I couldn't understand. I went upstairs, talking to her as I climbed.

"Are you calling me?" I asked.

"Yes. Didn't you hear me calling you?"

"Yes, but I was on the phone. I couldn't understand what you were saying."

I opened the door and she said, "Close the door quickly! . . . Look at me." She was on her back, naked, in bed as the prostitute had been in her pallet with her legs opened. We had gone to see her through the window after Father Procopio had told us not to ever go near the whorehouses, not realizing how much more we wanted to go when he spoke reverently with his hands locked in front of his generous stomach not realizing that he was creating with his thumbs and forefingers the sign of the vagina, speaking of the unspeakable things that were going on in the small houses out back where the prostitutes lived. It was the first time that we had seen two humans copulate, struck by its violence, and as I watched along with Willie and Louie and Frankie, I thought of the time when I was sheltered in the house with the women, not being allowed to see my beloved mare bred by a black and tan donkey.

"Where's Andy?" she asked

"He's outside," I answered, thinking still of the surprising mule that the mare had borne.

We heard the kitchen door open and close. Andy was back.

"If you want it, you'd better make it fast," she threatened. "You've been drinking, haven't you?"

Andy knocked on the door.

"What is it?" Rene yelled right next to my ear without stopping.

Andy waited for a second, sensing the harsh irritation in the voice, realizing that he had interrupted something intimate. And then he asked through the door: "Are we out of dog food?"

CHAPTER 6

"I killed three people on Friday," the illegal, Alfredo Gomez, said. His small delicate brown hands were trembling. "The police had me until yesterday afternoon. But they started to mess around and I escaped. They are looking for me because they want me to be in jail for the killings. I do not want to be in jail. I had to kill the three people that I killed."

Andy had let him in while I was upstairs getting ready for tonight's party. Andy had run to tell me that someone was looking for me. I had no idea who he was when Andy told me about him. I felt very apprehensive when I descended the stairs. Through the years I had been involved in a lot of cases where the person I defended had not been punished to the satisfaction of the victim's family and friends. It was not unusual for people to threaten to kill me the first chance they had. As I walked down the stairs I thought that this might be the final moment that all my life had been leading to and my frail son had been the inadvertent accomplice by letting the man in. Whatever, if it was coming down to this, I would be man enough to take it. When I saw that he was dressed in prison whites I knew instantly who he was. He was standing in the foyer shaking in fear and I invited him to come into the kitchen. He appeared very small and gentle and refined, with long thick black hair combed back, his arms thin like Andy's, his chest small and flat. He had a red streak that I could see in the light of the kitchen that extended from below the ears down and across his throat. The police had put a choke chain on him.

"Why did you kill them?" I asked, once we were settled down and little Andy had left the room.

"May I speak in Spanish?" he asked.

"Whatever you want," I said, "although you speak good English."

"I feel more comfortable in Spanish. It's a long story but you must know it to understand. I came to this country from Mexico in 1980. I had already been married for three years, but in Mexico I was not making a living. Sure I could find jobs and work all day and night, but I was not making a living. My wife and I were having to live with my in-laws. They were very mean with me, but that did not cause any problems with me. I knew how they were. They did things to me that you would never believe if I told you. I could not take it anymore, so one day I forced my wife to move out with me and we went to live with my parents. My father was indifferent, but my mother was a fine lady and she treated us with respect. That's all I wanted . . . respect. I could take anything in the world except lack of respect for what I was and what I was trying to do. One day after not finding work I decided that I would come to the United States to work. I was looking for a better life for me and the family that we would have. I left my wife with my mother, but she and my mother began to argue. You know how it is with a young girl and her mother-in-law. My mother would never say what it was that they always argued about. I suffered much trying to get into the United States. I was crossed into the United States north of Laredo along with about fifteen other men. We were each given a small compass and a bottle of water. I tell you this because you should know in order to understand what I did. We were told to start walking through the woods in a certain direction using our compasses. We were to walk for three days and two nights. In three days we would have crossed four highways. At the fourth highway we were to stop and wait for the sun to set. At that time a large truck would come by and slow down. One of us was supposed to stop the truck. Once we were sure we had the right truck, then we were to run to the truck and jump in. At the end of three days we had lost five men. One man developed a fever and we had to leave him there in the brush. We were afraid that if we were delayed because of him that we would miss the truck. God only knows what became of him. Two men were bitten by rattle-snakes and had to stay behind. One man ran out of water. He had trouble with his kidneys and he needed more water than he had. He fainted and we had to leave him behind. The last one acted like he had a heart attack. We did not have time to bury him. We covered him with dead wood. By the time we reached the road, we were like animals. I had started out as a human being and in three days I had become an animal with all the instincts for survival that an animal has. The remaining ones, myself included, reached Houston the following day. We were lucky that we found the truck. Many illegals never find the truck and have to return. Many more don't make it back. Sometimes they fool you and there is no truck. I don't have to tell you that it was a horror trying to get to Houston. But I was able to survive and find a job. I took an apartment with another illegal. He gave me trouble. He stole from me. I had to move out. So I lived alone in a smaller room and saved my money and sent some of it home to Mexico to my wife. One day I decided that I had enough money for her to come to live here. By that time I had identification. A lawyer such as yourself arranged for everything. It cost me a lot of money. Later I found out that this lawyer was a thief. Do you want to know his name?"

I shook my head. I didn't need to know the name of yet another lawyer that was a thief. I got up and poured two drinks. I brought them back to the table and sat down. His border crossing was a story I had heard many times before. "Why did you kill your wife and her parents?" I asked him as I handed him his drink.

"They betrayed me," he explained, apparently surprised that I did not realize that that would justify killing them. It was all very logical to him. "My wife brought her parents with her to live in the United States. But this time the shoe was on the other foot. They had to respect me. I did not have to respect them. But still they were doing things to me that are best left unsaid. We were doing well with money. I had a good job. Then Thursday night me and my friends were at a beer-joint and I overheard something that I could not believe. These men from my old town in Mexico were talking about my wife. They said that she had been seeing other men when I was in the United States. And her parents were the ones that were telling her to go out and have a good time. They were laughing about me. They knew my name. I was hiding behind the partition that led into the restroom. I heard it all. I became like a rabid animal. A man cannot live without pride and self-respect. I would have to kill my family to avenge my honor. I had a pistol that I had bought a long time ago. I took it and killed the three of them. First I killed my father-in-law because he had not protected my wife's honor in my absence. She was his daughter. Then I killed my mother-in-law for the same reason. If a mother cannot lead her daughter to do the right thing, then she has lost her honor. Then came my wife."

"Do you understand that there is a very good chance that you will spend a long time in prison for what you did?"

"It does not make any difference to me. I have extracted my revenge. I would even die if they so desired."

"Have you thought of the possibility that the men you overheard were lying, that they were talking so that you could hear them and become jealous?"

"No. They were speaking the truth. I am sure of it."

And he said this with such conviction that I was sure that even if it were not true, I would never be able to convince him. And, of course, he would never admit having made such a horrendous mistake. From now on he would have to believe the worst about his wife and her parents.

"Did you have any children by this woman?"

He turned his face away in disgust. "No . . . that is something else . . . something that I must tell . . ." At first the question had flustered him and then he began to cry. "It's all part of what they did to me."

I poured both of us two more drinks and sat back down. I had to figure out what to do with him. If I called the police, he would never trust me again. Besides, the police might take it out on him for having made a fool of them. I thought about that and I was certain that they would beat him or maybe even kill him. They had been known to have throw-down guns. They had been known to throw handcuffed prisoners into the bayous. If I called the Judge he would call the police and the effect would be the same.

He was looking at me patiently, trying to figure out what I was thinking about. Andy came in and asked me what I was doing. "Thinking," I said.

"Has he told you who he is?" he asked.

"You let him in," I said.

"I thought you knew him."

"In a way I do. Just a friend paying me a visit."

"Why is he dressed like that?"

I said, "White is his favorite color," and then a thought came to me. I got up and dragged my friend off with me. I told Andy, "Tell your mother I'll be right back. Tell her I had to run an errand."

I got him in the car in the garage and we took off for Louie's place. When we arrived we got off and I knocked on the door and I could hear Louie cursing about something. "Who the shit is it?" I could hear him yell.

"It's me," I yelled back.

Louie came to the door and greeted us, a drink in his hand. "What the hell is going on?" he asked, holding the door open for the illegal and myself.

"Nothing," I said.

"You all want breakfast?" Louie asked. "Donna Marie is cooking breakfast . . . aren't you Donna Marie?"

We walked into the kitchen and Donna Marie was in her short night-gown cooking for Louie. The illegal's eyes were taking her all in, stunned at her beauty. She looked back from the stove at us and said, "Hi." She was stirring something as we sat down at the table. "Andy," she said coming over to kiss me, "how do you feel?"

"I feel fine. It's you that had a lousy night. How do you feel?"

She sat on my lap and pretended that she was falling asleep. Louie thought that was funny. "And she wants to go to Hollywood . . . That's bad acting . . . Get off my brother," he yelled, acting like he was going to slap her.

She jumped off my lap and went laughing back to the stove. She turned to me and said, smiling, "Louie wants to be my agent. What do you think of that?"

"That's great," I said as Louie winked at me.

"Then," she kept on, "after I get some parts and get to be known, Louie wants to direct a movie. . . . Right Louie?"

"Sure sweetheart. Anything you say. Welcome to Hollywood."

I did not want any more to eat, but I was sure the illegal did. "Alfredo here is starving," I said. "Maybe you could put some extra eggs in for him." I asked him in English if he was hungry and he acted as though he didn't want to understand me. When I asked him in Spanish he answered that he was very hungry.

Donna Marie opened the refrigerator without being told and took three eggs out and cracked them and began to fry them. Louie was smiling, trying to figure out what I was up to. He knew there was something going on with me and the illegal, that I would never bring anyone dressed in prison whites to eat breakfast, without being in some kind of trouble. "What do you want?" he asked.

"What do you mean what do I want?"

"Don't bullshit me. What do you want? What kind of trouble are you in now? Does this guy speak English or doesn't he? How come he made a face when you spoke English to him?"

"He speaks English but he is a very quiet and reserved man, the type that keeps everything to himself. He's very suspicious but very smart. But you just won't get him to talk. Many times he has told me that talk is cheap. He doesn't waste energy talking. He's what the gringo calls a man of action . . . like John Wayne."

"John Wayne?" Louie asked, laughing, and Donna Marie laughed too.

"Yep . . . like Gary Cooper . . . but shorter."

"Bullshit," Louie said.

"Louie?" Donna Marie complained, "don't talk to Andy like that. Do you think we'll get to meet John Wayne and Gary Cooper?" She served Louie and Alfredo their plates and coffee and came to sit by me.

"Only if you piss me off enough to kill you. They're both dead. Anyway, I'll talk to him any way I please. Ain't that right, bro?"

"Let him talk anyway he pleases," I told Donna Marie and she laughed.

"I think it's cute the way you let Louie and Willie talk to you like that," she said.

"They love me, that's why."

Louie was eating, pointing to Donna Marie. "She ain't never had family, so she don't know about that kind of love."

Donna Marie looked down at her precious thighs. "Louie's right. I never had no family. That's why I love you and Louie and Willie so much. It's fun being around you guys."

Alfredo was eating everything that he could get his hands on. Even Louie noticed it. "Hey, bro," he said to me, punching me in the ribs, "this friend of yours looks like he hasn't eaten in days. What you got up your sleeve?"

"What do you mean?"

"Goddammit . . . cut out the bullshit. This guy is in prison whites and you're acting like he's dressed to go to church. What gives?"

"Do you trust me?"

Louie nodded. "Yeah," he said, "I trust you."

"Promise that you'll help us?"

"Yes. But do you remember that I'm on probation?"

"Yes. But that is why I don't want you to ask any questions. Will you help us? I promise that you will not get in trouble."

"Yes," he answered.

"Will you put this gentleman up for me until Monday morning? That's all I ask. Just keep him here in the apartment and don't let him out of your sight?"

"Sure. That ain't hard to do."

"Of course, I'll pay you."

"You don't have to do that," Donna Marie said. "You're family and he's family," she said pointing at Alfredo Gomez as he licked his plate like a dog. When he was finished he stood up and in English began to tell us that he could afford to pay his way. He wanted to pay me right then and there. He reached inside his shirt and he undid a brown cloth money belt from around his waist. He whipped it out from inside his shirt and slapped the belt on the table. He began to unzip compartment after compartment, each bulging with large bills, mostly hundreds, some fifties and a few twenties. "I pay my way," he informed us in English. "No man needs to pay for me."

"Why didn't the police take this money away from you?" I asked him.

"I wasn't wearing it when I was arrested," he said. I stopped him there. I did not want Louie to hear the rest of the story.

"Arrested?" Louie screamed, jumping out of his chair. "What the hell is going on?"

"Nothing. Forget it. You didn't hear a word."

Louie walked to the stove and poured some more coffee. "Shit," he said coming back to the table looking into the cup, "what I need is scotch, not this black shit. You got me worried, bro . . . I'm on probation."

Donna Marie appeared distraught. "Is he in trouble? Maybe we'll all get in trouble? Is it going to ruin our plans?"

"Don't worry. I wouldn't do anything to get anyone in trouble. Just don't ask questions."

Louie eyed the money piled on top of the table. "What are we going to do with this?"

"I'm taking it and putting it in a safe place. That's were it's going."

"Can't I even take a little bit for all the trouble the bastard is causing me? Who's paying for the food, for instance? And the bed? He's a lot of trouble. I can tell already."

"Tell you what. You keep records of what you spend and I'll make sure you get reimbursed."

"Yeah, bro, but that takes a long time . . . Why are you hiding him? Is he a witness?"

"I can't tell you."

"He's a witness. Bet you he's a witness. Ain't that right?"

"Can't tell."

"He's a witness, you bastard. You're hiding a witness with me.

I knew it. You smart shit-head. Why didn't you tell me before?"

"You never asked," I said.

CHAPTER 7

I took the belt full of money that the alien had given me and I hid it in the trunk under the mat and I remembered that Father Procopio would make us hide his liquor in the trunk of his car when we went out on Sundays to say Mass at the ranches in South Texas. He would share the liquor with us on the way back when no one wanted to sit in front with him, because he insisted on trying to burn the child next to him with his cigarette.

Rene was sitting at the kitchen table doing her nails when I returned. She looked past me as I came in through the kitchen door and acted as if I had not arrived. She concentrated on her nails. She was dressed and ready to go to the party.

"Hi," I said, trying to make light of my sudden absence.

"Hi," she barely said, more to her hand than to me, as she held her hand in front of her face blowing on her nails.

I went and got a drink. I drank it all in one swallow, an act odious to Rene. I poured another drink and drank that one in one swallow. She got up without speaking, blowing on her nails and went upstairs.

I went up and showered and got ready while Rene went back downstairs to wait angrily for me. When I was ready I went downstairs and Rene got up and walked out the door without speaking to me. I followed her and we got in the car and drove off without saying a word to each other.

It was dark outside and the fog had started to move in from the bay. Here it was December and we had only had a few cool spells. It would probably rain before the night was over. I drove in silence wondering what in the world our lives were coming to when someone next to me in the Houston traffic passed me on Rice Boulevard on the wrong side and honked. When I looked to see who it was, the driver, a young girl, was rapidly wiping the condensation from her window so that I could see what all this was about, so that I could see that she was shooting the finger at me. I must have done something to her that aggravated her. I politely nodded and accepted her gesture like a gentleman. She cut in front of me and made me slam on my brakes. Rene shot forward and hit her head on the windshield as the young girl took off. Rene bounced off the windshield and fell back in her seat. "Fuck you!," she yelled at the young girl as she felt her forehead. "What the shit is the matter with that bitch?"

Not knowing what I could have done to aggravate her, I answered, "God only knows," and kept on driving, slowly, as always. I didn't know what aggravated anybody anymore. The whole of Texas was going crazy.

"Must you drive so damn slow all the time?" Rene complained as she rubbed the back of her neck.

"Yes, I must," I told her. "Houston traffic is crazy. You never know who's drunk and has a loaded gun in their car. Let them shoot the finger at me. Who cares? As long as they don't shoot bullets . . . Are you hurt?"

"No," she answered. "At least I don't think so . . . My neck hurts just a little bit, but I'm all right. What's the matter with people?"

"It's the sesquicentennial," I told her and she looked at me with a look worse than the one the young girl had given me.

"What was the excuse for them driving crazy last year?"

"They were just practicing for the sesquicentennial," I told her.

I took a slow left on Shepherd again as I had this morning, but just before I got to the Southwest Freeway I turned right on Vássar. The fog was worse in the low areas beside the elevated freeway and it was hard for me to see, but half-way to the deadend was the house, a very old and expensive renovated wooden frame with brick veneer walls, with its popular contemporary roof, a sloping facade used to hide the old roof and the old boxiness of the original. The house was bigger than it looked from the outside, an illusion of smallness created by the brick fence that went completely around the yard. There was a heavy wrought iron gate in front, right next to the wooden garage gate. We were late, as usual, and angry and hungry. Rene had never wanted to eat before one of these get-togethers because everyone was such a good cook, although no one had ever attempted to cook intestines and spleen and offal and brain and tongue and the ceremonially aphrodisiac crotch of the cow. I had to drive to the deadend and come around and park on the far side of the street, since all the cars were parked at the curb next to the house. Rene had to get off into a soggy weed bed by the side of the car. She cursed as she almost tripped among the weeds. "Why didn't you let me out in front?" she demanded.

"I was going to, but you're such a bitch that I wanted you to fall in the weeds," I said.

She crossed the street at a run, cursing, and stopped at the gate and waited for me to cross the street and punch the bell. She was scratching the winter mosquitoes off her hose. Electronically the gate buzzed and unlatched and we walked in and Matt, our host, opened the front door.

"Where have you all been?" he asked. Rene walked past him and gave him a peck on the cheek. "Gosh you smell good, Rene," he said to her. "Good enough to eat." She smiled wickedly and she said, "As always."

"Yeah," Matt agreed and gave out a leacherous stare. "You wear the greatest perfumes. Where do you buy them? I can't get Christie to buy something I like."

"Oh, I shop around. Never all in one place," Rene said, telling him in a typical womanly way that she was not about to tell Christie where she bought her perfumes. Christie was going to have to find out for herself.

"Sorry we're late," Rene said to him, "but we had a slight accident."

Matt looked at us to see if he could see the injuries. "Oh? Was it serious? . . . I hope no one got hurt."

"No," I said. "Just someone cut in front of us and made me slam the brakes and Rene hit her head on the windshield."

He looked at Rene. "You don't look hurt," he said.

Rene looked at him and said, "It was just a tap. I'm all right. Thanks to God."

"Anyway, it's over and no one got hurt," I said. "Still we're sorry we're late."

He was a frail dermatologist with sparse hair and liver splotches on his arms, born and raised in Texas. His second wife Christie, who I saw standing in a circle of friends in the middle of the den, was a housewife now. She had been his nurse. They both divorced to get married and now Matt's first wife, Angela, had had to go back to work and Christie had retired. They just had to get married. I couldn't see her as sexually attractive, not like Rene, not with her caved-in rearend. I couldn't see Matt having an affair either, being so thin and old-looking for his age. I thought that he would have been securely settled for life with his first marriage.

"Oh, that's okay," Matt answered. "We're just now getting started. How're you doing?" he asked me and shook my hand. "Want a drink?"

"I'm dying for one," I said and he laughed as I followed him to the kitchen. On the way everyone greeted Rene and me. Rene stayed with a group to talk. I went into the kitchen.

"I've got bourbon," Matt said. "And I've got gin and tonic for Rene. Is that okay?"

"Sure," I said.

"The ice is in the freezer," he pointed out and left me alone to mix our drinks. Alone in the kitchen I could hear the laughter in the next room and somehow it made me feel a sudden awkward loneliness that I was listening to it and not being a part of it, like the oppressive solitude of a stranger in a foreign land. I had felt like that all throughout Korea, and even on R and R in Japan when I ran into Sergeant Rodriguez on a street in Tokyo, the same Rodriguez whose head was to explode in my face when the bullet entered his skull in a steamy trench in that forsakened and overgrown

171

Lionel G. Garcia

land. No . . . not even when we met Martinez and Garcia and Soliz and Benavidez to get drunk to forget what we were doing there did the inescapable feeling ever leave. Engulfed in the loneliness of my memories, I quickly fixed our drinks and brought them out, anxious to join the crowd before my thoughts got out of hand. I gave Rene her gin and tonic. She studied the glass for a second and said, "You didn't put a lime in it."

I wanted to get to my friends to say hello. I couldn't be bothered with trivial things such as lime in the drink. "They don't have any limes," I told her as I forced the drink on her.

"That's not true," Christie said. "We do have limes. Don't be an ass and get sweet Rene her lime."

I went back into the kitchen and there on the counter were the lime wedges cut up neatly and placed in a circle on a saucer.

After I had satisfied Rene I went over to talk to Matt. I had already taken pains on the way to the kitchen to shake all the men's hands and kiss all the wives. Matt was standing with John and Jim and Sue. John was a computer engineer born in Olean, New York. He was on his second marriage. He was tall and had bad teeth. He and his wife, Peggy, hated Texas . . . and Houston, especially. Peggy had been married before and had children from both marriages, plus an illigitimate child. Their dream was to get transferred back to Long Island from where they had come, where the water was beautiful and not muddy like Galveston. What they didn't blame on Houston they blamed on Galveston and they still had room for Texas. Peggy hated the humidity so much that she cut her hair short and would not do anything for it, blaming Houston for her oily disheveled look. She wanted everyone to believe that in Long Island, where there are no roaches, she would have looked absolutely beautiful.

Jim sold insurance, but not the Mexican way, where the agent went from house to house pestering for his three and four dollar monthly premiums. He didn't sell burial insurance, but big time insurance, big money. He was typical in his offending enthusiasm of those selling insurance, so we did not allow him to talk about insurance around us. He was told early in our friendship, when we had first allowed him and Becky into our group, that just as a gynecologist does not go around talking about vaginas he was not to go around talking about insurance. And still he always looked like the persistently begging dog that will not take a hint, that lives for a breakdown in someone's defense. He was from South Texas close to San Diego where I was born, and curiously now that we were both out of that area, we were friendly with each other. If we had both stayed in South Texas, where the division between the two races is so much a part of life, chances were that we would not have spoken to each other. Jim was married to Becky.

Sue was a frustrated high school English teacher, beaten down by unruly classes of children that did not want to be bothered by learning. She was married to Doyle, the stockbroker. Doyle had been born and raised in East Texas and had that East Texas speech pattern that makes them all sound happily ignorant. Like Jim, we did not allow Doyle to sell stocks and bonds when we got together and, even if we had, I did not know of anyone of us that would risk his hard-earned money on Doyle's advice. There must have been some clients though, because he lived the good life like the rest of us. Sue was from Dallas. She thought everything she did was perfect and she hated Houston, but she loved the rest of the state and the Dallas Cowboys. She thought, in a peculiar twist of logic, as did a lot of other ignorant Texans, that since the Cowboys were better than the Houston Oiler football team, that that made her better than us and Dallas better than Houston. Sue and Doyle were both on their second marriages.

"How've you been?" Jim asked me as I approached the group. They opened up a space for me between Sue and Matt.

"I've been okay," I replied. "Okay. Working hard," I kept on.

"Or hardly working," John said and everyone had to laugh at the oldest reply in the world. Why did he have to say that? "Looks like you've been busy. We hardly ever see you anymore."

Jim remembered that I hadn't been with them in a long time. "That's right, Andy. John is right. We haven't seen you in a long time. Every time we go out to play golf you're busy. What gives? You ain't that busy, are you?"

"Sure he is," Matt spoke. "Doesn't have time for his friends anymore. Hell, we used to play every Saturday. Now it's been forever since you played with us, Andy."

"I just don't have the time. Golf takes too much time for me."

Even Sue got into the act: "What are you so busy with? I mean, Saturday and all. What are you and Rene doing on Saturday mornings? Tell us, Andy. Oh, tell us. Now don't be bashful."

The group started laughing. They were all drinking white wine. I was the only one with bourbon, but no one had been to Korea except me.

"Hell, he ain't going to tell us anything," John said. "Andy's really very bashful. Aren't you, Andy?"

"I'm bashful sometimes and sometimes I'm not," I replied.

Jim said, "You're not very bashful in front of a judge and jury, are you?"

"No. For some reason I like to talk and think on my feet."

John wanted to know if anyone had bought any stock. "I'm into penny

Lionel G. Garcia

stock now," he told us and waited for someone to ask him how he was doing.

"When did you start that?" Matt asked him.

"Oh, a couple of months ago. Doyle got me into it. But you know how stupid Texas law is. You can't get into the first issue. Texas law says that you've got to wait one year, one damn year, before you can buy penny stock. Some of these stocks are issued at nine cents and in a year they're worth twenty-five cents. But you can't buy them in Texas."

Jim and Matt were very resentful of all criticism about Texas. I could sense that they were hurt. Jim couldn't hold himself back. "When are you leaving for Long Island?" he asked.

"As soon as they transfer me," John replied. "You guys don't know what you're missing living in Texas. You ought to go out and see the world. Hell, Texas ought to join the United States."

I laughed. "That's old stuff," I said. "Have you got some new gripe on Texas?"

John was hot now. I could tell that he had a well thought out speech, maybe his last before he left the state. "You really want to know what I figured out about Texas?"

"Yeah," I replied. "But I may be the only one listening."

"Well, it seems to me that the more ignorant you try to act the better everyone likes you. Look at your politicians, look at all your governors . . . and I mean all . . . I can't believe it." He laughed to himself before he said it. "All your governors sound like Mortimer Snerd talking through a turd. Have you noticed that? You cannot get elected in Texas unless you sound and act ignorant. The first commandment is: You must not use the right verb tense. And what gets me, and this tickles me coming from out of state, is that the more ignorant you are the higher the elected office. I talked to a dog-catcher the other day and I swear to God that he speaks better than the governor. Texans adore ignorance. They think that being smart and having a good vocabulary is enough to suspect a man. They would probably lynch a great mind."

Jim straightened up and cleared his throat when he heard John's words. He was offended. Matt wanted to change the conversation. His face was red. I knew he was trying to control himself, being the host. He wanted to know about our near accident and I told them about it and, from looking at Rene standing with another group, she was not showing any signs of hurting. Then he wanted to know if our roof still leaked. Outside of my good hearing range I could only hear the noise Rene was making. She was laughing, but I couldn't understand what her group was talking about. As of the last big rain, the roof had not leaked, I told Matt. He looked to me terribly disturbed. John had always been very critical of Texas, as had all the out-of-staters, but tonight he had attacked with unusual hatred, a characteristic usually found in out-of-staters who are about to leave Texas. Matt and Jim, as always, had taken it personally. Matt put his arm around my shoulder and squeezed me. He was trying to get my support against John's criticism of Texas. We were supposed to be partners now in defense of our state. I could not see myself arguing against John. Being a lawyer, I had seen too much truth in what John had said. It was too late for Matt to ask for my help: a hundred and fifty years too late, in fact.

John was through, or at least we hoped he was through. He was trying to keep a smile on his face, just to show us that he had no remorse, that his criticism stood.

For some reason Sue wanted to talk about me. "Andy, do you buy any stock? What do you call it?"

"Penny stock," I said.

"Do you?"

"No. I've never bought any penny stock," I replied.

"How about the Mercedes? How're you doing with that? Do you get good mileage? Oh, but you probably don't care . . . not charging two hundred and fifty dollars an hour." She was not giving me a chance to answer.

Rene was standing right behind me. She let out a scream and everyone looked at her. Someone had thrown a plastic cockroach on the floor at her feet. Pete, another native Texan, a chemical engineer was standing next to Rene and he was doubled up in laughter. I supposed it was he who had thrown the plastic cockroach on the floor. He was hugging Rene, as Rene kept on screaming and laughing. The rest in her group were enjoying this tremendously. I could see Rene's precious buttocks bounce as she laughed with Pete, as Pete kept his arm around her waist just above where her butt began. Our group was dead.

John had killed it. Matt and Jim were thinking to themselves, trying to mentally chew and digest this tough piece of meat that John had thrown at them. I knew that both of them had voted for the governor. I had not. As a matter of fact, I had not voted in Texas ever. I was not to be held partially responsible for the mess John had talked about. Finally, Matt took a sip of his wine to signify that all was well again with him and said to the group, "How's business been everybody? I don't know about you all's business but medicine is hurting. We're seeing less and less patients all the time. It's scary."

John agreed. "The computer industry is bad. We aren't selling computers like we thought we would. I know we're hurting. I just read today that CompuStat has declared Chapter Eleven. They've got stores all over Houston and in Texas. Texas is not where it's at anymore."

Jim asked, "Isn't CompuStat out of Dallas?"

"Richardson," John said.

Sue took a deep breath and said, apologetically, "No one asked me, but teaching is bad now. We had to take the competency test and all of us are up in arms. We've got no-pass, no-play. The children are horrible. They're a bunch of animals. The blacks and the Mexicans are horrible." She touched me gently on the chest with an open hand to calm my nerves and said, "Of course, Andy, I don't consider you Mexican like they are. These are people coming in that don't know how to speak English. I'm scared of the blacks, scared that they're going to kill me. They run around in the hallways running over people. We find guns on these kids all the time. They cheat. They steal. You can't keep anything out because the blacks steal it. I don't care what it is. They'll steal it. No respect. The blacks have no respect for authority. At least the Mexicans are more respectful. Thank God. I don't know what we'd do if they weren't. They don't steal, not like the blacks. Houston is going to be almost all black like Washington D. C. And when we are . . . I'm leaving. All I'm doing is trying to get through the day alive. Forget about teaching. And then we've got tons of paper work. We're really overworked and underpaid. We had one teacher quit the other day, right in the middle of class. It had never happened before in the history of the Houston Independent School District. Some black kid called her a whore, right in front of all the other students. She couldn't take it anymore."

I asked her, "How much do you think a good teacher ought to be paid?"

She looked at me and I knew I was embarrassing her. "I don't know," she said. "But whatever it is, it still won't be enough." And with that she took a sip of her wine and excused herself.

"Goddam teachers," Matt said. "They take a competency test that a ninth grader should pass and they bitch. I wish they would sit down and figure out how much they make an hour. High priced baby-sitters. They don't have to live with their problems. I wish they could spend a day with me to see what pressure is all about. I wish they could spend a day with Andy. They really don't know what the outside world is all about. They could call me a whore all day long, as long as I got paid what they get paid for what they do."

I needed another drink and went to get it. Matt and John and Jim went with me to the kitchen. Matt and Jim had forgiven John for his indiscretion, choosing to ignore what he had said.

"The goddam hospitals used to be full not two years ago," Matt whispered, continuing with his preoccupation for the medical facilities in town. Now that Sue was not around he was cursing: "Fuck! We used to put two or three people in the hospital every day with something . . . psoriasis, poison ivy, shit like that. Now we're lucky if we get one a week. People are just not accepting our opinion. The surgeons are sitting on their hands doing nothing. People are not getting operated on like they used to. The fucking insurance companies are not paying unless they are absolutely sure the surgery is needed. The whole economic system is falling apart. Shit. Nobody's raking it in anymore. I've heard of more doctors going bankrupt this year than I have in all my years in practice."

"And you Andy?" Jim inquired. "How's the law business?"

"I'm doing all right. Let me put it this way. I'm doing as much as I want. This year I don't want to do too much."

"What's the matter, Andy," Jim said, laughing, "are you celebrating the sesquicentennial?" and Matt and John laughed with him.

"Oh, I'm not celebrating that."

John asked, "How do you feel about that?"

"The sesquicentennial?"

"Yeah . . . How do you feel being reminded about Santa Anna and the Mexicans taking a siesta at San Jacinto every fucking day of the year? Hell, it's driving me nuts and I'm not Mexican."

I laughed. "Since I know the truth I don't mind it," I said.

"That's right, Andy. You shouldn't mind it," Matt said. "That had nothing to do with you."

Jim said, "Shit . . . Andy . . . All he cares about is making money. He's a fucking Mexican Jew. He don't care about all this other shit . . . Santa Anna . . . Houston . . . fucking crazy people."

John said, very seriously now, "If you're doing well you ought to consider yourself lucky. Lots of lawyers are hurting. That's what I hear."

Darrell, the dentist, came into the kitchen for a drink and stayed to hear the conversation. He and his wife Pam were Canadian. They were the only ones of the whole group that had not been divorced. They loved the humidity and the heat, but did not like what they described as Texas' lack of culture. At first, when we first met them they had said that they had escaped Canada because of the cold but later they admitted that economically Canada was worse than the United States. "Fucking socialized medicine," he whispered to us. "Fucking socialized medicine is doing Canadian doctors in." He had a mid-western accent. There was nothing about him that would give him away as a Canadian. He could just as easily been dropped into Texas from Iowa. "That's why we left Canada. They can keep it. You guys don't know how well off you have it in the United

States. Do you know that in Canada right now a dentist is getting ten dollars to fill a tooth? Do you know that in Canada a lawyer is lucky to make forty thousand a year?" He looked at us all to see if he had astonished us with his information. We all dutifully shook our heads and looked at our shoes. We were faking our disbelief since we had heard this so many times before.

"Fuck," Jim said, "that's what Andy makes in a month," and we all laughed.

"How much you make, Andy?" Matt asked me.

"I don't know," I replied. I knew to the penny how much I made but that was my secret.

"He knows," John said. "Sonofabitch can't play golf anymore cause he's at home counting his money."

"How much money did you get in that personal injury case this year?" Jim asked.

"Which one?"

"You know which one. The one where the child was run over by the bus."

"Oh, that one," I said. "I don't know."

"Six hundred thousand," Matt said and I wondered how he knew.

I would never admit anything but we were having fun, kidding around, as usual.

Darrell left to join another group.

"Things must be doing pretty bad in Canada," Matt said.

"Yeah, but it's not bad enough for anyone to come to Texas," John said, rubbing it in one more time.

Matt couldn't take this anymore. "What the shit is your problem with Texas anyway? If you hate it so much, why don't you leave?"

"I am," John said. "I've got my transfer."

"Oh," we all said at this surprise. Suddenly we felt a sort of kinship toward him. He was a friend in spite of his manners. It was unofficially left up to me to do the honors since no one else was going to speak. "We're really going to miss you, John," I said to him. I thought I would be speaking for the entire group.

"In a way I'm going to miss you guys too. I like you guys. I never said that I didn't like you. You guys are the closest friends I've ever had. It's the fucking Texas mentality that gets a man down. If only that would change, then this would be a great place."

"Oh fuck, John," Jim said. "What about the fucking humidity and the heat that you always bitch about. Don't tell me that suddenly you love that."

"I could take that. Shit, everything is air-conditioned in Texas. I could. I could take that."

"Well, now we know what it would take to get you back," I said. "Just a small matter of changing the Texas mentality. Come back in another one-hundred and fifty years."

"Yeah," John agreed. "By then you Mexicans will have the state back and we'll have more culture."

Christie, the hostess, came into the kitchen and had to get some *hors d'oeuvres* out of the oven. Matt helped her while John and Jim and I watched. Christie and I watched. Christie was placing the stuffed mushrooms on a silver tray. You could tell she felt pained at seeing us in the kitchen. "You guys get out of here and circulate. What are you all doing in the kitchen? You all look like a bunch of women. Get! Get out of here."

We went out into the den. Rene was laughing about something else. She was holding onto Bob's arm. Bob was an aerospace engineer at NASA. He and his wife, Allison, were from Florida. They had been married three times each. They could care less where they lived. They were the only couple from out of state that did not hate Texas and most Texans. He was a pleasant man, but after a few minutes of conversation he was through. He did pride himself in knowing such things as the square feet in his house and how many BTU's his air-conditioner turned out or put in, whatever. He knew the R-factor of his insulation and why his water heater sweated. He changed his own oil and tried to do minor tune-ups on his car. He bought almost everything wholesale. He watched television every day in order to decrease his cost-use ratio, a simple little ratio formula that he had devised to apply to all his big ticket purchases. It was he who kept the group up to date on the soap operas and the evening shows. Allison, his wife, was with another group made up of women. Allison was very shy and yet she owned a dress shop, although Rene and the other women insisted that someone else owned the shop and Allison just ran it. They could not admit that poor little Allison would have the nerve to go into business for hersef. What no one realized at the time was that shy Allison was having an affair with Pete, Cathy's husband. But one couldn't feel badly for Cathy because she had been having an affair with Tom for a long time. I noticed that Matt had come into the room while Christie was arranging the food on the table and had gone to talk to Pam, Darrell's wife. He was holding her hand and playfully trying to bring it toward his crotch. Pam took her hand away suddenly and gave him an ugly stare.

I needed a refill and I walked back to the kitchen. Tom was there. He was from California. He never said how much he hated Texas and Texans, but he didn't have to. He ignored the whole state. He was a solemn sort that sold, of all things, industrial glue. The first time he had told me what he did I was fascinated, fascinated that someone could make such a good living selling glue. It was not, I found out, a plain common glue that you and I know about. This glue works. It saved the petrochemical companies millions of dollars. When dry the glue could replace gaskets, or sealants, just about anything that stopped leaks. It amazed me that someone like Tom could make a living doing this shit. Leave it to an Anglo, and a Californian to boot, to show us how to make a good living by finding a need. I was used to seeing my ancestors making a living working hard, back-breaking work, with an axe and a pick and a hoe. Now comes Tom and tells me that you don't have to go to college, that you don't need to suffer, that all you have to do is sell glue to the refineries of the world. Of all my friends, I admired him the most because I felt that he had the most guts of any one person I knew. He never seemed to worry about money. He and Mary, his wife, seemed perfectly satisfied in their second marriage. Mary, of course, did not know of his affair with Cathy. She and Cathy were vey close. Tom an Mary had two sets of children. They owned and owed what everybody else did. And the only thing he did was sell glue. I was so interested in this magical glue that at one party I asked him to bring me some and the next day I had it in my hands, a small dab, for it was expensive. I rolled it in my fingers and could feel the warmth as it set. Tom had warned me to get it off my hands and put it on the work bench in the garage. I did as he told me. It had been a serious warning. "If it sets between your fingers it won't come off for a long time."

"What's in this shit?"

"That's the secret," he had said. "We're the only ones that know what's in it and we've got the patent working."

"You know that patents are a matter of public record and that they can be stolen."

"Yes, we know. That's why we try to keep as low a profile as we can. You notice we don't advertise."

Tom was hiding in one of the far corners of the kitchen. He had poured a large glass of wine. "How you been?" he asked.

I refilled my glass with bourbon. We could hear the women, especially Rene, and the men screaming in laughter in the den. "Fine," I said. "And you? How's the glue?"

"Selling like hotcakes. We have a hard time keeping up with our orders."

"That's great. How's the patent going?"

"Slow, but you know how that is. There's another company making glue like ours, but it's not as good. We really have no competition in the market place. And you? How's the law business?"

"All right," I said and I remembered that I had a fugitive hidden in my brother's apartment. I hoped for everyone's sake that Louie did not take him out to go drinking. He could turn violent again. I thought also of the luck that Tom had had in finding this magical glue to sell to Texans. He looked at me more solemnly than usual. "Mary's mother died last week in California," he told me, but he said it as if the cat had died.

"I'm sorry to hear that. I didn't know."

"Well, you know Mary. She did not want to bother anyone of her friends. You know that if anyone has trouble she's the first one that volunteers to help, but when it comes to her, she won't let anyone help her."

"Yes, I know," I said, wondering why anyone would want to be that way, unless Mary felt that everyone else needed help through life's tribulations but her. In that case she was being very pontifical. "Where did she die?"

"In California, close to Santa Barbara. They buried her there. Mary was really hurt that her father did not attend the funeral. Mary's parents were recently divorced, you know."

No, I didn't know. I didn't know what else to say, either. So Mary's father didn't make it to the funeral. Mary was hurt. In this culture no one cared about your mother dying. (It was always a blessing that your parents died.) We had not even been told. It had been too much of an inconvenience. "Mary is always ashamed to bother anyone," he said.

Peggy and Becky came into the kitchen followed by Christie. They saw that we were there and they stopped their conversation. They had been busily talking about Cathy and her affair with Tom. Tom acted as if he had not heard. Christie asked us to leave. They had some things to discuss in the kitchen and we were in the way. She and Peggy and Becky took some more food out of the refrigerator as we walked out. I walked over to Mary and told her how sorry I was to hear that her mother had died, which was a revelation to everyone else there. Everyone faked a shock expression for a few moments and offered condolences, which Mary very graciouly accepted. Pete, not to be outdone, then informed us that Cathy's father had died the week before that and again everyone faked deep regret for just a few seconds. A man didn't need to be reflected on as long as a woman. But this was all soon forgotten.

Jim said, "How about you Andy? Anyone in your family died recently? If they have, let's get it out so we can all grieve at the same time."

It was as if he realized how I feared death. I didn't answer. I couldn't. Rene answered for me. "Nobody's died. Are you kidding? His parents are healthier than he is." And everyone laughed. We were now in a large single group in a circle. "His aunt Victoria is going to be one hundred years old tomorrow."

"Someone's going to have to eat all this food," Christie said. "I'm not going to store it in the refrigerator."

"Why didn't you say so," John said. "Heck, I've been holding back. Let me at that food."

"Seriously gang," Christie informed us. "We need to eat the caviar."

"Is that what those little tiny salt balls are?" Doyle, the stock broker, laughed.

"Oh Doyle," his wife, Sue, said to him, "you embarrass me. You know perfectly well what that is. We always have caviar at our parties."

Rene said, "Andy doesn't like it, so he never lets me have it."

Pam, the Canadian, scolded me. "Don't pay any attention to the Mexican. He doesn't know any better. He wants to eat his tacos and enchiladas and nachos." And again the whole circle laughed.

"Did you ask Andy?" Becky asked Jim, once the laughter had died.

"Ask him what?" Jim said, sipping his wine.

"About the maid, Jim. Don't you remember."

Jim remembered. "Oh . . . yeah . . . Hey Andy, our maid don't know shit about English. Can you talk to her one day to straighten her out? I mean . . . shit . . . she don't understand. We need someone to translate for us."

Becky laughed and said, "Andy isn't going to talk to her. What I need is for him to tell us what to say to her."

"Yeah," Jim said. "That's what we need . . . How do you say: Clean the windows, goddamit. Real tough like . . ."

The circle broke up laughing as we all went to the table to eat stuffed mushrooms, quiche, bacon wrapped chicken livers, fried octopus, cheese balls, delicatessen cuts, olives, fried chicken wings, but never the offal and the crotch of the cow. And at the end of the table with the caviar, Matt was opening bottles of champagne after having iced them down.

"Ah, champagne and caviar," bashful Allison said, drunk, mimicking a southern belle, "this is the real life. I wonder what the poor are eating tonight?"

Jim and Doyle and Matt had gone into the kitchen to eat. I walked in and mixed a drink. "How about the Oilers?" Jim said. "They're looking pretty good."

"They still don't play worth shit to me," Doyle said. "They're like the Astros. They're all on cocaine. Besides that we need a new owner, a new coach, a new quarterback and whole bunch of other mother fuckers that can play. We need mean niggers, not that shit we got."

"You think we got too many whiteys on the team? Is that it?" Matt asked.

"Fuck no," Doyle said in all seriousness. "We need all the whiteys we can get. Them niggers ain't going to learn nothing. A team like the Oilers needs whiteys to keep everyone on the same page. All you have to do is look at them and see that they don't know what the fuck they're doing. Ain't that right, Andy? Hey, don't you have season tickets?"

"I used to," I said. "I got tired of seeing them lose."

"Don't you care what happens to the Oilers?"

I had to admit that I did not. There were so many more important things in my life.

"And the Rockets? And the Astros?"

"Nope," I answered again.

"What about the Dallas Cowboys? You like the Cowboys, don't you, you sonofabitch?"

"No I don't."

"Why?" Matt asked me.

"It's very simple to me. Do you think that the Oilers care about me? And the Astros and the Rockets? Whenever the Cowboys take an interest in me, I'll take an interest in them. They could care less if I win or lose a case. I don't see any Oilers down and out after I lose a case. Fuck the Cowboys and the Oilers and the Astros and the Rockets. I can't stand them. They're worse than a bunch of brats bitching all the time."

Christie walked into the kitchen laughing. She said, "Did you all hear what Allison said? She said 'Ah, champagne and caviar. I wonder what the poor people are eating tonight?' and Pete said, 'tacos and enchiladas and nachos.' Isn't that cute?"

CHAPTER 8

"Well, anyway," Rene said, driving me home, "I had a great time. How about you? Did you have a good time?"

"Yes," I said. I was feeling good. As a matter of fact I could have driven, but Rene always was one to exaggerate the situation. It gave her enormous pleasure to have things go her way, the way she had predicted them. She had told everyone at the party as we left that she was driving, that I was in no condition to drive.

"You wouldn't think that there is so much going on in a small group like that." She thought for a moment. She turned left on Greenbriar. Traffic had slowed down. I looked at the clock and it was twelve thirty. The fog was distorting the lights from the incoming cars and was making Rene use the windshield wipers. She turned on the defroster and it made such a noise that she turned it off. "You'd think, as much as we paid for this car, that the defroster would work without making so much noise," she complained. "Anyway," she said, cleaning the fog from the inside of the windshield with a napkin, "did you hear the scoop?"

"About what?"

"About Cathy." Rene was having to shade her eyes to soften the glare of the incoming headlights. Now I was glad she had insisted on driving.

"That she's having an affair?"

"No, silly. Everyone knows that, even Pete. I wonder how he feels?" she asked, neither of us knowing that Pete was having an affair with shy Allison.

"No telling. Tonight he sounded happy to me."

"But deep inside . . . I wonder how he feels?"

"What's the new scoop?"

"Well Cathy, broke up with Tom and she's having an affair with someone else now."

"I spoke to Tom about his glue and he didn't seem concerned."

"You know how those Californians are . . . they try to be real cool. Anyway, he's probably with someone else by now."

"Who is Cathy going out with now, if it isn't Tom?"

"An airline pilot, or something like that. It's hard to believe, isn't it? Then Cathy tells Pam . . . Pam's her favorite friend . . . that she's been having affairs for many years, even before she married Pete. And Pete knew all about her before they got married and she told him flat out that she needed more than one man to keep her satisfied. And Pete said that he loved her so much that it wouldn't matter to him. But do you believe that? Do you think that Pete doesn't mind it at all that she's having all these affairs?"

"It's hard to say."

"How would you feel?"

"Me?"

"Yes, you. How would you feel if I was like Cathy?"

"I wouldn't have married you in the first place."

"But what if I tricked you. Misrepresented myself."

She didn't know how close to the truth she was getting. "I'd resent it, sure. But she didn't lie to him. You've got to admire the lady for coming up front with the truth. She was saying 'Take me or leave me.' Pete went for it."

"You wouldn't have married her?"

"Nope."

"Well, now comes the bad part about Cathy. The second scoop of the night. She got herpes from this new friend. Did you notice that she couldn't sit down?"

"No. I didn't see anyone sitting down all night long."

"Well, she couldn't. Pam says that Cathy has sores all on the inside and outside of her vagina and up between her buns. Little tiny blisters. She showed them to Pam. She could hardly walk at first. She had chills and pain and fever. She was really sick all last week. She's really depressed. Of course, Pam says that Cathy could kill the guy for not telling her. He was kind of chicken shit, don't you think? What kind of guy would do that to a girl?"

"You've got a red light coming up," I told her, pointing to the corner. I was afraid that in our conversation she had not seen it. "You've got to admit that with the way she's been living, it was bound to catch up with her. She's not associating with the best of people, you know."

We stopped for the light. "Next thing. Allison is quitting the shop." There was a certain glee to her voice. I couldn't imagine why the women were so jealous of shy Allison.

"Why? I thought she was doing great."

"She says she is, but the hours are killing her. She says you need a younger woman to run a place like that. She's putting in like eighty hours a week. She figured her salary by the hour and she's making a little less than five dollars and she has all the headaches. She's caught some girls that work for her stealing clothes and selling them. Her cash register, she says, is always coming up short. It's just a headache for the money she makes. And I asked her if she really owned the shop and she didn't answer straight. She said she was the principal partner or something like that. She had told us a long time ago that she owned it by herself. Do you remember her saying that?"

"The light's green," I told her and she took off slowly. "I really don't remember things like that," I said, defending the shy and cute Allison, knowing that that would aggravate Rene—just a little dig. Rene knew that I liked Allison. She was everything Rene was not: sensitive, shy, forthcoming, beautiful face, average body . . . great subdued personality that made a person want to explore her.

She took the bait. She said, "That's because you like her."

"Allison?" I mentioned innocently. "Me? . . . like her?"

"Yes, Allison, you motherfucker. You've always flirted with her."

"Me? Tonight?" I asked, laughing.

"No. Not tonight, but you always do when you're sober."

"I like her as a friend. I admire her. She's so small and feisty. So cute and huggable. You wouldn't expect her to own and run a dress shop. She doesn't look like she would be in business for herself."

"Well," Rene said, angrily, "she doesn't own the shop. She's only a partner."

"However . . . That takes a lot of guts . . . to run a business, I mean. Who's she going to sell it to?"

"The other partners are buying her out. She and Bob are going to retire in Florida pretty soon."

She turned right on Rice Boulevard and accelerated violently, disturbed that I would defend Allison.

I ignored her tantrum and began to fall asleep. I yawned and closed my eyes.

"You want to hear something else?" she asked. I could tell she was in control of herself again. Allison was no longer on her mind.

"Not really," I said, tired from the long day. "I'd rather go to sleep."

"Oh yes you do. Listen to this. This'll wake you up. Matt is having an affair."

I was staggered with the news. I opened one eye and looked at Rene. She was smiling widely. I said, "You've got to be kidding."

"No, I'm not. Why would I kid about something like that? Guess who with?" She waited for me to turn my face completely toward her, my eyes still closed. "Peggy!", she screamed, delighted.

"You're out of your mind," I said. "You've got to be kidding."

She shook her head in a childishly stubborn way. "No, I'm not. I'm as serious as can be. Matt and Peggy are having an affair. Now Peggy is trying to convince John that she really loves Texas and she doesn't want to move to Long Island. Isn't that the shits? Can you imagine that? In your wildest dreams, did you ever think that would happen?"

"No," I said. I was awake now. That bit of news had been shocking. "Does John know?"

"No. Pam swears he doesn't."

"How does Pam know all this shit?"

"She's the type women like to confess to. She knows everything. You need to be careful what you tell her, because she'll tell everyone."

"I hope you don't confess to her," I said.

"No. I wouldn't dare. I tell you and no one else. That's why I love you so much."

So we were back to being in love?

I couldn't believe what I had heard about Matt and Peggy. I said, "I saw Matt trying to put the make on Pam . . . trying to get her to touch his crotch. Did you see that?"

Rene looked at me as though she couldn't believe that I was so naive. "Oh . . . you know Matt. He does that to all the women he knows."

"Well, I guess he did it to Peggy and she took him up on it."

"That's it . . . that's exactly what happened. I know it's hard to believe. That's why you'd better be careful. There are a lot of women . . . women like Allison . . . who'd take you up right now," Rene informed me as she drove us closer to the house.

It had begun to rain. A mild cool front was coming in from the west, just enough to cool the city and make it pleasant for Aunt Victoria's party. I thought for a few pleasantly erotic moments about grabbing Allison's small and dainty crotch, thoughts so real that I could feel the seam of her pants and the excessive warmth of her female part on my bunched-up fingers.

No one had mentioned it yet, but in two weeks it would be Christmas.

"I saw Pam get away from him," I explained, "but you never know . . . I thought you were going to say Pam. It really flattened me out when you said Peggy. Is that all?" I asked. "Can I go back to sleep or are you going to surprise me with something else? You know, I still don't believe it."

"Matt and Peggy?"

"Yes, Matt and Peggy. I mean, they're entirely different. A dyed-in-the-wool Texan having an affair with a Long Islander? It's hard to believe. What in the shit do they talk about? Matt still acts like he's a freshnman at the University of Texas and Peggy is always complaining about Texas. But come to think of it, she did look a little bit cleaner tonight."

Rene laughed. "She's taking pains to look pretty, like she's got a new lease on life. Didn't you notice? And besides, I don't think that there's much talking going on. There's a lot of screwing, that's for sure."

"Pam told you?" I whispered in my sleep.

Excitedly she said, "Yes. Pam told me."

"What about Christie? What does Pam say? Does Christie know what's going on?"

"No, she doesn't. She does know that things are not what they've been. She's noticed the change in Matt, but she thinks it's his menopause. That's what she told Pam, anyway."

"How does Pam keep all her stories straight?"

"Oh, she's very good at it," Rene said and turned into the drive-way.

"Thanks for driving," I said, suddenly feeling a warmth toward her. I only wanted us to be happy. That's all I wanted. It was Rene who could not be happy and who could not make anyone happy.

We walked in and turned on the lights. Andy was asleep. I dialed Louie's phone from the bedroom to make sure he and the Alien were all right. There was no answer and it worried me. I tried again several minutes later and again no one answered. Rene came out of the closet naked and she was doing her erotic dance in front of me as I sat on the edge of the bed. She was thrusting her pelvis back and forth in my face, rubbing herself with both hands. I was dialing once more when she straddled me and she gently forced one of her large pink nipples in my mouth. I could hear the phone ring at the other end and no one answered.

"We didn't make good love this afternoon," she whispered. "We need to finish it off. How about it?"

"I'm worried," I said, taking the nipple out of my mouth and putting the phone down.

She jumped away from me. "About what? Are you calling Louie?"

"Yeah."

"That kind of puts a damper on the whole thing. Here I am trying to fuck you and you're thinking about Louie."

"He's not home," I worried out loud.

I could see the flush of anger beginning to overwhelm her. Her look became so intense and so abnormal that I thought that some day she would hopefully die from one of these fits. She screamed, "Shit, Andy. The fucker is never home. How come all of a sudden you're worried because your brother, who is a pimp, is not home at one o'clock? What the fuck is the matter with you?"

She ran angrily into the bathroom covering her body with her soft hands and slammed the door. I could hear her throwing things against the wall. In a while she came out subdued, but bitter and dressed in her long sleeved nightgown, buttoned all the way to the top. She fell into bed angrily giving me her back, throwing the blanket over herself, making a cave as Dolores had done when we made love. But there were to be no screams that polarized the hemispheres and no screams to send visions of parrots flying between the eyes. She did give out not a scream but a huge angry sigh, as if she had gotten to the part where she killed me in her thoughts.

"Are all marriages like this?" I asked softly, trying to gather the ghosts of my antecedents. Rene, thinking I was pestering her, sighed once more, this time with even more feeling, and I thought I had better keep my mouth shut.

I went outside and decided that I had to go see Louie. I was feeling better. Surely the adrenalin charge that Rene had given me had sobered me enough to drive. I checked my reflexes and I was perfect. I drove in the light rain to Louie's and knocked on the apartment door until the neighbors turned on their lights and yelled that they were going to call the police if I didn't leave. I drove back and was undressing when Rene turned and said, "Hi, sweetie pie. You've been asleep all this time?"

"Yes," I told her, rubbing my eyes with one fist and holding up my pants with my other hand, "I just got up and got dressed to take a leak."

"That's cute," she said in her stupor. Then, "I love you sweetie pie."

Once I was in bed, she cuddled up to me and kissed me on my back. I sighed the one-thousandth sigh, the one where I got to the part where I killed her in my thoughts.

CHAPTER 9

The ghosts that I had tried to conjure up last night were all around my sweat-soaked bed this morning. I could see the familiar file of two abreast through the gunshot smoke of the cannonade and, at the head of the file, limping with his leg swaddled, the jovial and sincere Colonel Fernandez bearing the Shroud of Tamaulipas on high, so high that he had to walk on the tips of his boots, so high that I still could not make out the figure on the shroud. Their faces and their tattered clothes were covered with the dust of more than a hundred years of death-bred idleness. There was my great-grandfather, Andres, the teller of tales and history, his eyebrows raining scaley bran-like pieces covered with dust, as I had remembered him when he spoke to us so animatedly and with so much conviction. I could see that there was still fight in the old thin man. He was wearing diapers. Standing by his side was his father, my great-great-grandfather Agustin, Captain, Mexican Army, in his uniform of light green serge and riding boots, the green grown faded by its long entombment, the tips of his dry cracked boots rolled up on his toes like an elf. Behind my great-great-grandfather was a young Indian woman moving her feet to the sound of a distant drum. She was Josefa my great-great-grandmother and she put out a hand to touch me to see if I, rather than she, was real. She pointed solemnly at her mother, who was more Indian than she and who looked a century older than she. And so it went, from introduction to introduction until finally I redozed during the time of my great-great-great-great-great-great-great-great grandmother and grandfather, a set of dried and dusty humans so small and so old and wrinkled and so far from me that I wondered from where in them I came. And I calculated through my vision that if a man is one half of each of his parents, then I was one-five-hundred-and-twelfth of these two creatures.

Beyond them stretched a faceless crowd, like a mural of a famous battle.

Rene rolled over, the bottom half of her body covered with the blanket and she stretched until her taut right breast fell out of her gown and she sighed so loudly that the vision disappeared as quickly as it had come. I was fully awake and feeling a lot better than I had expected. I checked the time and it was a few minutes past eight. I got up without waking Rene and I showered and dressed and left for Louie's apartment.

Donna Marie was at Louie's but Louie and Alfredo, the alien, were not there. Donna Marie was eating breakfast and she invited me to eat, but I wasn't hungry. I had not been able to digest the quiche and caviar from last night and I periodically felt the mixture come up and burn my esophagus. I did have some coffee. Donna Marie was sitting across the table eating very daintily, picking at her food, taking a considerable time to choose what she would or would not put on her fork. She appeared helpless as she ate, but her body cried out for physical mayhem. In a way I could have felt sorry for her, but I didn't. She was wearing a cut-off T-shirt and panties. I could partially see her young breasts at the hem of the cut-off and at the loose sleeves every time she lifted her arms, the area that the nuns and the priest had cautioned us about and the area which had become so eroticized for the rest of our lives. Donna Marie was not concerned to be showing me her breasts. I had tried not to look at her body when she had walked in front of me as she had let me in and again when she got up to get the coffee.

"And you don't know if they came home last night or not?" I asked her.

"I don't know. I don't think so. I came in at three and they weren't here. They may have come in afterwards and got up and left early."

That was hard to believe.

"I was with Louie and that guy until one in the morning."

"Where did you go?"

"Cruising. Like we always do."

"Did Louie do anything foolish with this guy?"

"Like what?"

"Like did he get him drunk? Stinking drunk? Could the police have picked them up?"

"I don't think so. Louie was being very careful with him. He even disguised him."

That struck me as funny. "How did he diguise him?"

She started to giggle childishly, covering up her mouth. "He put one of my blond wigs on him and made him put on a black cowboy hat. He looked funny. He really did. He looked odd."

"I can imagine," said I, trying to think of how the man would look.

"But Louie wouldn't let him out of his sight. He said that you'd kill him if the guy got lost."

"He's right. I could kill him right now. God only knows where he's at. Did he give you any clues? Like, did he say he was going somewhere after they left you?"

She was chewing slowly, thinking of the night before, and looking at me with a seriousness that made me want to smile. You could tell she was really trying to help. She seemed disappointed when she couldn't remember. She pouted, pursing her lips. "They didn't say anything," she said. "Not that I remember, anyway. Hey, what's wrong with the guy? He don't look too swift. He understands but he don't look like he likes anybody. I was scared of him. Louie said he was a big witness for some case you're involved in. Is that right? Why is Louie taking care of him?"

"Louie's right," I said, wondering where Louie and the alien could be.

"Here," she said, noticing that I had run out of coffee, "let me get you some more." She walked over, leaning over me, and grabbed my cup and saucer and took it to the stove and poured coffee for me. I could see her small rounded buttocks through the panties alternately pulsating like biceps as she walked away from me. Walking back, from the front, I could see her indescribably generous part, the same one that the nuns and the priests had bashfully failed to mention: as usual, the most important part. She was smiling. "I like to wait on you," she said, carefully putting the coffee down for me and sitting down. "Louie's tough to wait on. He's so demanding. But he's always been like that. At least he's been like that since I've been with him."

"How long have you been with Louie?"

"We've been together five years now."

"That's a long time for Louie."

"Yes, I know. He's told me that before."

She was through eating and she shoved the plate away and took a cigarette from the open pack on the table. She lit it herself, not waiting for me to help her. After she lit the cigarette she offered me one. I declined. I had not smoked since that day in the office with Rene.

"He must really like you," I told her and she looked pleased.

"He says he does," she whispered, looking down at her lap. She was almost bashful and child-like. She looked at me and bit her lip. "And I believe him. He's the best I've lived with. Most of the other guys were really bad. They wanted to control every little thing that I did. Kept all the money. Louie let's me have all of it. With his job, he doesn't need me to survive. The other guys, they were white. You know what I mean. Louie's the first Mexican I ever lived with. If I'd of known what I know now, I'd of lived with a Mexican long before I met up with Louie. Louie's nice. You Mexicans are nice. I never knew that. My mommy was a hooker too and she always said that the Mexicans were real mean, that they were out to kill the white man all the time. She had me scared. And then I met Louie and I just love Louie. We have a lot of fun together. He doesn't hassle me about nothing. I work when I want and he doesn't beat me. That's the best thing about Louie. He doesn't beat me." She rested her face on her palm and looked toward the door. The cigarette smoke was curling around her hair. "No sir, he doesn't beat me," she sighed.

"You love Louie. Is that it?"

She thought for a moment. "I don't know. I don't know if I've ever loved anyone . . . You know what I mean? What's love anyway?" She blew smoke toward me, playfully. "How 'bout you? You in love?"

I laughed and it was my time to think for a moment. "No," I answered.

She found this funny. "Oh, come now . . . you don't love your wife?"

I shook my head. "No," I said. "As a matter of fact, I can't stand her."

"Oh . . . right now you probably can't stand her but tomorrow or the next day you'll come around . . . I know you."

"I hope you're right," I said.

"I'm right," she cooed. "I'm always right. Just ask Louie."

"Miss Right," I said.

She giggled and said, "That's me . . . Anyway, forget all that. What do you think about me going to Disney World to work?"

"Just what is it that you and Louie want to do there?"

"Perform . . . You know what I mean . . . anything to open the door. Then maybe I can dance or sing. Then Louie gets somebody to notice me and we can start my career."

"I thought you were going to Hollywood?"

She pouted as I spoke. "You say Hollywood and Louie says Disney World. You've got me all confused."

"Well, where do you want to go?"

"I want to go to Hollywood . . . wherever you want me to go. Louie doesn't know."

"Then Hollywood it is."

She blew some more smoke my way and said, "Would you go with me . . . would you?"

"Oh, no," I said. "That's for Louie and you. You both care for each other."

She made a face. "Yeah. You know Louie wants to get married some day. He doesn't want me doing this all my life. You know what I mean?"

"Yes, I know what you mean. Hey, maybe you two can get married in Hollywood," I said and she did not seem to be interested.

I looked at my watch. It was almost eleven. Donna Marie offered me another cup of coffee and I accepted, just to see her walking away and toward me.

She lit another cigarette after she returned. "You know," she started, "that Louie thinks a lot of you. He's proud of you. He says that you're the only one in the family that's amounted to anything."

I laughed. "So Louie has you thinking that too. That's his favorite way

Lionel G. Garcia

of getting something from me."

"Tell me about Louie," she said.

"What do you want to know?"

She smoked her cigarette and blew the smoke high above her head. "Well, he's kind of mysterious."

I had to laugh again. "Louie has always been like that. You get used to that. You never know what he's up to."

"Yeah . . . that's what I mean . . . but his past. Has he ever been married?"

"Louie? Are you kidding? He never told you that part of his life?"

She shook her head to show me that he hadn't. "No," she answered.

"Well, Louie's been married two times and I don't think he'd mind me telling you."

"Are you sure he wouldn't mind?"

"Sure, I'm sure."

"Who were they?"

"Louie married very young the first time, to a gal named Helen, and then about four years later he married Susie. He has one daughter named Margaret from his marriage to Helen and a son, John, from Susie."

Donna Marie thought out the newly discovered information and smiled a smile of appreciation, relieved that someone else had loved Louie besides herself. "Well, I'll be," was all that she could come up with.

"Can you keep a secret?" I asked her and by now she was willing to do anything for me to tell her more about Louie.

"Yes," she said right away without giving it a second thought.

"When Louie was working in the oil fields at night when he was young, Helen went out on him and he found out about it and he almost killed her and she took Margaret with her and left town. She lives somewhere in Lubbock or near there somewhere."

She thought about Louie's misfortune. "And the other wife? What happened to her?"

"Louie was never the same after that. He married her on the rebound. She got pregnant and Louie married her. But there was never any love in that marriage."

"And the son?"

"Susie's son? . . . he's married and has a family. Got a good job. He lives here in town, but you know Louie. He never sees him."

"I feel sorry for him now. Maybe I shouldn't have asked about him."

"You have a right to know some things. Don't feel bad."

"You know Louie feels bad. I knew there was something in his past. I could tell. Louie's not happy. He acts happy but he's not; he's not a happy person."

"I know that. None of us are happy."

"But you all act happy all the time. He thinks you're happy," she said, blowing the last of the smoke and crushing the cigarette on her plate.

I had to let out a small laugh. "He's always thought that. If only he knew the truth."

"Why don't you tell him you're not happy?"

"Because we never tell each other the truth, that's why."

She kept on. "Louie says that you were always the smart one in school. You were real smart, he says. He says no one wanted you to go to college. Your teachers and the people in your school wanted you to go to work at the cement plant, like your daddy. He says that he and Willie put you through college after you got back from the service."

"Louie's right. He and my brother worked and sent me to school, but I worked too. So did Dolores. Frankie helped some, although he never could find a good job. He was so frail. Anyway, it just wasn't them. Becky and Connie helped and so did my parents. But you know Louie. He's going to brag a little on himself if he can. They helped me out a lot. I couldn't have done it without them. I wasn't the smartest one, though. Becky and Connie were smarter and so was Frankie."

She smiled and said, "That's not what Louie says."

"You know Louie. You're not going to change his mind." I stood up and said, "Well, I'd better get going. No telling when Louie is coming in. Tell him I'm worried and that I'll see him at the party. If he ever comes in."

"Don't go," she begged, turning on her chair to face me. "I'm enjoying talking to you. I never got to talk to you before, with us alone. It's always been when Louie's around and I don't get to talk much then. You know how it is. And you know me. Maybe . . .? Just maybe . . .? No, I won't ask."

I was standing by the door. My curiosity was getting the better of me. "Ask what?"

"I was wondering . . . maybe you wanted to touch me up a little while you're waiting?"

"I couldn't do it," I said. "I couldn't do that to Louie . . . not that I don't want to, you understand?"

She laughed pleasantly and ran to me, the bottom halves of her breasts exposed, swinging like ripe canteloupes under her T-shirt and she gave me a long kiss and made me hold her tight by her small naked waist. "I knew you wouldn't," she burst out, then letting go of me, "but maybe you would. Who knows? Like my mommy used to say, 'Child, it don't hurt to try.' "

CHAPTER 10

On the night of December 31, 1964, at the age of thirty-eight when he couldn't take another year of the pain of living among what he believed to be diverging people, my brother Frankie stuck a gun into his mouth against the hard palate and pointed the barrel up toward his brain and pulled the trigger. He scattered his head in a violent spray of bloody fragments throughout the room. He had been drunk in the front bedroom of my parent's house and when my mother heard the explosion, she dropped the dish rag on the floor by the table that she was cleaning and she ran barefooted into the bedroom, inadvertently stepping on sharp bits and pieces of his shattered head.

A few days before he had died he had come to the office to talk to me. I was busy at the time, but I had relayed the word through Maybelline that I could see him as soon as I got through. He had not had time to wait. I called him at his home and spoke to him, but all he did was apologize timidly in his alcoholic way for any embarrassment he might have caused. It was I that should have apologized for not seeing him, I told him. I asked him if there was anything I could do and he said to forget it that he had already solved his problems. I did not know that he had not been working steady. At that time I did not see my parents often and had no way to keep up with him. I was busy making money and I was having trouble with Dolores and our marriage.

Frankie had always been the quiet one. In his heart he was storing all the anguish and pain that he could not relate to others. In the end, that anguish and pain of living among the diverging people had been too much. He had been drinking heavily for many years, a fifth of whiskey— sometimes more—a day for fifteen years. He had lost his job of twenty years when he could no longer bend down because of the size of his liver. He left his widow, Mary Lou and his children: two daughters, Rebecca and Mary Frances, and two sons, Frank and Joe.

He had never belonged to the family, being too sensitive. No one knew why he chose to kill himself at our parent's house. The shoe store where he had worked for twenty years closed for the morning in memory of him. It was the least Mr. Lipshitz could do.

It was shortly past twelve and in Texas on Sunday that meant that beer could be sold legally. The over-head garage doors on opposite sides of the ice-house were down to keep the mildly cool air from blowing across the width of the metallic building. In the warmer days of summer the doors were raised allowing a cross-ventilating breeze. I walked in by a small door to the side of the front garage door. Inside were a few diehard beer drinkers with swollen red eyes smelling of last night's alcoholic saliva. They had not slept and looked at me with uncertain suspicion, since I was not one of the regulars. The men had been waiting since eleven for the clock to strike twelve to begin drinking as a cure for their hangovers. They had not bathed or shaved. Carlos, a large stout man, was at the bar. Him I knew. He had been my parent's neighbor for many years and had owned a tavern since we had moved to Houston. He was typical Houston, changed and gone modern. He had graduated from the Mexican beer-joint establishment with its small clapboard room and bar and outside toilet to the Americanized metal ice-house: steely, airy and windy and cold in the winter and unbearably hot in the summer. In the steel girders that supported the roof lived innumerable amounts of birds, each species with its own distinctive nest and call and at times it was necessary to kill some of them with pellet guns when they became too prolific and would interfere with the sounds of the jukebox. At the bar on a wooden stool was a solitary alcoholic, a thin misplaced unshaved Anglo in wrinkled khakis, his hair plastered down to tell us all that he had touched water. His eyes were smaller than a squirrel's. He was enjoying a short unfiltered cigarrete while sitting effeminately with his legs twirled around each other, showing no socks and pale blue-veined ankles above his work shoes. He had no teeth and when he drew heavily on the cigarette, the sides of his face collapsed and partially disappeared into his mouth. He blew the smoke from both sides of his pucker, like a steam locomotive, a habit that had probably taken him a long time to develop in order to impress the prostitutes in his younger days. He took a deep pull on his beer and reset it down exactly on the original water ring. His attention was on the football game that had just started. It was hard to believe, but Willie and Louie and I had been here two years ago and we had seen this same man sitting on the same stool, drinking beer after beer without ever urinating.

Carlos waved at me when I came in and I waved back. He was smiling. The birds were being very quiet this time of the year. They had mated in the spring and their young ones had left for safer girders. "Come over here," he yelled and I went and I sat at the bar.

"Do you want a beer?" he asked, shaking my hand with both of his for the longest time to show me once again how proud he was of me.

"No," I replied.

"Long time no see," he smiled.

"It's been a long time."

"You were here with Louie and Willie last year."

"Two years ago," I said. "Time flies."

"Goddamit it sure does," he said, shaking his head, bewildered by the quickness of the passage of time.

"I see you've still got some of your old customers," I said, nodding to the thin man at the bar, the one who refused to urinate.

He looked at the man and frowned. "Oh, him. He's pickled. At night we just put him back in his jar. Sonofabitch is like a statue. Don't you think?"

"He was here two years ago watching a football game just the same as he is today."

He laughed and shook his head and excused himself while he carried two handfuls of beers to the men at the table. He came back wiping the ice from his hands. "That sonofabitch is going to stay like that all day long. I just set 'em up for him all day long. He was here all day and night yesterday."

"I'm looking for Louie," I told him outright. He looked at me in a pained way.

"He don't work here part-time anymore," he said.

"I know that, Carlos," I said, "but he's gone from his apartment and I need to find him."

He walked away from me and he stopped at the end of the bar. He was jerking his head and looking at me, wanting me to go over to where he was, alone, away from the small crowd. I walked over to where he stood and he walked me to the back of the building. When we reached the storeroom he turned the lights on and he began to whisper. "I don't want anyone listening," he said. "Louie was here last night. He wasn't here for a long time, but he was here long enough for me to know that he's headed for trouble."

"Louie always looks like he's headed for trouble," I informed him.

"Well, that's true . . . Louie don't come here very often anymore, not since I caught him stealing from the register . . . ." He stopped momentarily and sighed deeply. "I hate to bring it up again, like I'm asking for something. I'm not. It's my fault for trusting him, so I figure I've got to pay. But he did steal from me and last night he walks in after all this time, after I ran him off, and he walks in like nothing ever happened. This place was full last night. You wouldn't believe it looking at the crowd this morning, but last night was a big night for us. Well, Louie starts asking for trouble. You know how he is. He wanted to talk to me, so I got him off to one side and we talked. He didn't have anything to say that was important. He was drunk. I thought he was going to apologize for stealing from me but, he never brought it up. He was just talking drunk talk. But that wasn't the problem. Sure I was busy as hell and couldn't put up with him too much. But, Andres," he whispered, "the men he was with."

"Men?" I asked. "There wasn't just one?"

"No," he said, "there were two. One was an illegal. Andres, when I was talking to Louie it hit me who the illegal was. He was the sonofabitch who's been in the papers since Friday. He killed his wife and father-in-law and mother-in-law. The police are out looking for this man. They had just been here not thirty minutes before Louie walked in. Louie has his friend disguised. You know Louie. He's got to make a big production of everything. He's got him wearing a blond wig and a large black cowboy hat, like the shit-kickers wear at Gilley's. The disguise caused more attraction to the man. Everyone kept staring at him. I know some guys recognized him. He's been here a few times. When I told Louie to leave before he got in trouble, he said some strong words to me. I don't think he knew who the guy was. And then I thought to myself that if he didn't know who the guy was, why is he disguising him? So I kept my mouth shut. Then he started about me owing him money. He said I was stealing from myself and blaming him. He said he had the IRS on my ass. He said he knew people at the IRS and that my ass was gone to the penitentiary. You know how he talks when he gets drunk. Anyway, it hurt my feelings. You know I've been your neighbor all this time. Hell, I still remember that my kids and I helped your family unload when you came to Houston for the first time. I hate to think of how long ago that was. But I helped raise you children and I like Louie. You know that he's a likeable guy. I always knew you'd be a success, Andres. And I knew Louie would be a mess. Willie? Well, he's done all right. I just didn't appreciate Louie talking to me like that. I told him I was going to call the police and he got scared and he left with his two friends and the dog."

"Did he say where he was going?"

"No, but you know Louie. He said he was working undercover and that he and the police were working on using the illegal as bait to catch a cocaine dealer. He had some shit up his sleeve. How're you going to believe him? If he's working with the police how come he got all scared when I told him I was going to call the police? There were some people here last night that started to get insulted by what he was saying. By the time he left, he had everybody in a bad mood. We had like four or five fights after that. Worse still, one man was killed. That puts me in a lot of hot water with the police. They said that they're not going to leave me alone from now on. Anyway, before the fights started, after Louie left, the police came in and asked about the illegal. Somebody tipped them off. Somebody had recognized him, so I had to lie to save Louie's skin. If they knew I lied to them, and with another illegal getting killed last night, well, I'm sure they would close me down. The Chief of Police and the Mayor are hot on our ass. We give Houston a bad name. They want Houston to have a good name. . . . They want us all to be Houston proud. You know how it is, though. These Mexicans and people from Central America, they come over here and make a lot of money and they start going out and raising hell. They don't know that you're not supposed to carry a gun. They all carry guns. It's a way of protection for them in their country. They're always getting insulted. Before you know it, they pull a gun and someone is dead. Last night the man was killed because he had not stopped to give this other guy a ride from work last month. He just drove by and didn't stop. This guy had been looking for a fight since then. His honor was damaged . . . Well, I finally got rid of Louie. I wished I could have called your father so he could have come and dragged him by the hair . . . That's all I know and I thought you ought to know so you wouldn't get into any trouble."

"He didn't give you any clue as to where he was going?"

"Never said a word. You know how secretive he's always been. He just got up and left with his two friends, the illegal and the blind man."

"Did you say a blind man?"

"Yeah. Remember I told you that the three of them left with the dog?"

"I just thought I had heard wrong . . . . What the hell is he doing with a blind man?"

Carlos shook his head. "I don't know," he said wondering along with me.

He started for the bar and as he did he yelled at the men there about Louie and no one had seen where Louie had gone last night. They seemed reluctant to talk about it. I was sure that no one would admit knowing anything. Carlos took me to introduce me at one of the tables, a group of his old friends. I remembered these men, but they did not remember me. I had been gone too long from the neighborhood. They had been my father's drinking buddies before Frankie's suicide. Since then my father had not gone out to the taverns. He drank at home alone, as if the shame of what Frankie had done would preclude him from having friends and having a good time. I could see the men change expressions as they heard my name and Carlos explaining who I was. I could sense that in their own mind they were in concert living out that night when Frankie had blown his head away while my father was at the tavern getting drunk. I could see in their eyes that they remembered me running into the old tavern, yelling to my father that Frankie had just killed himself. I felt like telling them that that had been twenty-one years ago, when I was thirty. Did they remember that we all ran home to find my mother running through the house screaming, as she tried to clean up the sharp pieces of fresh bone from the soles of her barefeet and Frankie dead in the front bedroom? Did they remember how cowardly I had been, that I could not go into the room to see, that I stayed outside the house and looked through the windows at my mother in the kitchen, crying and pulling at her hair while two of the neighborhood women tried to calm her down and two others cleaned the bones from her feet while a fifth cooled my mother's head with the wet dishrag that had been found on the floor? I remembered the men coming out of the house with crumpled newspapers that had been used to wipe the mess of brains and blood and bone and skin and hair from the floor and the walls and the bed in the room. Did they remember who started the fire, the fire to burn the newspapers and the sheets and the mattress and the pillows and the pillow cases, the fire to burn Frankie's brains and skin and bone and hair, the smell of burning human head? And finally, did they remember who threw the reddened mop on top of the burning pile?

They each shook my hand apprehensively. I wanted to apologize for that night. What an unforgettably traumatic inconvenience it had been for everyone.

There was a larger group at another table: younger men, illegal aliens that Carlos didn't pay much attention to. He looked their way and they nodded. These were small leathery brown men far away from home that did the work that no one else would do—garbage collectors, concrete laborers, grounds and street maintenance, dish washers—the menial labor that is so demeaning to the Anglo, but so essential to the survival and growth of a city. They looked at us and kept on talking quietly among themselves.

Carlos talked to them. "If you men ever need a good lawyer just call on him," he said to the aliens, pointing a thumb at me. I grinned and walked over to them and shook their small rough cold hands.

I came back to the table of old forgotten friends and Carlos nodded to me and insisted that I sit down. Room was made for me. It was the custom for someone like me to sit for a while with these older men, even if I did not drink with them. They were of the old school and even if we had not had a mutual tragedy in our history, it would have been an insult to simply walk away. These men were not to be feared physically, but one never knew. They had children who would be insulted because their fathers had been insulted. And there were children of these children, each generation carrying the insult to a higher degree, that one had to watch out for.

They asked for my father and mother and their health. Don Tomas and Don Pepe said that they visited my father once in a while, not as often as they should, but they tried. That was good enough for me and I told them how much I appreciated that they were concerned for my parents' well-being.

"Well," Carlos said, "you have to remember that this group was always very close. We were and are the best of friends. We were Mutualists and in the Catholic Church together for many years . . . ."

"Still are," Don Arturo reminded the others.

"Yeah," Carlos answered him, "but we don't go to the meetings anymore."

"You want to know why?" Don Arturo asked me, as if he needed for me to answer in order for him to keep on. "The priest wants younger men that have good jobs so that he can get more money for the church . . . everything is money."

Don Pepe said, "You can't blame the good Father Rodriguez. He's got to survive just like the rest of us."

"It's Father Diaz that's the culprit, not Father Rodriguez," Don Filimon told them and one could tell that he was repeating his wife's words exactly. "To Father Diaz the church is only money. Especially since the Altar Society got Father Rodriguez to use some of the Bingo money to buy Father Diaz his new artificial leg. And they say Father Rodriguez is worse now instead of better. He's cursing a lot now, my wife says. He started his sermon Wednesday night at the blessing of the Holy Sacrament and he told everyone that they were a bunch of bastards."

Carlos grinned at the thought of what the senile Father Rodriguez had done. "Hell," he told them, "that ain't cursing. That's the truth."

"Why does Father Diaz let him get in front of the people?" Don Tomas asked. He was staring at his beer absentmindedly.

"He's jealous, that's why," Don Filimon said before taking a short drink from his beer. "He wants to see Father Rodriguez ridiculed by the parishoners."

Carlos said, "I don't think so. Father Rodriguez is stubborn. No one is going to tell him what to do. Remember the Altar Society tried to cover up the Saints with purple cloths right after Palm Sunday and he ran all the old hags off? Remember he did not want to pay out the big pot at the Bingo one night? Remember he did not want to replace the broken crucifix that fell off the altar? And on and on . . . You know how stubborn he was."

"He was always angry," Don Pepe said, shaking his head.

Carlos shook his head. "Anyway, we feel for your father," he told me. "I go see him two or three times a week, but I just live next door. It's easy for me. These other men live farther away. And God knows we're getting older and we just don't get out too far anymore. Just to the beerjoint and back."

"And that's getting dangerous," Don Filimon said. "Someone got killed last night," he informed me, seriously.

"That's what Carlos was telling me."

Carlos said, "Well, you've got to consider who these people are we're dealing with. In the old days we'd have a fight or two and that would be the end of the thing. Now? My God." He shook his head in disbelief. "Everyone gets insulted for the littlest thing. The last killing we had before last night was last month and it happened because someone rubbed up against this guy from behind. He felt insulted and he shot the guy right there." Carlos pointed to the area between the counter and the door. He shook his head again. "Let's forget about that . . . . Have a beer with us, Andres."

"I don't drink beer," I said.

"That don't make no difference," Carlos said. "You like scotch? Bourbon?"

"Bourbon," I answered.

He got up and went behind the bar and somewhere underneath he found a hidden bottle of his best bourbon. He showed it to me and I said it was all right. I didn't care what brand it was. I was beginning to crave a drink. I could see him pouring the bottle into a paper cup. "Water?" he yelled and I agreed. He poured water into the cup from a single faucet behind the counter and brought the drink. He had filled the cup to the brim and had spilled some on his hand. "Goddamit," he said, "just look at what I've done." He set the drink in front of me and all my companions felt pleased that I was drinking with them.

"The only thing I've got to tell you, Andres," Carlos warned, "is that if the law comes in here, you better throw the goddam drink away or hide it so no one can find it. I don't have a hard liquor license. It's against the law. But you know better than me. These Texas laws are crazy. You can buy a hammer on Sunday but you can't buy goddam nails. Or you can buy nails and not a goddam hammer. I don't know which one, but it goes something like that. You can't buy beer before twelve on Sunday, but who's to keep you from drinking it if you have it? These Baptists think that we're going to church if we don't drink on Sunday morning. How messed up can you be? All it does is that it makes it a lot more fun to get a beer on Sunday morning. Ain't that right, men? You think those boys over there are going to church because they can't get beer on Sunday morning?" He pointed his thumb at the Salvadorans.

Lionel G. Garcia

He started scratching the label off his beer bottle. "You know, Andres," he whispered, "that your father still cries for Frankie." He took an old handkerchief and wiped his eyes and then blew his nose. The other friends were teary-eyed along with him.

The television announcer was informing the alcoholic that the Oilers looked bad today. "Goddam Oilers!," one of the illegal aliens said, and for the first time since I had gotten there the thin alcoholic turned from his stool at the bar and looked to see where the comment had come from. "They ain't worth shit," the alcoholic said grinning, the garbled voice coming from his concave lips. He was fanning the cigarette smoke from his eyes, agreeing with whomever had spoken the words of wisdom about the Oilers. For a while my skin had prickled at what the alcoholic had said. I thought that he had said that the Salvadorans were not worth shit. But the illegals understood that he was agreeing with them about the Oilers and they laughed. These were the types of misunderstandings that could lead to death in a tavern.

Carlos, startled for a second as I had been, looked at the man at the bar and said, "Forget the Oilers. They ain't never going to win. Hell, a man ought to have something better to do than to put his hopes on a football team."

Our table was not interested in the game. Before Carlos and I had joined them, they had been busy talking about other things, important things like why do dogs get tied up when they copulate? Does the possum screw through the nose? Important things. When we sat down we had interrupted the conversation on the famous Mexican hoop snake, the *alicante*. I had heard bits and pieces of the end of the story that Don Tomas was telling his companions. Now we were back to the imaginary snake.

"And you saw this happen?" Don Arturo asked Don Tomas.

Don Tomas peeled his eyelid down with a finger and said, "With these two eyes I saw it."

Don Arturo looked at me and asked, "Andres, you are an educated man. Do you believe the stories of the *alicante*?"

I did not want to destroy the fantasy that was so important to these people. "I believe some of it and some I don't. I'm sure some of it is true," I said.

Don Tomas slapped the table and said, "There! There you have it. A man trained in the law has spoken."

Don Filimon, the oldest one of the bunch, could not contain himself. "I've seen some strange things occur with the *alicante*. Things that if I told you you would not believe."

"You've told us all there is to tell," Don Pepe said.

Don Filimon looked at him in disgust. "That's what you think," he informed Don Pepe, as he hitched up his pants. "One day my brothers and me were bailing hay. You know the small bales we used to make. We didn't have no machines in those days. You men know that everything was done by hand in those days." All of the men knew. Their childhood had been spent on farms. The Hispanic migration to the cities had not occured until the 1940's. "Well, it was in the morning . . . oh, about ten or eleven. Or maybe a little earlier. Who knows? Time in those days was different. Now I see these young people running around like they don't have time." He showed us how the young people scurried around by moving his fingers quickly over the table top. "They say they're late. They're always late. We were never late. You're never late until you buy a watch. That's why I never carried a watch in my life. What's a watch for, anyway?" He took a long swallow from his beer and he drooled off the side of his mouth when he set the bottle down. He smeared the drool across his mouth with his arthritic claw-like hand.

The other three drinking buddies sighed. They wanted the man to get to the point. He was cutting into their time.

"Well, anyway, I picked up this bale and I felt something go around me . . . fsssssst . . . fsssst . . . fssst. Round and round . . ." He embraced himself to show us how he had been bound. "But it was fast, so fast that I could not make out what it was. It had the bale and me together and it came across my back. I couldn't see what it was. Finally I raised my arm and I could see under my arm pit that it was the dreaded *alicante*. It was trying to suffocate me as if I were a raccoon or something."

"Did it kill you?" Don Arturo asked and we all started to laugh.

"No," Don Filimon said quietly, his feelings hurt that someone had made fun of him. "The *alicante* is a weak snake. It could never hurt you by squeezing like that. It can kill a small animal, but a man? . . . No. I don't think so. The *alicante* is weak but treacherous."

The Oilers were now trailing by three touchdowns and the illegal aliens and the Alcoholic at the bar were cursing. The two cultures had found a common ground to agree on at last.

"The *alicante* can rob a mother of her milk and the baby can die. I've heard of that. That happened at a ranch near where I was born," Don Tomas said.

Apparently they had all heard that story, because we all agreed with him and he was not allowed to tell it. Even I had heard the story.

"Let's not talk about the goddam snake anymore," Carlos said. He got up and fixed a bourbon for himself also. He took a sip and wiped the excess off his mouth with his fingers. "That shit is tough," he said, referring to the bourbon. "What's in that shit, anyway?" He looked at me seriously and asked, "Does your drink taste like shit?"

"I don't know what shit tastes like," I said and everyone laughed, including Carlos.

"Well, I do," he said, grinning from ear to ear. "And this sure tastes like it. But forget about the goddam drink. Let's not talk of snakes either. I hate snakes. Let's talk about life. Like what is life?" He waited for someone to say something. We were all looking at him. "Just as an example, what is life? What is this shit we call life, anyway?"

By this time we were all depressed, looking down at our drinks. I was thinking that somewhere in Houston Louie had an illegal alien that had murdered his wife and both his father and mother-in-law and he had him disguised with a blond wig and a black hat and in the company of a blind man and his dog. I wondered where he was. Don Pepe said, finally, that Father Rodriguez had told him that life was a dream and Carlos jumped on him. "What do you mean a dream? If someone beats the shit out of you, don't you feel it?"

We all agreed. So life was not a dream. Father Rodriguez was wrong.

Don Filimon said that to him life was a voyage and we all agreed, except for Carlos. "Where are you going and where did you come from? To me a voyage is when you're going somewhere. Hell, we're sitting still. This ain't no fucking voyage."

Don Filimon shook his head. He had been wrong. What did Carlos believe then?

"Shit, I don't know. Life is not what you think it is. Just when you think you know about life, well, then it changes and gets you all messed up. There's no meaning to the sonofabitch! You take the bible. Who's going to believe all that? You think Father Rodriguez believes all of that?"

Don Arturo said, "I bet you one thing . . . Father Diaz doesn't. To Father Diaz all it is is money so he can buy the new leg."

"Give me something that I can believe in," Carlos begged. "See old Joe there sitting at the bar? Do you think he gives a shit about life? Shit no! You could go up to old Joe right now and tell him everyone in his family just died and he wouldn't give a shit. Right, Joe?" Joe had not heard the conversation, but he turned around when he heard his name and grinned mildly, trying to cover up his gums with his lips. We could plainly see his tongue inside his mouth moving slowly like a broad pink worm. Carlos whispered, "Sonofabitch don't know what the shit's going on. He just gets up and drinks and then he goes to bed at night. Next day is the same for him. That's his life. But that's not important anyway. We ain't here for long. What is important is this: Who is man's best friend?" He looked around and smiled. I took the last of my bourbon. He was right. It didn't taste right. I could see that Carlos was setting us up for the grand finale.

He repeated the question heavily. "Who is man's best friend?"

Don Arturo spoke up and informed the group that the wife is man's best friend. He received considerable opposition, to the point that in defending his choice he almost lost his dentures. Carlos was faking outrage and laughing. "What the shit did the wife ever do for a man? At least my wife? That's who I'm talking about. The wife is meant to be the servant of the man and not his best friend."

"Well then," Don Tomas said, "how about the dog? . . . when he's not all tied up screwing? Shit," he said, "my dog treats me better than my wife."

"That's the truth," I said, much to their surprise.

"Shit," Carlos said to me, "you ain't got no problems. You've got it made. You got money, a beautiful wife and home and cars. You got all a man wants. Don't tell us you got problems."

"Well then," Don Filimon said as he tried to unravel the mystery, "the horse would be man's best friend. He takes you places. He is your companion."

No one agreed about the horse.

Finally when they could think of no one else, Carlos raised his hands for silence. He had a pronouncement. We were quiet like school children anticipating the knowledge that was to be ours shortly. "Man's best friend," he said very seriously, "is his own ass-hole."

"You're crazy!" shouted Don Tomas, barely able to contain his laughter.

"How can an ass-hole be man's best friend?" chided Don Arturo.

"Well," Carlos responded, very calmly and taking the time to sip his drink, "just think about it. Your ass-hole saves your life all the time."

"How can that be?" Don Filimon inquired incredulously, his old lips quivering and being smacked in obvious delight.

The explanation began: "Well, this is what I was thinking the other day. Suppose you're at a beer joint and you get into an argument and the argument continues into the night and it's getting hotter and hotter. You know how hot-headed the goddam Latins can be. An argument over nothing. And then you say the wrong thing and you know you're going to have to fight it out. There might be guns fired or knives unsheathed. You're not sure if you're going to get killed. Forget about your heart pounding . . . ." He grabbed his chest and shook his head. Then he held out his fist in front of us and he rhythmically opened and closed it to demonstrate what he was talking about. "If at that moment your ass-hole starts puckering in and out, in and out, in and out, like this . . . Well, my friends, that's the signal that will save your life and you'd better pay attention to it and start running, because if you don't, you're going to get the shit beat out of you!"

When we stopped laughing I got up and shook hands. They appreciated the fact that I, an educated man and the son of their old friend, had honored them by sitting down with them. Frankie's suicide and what had happened that night had been temporarily forgotten. I waved at the illegals as I went by their table. The alcoholic waved at me without taking his eyes off the game. He had five empty beer bottles in front of him. The Oilers were down by four touchdowns and a field goal and still the man refused to urinate.

CHAPTER 11

At the beginning of World War Two when we took Willie to the courthouse for his trip to Fort Sam Houston in San Antonio I was afraid that we would never see him alive again. But he came back the following day and then was called to active duty in one week. He rode the bus from San Diego, Texas, to Fort Benning, Georgia, for Infantry training, wearing the new shoes that our mother had bought him in Alice. He fought in the Pacific Theater and went through the Death March of Bataan. And he made it back. He arrived weighing one-hundred and ten pounds and he came in earlier than we had expected, so he had the only taxi driver in town, the one that ran the errands for the prostitutes, drive him home. Louie had already been discharged and he was working at the beer joints, taking the fat woman with him so that she could show the drunks how dollar bills should be folded and cigarettes should be smoked.

It was cold that night and the doors were closed. There was the winter smell in south Texas of burning kerosene lanterns and mesquite, the smell that penetrated our clothes and bodies, the smell of the illegal alien of today. We were eating our favorite supper, potatoes with eggs and tortillas and we were all drinking coffee. I was ten years old and both proud and scared that my brother Willie was in the Army. I had followed the war in the newspapers in school and on the radio at home every day. I had known where Willie was most of the war except when the Japanese held him prisoner. Those had been bad months for all of us.

In the lonesome darkness of the night we heard the car stop. The heavy-metal sound of the car door slamming shut startled us. It was so dark outside that we could not see through the windows. Whoever was outside had the advantage over us, for we knew that we could be seen as we sat eating our meal and we felt naked and vulnerable. We shivered as we looked toward the door. The neighborhood dogs had been warming themselves under the houses directly underneath the wood-burning stoves and now had come out and were beginning to bark. My mother got up and very hesitantly went to the door and cracked it open. She said, "Someone's there." She stood for the longest time peering with one eye through the crack in the door, allowing the gentle howl of the wind to enter the room. We heard another car door slam shut. "There are two men getting out of the car," she said. The dogs were now howling in force.

"Is it daddy?" Connie asked, scared of whom it could be.

My mother had put her hand to her mouth. "No," she answered, "I don't think so."

We could hear the men talking. One of them was laughing in a carefree manner as if nothing could ever bother him. By this time my mother had opened the door slightly more to see who it was. She was holding her face between her hands and she was shaking her head. As the men approached she turned to us and let out a sigh. "It's Willie," she said. "He's finally home. Now I can cry."

She wept and Willie wept with her. "Oh, Willie," she sobbed, "if you only knew how we missed you." Then it was the girls turn and they hugged him and cried. Finally it was my time and he hugged me and he smelled stale. He kissed me on the cheek and it was all I could do to keep from crying. He didn't look like Willie to me. He was so thin. "How you been?" he asked me. I could feel the boniness in his body. He was not the same Wille. It would take him a while before he recovered. "I've been fine," I said.

He looked me over and said, "You've grown, you little fart. You look good."

"How's the war?" I asked, like I was asking about the weather.

"Okay," he answered and sat down. He was carrying his duffle bag all this time and he set it down by his chair. My mother had brought him a cup of coffee by now. "Have you eaten anything?" she wanted to know.

"No," he said, "I haven't eaten anything all day long. We never had time on the bus. We were running late and the bus was full. Everywhere we stopped we just didn't have time to order anything."

"It's just as well," mom said to him, running her hand through his hair. She could not believe that Willie was home. "That way you can eat some good food."

The taxi driver had been standing at the doorway with his hat in his hands. He was smiling at our good fortune. Willie turned to give him some money, but he refused it. "No, no, no," he cried, shaking his hat at Willie, "you've been through a lot. I've heard all about it from your father. I don't want any of your money. I'm just glad you're back. I just wish I could have gone. I would have shown those goddam Japs a thing or two. I just hope you did."

Willie grinned and walked over and shook his hand and thanked him and the man left.

Mother fixed Willie a good meal, better than what we had eaten. She had some pork sausage that she had cured in vinegar and she cooked that with refried beans and eggs. She fried potatoes on the side. She sliced some onion and opened a can of tomatoes and mixed the two in a hot skillet with chilipitin peppers. She poured the hot sauce over the eggs. For him she quickly made new dough for tortillas and fresh coffee. Willie ate slowly as we watched him, stopping once in a while to tell us of the incredible things that had happened to him. We listened in silence. As he spoke, my mother, who had not sat down, brought hot tortillas to the plate in the center of the table. But they were just for Willie, our deserving warrior, not for us.

The dogs began to bark once more and mother went to the door and peered outside into the darkness. The wind was beginning to pick up and it was beginning to fog, so she came back to the window by the sink and she lit the extra kerosene lantern and took it with her and she held it high over her head to illuminate the barren yard as she held onto the door. She looked beyond the front yard across the ditch and to the street. "There's a man walking," she whispered to herself and looked for a while. "I think it's your father . . . It looks like he's crossing the ditch and coming into the yard . . . He fell down . . ." She covered her mouth as she let out a moan. "He's up now . . . He's all right . . . Yes, it's him," she said, definitely. "He's drunk again. Thank God, he's home."

She blew out the lantern and opened the door fully.

My father staggered in and in the poor light could not make Willie out. He rubbed his eyes at what seemed to him an errant shadow cast on the chair. He teetered back and forth in his drunkenness, suddenly shifting his right foot backward and outward to maintain his balance to keep from falling. Every movement was an exaggeration of the normal. He brought up his right hand to shield his eyes from the lantern on the table and he did so in a large outward arc as if saluting Willie. He approached Willie in slow fearful steps, holding on to the chairs.

My mother was crying as she saw the transfiguration my father was going through. "Who do you think it is?" she playfully asked my father.

My father, for all he knew, was seeing an apparition. He put out his hand to touch Willie and Willie grabbed his hand and shook it. My father recoiled as if he had been shocked by Willie's hand. He looked at his hand and then at Willie. Willie said, uncomfortably, almost apologizing for having come home, "It's me, Willie, Dad. Don't you recgonize me? Have I changed that much?"

"Willie?" my father cried in his drunken state, "is it really you?"

My mother wanted to help him out in his stupor. She said, "It's Willie. Your son. He just came in not an hour ago. He's early. They let him come home early for Christmas."

It finally dawned on my father that it was Willie and that he was not seeing a ghost. "Willie . . ." he said softly, embracing his son. "Willie. Willie. Willie . . . How good to have you home. Goddamit, son. When did you come in?"

"I just told you. . . . Not an hour ago," mother said.

"Goddamit, son. I didn't recognize you. What did the Japs do to you? How come you're so thin? The sonofabitches didn't feed you, did they? Those little sonofabitches are cruel." He sat down and started to weep at seeing the physical condition that Willie was in. "Look at what those bastards have done to my son. He doesn't look like Willie anymore."

"Now, now," my mother said to him, "it's not the end of the world. Thank God, it's something that can be corrected. It's not like he lost an arm or a leg . . . What did the doctors say?"

"They don't say much to us. All I know is that I suffered from malnutrition and worms. I just didn't get to eat when I was in prison."

"See what I mean?" my father murmured. "The goddam doctors don't say nothing to my son. The goddam Japs didn't feed him."

My mother was stern with my father. "Don't talk like that. You're not in some beer joint. You're in front of me and the children."

"It's just that it makes me angry for anyone to treat my son like the Japs treated him."

"We're all angry," mother wept. "Can't you see?"

"I'm angry, that's for sure," Willie said. "But you know what the Japs say. 'He who fights and luns away lives to fight anothel day.' " Connie and Becky and I started to giggle at what Willie had said. He laughed with us as our parents looked sternly about, worried at what Willie looked like. Then Willie said, "Maybe I'll have a chance to go back."

"Oh, no!" mother gasped. "God forbid. Let someone else do the fighting from now on. You're not going to be in any condition to fight anyone. Let the doctors talk to you. They'll tell you exactly what I'm telling you right now."

The joy of homecoming was short lived. Willie started going out with Louie and they both were drinking heavily, taking the fat lady around to perform at the beer joints and staying out late, drinking heavier than my father and staying out later than my father. I don't know who was angrier, my mother or my father: My mother with Willie and Louie for being so much like their father, or my father because Willie and Louie were coming in later than he and waking him up and bothering him. Our father felt that he had lost control of his own home. Willie, along with Louie, was kicked out of the house long before Willie was supposed to report back to his army base. Before he left he came to say goodbye, wearing his uniform as he had that night. He had lost his duffel bag and most of his clothes and was carrying what he had left in a pillow case. He returned in one month, discharged and ready to put on some weight.

And when Louie and Willie brought the ugly fat lady to the house our mother objected and she made our father board up the house and all of us moved to Houston.

It was a beautiful clear afternoon and I could still smell the sweetness as I had yesterday of the on-growing honeysuckle that had lingered on through the fall, the still green vines strongly clinging to the side of the old house reminding me of my great grandfather's death. Across the back yard on the north wall of the garage the honeysuckle that Frankie and Louie had planted as punishment for their poor grades was blooming heavily and the swarm of bees around it appeared like a cloud of faded yellow smoke. On the gables of the house and the garage the runaway birds from the ice-houses watched our every move below. Rene and I went inside and everyone was there except Louie. That would come later. My father went out with Al, Becky's husband, to unload the beer and ice I had brought. Becky and Connie were sitting at the table with Victoria. Connie was already drinking a beer. Fat Angie, Willie's wife, was sitting with them. Everytime I saw Angie I remembered her on her wedding day when she was young and beautiful and thin. Her mother had had to pin her wedding dress at the back to keep it from falling down. She could have worn the dress on her thigh this morning as she jovially slapped Connie on the back to compliment her on something she had said. Becky was not thin anymore, but she was not as fat as Angie. Becky was a larger, taller woman than Angie, bigger boned, and she carried her weight without problems. Connie, on the other hand, was still slim. She had to be. She was always on the verge of getting married again. Today she was alone, as far as I could see. I would be proven wrong. Connie had been married five times. She had turned out to be the loudest one in the family and could curse with any man in town. Nothing embarrassed her. "Why should I be embarrassed?" she would ask. "I'm only a human being. What's the worst thing that could happen to me? Someone could kill me." She would stop and think about that possibility and chase it out of her mind. "Nah," she'd say. "No one is tough enough to do that." I could hear her laughing as we walked past the kitchen. She was telling the other women a joke. Both of Connie's daughters had gotten pregnant as teenagers and she had made them have their babies and raise them. "Shit," she had told everyone, "everybody thought I was crazy for making them do it. But I believe in people taking responsibility for their fuck ups."

Becky, who we had all thought would be the live wire in the family, turned out, in her middle age at least, to be more subdued. One could tell that she was not happy with her life. She had been the one that had dreamed of being rich, of getting married to the rich man that came from England on the Queen Elizabeth, of taking cruises on large ships like the ones we saw on the newsreels in the dark theater on Saturdays. She always assumed that Connie would marry poor. She was the chosen one. Unfortunately she married a poor ignorant Anglo longshoreman named Al who earned over ten dollars an hour when he worked. The trouble was that he seldom worked. He was too expensive to hire.

My mother was working in the kitchen, peeling potatoes, cooking a large skillet of rice. Rene yelled hello to everyone and they all greeted her. Rene stayed in the kitchen. She kissed my mother and began to help her with the cooking. I walked over to my sisters and my sister-in-law and Victoria and I went around the table kissing them all. Connie, of course, made the most commotion, feigning a collapse into the chair after I kissed her. Everyone was laughing. "Goddam, you're handsome," she mocked.

"Connie will never change," mother said, looking across the room to where we were. She didn't know whether to be embarrassed or not. She looked to see what we were doing.

Connie said, "Goddam, Andy, you made my knees buckle with that kiss. It's a good thing I'm your sister. If not I'd be on you like a goat in heat!"

"Be quiet Connie," my mother begged. "You take things too far some times. I'm sure you're making Andres feel bad."

I was laughing. What else could one do with Connie? "I'm not making him feel bad," Connie yelled. "Look at him. The little fart is laughing."

My mother realized that it was impossible and she went back to her cooking. Rene was talking to her. By now I would have thought that my mother would know better and stay out of Connie's way. Connie took a drink from her beer. She asked Becky if Becky wanted a beer and Becky said no, not just yet. Al was going to bring her one.

"Andy, no one brought ribs," Connie said. "Can you believe that?"

"That's okay," I said. "We've been eating too many ribs as it is."

My Aunt Victoria remained silent, not paying attention to what was being said. She seemed so preoccupied with the passage of time. I asked for Willie and was told that Willie was outside starting the fire for the barbecue. I got up and went by the kitchen to go to the back yard. My mother and Rene were talking very animatedly, all the while butchering the side of goat we were going to barbecue. Rene looked so beautiful. Her rear end was sticking out from the flowered apron that she had put on and I could imagine her naked and how good she still looked. I was back to loving my wife. She could be . . . no . . . she could *look* so tender at times that it was hard for me to believe that this was the same woman that caused so much hatred in me so often.

Mother looked at me as I crossed the kitchen on the way to the door. I could tell she was going to talk to me. "I didn't know," she said, "that you had been in the hospital Friday night?"

I stopped and hugged her. Rene was smiling pleasantly at me. "I didn't want to worry you," I told her. "It was all a misunderstanding. The doctor thought I was sick, that's all. Who told you?"

"Willie . . . and now Rene," she answered. She inspected me to see if there was something about me that she could see wrong. "Are you sure there is nothing wrong with you?"

We could hear the laughter coming from the dining area where Connie and Becky and Angie were sitting with the aged Victoria.

"I'm sure there's nothing wrong with me."

I could tell that she did not believe me. "No doctor puts a man in the hospital unless there's something wrong with him."

Rene came to my defense. "There's really nothing wrong with him that a good restful vacation and less alcohol wouldn't cure. He's been very restless, very nervous lately. Always jumping on me for the slightest things." I resented that she had added the last part when she knew I couldn't defend myself. She sensed my mother's worry and grabbed her by the shoulders from behind and hugged her. My mother, unfamiliar with physical love, felt embarrassed by Rene's embrace. She flushed red and froze solidly in place.

I saw my father and Al carrying a wash tub loaded with ice and beer as they passed outside by the door. They were bending under the load and were heading for the back yard to where Willie was building his fire.

"I've been nervous," I said. "I think that's all they found. I didn't want to stick around all night long for them to tell me that. You know how the hospitals are nowadays. They need patients.They're going to try to keep you in there whether you need it or not."

"I've never heard of such a thing," my mother said, innocently.

"He's doing all right," Rene said of me. "He just needs rest."

To the still clinging Rene my mother said, "You need to see that he rests. He's restless and nervous. I can tell. He's always been nervous, even when he was a little boy. Of all of them he was the most nervous and anxious, like he had worms . . ."

"Is Maria Luisa coming?" I asked her, inquiring about Frankie's wife.

"No, she couldn't make it," mother said. "She's got to baby sit for one of the children."

"Someone did invite her?" I asked.

"Don't be silly," my mother said. "We'd never forget to invite her. Connie invited her and Becky and your father and I invited her. It's just that she couldn't make it . . . Did you go to Mass today?"

I sighed in resignation for the sermon that was to come but today mother felt kind. She only said, "Everyone here has gone to Mass today except you . . . and probably Louie. If you don't go to church you are only half a person. That's what Father Rodriguez says."

Rene turned loose and I kissed my mother on top of the head and walked out. Willie was throwing wood on the fire that he had set on the ground by the garage. He was holding a rusty axe in his hand. My father and Al were under the tree. They had opened a beer apiece. They offered me one and I took it, since I knew I was going to have to drink beer today. Willie had his beer tucked in his belt. He took it out like a gunfighter and took a long drink. Whispering so that our father couldn't hear, Willie said, "Goddam axe. Nothing around here is worth a shit. He never had anything worth a shit. Look at this goddam axe, will you? It hasn't been cleaned or sharpened in years. I almost broke my goddam hands when I swung it the first time. The sonofabitch bounced back like a rubber ball. Talk about getting a shock."

"What did you tell them about Friday night?" I asked him.

"Nothing really," Willie said, tucking his beer back in his belt.

"I just told them that you had been in the hospital for tests and that everything was okay."

"You didn't tell them about rescuing me from the hospital?"

"Shit no," he said, looking at me as if I were crazy for asking.

He swung the axe and broke, not cut, a small piece of wood in half. He threw the two pieces into the fire. My father and Al went into the old garage and we could hear them moving things about. They came out rolling the old washing machine that my father had made into a barbecue pit. Al had the extension cord hooked around his shoulder. We went over and helped them roll the washing machine under the tree right beside the beer.

My father had removed the agitator on the old washing machine but had kept the shaft intact. He had cut a circular grill with a hole in the center and it fit perfectly over the remaining shaft. With the washing machine motor running the grill would move back and forth over the hot coals. When he first unveiled it, it was the talk of the neighborhood. The idea was that the meat would not catch on fire if left unattended.

Al connected the washing machine to the extension cord and ran the extension cord into the garage. He came out dusting himself. "Goddamit Dad," he shouted, "when are you going to clean up that old garage. Hell, one of these days I'm coming over and we ought to go ahead and do it. I'll help. You know I can help you. Hell, me and Becky'll come over one day and spend the whole day and you and I can clean the garage."

Al walked over in his familiar swing, taking long strides. He reached us and pulled out a cold beer from the tub. He opened it and drank. He shook his head at the coldness of the beer. "Goddam, they're getting cold. That's the way I like them. Right Dad?"

Willie and I were smiling, watching my father. He did not like to be called "Dad" by Al. It was beneath him. My father swallowed his beer and said nothing about the invitation to clean the garage. He was angry and insulted. Twice he had been called "Dad" and he had been told that he had a dirty garage. When Al had to go in to the john, my father could not contain himself any longer. "Who the shit does he think he is? He know he's not supposed to call me 'Dad.' But still he does it. Becky has told him not to call me 'Dad.' I am not his father. I always hoped that Becky would marry a good decent Mexican man with money."

"It's hard to find a decent Mexican with money," Willie said. "You almost have to be a crook. Unless you're like Andy here."

My father misunderstood. "Andres is not a crook."

Willie said, "I didn't say he was. Andy's the exception. But how many Andy's are you going to find?"

"Goddammit," I said, "I'm tired of being used as an example. Don't use me as an example."

"Andres is right . . . Anyway," my father said with Al still gone, "I thought Becky would do better. How long is it since the bastard has worked?"

We both shrugged. We didn't keep track of Al's work. "I thought he worked this week," I said. "Isn't that what Becky said?"

"That's what she always says," our father informed us. "He hasn't worked in God knows how long. Poor Becky. She was always so proud. She had such high hopes for herself. I remember when she was little that she used to sit on my knee and tell me all the things she was going to have when she grew up and how many places she would go to. She was going to marry rich . . . And look at what she married. A damn Gringo with no money, no future, no education. What got into her?"

Al came back out of the garage. He was singing a little rhyme and laughing to himself: "No matter how you shake it and dance, your last drop goes down your pants."

He opened another beer and he stood silently, as though having gone to urinate had alienated him from us. We, and most importantly he, could tell that he didn't belong and that we had been talking about him. At this point, knowing how my father felt about him, I looked at him as he stood alone and destitute and yet so near to us and I had to feel compassion for him. He tried his best to be one of us.

The fire had produced enough coals. Willie went into the garage and came out with an old rusty shovel. Al laughed and yelled, "Be careful with that fucker so you don't get lock-jaw." Willie ignored him by smiling. He carefully took shovelfuls of hot coals and dumped them into the bottom of the washing machine. When he was through he spread the coals evenly with the shovel and slid the famous grill over the agitator shaft. "This sonofabitch is going to be good," he said.

Said Al, "You're fucking A." If only he hadn't had an opinion on everything, I'm sure our father would have liked him.

I could feel my father seething. Rene came out with the platter of goat meat for the barbecue and gave it to Willie. That was Willie's job, to barbecue. If I had tried to intervene there would have been a fight. The only way for me or anyone to ever get to barbecue was for Willie to die. Willie looked at the platter of fresh meat and he picked up several pieces as if looking for something. "Shit, Andy," he said, looking at me, "you mean to tell me Rene didn't find the crotch of the cow?" And everyone laughed, except Rene and our father.

"You should show more respect for Rene," father said to Willie.

"Oh, Dad," Willie replied, "we're only kidding Rene . . . Right Rene?"

Rene looked at me and said, "I don't know. I don't know when you guys are serious and when you're not."

Our father looked hurt for Rene. "Don't pay them any attention, Rene. They've always been renegades. And Louie's the worst one." Willie took each piece from Rene's plate and placed the meat tenderly down into the hole that was the old washing machine drum. When he was satisfied with the way things had gone, he started the washing machine motor and stared down into the pit as though he were looking at movie film. Satisfied again that everything was all right he came to where we were and opened a fresh beer. He was ready to accept any compliments that we might have going his way.

Contrary to Mexican culture, Rene had stayed outside with us. She was standing by me holding the bloody pan by her side. She refused a beer when my father offered her one. It was too cold for her. She was drinking a glass of white wine inside.

The silence that followed was out of respect for Rene being there, as our father had just reminded us. No one wanted to talk for fear of saying something offensive in the presence of a lady. Al, not known for being quiet, finally decided to talk. "That sure smells good," he said of the aroma coming out of the pit. The motor was humming away nicely, the chuga, chuga, chuga sound intermingled with the hissing sound of the fat dripping over the coals. "How long you figure it'll take to get done?" Al asked. He did not mind exchanging pleasantries over the barbecuing of goat. Willie loved to be asked these technical question as if it mattered as much as to calculate the orbit of the comets. In other words Al was not above giving Willie all the rope he wanted.

Willie looked toward the washing machine on fire and cocked an eye for good measure and said with so much certainty, "We'll be eating in two hours," as if nothing could ever occur to prove him wrong.

I said, "Rene, go inside and tell mom that we'll be eating in two hours. I'm sure she wants to know."

Rene left, swinging the pan away from her side, and everybody watched her as she walked. When she rounded the corner and disappeared from view we were able to concentrate on the goat. Willie had gone over and was turning the meat. My father had gone with him and so had Al and they were saying how wonderful it smelled.

Two cars came slowly down the road and they both stopped in front of the house. Two men got out from each car and walked to where we were standing under the tree. As they approached one of them spoke: "Is this the house where the lady is celebrating her one-hundredth birthday?"

We told them it was and they introduced themselves as reporters and photographers for the two daily newspapers, the *Post* and the *Chronicle*. My father said that he would show them the way and he took them inside the house. We could hear Connie and Becky and Angie screaming and laughing inside the house as the newspapermen interviewed Victoria and took her picture. Later we were called inside by my mother. We were wanted for a complete family picture. Once that was done, we returned outside.

I was drinking a beer and looking into the embers and the constantly moving roasting meat and I started to think of Victoria, of so many years ago, of how she had taken care of my great grandfather for all those years, how in some ways she had mistreated the old man and how I had never blamed her for it, how she had sacrificed her life for him and how many people I knew, all women like Victoria, who had done what she did, becoming care-takers of old men, old men whose only joy to give is the

Lionel G. Garcia

joy of being taken care of, causing more trouble than they're worth, women who are saddled with troubles that are not even theirs, women who are known as loving aunts by rascal nephews and nieces, women who enjoy being stepped on and abused. What type of mentality was this? Of what good were their lives if they lived for someone else?

The smell of the embers became the smell of gunshot. I went from my Aunt Victoria to Korea and my ears began to ring and hum and I tasted Sgt. Rodriguez' metallic blood in my mouth once more and I tried in vain to wash the taste away with beer. Then I shifted to Willie's son Chris who was killed in Vietnam during the Tet Offensive. He had gone to fight like his father Willie and his Uncle Andy to see what it was all about. He would come back, he thought, and be a lawyer as his uncle had done. We never saw him alive after he left for Vietnam. The earlier premonition of death that I had had about Willie when he left for the war came true for Willie's son. The night before he left, Willie, Louie and I had taken him out and had gotten drunk with him. We looked for a place that had a naked fat woman dancing on the bar picking up dollar bills and smoking cigarettes with her most intimate of parts, but we could never find one. We could not give him his good luck, could not find it in all this metropolis. He came back in a metal casket. Willie was never the same again, as our father was never the same again since Frankie had died.

The drippings from the meat created a giant sizzle and smoke and I awoke from my dream. "What were you thinking about, son?" my father asked.

"Lot's of things," I answered.

"Willie says the meat is almost done," Al said.

Willie had to add, "Almost. Maybe a few more minutes." He reached down to the meat with a long fork and brought out a piece of meat and he placed it on a cutting board that my father had brought from the house. Using his pocket knife, he cut a piece off the end and chewed it. His eyes closed to describe the delicacy of the meat. "Ummmmmmmmmmmm-mmm," he went, chewing slowly. "It's great."

At this time Louie arrived. I saw the car, but I could not recognize it. Neither could anyone there with me. We all wondered who it could be. It was not Louie's car. This one was a long low white Continental with chrome spoked wheels and red leather interior. Louie was resplendent as the driver. He wore a white suit and dark glasses. When he got out of the car we could see that he was wearing white shoes and all the artificial jewelry that he owned. With him in the front seat was the lusciously edible Donna Marie and in the back seat was Alfredo the illegal and a man who I did not recognize. Louie was having a difficult time getting this man out of the car. After a while he got the man out and it was obvious that the man was blind. Louie was waving at us and leading the blind man along. Donna Marie was wearing a tight-fitting white dress and white shoes. Alfredo was in his disguise: Donna Marie's blond wig and the black cowboy hat and now something new, a pair of sunglasses. He was wearing Louie's old clothes, an old black wool suit with a white shirt and an old wide tie. The blind man was in khakis and cowboy boots.

The errant birds, observing the arrival of such a group, began to fly off the gables and return to the ice-houses of the neighborhood.

As Louie approached, pushing the blind man in front of him, he was laughing. "Shit man," he said, "we lost the fucking dog."

"What dog?" Al asked.

"The fucking dog for this man to see," Louie said and it started us laughing.

"We forgot the dog at the beer-joint," Donna Marie explained.

"Donna Marie," Louie said, "will you please go inside with the women. This is a Mexican party."

Donna Marie smiled at us and said, "Louie, you need to take me in to introduce me."

"Just go in there and tell them you're with me, Donna. No one is going to say anything."

Donna Marie turned after smiling at us one more time and started dutifully toward the house, but not before saying, "Hello, Andy. How ya doing?"

Playfully, Louie said, "Quit flirting with my little brother and get into the house."

And that was when she left.

"What . . . What happened with the dog?" Willie asked Louie. He was still laughing.

"We . . . We . . ." Louie tried to begin but he started to laugh at seeing us laughing. "We . . . We were all drinking beer at some place, and hell, I realized what time it was . . . it was . . . and I knew I was in trouble. I knew if I didn't get here for the barbecue and Aunt Victoria's party, that Mom would kill me . . . Shit man . . . I got up running and Alfredo grabs our friend Clete here and throws him in the car while I'm trying to pay . . . Fuck it! I've got money to pay. But I'm keeping tabs, Andy . . . Anyway, the little shit-head takes Clete and throws him in the car . . . They haven't been seeing eye to eye all day long anyway." The pun started us laughing again. "That's true," Louie said trying to get serious. "These two fuckers have been fighting all day long." He placed his cupped hand to the side of his mouth so that Alfredo and Clete could not hear him. "The

221

illegal thinks that God hates Clete. Can you believe that shit?" Louie readjusted the large medallion that hung from his neck.

"Why is it that he thinks that God does not love the blind man?" our father asked innocently.

"Who knows why these Mexicans think the way they do?" Louie said. "But back to the story. I run out and get in the car and we take off. Right now . . . just right now when we pull up, Clete asks for his dog. It blows my mind! I start to laugh. We left the goddam dog in the beer joint!" Louie glanced at Clete and it appeared as though Clete was about to cry. "Don't worry Clete," Louie advised him, "we'll go get it later. No one's going to mess with the goddam dog. Mexicans are afraid of big dogs. They won't mess with him."

Willie was laughing hard. Al was slapping one of his short legs, doubled up in laughter. Clete was standing next to Louie holding on to Louie's arm. Alfredo had gotten some of Louie's gall rubbed off on him. He reached for a cold beer out of the tub without being invited. Louie wanted a beer and Clete wanted a beer. Alfredo was nice enough to give them each one.

Clete swayed back and forth as though he was wired to some internal beat that only he could hear and the swaying made Louie move with him. Clete looked skyward and said that he was worried. "Maybe we could call the place to be sure the dog is all right," he said to the sky.

Louie made a face showing disgust. "Yeah," he answered abruptly, "just wait a goddam minute will you? Can't you see that we just got here? Give me a break, will you? You're getting on my nerves too, you know that."

"I'm sorry, Louie. I just worry about my dog all the time."

"That goddam dog gets treated better than you do, so what's the problem?" Louie said.

We were all feeling sorry for the blind man, but it seemed as though he and Louie knew each other well and both enjoyed the give and take. The one that was not enjoying the banter was my father. He did not like Louie to be disrespectful to our guests and, rather than create a scene at such an important occasion, he took his beer with him and went inside. He could not bear to listen to Louie talk. We did not ignore his leaving, but neither did we talk about it. Louie knew, we all knew, why our father had left.

"Where were you last night and this morning?" I asked Louie.

"Man, you wouldn't believe it," Louie said. He had gotten Clete's arm off him and had gone to put his arm around Willie. Both were looking at the meat and admiring it. "Goddamit. Last night Alfredo and I took off with Donna Marie. We had a good time, didn't we Alfredo?"

Alfredo was on his third or fourth beer and he nodded his small head inside the blond wig, moving his extra large hat up and down. He was looking at the washing machine contraption through his sunglasses and wondering about it.

Louie said, "Hey Andy, get Clete over here so he can see this washing machine." He laughed to himself. "Goddammit, I keep forgetting that Clete can't see."

I took the shaking Clete with me to the washing machine and he could feel how hot it was. He had the palm of his hand almost touching the metal drum.

"Can you tell what it is, Clete?" Willie asked him.

"It sounds like a motor but it's hot on the outside," Clete said. "What is it? It sounds like one of those old washing machines."

"That's what it is," Willie said proudly. "What do you think of that? Making a barbecue pit out of an old washing machine?"

"That's cool."

"Shit man," Louie said, "it's great. My dad's a smart man."

Louie kept on hugging Willie. Willie said, "Andy was looking for you. Where in the hell've you been?"

"First of all, last night we got involved in a fight. So this illegal gets killed."

"At the Four Roses," I mentioned under my breath.

Louie looked at me in disbelief. He said, "How'd you know? This only happened last night."

"I was at the Four Roses this morning tracking you down."

"Then you know about the fight?"

"Yeah, I know about the fight. I heard all about it."

"Do you know that this morning they're blaming me for the fight? Shit man, I didn't do anything. But you know how it is. If anything goes wrong . . . hell . . . blame it on Louie. I get the blame. I didn't have nothing to do with the fight. I was gone as soon as it started. What do they take me for, a fool? I ain't hanging around no Mexican fight. No sir. I've been around too many to know that you get your ass out of there fast. Then I found out that this guy gets killed. And you know what? I also found out this morning that no one wanted to leave. They just let the guy die. People were shooting pool, playing dominoes, watching TV. Well, when the police finally show up, they call an ambulance and then they want to know what happened. Everybody says that they don't know. No one saw a thing, man. Everybody was in the rest-room taking a leak. The police counted forty-five guys taking a leak when the guy gets shot . . . Did Carlos tell you that, Andy?"

"No," I answered.

"I knew he wouldn't. He blamed me for the whole mess, didn't he?"

I wasn't about to start any more trouble between Carlos and Louie. "No, he didn't," I said. "He didn't blame you at all."

"Well," Louie said, arranging his bracelets around his wrist, "that's a change."

We heard the commotion in the house as the door opened and the two reporters and photographers came out. They walked toward us and Willie invited them for a beer, but they said they had to leave and thanked us. All four of them stared at the washing machine contraption spewing barbecue smoke. They thought it was better not to ask what it was we were doing.

My father had accompanied them as far as the corner of the house and he waited for them there. Now, as they left, he walked them to their cars. We could hear him talking about Victoria.

After they had left he called me over as he walked toward the house. I walked over to him as he stopped midway between the house and the tree, undecided whether to go inside or not. "Is Louie still talking trash?" he wanted to know as I approached him. "I'm not going back there if he is."

"You shouldn't pay too much attention to him."

He gave a fatherly look of exasperation. "He's getting worse, you know. He's never brought anything but dishonor to this family, Andres. You know that. Today he shows up with that prostitute. Who gives him the right to bring a prostitute here? Doesn't he have better sense? Isn't that an insult to your sacred mother? The prostitute's in the house as one of the family. I was raised to believe that that is wrong. Sure I knew the prostitutes of my time in San Diego, but this is wrong. Wrong. Remember how he and Willie brought the fat lady to the house after the war? Isn't that one of the reasons why we're here in Houston? . . . He dressed like a pimp in his white suite. He wears all that fake jewelry. Where's he working now?"

"I thought he was working with Willie at the can company? Didn't Willie get him a job?"

"That's it, I don't know. I don't know what he's doing, except hiring out that girl friend of his and making money off her. He's into dope too."

"How do you know?"

"I don't have evidence, if that's what you want. But I've suspected it for a long time. Sometimes he acts like he's on cocaine. You just watch him. He'll be real happy and then he wants to fight."

"How do you know so much about cocaine?"

"Cocaine has been around for a long time in Mexico. I've known a lot of people on it."

"Well, knowing Louie, I wouldn't doubt it."

"And where did he get the car?"

I was trying for the sake of harmony, at least for today, to take Louie's side. "He probably borrowed it from a friend," I surmised.

"I hope so," my father sighed hopefully. "And what about the two men he's got with him? One of them is blind and the other one looks like a crazy person . . . dressed crazy. Who would dress like that and be sane?"

I had to admit some of that was my doing. I said, "One of them is my fault. The one dressed like a crazy person with the blond wig and black hat is a client of mine. I'm taking him to the police tomorrow morning. He's giving himself up."

"What did he do?" my father asked, disturbed. "Is he a wanted man?"

"You'll find out about it in the newspapers on Tuesday," I said.

He looked at me and shook his head. "And you too? Are you bringing criminals to the house to visit your parents?"

"I didn't know that Louie was bringing him here."

"Doesn't Louie know about him?"

"No," I said. "It's all my fault. You're the only one I've told about this. I'd appreciate it if you don't mention it to anybody . . . I'll get in trouble if you do."

"Don't worry, I won't mention it," he said, disappointed, and started to walk away.

I couldn't let him go off without trying to help him. "Louie's a better person than you give him credit for," I told him. "Louie's got a big heart."

He slowly turned back to face me, stared for the longest time and said, "If you believe he has a big heart, answer me this: What's the blind man doing with him?"

"I don't know," I admitted.

He thought for a while. "What is he getting from Louie? What is Louie getting from him?"

"Louie takes him out . . ."

"But is that all? Would Louie put up with a blind man just to take him out?"

"You're saying that he does more for Clete than take him out . . . is that it?"

"Yes . . . That's what I'm saying."

"He gets dope and liquor and sex from Louie. Is that it?"

My father shook his head and stared at Louie from that distance as Louie joked with Al and Willie. "He's incurable," he said. "What I wonder also is what is he doing with the blind man's wife? With Louie you have to look at the woman. What's going on with the woman? What's the blind man's wife doing while Louie has him out in the beer joints?"

"You mean to tell me that you think that Clete's wife is having an affair while Louie takes him out?"

"More than an affair. I believe he's pimping for her."

"Have you seen the wife?"

"No," he answered, and I could see in his eyes that the solution came to him even as he spoke. He said, "But I would be willing to bet you that she is a beautiful woman. Louie wouldn't be with the blind man if she wasn't . . . Trust me," he said when he saw that I was thinking about the possibilities. "Louie's incorrigible," he said as he walked away.

I couldn't help but grin in amazement at how uncommonly serious our father had become in his old age, at how much he had changed. It had always been my mother who had worried about the family. My father had had a good time at the beer joints as we were growing up. His many years had blunted the tip of his memory and he had forgotten how much like Louie he had been in those days, his uncaring selfishness a badge of his *machismo*, just as it had been for every man in town. Nonetheless, for many years now the family had forgiven him his sins of neglect because we felt that during our destitute years he needed to belong among the *machos* in order to maintain his self-respect. I had studied him this afternoon as he sat next to Aunt Victoria for our photographs. I saw a shadow of what was once a care-free man; he was bothered unconsciously by the unpredictability and mystery of death that was ready to take him, thin and frail, infinitely smaller than he once was, his eyes retracted like heavy metal bearings into his skull, his nose grown larger, pocked and flatter, looking more each year like his father, his mouth smaller almost without lips. And I remembered at that instant, as the photographers made him stand and then sit as they arranged him and Victoria for their photograph, that one day out in the fields when we had been picking cotton when there was no food to go around, that he gave what little he had to us and walked away like the dominant lion shunning food, saying that he was not hungry.

A car approached slowly as though looking for a house number and the driver, a middle-aged man very neatly dressed and groomed, turned into the old unused driveway, the one that at one time had led past the tree to the garage. He rolled the window down and asked me if this was where Connie's parents lived. When I said yes, he parked the car away from the house, got out and said that he was Connie's friend. By this time my father had walked back to where I was to see who was in the car. We introduced ourselves to him.

"Connie's inside," my father said, brusquely.

The man thanked us and started toward the house. He was dressed in a dark suit with a perfectly white shirt, red tie and black cowboy lizard-skin boots. As the saying went, he looked as clean as a drop of water.

My father drew in a deep breath, as if it were his last. "I wish Connie would not invite anyone to our house. God only knows who this man is."

Now I had to defend Connie. "He seems like a nice guy," I said. Willie was yelling for us to join their group, so we walked over there and I told my father not to get angry with Louie. "Just ignore him," I begged.

He was holding on to my arm as we walked slowly. "Son," he said, "I can't ignore him." I could feel the boneyness of his fingers as though some claw had hold of my arm. "I'll stay a while, but that will be all . . ." He stumbled on a hole in the yard and he had to re-grab my arm to keep from falling. He ignored almost having fallen and said, "Sometimes I wonder how much better we would have been if we had stayed in San Diego . . . Grow up in a small town . . . Small schools . . . more around our people. Maybe Frankie would still be alive, don't you think?"

When we got there Willie was telling a joke and out of respect for us he began again, "This bad-ass gringo cowboy, he walks in this Mexican beer joint and he's raising all kinds of hell, shooting his gun off. There's a Mexican with this big moustache and a big hat playing the piano. The gringo shoots at the piano player and shoots a button off the piano player's cuff. The piano player just keeps playing, his back to the gringo. The gringo says, 'Give me a double whiskey' and he pounds on the bar. The bartender says, 'You want some butter with your whiskey, señor?' The bad-ass gringo says, 'What the shit do I want butter for? I'm drinking my whiskey, not cooking it!' The bartender says, 'The butter is for the gun, señor.' The gringo says, 'For the gun? What the shit do I need butter for my gun for?' The bartender says, 'So that you can put it on the barrel, señor, because as soon as Pancho Villa finishes playing his mother's song, he's going to ram the gun up your ass.' "

We were laughing when Connie came out of the house carrying a pan and bringing along her boy friend. By that time the jokes had started and if she had not intruded, we probably would have kept on. She wanted to introduce her new boy friend to all of us. His name was Ellie, but that was in Houston, in that part of the Mexican community that was trying to be Anglicized. His real name, we found out, was Eulalio Barrera, born in Alice, Texas, a town bigger than San Diego and ten miles east. He no longer pronounced Barrera with the trill on the double r's, instead he Anglicized it with much difficulty.

"Ellie Barrera," he said, speaking self-consciously like an Anglo, introducing himself and shaking everyone's hand, the feeling of despair coming over him every time he spoke his name among the hostile crowd. "No one calls me Eulalio anymore," he apologized.

"It's too difficult," Connie explained, parroting his words.

"I don't know why they named me like that. You know how parents are. I've had a lot of ribbing in all the years I spent in the Army. You see, I had to use my real name for military records. No one knew who I was every time my records caught up with me. It was all very confusing. I tried to have my name changed but . . ." He let the sentence hang there, realizing he had already made too much of his name.

"That's nothing," my father said, chiding him, "I had two uncles named Nepomuceno and Hermenegildo. That's worse. How'd you like that?"

"That would really fuck you up," Louie said.

Ellie laughed and said, "Then for sure I would have changed my name."

"I'm glad my name is Alfredo," the illegal said in perfect English, leaning against the hackberry.

"Cletus ain't bad," Clete said, swaying to the rhythm of the washing machine.

"I knew a lot of Barrera's in Alice," my father told him, looking to the ground and trying to remember who they were.

"Oh," Ellie said, in his Anglo voice, "I haven't been in Alice in years and years. Ever since I joined the service. Over forty years. I went in when I was eighteen." (Everyone quickly added up how old he was. He was just right for Connie.) "I never went back. When I retired I came to live in Houston. This place is the only place for me. This is a cosmopolitan town. You've got everything in Houston. Better than New York."

"Yeah," Willie said, "we've got crime in the streets, murder, rape, burglaries, hold-ups, assaults, pollution, you name it."

Our father offered Ellie a beer and Connie gave Willie the pan and went back inside, secure in the thought that maybe we had taken a liking to him. Our father walked Ellie to the tub of iced beer under the hackberry.

"What's that?" Ellie asked him, stopping and pointing at the smoking washing machine whose motor was groaning its chuga-chuga under the stress of the intense heat.

"It's a barbeque pit made out of an old washing machine," our father explained again and then he stopped before he gave him the beer to see what Ellie's reply was going to be.

"I've never seen anything like that," Ellie said, diplomatically, studying the contraption. And, of course, our father took it as a compliment and handed him the ice-cold beer.

Finally we were called in to eat. Willie and Louie took the meat out of the pit and put it in the large clean darkened pan that Connie had brought out. Al, without being told, went inside the ominously tilting garage and unplugged the washing machine. It gave out a long hot moan of relief before it hissed to a stop. Willie and Louie carried the hot pan between them, the meat trailing smoke toward us as we walked behind them. Alfredo the illegal walked next in line, staggering from the beer, his loose fitting suit making him comical, his blond wig slightly off center. Al had run back from the garage and had grabbed Clete's arm and was guiding him behind Alfredo. My father and Ellie and I were at the rear talking about small town life in South Texas, the life that my father felt had eluded us, the life that would have made us more responsible.

In the silence of the neighborhood as the sun was setting on another day, we heard Clete's lament as he shook his sun-glassed head at the sky, "I wonder where my dog is?" he cried.

CHAPTER 12

After dinner the men went outside into the twilight to drink while the women cleaned the kitchen. Al had come out ahead of us and had turned on the lights from inside the garage, the lights from the naked bulbs that hung from the hackberry. Louie had called the ice-house and the dog was safe. The dog was sleeping and only once in a while, he was told, did the dog get up and look for his master Clete. At those times he appeared disoriented and would sniff out some newly arrived illegal alien in hopes that it was his master that had come back to rescue him. Clete was relieved but still concerned as he looked down at his shoes without seeing the small ant hidden under the leaf that it carried as it tried to cross one of his wing-tips. "I'll never feel right until my dog is with me," he said after taking a long drink from his beer, the lenses on his sunglasses full of grease from the meal. "I've never left my dog behind," he worried. "I don't know what got into me." Louie took Clete's sunglasses and fogged them with his breath and cleaned them.

Ellie had quit drinking beer. He complained that it gave him heartburn. To take the place of beer he had gone to the car and had brought back a fifth of bourbon. He was drinking it straight out of the bottle. He started passing the bottle around insisting that we all drink. Each trying to outdo the other, we finished that bottle in a short time and Ellie went back and this time opened the trunk and brought out another bottle. He had a case of bourbon in the trunk. "I always carry a case everywhere I go," he explained. "A habit from my Army days."

I was feeling a detached presence to those around me from mixing the whiskey and the beer. For some reason we were standing perfectly satisfied around the hot washing machine, its bowels now empty except for the burning embers, its motor now as still as the wings of the birds that had returned to the gables of the house and the garage, as though we were paying homage to the contraption for the good food it had provided us. Perhaps it was the warmth we were seeking now that the sun had gone down and the chill had returned to the air. Regardless, I was not cold. I was not anything. I was numb and drunk.

Louie wanted to show off his car, but by this time we were not very interested in walking any distances. He insisted and we went, reluctantly. Who cared what the car looked like. The car was a customized Continental with a long hood with red leather interior, a built-in bar and car phone. Louie wouldn't deny that it was his nor would he deny that it wasn't. He enjoyed trying to keep us guessing, although we knew that the car could not possibly belong to him. Anyway, none of us showed too much interest in the car and we took a cursory look and came back to the comfort of the hackberry.

Three more people showed up at the party before the trouble began: Dolores, Father Dominguez and Father Diaz.

Dolores arrived and I almost missed seeing her. She had parked at the opposite side of the house, behind my car. She had planned on being there for a very short while. She had come to bring her annual gift, since she and Victoria loved each other so much. I had gone in to tell Connie that Ellie was very drunk and that she should be thinking of taking him home. When I entered I saw Dolores standing by Victoria, hugging her, and she looked very classy, married to the very successful physician, Dr. Obregon, and it showed in the long mink and diamonds that she wore. I couldn't help but think of how far she had come, from an insecure dark skinned girl that fretted about being in the sun, who had run screaming through the hallways on our wedding night, scaring the old people because I had tried to claim my husbandly rights, who had only learned to make love inside the cave that she made from her blanket, who had disturbed a whole law firm when she caused the senior partner to jump from the balcony at the Warwick Hotel to escape her scream, taking his wife with him in the fall and injuring themselves as well as the pruned ligustrums, all because when the lights were turned off he had attempted to touch her most initmate of parts. She saw me as I entered and she helplessly blushed crimson, as I remembered her delicate intimate part at the point of my mind and I could sense that she remembered that I had not seen her for many years and she wanted to tell me that she no longer screamed enough to depolarize the hemispheres and that the only visions of flying parrots were not between the eyes but between her legs, that there at the seat of her most intimate hairless self, parrots flew and spoke the truth. Immediately I realized that I desired her more than ever, not because she was more beautiful than Rene or Donna Marie, but because she had been such a distant figure all our years and at my age I wanted all the things I could not have. As I heard her new-found guttural laugh, I could have kicked myself at that moment for not having taken the shine of youth off her. That job, lamentably, had been accomplished by her present husband and how I hated him for it.

She kissed Victoria on her hollowed cheek and very bubbly, vibrantly, gingerly, walked out, almost ran out, waving goodbye. Everyone was shouting happily at her. Finally as she reached the door, she greeted me and my heart raced like it had when I had first seen between the legs of the fat lady that smoked the cigarettes and folded the dollar bills with her offensively large cunt. She was gone as an apparition would leave and the quiet in the room was embarrassing. It was Rene's turn to blush. Not only did I know what everyone was thinking, everyone knew what everyone else was thinking: Who would have thought that dark little nun-like Dolores would steal the spotlight from Rene one day?

Father Rodriguez and Father Diaz were another story. They arrived late because they had had to say the afternoon mass by themselves since there were no altar boys to be found when the Oilers were losing. Father Diaz was not wearing his new artificial left leg. He was having great difficulty with a substitute, what looked like the end of a table leg protruding from under the hem of his black trousers.

"Goddam Altar Society," Father Rodriguez said as he started on a plate that our mother had fixed for him and Father Diaz.

"Aren't we going to bless this food?" asked the young Father Diaz.

"No," Father Rodriguez scolded him. "Let's eat."

Our mother winced when she heard the priest. "Goddam old crows," he kept on. Father Diaz was eating silently as we gathered around the table to watch them eat. Louie, Willie, Ellie, Clete, Al and Alfredo had stayed outside to keep on drinking. "Who would think that the sonsofbitches would take away poor Father Diaz' leg? And for the smallest of things."

Father Diaz shook his head at Father Rodriguez, but the ancient priest was not to be denied. "For the smallest of things," he repeated. "And they almost had it paid for. How cruel the old whores were."

"That's enough, Father Rodriguez," Father Diaz warned him.

"It's all in the Bingo," Father Rodriguez said. "The whole church has become one big Bingo."

We could tell that the conversation was the last thing Father Diaz wanted to hear. "Forget it, Father," he said, eating, with his mouth full.

"How can one forget," Father Rodriguez explained, "when our own congregation turns against us."

"It can't be that bad," our mother said.

"It's worse," Father Rodriguez informed us, eyeing us all solemnly. "They've taken away Father Diaz' leg and now there is talk that I'm to be retired." He looked all around us once more, this time counterclockwise, tears coming to his eyes. "I ask you . . . is it that important?"

"That's enough, Father," Father Diaz said. And to us he tried to explain: "It's not as bad as Father Rodriguez thinks. The poor ladies of the Altar Society ran out of money. That's all. I can get the leg back shortly.

The congregation does not have to lose all the money invested. Shortly I will go by the bank and pay the last payment and everything will be all right."

Father Rodriguez shook his head as he finished the plate and pushed it away. "They could have taken out one bingo pot, that's all. One large pot, the one next to the Grand Pot could have been eliminated and the leg could have been paid for. What's the name of that pot?"

"The Little Holy Pot," our bingo playing mother said.

"Yes . . . that one," Father Rodriguez remembered.

Father Diaz arose with the same difficulty he had had sitting down with his new leg. Father Rodriguez arose also and thanked our mother for inviting them. As Father Rodriguez reached the door he turned around and blessed us in Latin, making an imaginary crucifix in the air with his powerful hand and he must have mistakenly thought that he was on the altar, for he turned around and genuflected before he opened the door and let himself and Father Diaz out. Father Diaz, as he was pushed out, made a circular motion with his finger around his temple to indicate to us that Father Rodriguez was insane.

"I don't care if he curses. He's a very good man," my father said outside after Father Rodriguez was gone. "He's been very good to us for so many years."

Willie said, "He's getting old, isn't he?"

My father looked at the silhouettes of the tucked-in birds on the gables and said, "Yes, he's getting old. And when one gets old, things don't work like they should anymore. He's in his early eighties."

"It's hard to believe," I said, "that he's that old. I remember when he came here he was such a young man."

"He's been very good to our family," my father defended him. "He's supported us through many difficult times. He buried Frankie when he didn't have to, when the Bishop told him not to."

"I thought you didn't like priests?" Louie asked my father.

"That was when I was young. They had done things to me when I was young. But this priest has been good. Very good. Your mother and I love him a lot. There are priests and there are priests. They're like anyone else. You find some good ones and some bad ones. We have been blessed to have had Father Rodriguez around for so many years . . . Now Father Diaz is another story, I hear. He's more interested in the money."

Here it was December and no one had mentioned Christmas.

CHAPTER 13

The trouble began with Ellie. The minute I saw him I knew that he was a troublemaker. I had been dealing with troublemakers for twenty-three years in the practice of law and I knew a troublemaker when I saw and heard one. Watching him drink was watching a time bomb getting ready to explode.

"There wasn't a sonofabitch that could keep up with me on a fifty caliber machine gun," Ellie said, trying to incite someone. "I could fire the sonofabitch and shoot a gnat's ass off at fifty yards." He looked around with a challenging air of defiance.

Willie couldn't take that lying down. He looked at him and said, "You're a fucking liar."

Ellie jumped toward Wille in a threatening manner. "What do you mean a fucking liar?" he yelled, stopping short of bumping Willie.

Louie was about to jump on Ellie. I tried to bring peace. "Let's just drop it," I told Willie. "Let the man have his say."

Willie didn't appreciate that. "Why not shut him up?"

My father raised his hands in a friendly gesture. "Gentlemen," he said as though holding court, "let's not get into an argument. Let's be civil. This man is our guest. He is Connie's friend."

Clete was holding onto the tree, drunk, and he cried, "Let's not start anything, men. Let's just have us a good time."

Louie said that if anybody was going to start anything he was going to finish it. Our father walked to the house. "Then there is not much I can do except go in and call the police," he said.

I said, "Please, father, don't call the police. I can handle this. There will not be any fighting. I guarantee that."

"Well, son," he replied, "then I leave it up to you. I will not be a part of this mess. I'm going in." And he started toward the house but before he had gone half-way, he turned back and said to Al: "Al, do me a favor, will you?"

Al was staggering under the darkness of the hackberry. "Sure Pop," he murmured in the solitude of his drunkenness. "Anything."

Father scratched his head and said, "Al, before you turn in will you roll the barbecue pit into the garage?"

"Sure thing, Pop," he said. And our father continued on his way, hating Al more than ever for calling him Pop.

Willie kept on. "Tell us more lies about how good you were," he said to Ellie.

Ellie pulled up on his trousers and tried to stare a hole into Willie. He spoke slowly. "I was the greatest that ever lived on any weapon. Anything."

"The way you drink you couldn't find your ass with both hands," Willie said.

Louie chuckled at what Willie had said.

"Be careful how you talk," Ellie cautioned Willie. "More than one man has paid dearly for talking to Ellie Barrera like that. Hell, judo, karate, I know it all. Served in the Orient for ten years. I can do anything, whip anybody's ass."

Willie and Louie laughed at him. Louie said, "Shit, man, I see little people from Mexico that can whip your ass good any day of the week. Little farts, like my friend here." He pointed at Alfredo the illegal. Alfredo was drunk against the tree next to Clete. Al, being more cautious, was beginning to move away from the group.

"Look," I told them, "why don't we just forget all about it. No one is going to fight. I'm not going to let anyone fight here today. This is a birthday party for our Aunt Victoria and we are here to celebrate it. Let's knock it off."

Ellie looked at me defiantly and rocked backwards on his heels, trying to focus on me, and said, "You're an arrogant mother fucker if I ever saw one. You walk around here like hot shit. Who the fuck do you think you are? Ain't nobody appointed you the General."

"All right," I said, "that's enough. This is our house and we need to respect it."

"Respect, shit," he said quickly. "You guys ain't showed me no respect since I got here. You mother fuckers know who the shit I am? Connie ain't told you fuckers who I am?"

"I'm sorry but Connie hasn't said a word to us about you," I told him.

"Fucking Sergeant Major I was. Division Sergeant Major . . . Could shoot a gnat's ass off at fifty yards. . . ." He took a drink from his bottle and wiped his mouth on his coat sleeve. "Could jump off a fucking airplane at any time any place." Louie said, "Seems to me you've had too much to drink. Your ass is overloading your mouth."

He should have never said that to Ellie. "I'm going to have to teach you a lesson, you mother fucker," Ellie said, enraged, and he started toward Louie, his hands extended in an Oriental manner, ready to strike. Willie got in between and pushed Ellie back. Ellie shouted, "Leave me alone. What's the matter, can't you fight your fights. Gotta have big brother defend you. And little brother too? What's a matter with you sonsofbit-ches? Can't you fight one on one . . . hand to hand? You're afraid I'll kill you sonsofbitches? You're afraid I know how to kill a man and not feel bad about it."

I was trying to cool him off. "No need to get so angry, Ellie," I said. Louie was anxious for a fight. The struggling Willie was the only thing keeping them apart. "Who cares about the machine gun?" I reasoned. "Fifty caliber, thirty caliber. Hell, I was the ammo carrier for a fifty in Korea. That's no big deal. I couldn't hit the side of a barn with the sonofabitch."

Al's voice was heard coming from the darkness beyond the hackberry, "Neither could I. Only John Wayne could fire a fifty caliber from his hip."

"Fuck John Wayne," Ellie said, backing off, knowing that he could not get to Louie without fighting Willie. "You mother fuckers are making fun of me now. Nobody makes fun of me and gets away with it."

Father had asked Connie to come out and take Ellie home. She and Becky and Angie came out of the house walking angrily through the semi-darkness illuminated only by the small naked bulb on the opposite side of the house. Connie started talking very gently to Ellie as she approached him, as one would a renegade animal, and it soothed his anger. Angie's and Becky's presence calmed Willie and Louie and they both backed off.

"You've been drinking too much again, Ellie," Connie said to him. "Let's get out of here. Just forget all about it. Everybody's going to forget about all of this, right?"

We all said it would be forgotten. "Take him home, Connie," I whispered to her. "You need to drive him home."

Ellie was beginning to retreat to the car. Connie was pushing him gently in order not to injure his pride and at the same time trying to keep him on his feet.

"I need a drink," Ellie said, smiling now.

"No you don't," Connie said.

"Yes, I do," he insisted.

"When we get you home."

"Right now!"

"No. How much have you had already?"

"Not enough. Not enough to block these mother fuckers from my mind."

Connie had him going in the direction of the house. She was trying to get him inside the house so that he could take his leave from Aunt Victo-ria, but she was having a hard time. He was drunk, but he was still very strong. He was more inclined to go toward the car.

"Take him home," I shouted to her. "Forget about saying goodbye to Aunt Victoria. She'll understand. I'll tell her goodbye for you and Ellie."

"Thanks, Andy," she said.

Ellie wasn't through. He said to Connie with the intention that we would over-hear, "Bunch of mother fuckers never served time."

Willie replied instantly. "Shut up ass-hole. I survived the death march of Bataan. I survived the fucking Japanese. Andy surivived the gooks. He had a goddam grenade go off in his face. Any scream sets him off. I can't think straight. We're all messed up and you say we didn't do nothing."

Ellie yelled back. "You bastards never had someone die on you."

Willie listened passionately to what Ellie had said and I could see in his eyes that we were going to have serious trouble if this continued. "My son was killed in Nam you no good sonofabitch," he screamed, tears rolling from his eyes.

Willie was walking toward the retreating Ellie and Connie. So was Louie. Becky and Angie were pleading with Willie to go inside, trying to hold him back. I was trying to stop Louie, my arms around his waist. Becky and Angie could not handle Willie. I let go of Louie to help them and still Willie kept on. He had one purpose and that was to get to Ellie. Ellie turned around as if to shout some more and he saw that Willie was coming after him and getting closer. Ellie broke free from Connie and ran, staggering, to the car and opened the car door on the driver's side and he reached under the seat. Instinctively everyone knew that he was reaching for a gun. Willie saw him and immediately stopped and pushed us out of the way. We started running, Becky and Angie toward the house and Willie and Louie and myself toward the tree. We were yelling, "He's got a gun! He's got a gun!" Clete tried to run but he fell over Alfredo, who had passsed out at the base of the tree. I jumped on top of Clete to keep him still. If it were possible, we were all going to hide behind the tree. Ellie turned on the car lights and hit the high beam. He lit up the whole back yard. We could see that he was using the open car door to steady his pistol as he aimed at us. We could hear Connie begging him not to shoot.

He fired two shots rapidly before Connie broke a bottle of bourbon over his head and he fell to the ground. The first shot hit the trunk of the hackberry and ricocheted upward into the branches causing a mild rain of dead winter leaves and twigs to fall on us. At the same time, the sleeping birds heard the powerful noise from the .357 Magnum and flew noisily from the gables back to the safety of the ice-houses of the neighborhood. We knew he had used a .357 Magnum because the other shot made a small entry hole, about an inch across, into the base of the washing-machine barbecue-pit contraption, but the exit hole, however, tore out an eight inch square section that irremediably ruined our father's well-known handiwork. We agreed later that he was lucky not to have been there to personally witness the death of his beloved invention.

CHAPTER 14

When the police arrived I thought that our father had called them from inside the house. They turned into the old driveway very deliberately, drove past Ellie's car and Louie's Continental and slowly came to a stop, even as we were on the ground protecting ourselves from Ellie's gunshots. Connie had helped the drunk and injured Ellie inside the car. The police helped to illuminate this scene with their headlights: Willie was on his knees peeping behind the hackberry and cursing at Ellie; Louie was propped with his back against the hackberry, next to Willie asking if anyone could see Ellie to tell us if the shooting was over; his white suit had gotten stained at the the knees and elbows when he had crawled behind Willie; his large gold-plated medallion had swung over and rested on his left shoulder. Louie said "Oh shit," when he saw the police car. "Oh shit is right," Willie agreed. Clete was moaning as if wounded, asking for Louie to help him. He couldn't move with the drunk Alfredo on top of him. Al had run off and was inside the garage. We could hear him whispering, "Hey guys, is the coast clear?" I was next to Clete and Alfredo, on my belly, and I jumped up when I saw the police car. My first instinct was to grab Alfredo. He had lost his large black hat and blond wig; both were lying on the ground, the wig inside the hat like a decapitated mannequin, close to where he had fallen. I got him on his feet and ran him inside before the police could get out of the car.

Becky was the only one in the kitchen. "Who called the police?" I asked running in with Alfredo and she looked at me like she didn't know what I was talking about.

"No one that I know called them," she said. "We didn't. I was just as surprised as you when they drove up."

I said, "Where's everyone?"

"They ran to the neighbor's before the shooting started. Dad kept saying that we better get out before Ellie went crazy. Mom and Dad took Rene and Angie and Aunt Victoria and the whore with them across the yard next door."

"They're hiding?" I asked.

"They're hiding," Becky confirmed.

"Why didn't you go?" I asked Becky.

"I just couldn't leave Al. I was scared for him. I was looking out through the window."

239

"Al's okay," I told her.

"Yes, I know," she answered. "I was glad when I saw him running into the garage." She studied Alfredo and asked, "What happened to his wig and hat?"

"They fell off during the shooting," I told her. "And you can take his sun-glasses off too. He isn't going to need them anymore. Hide him for me, will you?"

I went outside and the police had started their emergency lights whirling. They were still inside the car calling over the radio. I could see Connie sitting in Ellie's car, parked alongside the Continental. She didn't know whether to leave or not. I was hoping that she would, now that the police were distracted with the radio. I couldn't see Ellie. He was probably on the floor of the car passed out from the blow to the head and the bourbon. When I returned to the hackberry, Louie was dusting Clete off by the light of the naked bulbs. Clete was looking up to the branches, asking what had happened. "Just a crazy drunk Mexican shooting at us," Louie told him as he straightened Clete's shirt and trousers. "What else is new?"

Willie had gone to check the washing-machine barbeque-pit that appeared to have exploded with embers like a shooting star during the second shot. We knew it had taken a direct hit. As he walked around to the back side he found the exit hole from the gunshot. "Goddam," he said, shaking his head. "Come and look at this."

We went and checked the hole that the bullet had made and we were relieved that none of us had gotten hit.

"I'll tell you what," Willie said seriously studying the enormous hole, "Dad's going to have a shit fit when he sees this."

"And he's going to blame it all on me too," Louie predicted.

"Hey guys," Al whispered from inside the garage, "can I come out now?"

"Yeah," I said to Al, looking at the hole along with Louie and Willie, "come on out."

The officers got out and walked to where we were and shined a light on us. "Good evening," one of them said. In keeping with the Mayor's campaign promise both policemen were Mexican-American. "What's going on?"

"Oh," Willie said, "we're just having a good time. Drinking a little beer and eating a little goat meat. You all are too late. There ain't much left."

"Thank you," one of the officers replied very politely, "but we just ate."

"It smells good," the other one said, smiling at the aroma coming out of the back side of the washing machine. They both walked around the washing-machine and inspected it, wondering what it was and now even more curious at it with the big gunshot hole. "What happened?" the policeman asked.

"Oh," I answered, "just a little accident . . . a melt down."

"Yeah," Willie said, "just like the Russkies."

"Is this a barbeque pit?" the other one asked.

"Yeah," Willie said. "You want to see how it works?"

"No," they answered. "We'll just take your word for it."

"What could we do for you?" I asked, wanting to know why they were there. Had our father called them from next door?

"It's the white Continental with the red interior parked by the side of the house. Does anyone here happen to know who's driving the car?"

Louie said, "I am, why?"

The officers shined the light in Louie's face. "What's your name?"

Louie said, "If you take your fucking light off my face I'll tell you. You're blinding me."

"I'm asking you a question," the officer said. "What's your name?"

"Get your fucking light off my face and I'll tell you."

"Why don't you put your flashlight down," I said. "There's enough light here to see who he is."

One of them replied, "Sir, would you please stay out of this?"

"I won't," I told him.

The officer said, "Sir, are you going to interfere with a policeman?"

"Damn right I'm interfering with a policeman. Who the hell do you think you are?"

Willie said, "Come on Andy, let them have their say. . . . . . What the shit are you two riled up about?"

"We're just asking what this man's name is. Will you tell us your name?"

Louie shook his head and said: "Not until you bastards take your light off me."

"Listen Officers," I said, "obviously you want to know his name. If it's that important to you why don't you take the light off his fucking face and let him tell you his name?"

"Sir, you're interfering with a police officer. The white Continental bearing those license plates has been reported stolen by its owner."

"Stolen!," Louie screamed. "That's a crock of shit. Who the fuck told you shit-heads that car was stolen? Who? Who the shit said that? Who reported that? You guys are wrong."

"Sir," the officer replied, "we don't make up calls for stolen vehicles.

We don't make the laws. We're paid to enforce the law. We got a lead and we double checked this car. The owner reports his car is stolen and we find it and we call it in. Now, whoever is driving that car is coming with us. He's under arrest."

Louie yelled, "Under arrest, my ass! No one is arresting me for something I ain't done. That car was loaned to me by the owner. Sonofabitch owes me more money than he's got. Sonofabitch owes me money. This is a favor he's doing." Louie started walking around angrily in a circle, his fists clenched. His medallion had fallen back to his chest. "I can't believe this shit. I can't believe this shit. Can you guys believe this shit?"

We were all beginning to back off. Knowing Louie, there was a possibility that the car had been stolen, not stolen in the sense that Louie would go out and steal a stranger's car, but stolen in the sense that Louie would get into a friend's car and hot wire it and drive off with it and think that it was a great joke. No one answered Louie when he asked us if we believed this shit.

"Don't you guys believe me?" he asked all of us. "Goddam it, if I can't get you bastards to believe me, who's going to believe me?"

"Look Louie," Willie said, "we believe you. But why don't you go with the police and we'll follow and you can explain it to the police once you get to the station. Then we'll get you back and we can keep on with the party. Man, it's just starting. We've only had one shooting."

"What do you mean, one shooting?" the policeman asked, confused.

"He's only kidding, officer," I explained.

Louie stood his ground. "No one," he said, expanding his chest, "is going to take me in for something that I ain't done."

"Louie," I reasoned, "just go with them. They aren't going to do anything to you. Once you get to talk to your friend then all will be settled. No sense in making more out of this than it is."

Al said, "If I was you, I'd go peacefully, Louie. There ain't no sense in aggravating the situation."

"Louie," the officer said, "they're right. Come on with us now. You're going to have to come with us anyway, whether you want to or not."

"What do you mean? . . . Whether I want to or not? Who the hell do you mother fuckers think you are? . . . Coming in here and disturbing our party."

The Officer said, "The party's over, Louie."

"Not for me," Louie said and he took a swing at the officer closest to him. Blinded as he was by the light, he missed badly. He fell, drunk, as he missed his swing and the two officers were on him immediately and had him handcuffed before Louie could do anything else. "Bunch of mother fuckers," he yelled. "Always picking on me. Why don't you pick on the big shots, the ones who pay you under the table, you sonsofbitches . . . Hey, you're fucking up my good suit. Let me up. What the shit's the matter with you guys, anyway? Let me up. You're messing up the expensive jewelry. . . . I'll go with you. There ain't any problem, see? I respect the law." Then he said to us, "You've got to butter up these sonsofbitches once they got you handcuffed. Or else they'll beat the shit out of you. You know our good ol' Houston police."

The officer said, "Now we don't want no trouble from the rest of you, so give us room to get him to the car. You men don't want to start anything you can't finish. One of you better follow us to the station in case he makes bond tonight. We'll go ahead and call a wrecker for the car."

Both of the officers grabbed Louie and escorted him to their car. I followed to be sure that they wouldn't hit him.

"He's all right," one of them told me. "We aren't going to work him over. He's going directly to jail. We aren't going to take no detours to the bayou with him."

"I just want you to know," I told them, "that I've got your names and badge numbers. If anyone lays a hand on my brother, both of you are going to be in jail for a long time. I just want you to understand that. Is that understood? If you take him to the bayou to see if he can swim handcuffed, I'll have both of your asses."

The officer started the patrol car and his partner got on the radio to tell the dispatcher that they had arrested Louie and that they needed the car towed. Louie was in the back seat crying, his once shiney white suit a rumpled soiled mess, his fake jewelry covered with the dust from around the base of the hackberry.

And that was when Connie started Ellie's car and slowly, unnoticed, drove off silently without lights into the drunken night.

CHAPTER 15

By the time the Police had cleared their radio, Connie and Ellie had reached the corner and Connie had turned on the car lights. The police backed out of the driveway, slowly crunching the old gravel bed long ago hidden under the grass, the gravel that my father had laid down when he had worked for the concrete company. I could see Louie in the back seat as the car went past me, his arms handcuffed behind him. He gave me a bewildered glance as if to let me know that he knew he would survive tonight but after that who knew, that he had had the misfortune of getting into trouble more than anyone else in the family, since before he and Willie placed the dead locusts on their tongue.

The police never noticed Connie and Ellie driving off and to think that I, at least, had been sure that Ellie was the reason the police were there. At the same time, as the police car was driving off with Louie, from the back of the house came our father and Becky and Angie and Rene and Alfredo with his blond wig and black hat on and the resplendently white Donna Marie, who seemed to glow in the dark, in her stiletto heels.

"What happened?" our father wanted to know as he hurried excitedly toward us. "Becky tells me that there were shots after all."

Rene said, "Andy . . . What in the world is going on? Was there really a shooting?" she asked, incredulous.

"Yes," I replied as we started to walk toward them. "We had a shooting. Ellie got drunk and he started getting crazy and we started arguing. Connie was taking him away . . . She had him on his way to the car. Then when he got to the car he reached under the seat and pulled a gun and started to shoot at us. You should have seen us all trying to hide behind the tree . . . Where's mom and Aunt Victoria?"

Angie was gasping in her excessive weight. "She's in the house taking care of Aunt Victoria," she said, the fat around her heart making it difficult for her to breathe.

"And Louie?" our father asked. "Where's Louie? Becky says the police took him?"

Willie looked at him and said, "Yeah . . . they sure took him. They said he had stolen the car."

"Heaven forbid," our father said trying to hide his embarrassment.

"Louie wouldn't steal no car," Becky said.

"He didn't steal that car," Donna Marie said. "That car belongs to one of Louie's friends."

"Willie," I said, "let's go check the car and see if it's been hot wired."

"It hasn't," Donna Marie informed us. "Louie had the keys."

"Then it wasn't stolen," I said.

"No," Donna Marie said, "I told you."

"Well," our father thought, finding some redemption, "that's in his favor. Where did they take him?"

"To jail, Dad," Becky said.

"Directly to jail? . . . Without a . . ."

"He's going to get booked," Willie told him.

"Without benefit of a hearing?" our father asked us, confused.

"That'll come later, Dad," I said. "Willie is right. They're going to book him for stealing the car. But then it'll probably get straightened out in the morning."

"What about bail?" Becky asked.

I said, "I don't think he can get bail this late at night."

Our father pulled out his small watch, the one that he had found without a watch-band at the concrete plant, and showed it to Rene, "Can you see what time it is?" he asked her.

Turning the little clock face around to catch the distant light of the naked bulbs on the hackberry Rene said, "It looks like it's almost ten."

"Andy, you don't think he can get bail this late?" our father asked.

"I doubt it very seriously, Dad," I replied, feeling sorry for the old man, realizing like everyone there just how preoccupied he was with Louie. "He's just going to have to spend the night in jail."

"Well, I'm worried for him," our father said, feeling useless, resigned to Louie's fate for the night. "At least no one was injured by that crazy man that Connie brought over." He set his jaw tightly, clicking his false teeth and looking intently toward the hackberry and the naked light bulbs that hung from its lower branches. "He better not have hurt the tree," he said. "That tree has been in the famiy for many years. That tree was here even before we moved here from San Diego. All my children grew up with that tree." He shook his head from side to side.

"Why would Connie go around with someone like that?"

"She doesn't have anyone else, that's why," I said.

My father shook his head again as he looked at his watch. He put it back in his pocket when he realized that it was useless to try to discern the hands on the face in the darkness with his poor eyesight. "Do you mean to tell me, son, that Connie has no other choice in men?"

"No, she doesn't," I said. "It's sad but she doesn't."

"Well then," he said slowly walking away toward the lights, "I feel very sorry for her."

"Where you going, Dad?" Willie asked him as he walked away. Willie grabbed me by the arm. He whispered, "We've got to get him away from the barbecue pit. If he sees it, he's going to have a shit fit."

"Dad," I said in desperation, "let's go in. . . . Forget the whole thing ever happened. Check it out tomorrow."

"No son," he replied. "I have to see it for myself right now. The tree is the important thing. If it is injured we must help it. I believe I still have an old can of creosote to treat the wounds . . . An old can that I've had forever . . . Creosote doesn't go bad, does it?" he asked as he walked steadily toward the hackberry.

"Pops," Al said to him, "you don't want to go to the tree. It ain't a pretty sight."

Our father stopped and looked at Al and said, "Al, will you please not ever call me Pops." And he kept on walking.

We followed behind him. I was in back helping Donna Marie, as she was having difficulty walking in the tangled grass in the dark with her high heels. "How am I going to get home?" she whispered to me.

"I'll take you," I said, "don't worry."

Still whispering, she asked, "Won't your wife mind?"

I had to smile at her innocence. I said, "Donna baby, my wife is going with us. You don't think she'd let me go off alone with you?"

Donna Marie smiled, tickled that she would cause a response from Rene. "She's jealous," she said, a huge understatement.

Alfredo and Willie were helping Clete in front of Donna Marie and myself. Rene and Becky were walking up front by themselves, trying to catch up with our father.

By the time we got to the hackberry, our father had already discovered the hole in the washing machine. He was staring at it blankly, as though he couldn't believe what had happened. "My God!" he said, having forgotten the tree. "How could all of you allow something like this to happen?" He contemplated the hole again, measuring it with the movement of his eyes. "I'll bet," he said, "that it was Louie's fault."

"Louie said that you would blame him," I informed him. "But it wasn't his fault. It was all our fault."

"That's right, Dad," Al spoke. "Louie didn't have any more to do with it than all of us. Right Willie?"

Alongside our father and commiserating with him were Rene and Becky and Donna Marie and Alfredo and Clete and Willie and Al and myself, all shaking our heads as on one string. "Al's right," Willie said. "And so is

Andy. Louie was crying when it happened," Willie exaggerated. "He was crying because he knew you were going to blame him."

Our father set his jaw tightly once more and said between his clenched false teeth, "The reason I blame him is that it is usually his fault. Don't you here agree?"

We kept shaking our heads, aided by the imaginary string.

"Just think," Rene shuddered, "what would have happened if he would have shot someone?"

Becky shook her body and covered up the chill by closing her blouse at the neck. "Thank God nothing bad happened," she said.

Clete looked up toward the naked bulbs and the dark cloudless sky and shook his head head vigorously like a hen swallowing water and murmured, "Thank God."

"He's right," Donna Marie said. "I mean . . . Clete's right. Thank God."

Our father bent down and inspected the hole closely for the first time. I got out of the way of the light so that he could see better. "For that we can be thankful," he said, poking his finger inside the hot tank.

"What about the tree?" I asked him when I thought that he was too preoccupied with the hole. "Hey, Dad . . . what about the tree? The tree got hit."

"I suppose I ought to check our good friend the tree," he said and he walked over, stooped to it and saw the gash that the gunshot had made. He felt the bark and took some of the heart wood that was exposed and peeled it off and rubbed it between his fingers. Then he smelled it. "If it hadn't been for the tree, someone would have been killed," he said. "Crazy people. There is no respect for anyone today."

After rubbing the tree he returned to his beloved washing machine and stared unbelievingly, his eyes set perfectly still on the monstrous hole once more.

"Don't you think we ought to go in?" Becky said when we sensed that our father was going to begin to cry. We had heard him sniffling and Becky had made a gesture with her hand that we should take him in.

Our father straightened up and wiped a tear from his eye with the joint of his boney finger. Then as we led him away he broke down and began to bawl like a calf. "How could you do this to me?" he cried to God as Becky and Willie and Rene held him up on our way inside. "After . . . after . . . after all the work I put into that barbecue pit . . . For the first time I let my sons use it without my supervision and look at what happens. . . Oh God! When will I get rid of the blight of my children? What have I done to deserve this cross? . . . My son is in jail . . . stolen

Lionel G. Garcia

car . . . murderers (No one caught on that he was referring to Alfredo) . . . whores (Everyone knew he was referring to Donna Marie) . . . crazy man brought home by my daughter, the daughter that has been married only You know how many times . . . He shoots . . . trying to kill my children . . . Only through Your grace and intervention and the presence of the tree was a tragedy circumvented . . . For this I am grateful . . . but for the rest? How can I be happy? Look down at all of us here, dear God . . . Could you not have been more gentle?"

"What's the matter with him?" Donna Marie asked as I helped her walk to the house.

Alfredo was helping Clete.

"He's just depressed over the barbeque pit getting shot," I told her.

"What about the tree?" she asked. "Is he pissed over that too?"

"Oh yeah," I said. "He's pissed over that too. He'll be all right once we get him to bed. He's had a long day. He's just never felt that he has been fulfilled in his life, that's all."

Donna Marie gave me a blank look. "What are you talking about?"

"He has never felt that he amounted to anything. His life has been useless."

Donna Marie took stock of herself for what I saw was an instant and said, "Oh," self-consciously.

Our mother was feeding Aunt Victoria her nightly pudding as we walked in. We sat at the table around them, our father crying softly, more composed and slightly embarrassed, glancing at Donna Marie, Clete and Alfredo—the strangers—from behind his handkerchief with an apologetic eye. He cleaned his nose on his sleeve, ignoring the handkerchief. "The police took Louie," our father told mother.

"I know," she answered. "Victoria and I saw it through the window."

"You don't sound worried," father said.

Victoria whispered as she swallowed her pudding, "All the good that comes to us has its roots in evil. Just mark my words."

"I'm terribly worried for Louie and for what happened here today," she said, ignoring Victoria, as though the old woman had not spoken. "Poor Louie . . . in trouble again." She scraped the glass jar and gathered the last of the pudding, enough to make half a teaspoonful and fed it into Victoria's opened mouth. She scraped the spoon across Victoria's hard palate. "Someone has to go see if he can get out tonight," she said. "I don't want him spending the night in jail if he doesn't have to."

"I'll go," Willie said. ". . . Angie and I'll go. Won't we Angie?"

"I'll go with you," Angie said. "When do you want to go?"

"You two go right now," Mother said. "And when you get there call us . . . call us no matter what time it is."

248

"Yeah," Clete said, shaking his head at the light bulb dangling from the frayed cord from the ceiling. "Be sure and call us all cause we're worried about Louie. He's a character that Louie."

"In the meantime," I said, "Rene and I will take Donna Marie and Alfredo and Clete home."

"What about my dog?" Clete asked, worried.

"We'll get him tonight," I said. "Don't worry."

"Everybody get going then," mother said. "I'll put Victoria to bed. You," she said to our father, "you'd better get some sleep right now because it might be a long night."

Our father started to sniffle again. "They ruined my barbeque pit and shot the hackberry," he moaned, his head now fallen on his arm outstretched on the table. "After all that work. God . . . God . . . why did Connie have to bring that horrible man?"

"Now go to bed and rest," mother told him and he obeyed her and stood up slowly and walked into the hallway and disappeared to his right. "We'll talk about it some other time," she said to him as we heard him shuffle into his bedroom, Frankie's old room. "Tomorrow we'll look at it from a different light," she said.

Victoria looked at all the people around her, nodded, and said, "Something good will happen from all of this. But we still have a lot to go. Mark my words. Haven't I always been right in matters like these, Clementina? Aren't we going through the same thing all over again?"

"Yes," our mother said. "It's just one of those things that seem to happen to this family every once in a while."

"Precisely . . . we ought to be used to it by now," Victoria said.

"Come," our mother said to her and Victoria docilely stood up on her own and followed our mother. "Let's go to bed." Victoria walked past her at the door where our mother stood and went into the hallway as our father had done and she too disappeared into her bedroom. "You had all better get going," she said to us.

Rene wanted to stay to help finish cleaning the kitchen, but mother insisted that she was not going to clean the kitchen until morning.

"Are you sure you don't want us to stay and help finish cleaning up?" Rene asked my mother.

"Yes, I'm sure," she replied standing by the door and watching the hallway to see that Victoria went into her room. "You go on home. It's just a little bit. I tell you I'm too tired. I'm very worried, but I'm so tired. I've got a bad headache . . . I'll feel better in the morning and I can do it then."

"Well, Mom," Rene said, "if you insist. We do have to take these people to God knows where."

Mother had prepared a package of left over food for me. "Eat this tomorrow. Have Rene warm it up for you. It ought to be good." She kissed me on top of my head. "Take care of yourself. Don't drink too much. I hear that you're having trouble sleeping. Now don't get after Rene because she told. She only tells me these things because she loves you. I hope you understand that. Besides, if she didn't confide in me who could she talk to? . . . Drink a glass of warm milk before you go to bed. Leave that cursed alcohol alone. Go to the hospital if that's what you need." To Rene she said; "Take real good care of him. Protect him with your life. He is so dear to us as are all our children. Remember I love Louie just as much as I love Willie and Andres and Concepcion and Rebecca . . . as much as I loved and still love Frankie . . . . If you have trouble with him, just call me. I'll fix it. If he needs to be in the hospital make him go. Hide his liquor."

We drove off, mother standing alone on the gravel driveway, waving goodbye to us in her black woolen sweater wrapped tightly almost twice around her in the darkness and chill of the late night. Not much was said inside the car at first. There was no mutual ground for conversation. So Rene and I talked in subdued tones about North 59 Freeway and the traffic and the Houston fog that settled in at that hour of the night. In the back seat were Alfredo, Donna Marie and Clete.

Finally Alfredo said in English from the rear seat; "Mr. Garcia, if I had had my gun, I would have shot it out with the man. I swear it on my mother's name."

"Forget that, Alfredo," I said. "You're in enough trouble already."

"When do I turn myself in? I want to turn myself in. I'm tired of all the disguises that Louie has for me."

"You turn yourself in tomorrow morning. I've got it all set up. You just do what I say."

"Very well, my good lawyer. And the money I gave you?"

"I'm going to deposit it in the bank. I'll get the legal papers ready and I'm going to be your trustee. Do you know what a trustee is?"

"Of course, I do," he replied. "I'm more educated than you think."

"I'm going to send some money to your parents every month by way of a money order."

"Yes, a money order. If not they'll never receive it. You know how the mail service is there."

"Yes, I know. That's why I'm going to do it like that. I'll send only the interest from the money every month, so that when you come out you'll still have some money and you can go back to Mexico with it. You won't be begging out in the streets."

"You already talk like I'm going to prison. Don't I have a chance?"

"No."

"And the story I told you? Will not that be taken into consideration?"

"Yes, it will. I have to see about it. It depends what course the trial takes. You understand? There are a lot of things we can do.

I'm going to see if I can get you ninety-nine years. That might be the best we can do."

"What if they want to give me the death sentence?"

"Are you kidding? In Texas? . . . For what you did? It just isn't done. So you're free from that. We'll plea bargain. Save the state of Texas some money, so that they can use it for the sesquicentennial."

Alfredo nodded his head at my words and grinned. "That's pretty good," he said, in pretty good English.

When we arrived at Louie's apartment, Alfredo, Donna Marie and I got out of the car and I could see that Donna Marie was staying very close to me. "Andy," she whispered, "I'm scared of him." She looked toward Alfredo who was walking in front. "Is that right, that he's going to prison? Is it true what he was saying inside the car? . . . He's not an important witness?"

"No," I admitted. "But he's harmless."

"Not for me he's not," Donna Marie shot back. "I ain't staying in the same house with him. If I had known he was going to be on trial, I would have never been around him. What did he do?"

"He's not a bad person. He just got himself into trouble with the law."

"I don't care, Andy. I ain't staying alone with him. . . . What's the deal anyway. Did Louie know that he was going on trial?"

"No."

"That wasn't fair, Andy," she complained. "You could have gotten him in a lot of trouble."

"Not if he didn't know. I never told him."

"Wasn't it in the papers?"

"Yes, but you and Louie don't read the newpapers."

She looked at me with ambivalance, not knowing whether to like me anymore or not. "I could be very angry with you, Andy," she said. "And Louie could too."

"No you can't," I said. "Remember I'm the one that Louie loves."

She walked away from me and said, "That's true. Still . . . ." And she didn't want to finish the sentence.

"You can go with us," I said. "You can sleep in the empty bedroom."

She turned back and said, "You don't have to, you know. I can take a cab and sleep at some friends."

I grabbed her by the arm and held her still and said, "No, you don't. You're going with me. We've got an empty bedroom." In a slight fit of jealousy I said, "Besides, you're right. You should be scared to stay with him alone. I don't know what I was thinking."

"That's what I mean . . . you should have thought of that a long time ago," she cried, exasperated with me.

Alfredo had already climbed the stairs to the balcony and was expecting us. I took the keys from Donna Marie and opened the door and Donna Marie walked in and turned on the lights and went into her room. I told Alfredo that he was staying there alone for the night and he was scared. "There's nothing to be scared about," I told him. "Just stay inside. Go to bed right now and stay in bed." I walked him into the bedroom that he had been using and he slowly undressed to his shorts, but first removed his black hat and blond wig and placed them on top of the dresser. He was shying away from me, trying to hide his frail body. He held the sheet in front of him and when he turned, I could see the scars that his father had impressed on him on the back of his thin legs.

"Please," he said, "stay with me until I get in bed." And he asked me to turn off the light and he crawled in bed and covered himself completely with the sheet as though he were dead. From inside his sepulcher he said, "Now you can go. I'm more pacified. Lock me in . . . until tomorrow."

"If God wishes," I said, in Spanish. "Remember that I'll come for you early."

"What time?" he asked, his voice deflected, like a child, from underneath the sheet.

"At seven," I said and checked my watch. "In about eight hours. So go to sleep."

"All right . . . Until tomorrow," he repeated.

In the front room Donna Marie had packed a small suitcase and was ready to go. "Is he in bed?" she asked.

"Yes," I said, "finally. And we've got to go."

Rene was obviously angry that Donna Marie had returned with me. She had not pulled her seat forward to let her and her suitcase in. Clete was surprised to find someone in the back seat next to him. "It's Donna Marie again," I told Clete as he felt for the body next to him. "I thought I recognized the perfume," he said, smiling toward the dome light. Donna Marie laughed.

Once we were on our way Rene said, "I feel like never speaking to you again as long as I live."

252

"Why's that?" I asked.

"Because you've carried me around with one of your criminals in the same car. I couldn't believe what you and he were talking about. What in the world did he do that he might get executed? . . . He must have killed someone."

"Oh, no!" Donna Marie gasped. "That's it."

"He just didn't kill someone. He killed his wife and mother-in-law and father-in-law," I said.

"Oh, my God," Rene said, holding all ten fingers to her mouth. "Is that him? In that horrible disguise that Louie thought up?"

"Yes," I said. "I'm afraid so."

"Andy!" Donna Marie scolded me with so much familiarity that Rene did not know what to hate me more about, her brush with Alfredo or bringing Donna Marie to sleep with us.

"Lordy, Lordy," Clete said with a touch of incredulity and now undulating his head like an earthworm caught in the sun.

The beer joint was on Navigation Avenue two blocks from the ship channel. It was half past eleven and Navigation at that time of night was very dark. Only a few of the street corner lights were lit and with the fog of the late night I had to slow down several times to read the block numbers on the street signs. The closer we came, the more Clete thought of his reunion with his beloved dog. He practiced his apology, admitting it was his fault that the dog had suffered through the day. "It'll never happen again, Thor," he murmured to his lost dog. Offering restitution, he said, "I'll make it up to you somehow."

El Gato Negro was a small run down building that had been painted white many years ago; it tilted much like our old garage, a weak light bulb lighting its front door. The view from the open windows showed a lot of activity. The once proud neon sign dangled in pieces between the gables on the wall over the door, having long ago been broken by someone that had angrily thrown a beer bottle at it after having been thrown out for fighting. I could see that it had been in the silhouette of a cat, but now the neon tubes were mangled and disconnected. Only the head remained entirely visible. Clete insisted on getting out with me. The dog would only go to him, he thought. I told Rene and Donna Marie to stay in the car and lock it. "Don't open the door to anyone except us," I warned them as we got out.

I took Clete by the arm and led him up the prefabricated concrete steps. "Man," he said, holding on to the fuzzy door-jam, "you don't know how much I appreciate this. Goddam Louie left me high and dry, man. I don't believe this shit. I feel so bad for the dog."

I threaded Clete through the crowd of drunks and got him up to the bar.

"You come for the dog?" the bartender said above the noise of the accordion and guitar, wiping the condensation from the beers from his hands. He was smiling at our predicament as though he had an amusing story to tell us.

I looked for the dog on the floor.

"He's gone," the bartender said. "No use looking."

"Gone?" Clete asked, a despair in his voice, his eyes looking at the ceiling as though he didn't want to believe what he had just heard. "Gone?" He shook his head twice, thrice, and began to weep openly and attract a crowd.

"*Que chingado tiene el bolillo ciego?*" one old man asked.

"*Se le fue el perro,*" the bartender told the crowd.

"*Que dicen?*" the deaf one wanted to know.

"*Perdio el perro,*" the bartender screamed above the noise.

"*Donde?*"

The bartender said, "*Aqui en la cantina. Se lo robaron.*"

"What are they saying?" Clete wanted to know.

"The bartender is telling them that the dog was stolen."

"Stolen?" When he said the word he lowered his head for the first time and I could see his shrunken eyes over the rim of his dark glasses. "Stolen? Did he say my dog has been stolen?" One eye was going one way, the other another.

"*Si,*" an old drunk man said. He approached us rather cautiously. "*Se lo robaron porque alguien dijo que el perro valia mucho dinero. Mil pesos dijieron. Lo cargaron entre tres personas y lo echaron en un carro y se lo llevaron. Pfffft. Asi se fue. Barbaros, esa gente. Gente muy corriente.*"

"What is he saying?" Clete begged.

"Someone said that the dog was very valuable, so these three guys stole it. Someone said it was worth one thousand dollars."

"Louie . . . . That damn Louie said it. I was sitting right by him when he said it. He was bragging to the people here how valuable Thor was. Goddam! They stole my fucking dog! My seeing eye dog! What kind of people are they?"

"They're just trying to make a buck, just like you and me," I said. "That's the best way they know how."

"Louie and his big mouth," he cried. He shook his head at the ceiling and tried to bang his fist on the bar but missed, hitting himself on the thigh instead.

I escorted him out and Rene let us in the car.

"What took you so long?" she asked.

"We were talking," I answered.

"I was scared. All those men going in and out. They're all drunk."

"They're all cursing," Donna Marie said from the half darkness of the rear seat. "It was awful."

Rene continued, giving Donna Marie an icy look for interrupting her, "One of them stopped and urinated on the front wheel of the car just like a dog . . . The dog. Where's the dog?"

Clete started to weep openly again. "They . . . they . . . stole my . . . my dog," he said between sobs.

Through the sobs Clete gave us his address and we drove him home. I helped him to the front door and he rang the bell. His wife came to the door. She was beautiful, tall, full breasted and long legged, her face more delicate than Rene's, her body more powerful than Dolores'. "What happened?" she wanted to know at the door, tying her housecoat around her waist.

"He's a little drunk," I said, holding on to Clete as he leaned across the threshold.

"You look drunk too," she said to me. "Where's the dog?"

"Somebody's got it. Clete'll tell you all about it."

"They stole my dog," Clete said staggering in, angrily resigned now to his fate. She took him over once he crossed the threshold.

"Stole your dog? Where?" she asked, supporting his weight.

"Somebody's got his dog and I'm sure they'll want a reward."

"Reward? . . ." Events were coming too fast for her. "What happened? Where's Louie?"

"Louie's in jail."

Stunned, she asked, "In jail? What for?"

"For stealing a car. He just got arrested."

"Oh no!" she cried, worried. "He owes me money."

CHAPTER 16

Jack and Marie were home by the time we got there. Jack was in the living room drinking scotch and leafing through a magazine. Marie was upstairs. Jack came over and opened the door for us. "Where have you been?" he asked, disturbed. "I've been waiting for over an hour."

"I see you didn't waste any time making yourself at home," Rene said to him. "You've helped yourself to the scotch."

"Why not?" he asked and he gave a toasting sign in my direction. "Care to join me?"

"And don't be bugging me, Jack. I'm pissed off," Rene said as she threw the package of food into the kitchen. We could hear her open the refrigerator and then slam it shut. I went over and got my drink from Jack. Donna Marie was standing in the middle of the entry-way, the suitcase by her on the floor. For the first time since I had known her she looked bewildered and out of place. Rene, now in her element, returned to the den complaining. "I'm in no mood to be bugged. I'm in no mood for anything, period."

Jack backed off. "Take it easy Rene. I was just saying you all were late."

"Ask *him* why we're late," she said, pointing with her thumb at me and indirectly at Donna Marie.

"This is Donna Marie," I said, taking this, the first opportunity, to introduce her to Jack. I didn't know her last name.

"Hello, Donna Marie," he said, staring wistfully at her. "You are beautiful, you know that?"

"Oh shut up," Rene told him.

"Oh, thank you," Donna Marie said, smiling at the compliment through Rene's tantrum.

"But I imagine everyone tells you that," Jack said.

Donna Marie blushed and said, "Almost." And it was too much for Rene as she ran up the stairs to talk to Marie.

I excused ourselves from Jack and took the suitcase and Donna Marie to the downstairs bedroom that had once been used by the maid. I showed her the room and the bathroom and she decided that she had had enough for one day and wanted to go to bed. I found clean sheets and a pillow case and a blanket in the bathroom closet and together we made up the bed. If she had asked me to stay with her until she fell asleep, like Alfredo had asked, I would have gladly done it, but she didn't.

"You'd better go," she said as she started to undress. "You're liable to get in trouble with your wife."

Marie was in the shower, so Rene had come down to be with us. She was sitting in a chair by the time I returned. Our son Andy had come in earlier from the football game and was asleep. Rene had awakened him to ask him how he had done. "We lost, mom," he said partially awake. And then the shadow of his dreams overtook him and delirious, he said, "The score was one hundred to nothing. The Oilers were run out of town."

"That's what he said," Rene was telling Jack as I walked in.

"He wasn't awake . . . Another drink?" Jack asked when he saw me.

"Okay by me," I said and he went behind the bar and fixed me a bourbon and water. At this late hour his familiarity, although abrasive, had grown acceptable mainly because I was tired of him and he had dulled my senses. And then I knew that to say anything now would only make me out as being jealous. I had learned the lesson well from the Anglo culture. I would bite my tongue and not try to kill him. ("Any sumbitch that touches my wife Angie is dead," Willie had told me when I had told him about Jack. "Why don't you kick him in the balls? That ought to teach him a lesson. Or maybe we can get Louie to get someone to cut off his balls and his dick. I'm sure Louie knows someone that can do that. To think that there he is and he screwed your wife . . . Man, I couldn't take it. Angie ain't much to look at now, but she was at one time . . . But I don't care. What's important is that no one touch my wife . . . that I had been the only one.")

"I wish you wouldn't drink anymore," Rene said as she looked at me. "You're killing yourself. Your own mother told me not to let you drink."

"Oh, come now, Rene," Jack said. "Don't be a spoil sport. Let him have his drink. The poor chap is just enjoying a drink with me."

"He's been drinking all day long. He's had enough. Don't you think you've had enough, Andy?"

I was thinking of Donna Marie alone in her bed when I replied, without the slightest idea of why I was saying, "No. I feel fine."

"I'm not begging you anymore," Rene said and got up from her chair. "You do what you want. I'm going to bed. I can't be responsibe for you. Kill yourself if you want."

Jack handed me my drink. "Get off his back, will you Rene. Give the poor chap some rein. Give him his head."

"Oh, shut up," she said as she walked upstairs. Then she remembered Marie. "How'd you do with Marie?"

"Oh, I don't know. Why don't you ask her. I'm tired of lying for her. Especially when she does a better job of it."

Rene ran up the stairs and we heard the door open and slam shut in Marie's room. We could hear Rene screaming.

"What's going on?" I asked. Jack looked troubled, looking up at the ceiling where Rene and Marie were having it out.

"Oh, you know women," he said. "Especially young women. Well, all women. They think with their cunt."

"I didn't know you knew Spanish sayings?"

"It's really not Spanish. It's Norwegian. The Norwegians believe firmly in that proverb."

"So do the Mexicans. That's why they have a saying for it."

"Well, Marie, thinking with her you-know-what, sort of escaped from my sight to go see her boyfriend."

"Weren't you expecting that?"

"Not hiding from Friday night till this afternoon."

"I thought you and she had an understanding . . . that she was going to spend the week-end with her lover."

"Well," he admitted, "more or less. Except that I needed to know where she was and I could never find her. She left and didn't tell me where she was."

"What difference would that make to you? You knew who she was with. You knew that she was not staying with you. I thought you and Marie were playing a little game with Rene . . . It's called keeping Rene in the dark."

"Well, Andy," he replied, "you know how persuasive Marie can be. I just didn't expect it to go this far, that's all. I never saw her this weekend."

"It seems to me, Jack, that as a father you would not be in collusion with her against Rene. You're taking on too much. You can't handle Marie. I know I can't. Not the way Rene can."

He looked despondent. "You're right, of course, Andy. I guess I'm just trying to be a super dad and I don't know how. I'm kind of an ass-hole . . . Well, you know me."

I felt sorry for him and I did the gentlemanly thing in not taking advantage by agreeing with him. "Rene hasn't said anything to me about Marie, but then again she's not my daughter. Do you think she knows?"

"I know Rene very well," Jack said, oblivious that he had acted like an ass-hole again, "and I know that she suspects something is going on. But Marie is so sneaky."

"Sneaky?"

"Sneaky. Like her mom. Takes after her."

I almost dropped my glass.

"You all don't have much to worry about, though," he informed me in a whisper, secretively. "I think she's moving out and moving in with the guy."

258

We both finished our drink and he took mine along with his to the kitchen and filled the glasses with ice. Then he came back and refilled them.

"When is all this going to happen?"

"Soon," he answered as he drank from his glass. "Like, maybe tonight. But that's Rene's problem. Rene wants to keep her here. I think Marie's old enough to do whatever she wants."

"If only she could afford it," I said.

"That's true," he agreed. "You want another one?"

"That was fast. Yeah, why not," I answered and gulped the drink down.

Upstairs the shouting between Rene and Marie kept on as Jack poured another drink over the same ice.

The phone rang. It was Willie.

"Bro . . .?

"Yeah?"

"They've got him dead to rights."

"What does he say?"

"Louie?"

"Yeah."

Willie laughed. "Shit, Andy, you know Louie. I don't know what's true and what ain't. The owner says the car was stolen. Louie knows him, but we haven't been able to get hold of him."

"Where are you now?"

"We're all still at the jail."

"Who's there?"

"Angie came with me and then Al and Becky."

"Have you called Dad yet?"

"I've been trying, but they don't answer. I don't understand it. Do you think something bad has happened?"

"I think they would have called. I've been here for a while and the phone hasn't rung."

"Well, we're still here."

"You aren't going to be doing any good there tonight. Why don't you just go home and I'll be there in the morning. I'll get him out then."

"Will you do that, bro?"

"Yep, I'll do that. Meanwhile, I need to hang up. All hell is breaking loose here."

"You and Rene?"

"Not yet. Right now it's Rene and Marie. They're going at it real strong. I can hear Marie screaming in pain . . . Listen, see you tomorrow. Call me in the morning. I ought to be in the office at ten or eleven."

"Thanks, bro. We had a good time, huh?"

"No problem. Sure did. Reminded me of San Diego."

As Jack brought me my drink, a red-eyed swollen-faced Marie ran down the stairs carrying two suitcases. Rene was right behind her screaming. "You ungrateful bitch! Fucking whore! Don't think I don't know where you've been all this weekend. Fucking your boy friend, that's where." As she ended the stairs she turned to Jack and looked at him as though she was thinking of killing him. "And you, fuck-head, where do you fit in this picture?"

"I don't fit anywhere," Jack said, nervously. "Maybe that's my problem."

"And you enjoy that, don't you? Playing the fuck-up and the dumb head. That way you don't have to do a fucking thing except agree with your little whore. You don't have the balls to make a goddam decision."

"I suppose so," he said and he turned his head downward in a submissive way. I had never seen him totally defeated.

"Fucking queer," Rene yelled at him. "Both of you get out of my house and don't show your fucking faces here again."

Marie walked hurriedly in weighted steps toward the front door, a suitcase in each hand. Jack gulped the last of his drink and ran. He was at the door before Marie got there and he opened it quickly, took the suitcases from Marie and they both hurried out. Rene, following close behind them, yelled from the threshold, "What you have in your suitcases, you whore, is all that you get," and she slammed the door on them.

But through the door we heard Marie's reply as clear as if the door had been open, "You're the fucking whore in this family, old lady," she said, calmly.

Rene, in a fiery rage, tore open the door and yelled, "Shut up or I'll kill you, you bastard." She slammed the door again, shaking the windows and came and sat down.

"What was that all about?" I asked, pouring another drink.

"Marie. That's what that was all about."

"Why are you so angry?"

"You really want to know?"

"No, not really. I'm going upstairs and going to bed. I've got a long day ahead of me."

"You really don't want to know? You don't care?"

"Goddamit, what do you want from me? First you act like you don't want me to ask and then you get angry because I don't want to know."

"Marie is going out with a married man."

"How did you find out?"

"I beat it out of her, that's how. She's not staying with her father on weekends. She's shacking up with this guy."

"So what are you going to do about that?"

"Nothing. I can't do anything . . ." Then she took a hurried deep breath and sighed for the longest time. She looked strangely around the room, as though she had been mortally wounded. She said, "The trouble is . . . she's pregnant."

That stunned even me. For some reason I thought that that would be the last thing that I would hear from Rene about Marie. "Get an abortion?" I asked.

She wiped a tear from her eye with the back of her fingers and shook her head. She sniffled and looked blankly across the room, seeking time to compose herself. "Problem number three," she cried. "She doesn't want one. She wants to have the baby."

"I feel sorry for you, Rene. And Marie . . . Does Jack know?"

She shook her head as she blew her nose. "No," she whispered.

"We're tired. Talk to her tomorrow. Don't get too worked up right now. I need to go to sleep . . . That's all I need, more complications in my life."

"You are her father now," Rene said.

"In a way, yes. Legally she still belongs to you and Jack."

"You do have some moral obligation to her," she said.

"True," I replied, "but legally she's not mine. She never wanted my name. Jack never wanted her to have my name."

"But those were old problems, Andy. She was afraid of the racial discrimination. I'm sure she feels different now."

"Well, Rene, it's too late. While we're talking about problems, let me tell you that you and I have another problem."

"Which one is that?

"That I'm seriously thinking of leaving."

She sat upright in her chair and she lost her forlorn look. She appeared confused and pained, as if trying to awaken from a nightmare, not really believing what she had just heard. She murmured, barely audible, without emotion, without thought, "I won't let you."

"How are you going to keep me here? Are you going to tie me down?"

"No . . ." she whimpered, abruptly. She began to regain her senses. "Get me a drink will you please, Andy? I need a drink. I need to slow this conversation down. Let's both of us sit down and talk it over."

I got her a gin and diet tonic. She took a long hard swallow. She was sitting slumped on the chair, the glass hanging limply from her small white hand. "I'm tired," she said, softly.

"What are you tired about?"

"Life . . . I'm sick and tired of life."

"I think we all are."

"If you and I could go to an island and hide forever. No one to bother us. No families . . . Wouldn't that be ideal?"

"I don't know. We'd still have a problem. We are the problem."

"You're right," she said, wiping some more tears from her eyes, "as usual." I handed her my handkerchief, but she refused, taking it for an act of pity. "I don't want anything from you," she said, angrily, referring to the handkerchief. She looked vacantly toward the far wall and said, "I just don't handle myself the way I used to, do I?"

"Oh, you're not that bad."

"You still love Dolores, don't you?"

"No . . . well . . . I don't know."

"You think you still love her, don't you?"

"I don't know."

"You fantasize about her?"

"No."

"But you're going to start fantasizing, aren't you?"

"It hasn't happened before. I had seen her many times after our divorce and I hadn't."

"But not like this. She made it a point to go to the party when you were there . . . to stir up old memories. She didn't do that last year or the year before that, or the one before that. We have a party for Victoria every year. Where has she been all these years? I had never seen her at a party for the family . . . She's always there and gone before we get there, but not this year. Aren't you curious? Why did she come today when we were there?"

"I don't know. I wasn't thinking of why she came today when we were there."

"But you have thought about her, haven't you?"

"Yes . . . I admit that. But it never has amounted to anything. You're making it sound worse than what it is. I don't dwell on her. I don't fantasize with her."

"Not much," she declared, sarcastically. She handed me her empty glass. "Get me another drink, will you?"

I took the glass from her and went into the kitchen and got some more ice. "What do you mean by what you just said," I asked, fixing her drink at the bar.

"What do I mean? I've seen you day-dreaming in bed in the mornings. What are you thinking about?"

"I have my own private thoughts," I replied. How could I tell her that I had been living among the ghosts of my antecedents all this time? "And what about you?" I asked, handing her the drink.

"What do you mean?"

"You and Jack. Jack is around here very frequently. Don't you think I get tired of seeing him around the house. Using my bar. Sitting on my furniture like he owns it. Walking around the house like he owns it. Looking at you like he remembers eveything about what you and he did . . . ."

"Jack?" she asked, looking at me, smiling at what I had just said.

"Yes."

"Don't be absurd. When I met you I realized I had never loved Jack. Jack could never be the man you are. I love you Andy and I admire you."

"Well, Rene," I said, "at least that's nice to know."

"I saw you today when Dolores came in . . . I still can't believe she came."

"She was just there. She came in to bring a gift for Aunt Victoria. That's all. You notice she didn't stay long? She could have stayed forever, through the shootings and the fighting, you name it. She was just paying her respects."

"I saw the way you looked at her and I didn't like it. I also saw the way your family looked at her. You bitch all the time about me, but I get tired of being treated like a second class citizen. I get awfully tired of you and your brothers and your sisters. Your parents are fine now. I love them and all that. I know that at one time they did not approve of me. They are kind enough not to show any resentment toward me and I appreciate it. They've taken me in and I love them for it. But the rest of your family is crazy."

"And what would you call what we just saw right now. Mental well-being?"

"Between Marie and me? That was mother and daughter stuff. It'll be all right after a while."

"I hope so," I said, "because Marie needs you."

"*I* need you."

I had to go into the kitchen to get some ice. When I came back I poured some more bourbon and filled the rest of the glass with water. I sat back in the chair next to her. "Yep . . ." I sighed, "I'm thinking of leaving."

She emptied half her glass. "And what are your reasons, you sonofabitch, if I might ask?"

"I'm not happy. Right now at this moment, at this time in my life, I am not happy. I'm fifty one years old and I'm seeing my life go out before me and I don't know what I've done. What have I done with my life? All I do now is work and come home and argue. So I drink. And I drink. And I drink. Is that all I'm going to do? Kill myself drinking because I'm miserable. That's not what I want. I want to be happy before it's too late. I still have my health. I'm still young. You may not admit it, but I see in you all the hatred for me that I want to see in one person. Sometimes I wonder why you stay married to me if you hate me so much. Why weren't you the one to make the first move?"

"Because I do not hate you. I love you. You can't see that? . . . Get me another drink will you? Oh shit . . . why didn't you stay in the hospital?"

I grabbed her glass and went into the kitchen again and got ice for her drink. From the kitchen I said, "I didn't stay in the hospital because I have nothing physically wrong with me. My problem is mental and unless I can straighten out my mind, I'm not going to make it. I'm slowly going crazy. You're driving me crazy."

"How could I be driving you crazy? I hardly ever see you. You come in late and if you're not drunk then you get drunk right away and then you go to sleep. I don't get to talk to you."

"Agreed. I don't see you that much. Then someone else is driving me crazy."

"Like who?"

"I don't know. If it isn't you, then I don't know. Maybe it's this whole fucking world. Everything bothers me. I'm even doing things myself that bother me. I'm not going crazy like insane. No one is going to affect me that much. I'm too strong for that. What I'm talking about is crisis. Depression. You make me nervous. You make me want to run away. I feel trapped with someone that doesn't love me."

"That's odd," Rene said, "that's exactly the way I feel too."

The phone rang and I got up to answer it. It was my father yelling into the receiver. The garage at the house was on fire. The fire trucks were there trying to put out the fire, but it looked like they had gotten there too late. Everything was destroyed. "We lost all your mother's and Victoria's old clothes, even the long dresses they wore to the dances in San Diego . . . and a lot of pictures of our family going back many years . . . I was sorting them out to give them to all our grandchildren." He stopped and I could sense that he was wiping the tears from his eyes with his red handkerchief.

"That's too bad. I feel sorry for you and mom. Willie called and said that he couldn't get you, so I was worried and I was going to see about calling you in a short while."

"And I lost Frankie's old clothes," he wept. "That hurts me a lot. Your mother and your Aunt Victoria are outside crying, waiting for the structure to collapse. Wait . . . Wait just a second."

"What's going on?" Rene asked. "You look so worried."

"It's Dad. The garage is burning down right now. He's really taking it hard. The fire trucks are there trying to put out the fire, but they think it's too late."

Rene got up to stand by me. "Do you think we ought to go?"

"I'll ask. I think he went to look out the window."

"How are your Mom and Victoria taking it?"

"They're outside watching the fire. Dad says they're crying."

"Son? Are you there?"

"Yes, Dad."

"Everything has fallen," he said. "I just saw it. Completely destroyed."

I asked him if he wanted me to go over and he said that I didn't have to. There wasn't much that I could do. He and my mother and Aunt Victoria were all right. He had tried to get Willie, but Willie was not home yet. I told him that Willie had just called from the jail and was probably on the way home. He asked about Louie and I told him that Louie was going to have to wait until morning to get out.

"Well, good night," he said, calmer now. "These things happen. As your Aunt Victoria says, all the good that happens to you has its roots in some tragedy."

"Do the firemen say what caused the fire?"

"They think it's electrical."

"Listen Dad," I said, "I told you not to be messing around with the wires around the house. Now you see how dangerous it is."

"I always did my own electrical," he said. "I know what to do."

"But it's different now. You were young and strong then. Now you just can't do it. In the old days the wires were different, or something like that. You don't know now about these new things. Everything is made of plastic nowadays. They don't even use that black tape anymore. They use little plastic things to connect wires with."

"You're right son," he said. "Everything has changed."

CHAPTER 17

Unknowingly, Rene had planted the seed in my mind for the mental ramblings of this morning. As I lay in bed, having spent a fitful night, I no longer wanted dialog with the ghosts of my antecedents, and as they approached my bed I waved them away, all of them, even the gregarious Colonel Fernandez and the revered Shroud of Tamaulipas. I was more interested in fantasizing about Dolores and it struck me as dumb that I had not thought of her for many years. So once again we sat on a sheet on a hot windless afternoon under the hackberry playing Hearts, she wearing her perfectly white shorts with her dark long legs crossed, like a maharanee, and I in front of her looking into her dark brown face, but then taking a very compulsively primitive stare at her crotch. There sticking out to one side of her shorts was a large clump of glistening black pubic hair, the hair the flaccid nuns had alluded to. My heart stopped once again as it had when I had seen the fat naked lady for the first time and I leaned forward to her and she thought I was asking for a kiss and she said, "Don't be silly, Andy. Let's play cards." And I whispered in her ear, looking around to make sure that no one was coming, "Dolores, look down and see what you're showing," and she looked down and gasped and hastily, with the adorable fingers of both hands tucked the clump of pubic hair back inside her panties.

"Then is when you should have screwed her," Willie said when I told him and Louie what had happened. "Right there on the sheet: Pow Pow Pow."

"What if someone had seen us? It was in the afternoon."

"When you want it bad enough, nothing's going to stop you. So what if somebody saw you. You think they're going to come up to you and say 'Pardon me, but you can't screw in the daytime.' Besides, you've got to be fast. Fast. Pow Pow Pow . . . Slam Bam."

"Dumb-ass," Louie said, "that was her way of showing you that she wanted to be taken. I can't believe you're so fucking dumb. If you were worried about being seen, why didn't you take her into the garage?"

Willie said, "Louie's right. You could have done something. She was giving you a sign . . . showing you her cunt hairs so you'd get aroused."

"And what did you do? You told her to put them back in place," Louie said, slapping the hackberry with his palm. "What a shit-head."

Little did I know then that I had just merely delayed finding out the truth, that if I had touched it that afternoon, the whole neighborhood would have run out holding their heads at the sound of the terrible screams that she would have let out and that not only I, the closest to her, but everyone within sound would have suffered the depolarizing screams and the visions of parrots flying between the eyes.

But I fell in love with the sight of her most intimate of parts and in those early years the thought of her occupied all my time, so much so that my concerned parents took me in my smitten state and enrolled me in summer school to study automobile mechanics, to see if perhaps I would return to my old self. "Take him and whip him if you have to," my father begged the principal as they left me there. "But get him back in shape." Louie and Willie in the meantime wanted me to rape Dolores.

As I continued to fantasize, my preoccupation extended not only to Dolores, but it took in a displeasure with myself for not having made love in my youth to all the girls that had given me the opportunity: Angelina, Anita, Alicia, Amelia, Arcadia, Belen, Belize, Beatrice, Conchita, Carmen, Cenobia, Celedonia, Dolores, Diana, Demeteria, Elena, Eugenia, Francisca, Fana, Graciela, Hortensia, Hermenegilda, Idolina, Imelda, Irene (not my wife), Juvencia, Juventina, Jovita, Leticia, Leonor, Leonarda, Maria, Marika, Margot, Naida, Noemi, Neta, Nepomucena, Octavia, Otilia, Otona, Prudencia, Pilar, Petra, Queta, Rosalinda, Rosenda, Roberta, Star, Sylvestra, Tacha, Taquita, Tacota (her fat sister), Uvalda, Umbelina, Victoria, Wilhemina, Winona, Yolanda and Zoila. Thanks for nothing.

Willie called at seven to tell me that nothing was left of the garage. He had been by last night and again this morning. It had burned to the ground and nothing had been saved. He asked me about Louie and I told him it was still too early to call the jail, but that I would get him out sometime this morning. He wanted me to call him the minute I got Louie out so that he wouldn't be worried anymore. He had not slept. Neither had I, I said. He asked me how it had gone with Rene and I went downstairs to pick up the telephone so that Rene would not hear. I told him I was leaving Rene and he did not say anything for a while. I was expecting something more definite from him one way or the other, but all he said was, "Well, you know what's best for you, shit head."

"I know," I said, disappointed.

"Do mother and father know?" he asked.

"No," I replied, "I haven't told anyone except Rene."

"How did she take it?"

"She was angry at first, but then she seemed to settle down."

Lionel G. Garcia

"You've got to remember that she's Anglo," he reminded me. "They take divorce in stride. If that would have been a Mexican girl, you wouldn't be alive this morning . . . You slept with her last night?"

"Yeah."

"Goddam, Andy, you are Americanized. How could you take that chance?"

"Remember . . . I didn't sleep."

"But still . . . she could have killed you very easily. But then . . . an Anglo woman wouldn't kill you. Dolores would have killed you for sure. Did you sleep with Dolores when you told her you were leaving? Didn't you have to move in with Mom and Dad?"

"Yeah. You're right."

"Damn right, I'm right. Be careful. Call me about Louie."

I knocked and went into Donna Marie's bedroom and she had already showered and was in her slip combing her hair. She would be ready in thirty minutes. I rushed up to the room and took a shower and dressed. By the time I got down again Donna Marie was ready and waiting at the breakfast table for me.

"Are you hungry?" I asked. "You want some cereal?"

She shook her head. "Not really," she said. "I can wait and fix something at the apartment."

In the car she said, "What was that all about last night?"

"Nothing," I said. "Just family problems."

She laughed and said, "I didn't think you had family problems."

"Oh, how wrong you are. I have a lot of family problems."

"But they ain't real serious."

"That's right," I said, thinking that, compared to hers, my problems were minor. And yet, she did not seem to be bothered by her problems.

"I just don't think about it," she said, stoically, looking out her window at the traffic in the early morning mist. We were going away from town on the Southwest Freeway toward Louie's apartment.

When we arrived I followed Donna Marie up the stairs, her smooth calves at the level of my eyes. She was wearing a very simple pink dress and a light coat, looking like a virgin. She unlocked the door.

If Alfredo had not been there this morning, drinking his coffee and reading the newspaper about himself, I would not have been surprised. "No, my captain," he said to me, "I would never run out on you. I am a man of my word. If I say that I'll be here, I'll be here. No question about it." He had not been able to sleep either.

I had a cup of coffee with him while Donna Marie made breakfast for herself. Neither Alfredo nor I were hungry. After we finished our coffee

Alfredo walked back into his room and came out with his blond wig and black hat, ready to put them on. I didn't think he should wear anything today. I wanted to make sure the police recognized him; so we left the wig and the hat there for Donna Marie. She was eating by the time we left. She said goodbye to us and gave me a kiss with her mouth full. "Be good," she said. "Get Louie out."

I was taking my time getting downtown. There was a traffic problem on the Southwest Freeway. About two miles ahead I could see a road crew of about fifty people milling about an overpass, only one or two appeared to be working, carrying reinforcing steel from a large pile to an area where new concrete was to be poured. The other forty-eight were looking at the traffic jam and playing early morning grab-ass.

"Do you know how long this freeway has been under construction?" I asked Alfredo.

"No sir," he replied, "but this is the one we used to take to go to Monterrey and it's always being worked on."

"This freeway has been under construction for twenty years."

Alfredo shook his head.

"And the goddam Gulf Freeway has been under construction for forty-five years. It is the longest lasting engineering project ever attempted by man."

"How could this be?" Alfredo asked.

"I don't know. It just got away from everybody. It developed a life of its own . . . like a monster."

Alfredo shook his head once more, looking forlornly at the stalled vehicles all around us.

This morning, as I was turning him in, I felt sorry for him and for his family for having been brought up in a culture that believes that a man's ego must be satisfied through *machismo*, the revenge sought for insults imagined or real. He felt perfectly satisfied that he had done the right thing. I was certain that there was not a trace of doubt in his mind.

(Once, when a man we knew in San Diego was asked by the judge why he had killed his wife, he replied with a reasoning that was astonishingly lucid. He said, "Because she was mine.")

"How are you feeling?" I asked him.

"Not good," he said and I was trying to figure out how to help the man.

"I have your money."

"How much are you going to charge me?"

"Nothing," I said. "The court has appointed me to defend you. The state will pay for your defense."

"What state? Texas?"

"Yes, sir. The state will pay me. They think you're broke."

"I could pay a small amount."

"No. That would complicate bookkeeping. They want to pay for all of it."

"What are you going to tell the judge?"

"First of all, let's get our story straight. Tell me what happened."

He told me his story in Spanish: He had come to the United States and had started to work and had saved his money. His wife joined him after a short while and she too began to work. She was a domestic. Eventually she grew homesick and, knowing that they could not make a go of it in Mexico, they decided that the next best thing would be to send for her parents. He had been hurt at first, but he had not said anything. He had wondered why *his* parents had not been brought over. Why only the wife's parents? He said nothing to anyone. He considered that his wife loved her parents more than she did him, since she was happier now than ever before. Her parents had never liked him, although he came from a better family. He was much too dark and Indian-looking for them. For a short while, from the day that he got married, his mother-in-law and his wife had made him sit in the tub daily in very hot water in which the root of the pomegranate had been boiled, making sure to ladle the juices over his testicles until his testicles became the size of grapefruits. This he was told was a ritual for increasing his virility. His mother-in-law had her daughter feed him cod-liver oil in large gelatin capsules that burst open in his esophagus and that caused him to belch all the time. But whatever they attempted did not work. Mysteriously, his wife did not conceive. His wife and mother-in-law had taken him one day to the Mission San Juan in San Juan, Texas, to have him go on his knees from the outside steps to the altar, praying one hundred rosaries while they waited outside and drank Cokes, seeking a miracle to make him fruitful. Nothing worked. In the meantime he was becoming suspicious. His wife was not as loving as she had once been. Her own conscious was being gently swirled by the spoon of her perfidy, he said. Her guilt was causing her to become another person, distant. All the things that had been done to him had been done to cover up his wife's guilt and her parent's guilt also. It was one night when he was getting drunk to forget his sorrows that he overheard the conversation of the men playing pool. They knew this lady they said and they described his wife and the events so exactly that he was sure that they were talking about her and her mother and her father. Her parents had encouraged her affairs in Mexico and had covered up for her all this time. He had thought of killing the men as they laughed about him. He went into the toilet and pulled out his gun and counted his bullets. He only had five, not enough to kill everyone except his in-laws and his wife. Maybe some other time he would take care of these other men. He weaved his way home, the gun in his belt on his back where no one could have seen it in the beer hall. When he got to the apartment where they all lived, he made a cup of coffee and sat down to think of the fate that had been dealt him. His rage was uncontrollable. The men had even made fun of his pomegranate baths. He walked into his in-law's room and found the couple asleep, snoring, the man with his arms folded over his chest so that when he killed him he did not have to be repositioned in order to be buried. He shot him in the head and the man twitched for a few seconds. There was only a small amount of blood that oozed onto the pillow. The mother-in-law had not awakened. He walked over to her side and gave her the kiss of death and shot her in the eye toward the center of the head. That had been a mistake. The juices from the eye and the large amount of blood that followed ruined the pillow case and the sheets. His wife was asleep, mysteriously hugging a pillow. At first, before he went into her room, he felt remorse, but once he saw her with the pillow, he became enraged. The pillow had become a man before his very eyes, a fact that he blamed on his mother-in-law's constant use of herbs. She had messed up his mind. He shot her in the head twice, once on either side and then he shot the pillow.

I let him off a half block from the police station and took his parents' address from him.

I told him that I wanted him to walk slowly and to go into the police station and tell the sergeant at the desk who he was and why he was there. I also told him not to say anything, not to sign anything and not to expect to see me for a few days.

He got out and I followed him slowly in the car until he climbed the steps and went inside. Then I went and parked the car and hurried back to see if I could find my brother Louie. By the time I got back, the station was swarming with policemen. Alfredo's arrival had caught them by surprise. I could see the Police Chief meeting with some of his men in the hallway, probably trying to get their story straight for the newpapers. The sergeant was too busy for me and he had me talk to the bailiff and I posted bail. One of the policemen brought Louie out for me.

"Goddam bro," Louie said, rearranging his dirty white suit, "this goddam jail is getting bad, bad. When in the fuck is Houston going to join the twentieth century? Goddam, bro. I had to sleep standing up with my ass to the wall. I saw two guys get raped. Right in the middle of the room. Those niggers are experts at that shit. Smooth as silk. Three guys hold him down and the other one rapes him. Faster than a rooster. The guy doesn't even have time to yell . . . . You paid bail?"

"Yeah."

"How much was it?"

"Not much." I laughed. "Don't worry about it. I have an account with these people. Here, take my car. You know where my parking spot is. Go home and clean up. Be sure and call Willie first thing. Tell him I couldn't call him. He's worried about you. Take care."

Louie got emotional. A tear came to his eye. "Goddamit, bro. You're something else. Who would have thought that little piss ant Andy would be keeping his bigger brother out of trouble? Shit head. I appreciate it. I just want you to know that I appreciate it. I'll pay you back. Don't worry about it. I'll pay it back to you first chance I get."

"Don't worry about it. I do this all the time for other people. Why shouldn't I do it for my own brother?"

He hugged me and I could smell the jail in his clothes. "You smell bad, Louie," I said. "Go home and let Donna Marie give you one of her baths. You need a change of clothes."

He laughed and winked at me and said, "Bro, that's exactly what I'm going to do. That and pour me a big glass of scotch."

Maybelline looked at me nervously as she handed me the phone messages. I greeted her and she followed me silently into the office.

"What happened to you Friday night?" she asked, worried.

"Nothing. Why?"

"You had a doctor's appointment in the afternoon. You never called. I was worried. I tried calling all weekend long but the phone was either busy or you weren't there."

"We were in and out all weekend. Nothing happened."

"You went to the hospital, didn't you?"

"Yes," I replied, wondering how she knew.

"They've been calling this morning to tell you that you left without paying. Your insurance does not cover anything unless you've been in the hospital for twenty-four hours."

"Do me a favor, Maybelline. Next time they call, tell them that we are thinking about suing them for medical mistreatment. See how they like that."

"Whatever you say. And they didn't find anything wrong with you?"

"Nope. I never gave them a chance anyway."

"You may want to eventually pay, because they say that they will not release the results of their tests unless you pay."

"Maybelline, please. I am not going to pay anything. I was there maybe a couple of hours. They ran all these tests and then I left. Please, let's not talk about the hospital anymore. In short, Maybelline, fuck them."

"Yes sir," she said meekly and closed the door gently as she escaped.

I returned Sol's call. He was busy with another phone call and he promised to call me right back. Then I returned my father's call. My mother answered and said that my father was out by the garage picking through the litter to see if he could find something of value. She called him to to the telephone and I got to talk to Mom while I waited for him.

"Louie's out," I told her.

"Thank God for that. Your Aunt Victoria and I have been praying rosaries all morning long. We even called some of the ladies of the Altar Society to help us pray. How did he look?"

"A little dirty but otherwise all right."

"Praise the Lord. I always know that praying the rosary helps. Father Rodriguez doesn't believe in the rosary anymore. Can you understand that? We don't pay too much attention to him anymore, anyway."

"How are you feeling from last night?" I asked her.

"Oh, we're fine. Your Aunt Victoria got pretty upset and your father is very depressed this morning. How did you and Rene do last night. Willie said you and her were having trouble with Marie."

"He's right."

"And that you were having trouble with Rene."

"I guess he's right. Mom, I want to leave Rene."

"Divorce? For good. Leave her for good? Who would you go with?"

"No one. I'm not saying yes or no right now, but I don't feel that I love Rene anymore."

"Son, it's hard for a parent to have an opinion. This is why the spider will not pee. Whatever I say now will be wrong later on. All I can do is tell you that whatever you do, we will always love you. You know you have your house here with us if Rene ever says anything and she doesn't want you around. And then there's Louie and Willie and Becky and Connie. Frankie would have loved you too under any circumstances. I can hear your father yelling . . . He wants to know about Louie. I'll tell him Louie is all right. He's saying that he'll call you back. He's too dirty to come to the telephone . . . ."

"Goodbye, Mom."

"Take care of yourself, son. I hope everything works out for you, that you find what you're looking for."

The phone rang and Maybelline told me that it was Sol. I picked it up and said, "Shalom."

Sol laughed. "You're not a Jew."

"My ancestors were though. But we were cowards. We became Catholics right away, when we saw that there was no sense being Jewish."

"My ancestors weren't that smart. We've suffered for it too. And for what? Isn't man a strange animal?"

"Tell me about it. I just dropped off a man at the police station that killed his entire family and at the same time I got my brother out of jail. And this was only one weekend."

"Your brother in trouble, Andy?"

"Oh . . . a little."

"Don't tell me you're involved with the famous mass murderer?"

"Yeah . . . I'm going to defend him."

"That'll be something. Be careful. There's some Texas politics involved in this one."

"You've got to be kidding."

"No . . . that's what I heard over the weekend. Even the governor is in on it."

"Sounds far fetched to me."

"It's not. The trouble with man, I think, is that he thinks he can think. Logically, I mean."

"You didn't call to tell me that, did you? What can I do for you, Sol?"

"Well, Andy, I have two reasons to call you. First and most important, I wanted to find out how you made it through the weekend. No repercussions from the hospital stay or anything like that?"

"No. Nothing. They want me to pay the bill, that's all. They're all worried about the bill. They won't release the test results until I pay."

"You shouldn't have any trouble. They're our clients. If you need the test results, I'll get them for you."

"Hey, Sol. I'm going to pay them. Relax. I just want them to work a little more for their money."

"I know you're going to pay them. What I was referring to was in the event that you were so upset with them and did not want to pay them and you needed the results of the test, then I could be of help."

"Thanks. And the second reason?"

"I've thought it over and discussed it with my wife and we feel we'd rather stay with the firm than start out all over again. You know how it is. I'm no spring chicken." He gave a short laugh at the thought of his age.

"I was hoping that you'd come with me, Sol. We could be a terrific team. Share office expenses. I wasn't even thinking about a partnership. I was just thinking that we could be office mates. Like the old days when they had the Jew and the Mexican together. Something real simple. But whatever you want. If you don't want to then, that's it. I respect your feelings."

"It's not that I don't want to, Andy. It's just that we're set over here. Oh, I know that there are prejudices and that some people don't like me. I know I'm not loved at the country club, but what the hell. I can't be taking my time to be worried about them. I do good here. I consider myself the best they've got."

"I know, Sol. I know you're the best they've got. My problem with that is that they don't appreciate it."

"Fuck them. As long as I'm making it, forget it. Know what I mean?"

"Yeah. I know what you mean. We'll talk about it some other day, okay? Call me for lunch and don't be such a stranger. You're only one block off, remember?"

"By the way, I've got to tell you . . . the rumor is that we're getting our first black."

"Hey, that's something. Are they going to let him go to the bathroom?"

"The word is that he'll be light . . . a light black. That way they can work their way to the real black one of these days."

"Have they got any school in mind?"

"University of Houston or South Texas School of Law."

"Why not Texas Southern? That's a black school."

"No one has passed the bar yet this year. They're having trouble."

At first I was thinking about Sol and how I hated to see a man of his talent go to waste in a huge law firm. And then I felt sorry for him because he had turned, through the years of constant acrimony, into someone else. I was sure that he would have sacrificed our friendship for the good of the law firm. I hated for him to have gone that far.

I was thinking about Alfredo's trial. First there would be the grand jury indictment. That would go fast. We could be hearing from them in a few days. I was sure bond would be set so high that it would be impossible to get him free before the trial. That wasn't necessarily bad. I would much rather have him in the security of the jail than out in the streets in Mexican town. No telling how long he would last alive there. And he was not about to get raped in jail. He wasn't pretty enough.

Maybelline buzzed and said that Dr. Silverstein was on the phone and he sounded angry. He had called her a nookie-head and she wondered if she should be insulted or what. I told her to tell the doctor that I was busy. I wasn't about to talk to a crazy doctor this morning. Maybelline came in and said that the doctor had called me a name, something she could not repeat. Then she surprised me by sitting down in front of my desk as though she had made an appointment and needed legal advice. She clasped her hands on her lap and she nervously tried to smile. I had sensed something wrong with her when I had first walked in. We had been close for so many years. She cleared her throat daintily.

"Andy," she said with a nervous high voice, "I've been your secretary for many years. I was remembering the other day that it has been almost twenty-two years that I started to work here."

"Has it been that long?"

"Yes. I started in January of 1964. In one month I will have been here twenty-two years. I checked the payroll from way back."

"And?"

The phone rang and Maybelline excused herself and went into the foyer to answer it. She came back and whispered, "Some lady wants talk to you, but it must be in Spanish. She sounds like she has something to hide."

I picked up the phone not knowing what to expect. It was about the men that had stolen Clete's dog. Louie had told them to call me.

"Are you the man responsible for the dog?" this woman asked. The men had had her call for them, as if I could recognize their voice.

"No, not really," I told her. "What did you have in mind?"

"The dog is safe. We need money for the dog. Your brother says that the dog is worth a lot of money."

"Well, my brother says things he doesn't know anything about. The dog is not that expensive."

"We want one thousand dollars for the dog."

"We'll give you two hundred and fifty," I said. "Take it or leave it." I could hear her talking to the men.

"They say that's fine," she said.

"Call my brother back and arrange a place where we can exchange the money for the dog. He'll call the owner."

"May God bless you," she said from force of habit.

Maybelline had sat down again in the chair in front of the desk, waiting for the phone conversation to end. "Well, I hope it wasn't anything too important," she said. "It sounded so mysterious."

"You were saying, Maybelline."

"It's very embarrassing for me to tell you this, Andy, especially since I've considered you like a son for such a long time."

"Are you having trouble?"

"No . . . No. It's not that. You see, my husband has been dead for many years . . . . Twenty three. I had just become a widow when I came to work for you. The truth is this: I have a confession to make. I've been seeing this man for several years. It hasn't been much for all those years, but you know how it is nowadays. Sex is everywhere."

I laughed. "Oh?"

"Well, yes," she said, self consciously playing with her dress. "I'm afraid we are on the verge of becoming intimate." She blushed as she looked out the window at the traffic on Milam street. The lady was almost sixty-five. "He's invited me to go with him to Las Vegas for a week . . . . Should I go?"

I said, "Why not?"

"Oh, there would be a chaperone with me. My cousin wants to go. It would amount to a threesome. My cousin and I would stay in one room. But you know how it is. There will be talk, you know, if I go."

"There's going to be talk anyway, Maybelline. You're not going to stop the tongues from wagging. You might make the newspapers and the ten o'clock news."

"Quit your kidding, Andy. Do you really think I ought to go?"

"Hell, yes. Take a chance. What have you got to lose? As my great-grandfather used to say, 'You're going to give it up to the ground someday anyway.' "

She blushed. "We could very well become intimate. He's very insistent. Very persistent. I'm sure he expects something from me. He's paying my way."

"Let him have it . . . How old is he?"

"He's seventy-four, but acts and looks sixty. You couldn't tell his age unless someone told you. Andy, he's very handsome and gentlemanly. You would like him. He's a lot like you."

"Well, Maybelline, if the gentleman is seventy-four and still wants sex as badly as he does, by golly, he deserves it."

"You do have a way of convincing people," she giggled. Then she turned somber once again. "One more thing, Andy, and I hope it doesn't shock you. I've known this gentleman for a long time . . . . He's my ex-brother-in-law . . . my late husband's brother."

That did bother me for an instant, but she seemed to anticipate my thoughts. "We never had anything to do with each other while Manny was alive, if that is what you're thinking. Oh, God, I would have never done anything like that to Manny. I loved and respected him so much."

"Well, go and sin no more," I said.

"Does that mean I can take the week off?"

"Sure. Go on. Have fun."

"I've arranged for my niece to come in and answer the telephone and do some light typing."

"That's very efficient of you, Maybelline. Go. When do you leave?"

"This afternoon. We've already got our reservations."

"Oh ho ho! . . ." I cried out trying to embarrass her. "You rascal you . . . You already had your mind made up."

She stammered as she spoke, very embarrassed, "Well . . . Well . . . Well, I kind of thought . . . well, I thought that you would agree with . . . with me. Oh, you can fluster me so."

"You're a good and decent woman, Maybelline. Have fun."

"One thing I need, if it's not too much trouble."

"What's that?"

"Can I get my pay check early? You see . . ."

I raised my hands to stop her. "Maybelline . . . you don't have to explain anything to me. Write the check and give yourself fifty dollars more."

"Oh thank you," she squealed like a little girl, giving a little jump, surprising me with her new found teenage personality. I hoped this womanly tendency that Jack and I had talked about last night would not apply to Maybelline and, if it did, I hoped it would wear out shortly.

"Control yourself, Maybelline," I cautioned her. "Act your age."

She turned demure and said, wringing her hands, "I'm sorry, Andy. It's just that I'm sooooo excited. I'm so happy that you said that I should go. I haven't had anything like this happen to me in soooo many years." She started to walk away and said, "Older women have feelings also."

"Don't go yet."

She returned to the desk. I said, "Two quick things I want you to do before you go home. First, call the trust department of the Bank of Commerce. Tell them we are in the process of setting up a trust account and we need forms . . . lots of forms. Tell them to send all the forms to us. When you get back I'm going to leave it to you to set up Alfredo's money in a trust."

"Who's Alfredo?" she asked.

"Never mind. I'll tell you all about him when you come back. Here take his parent's address and put it somewhere for safe-keeping until you return." I took the paper that Alfredo had written on and gave it to Maybelline. "Then call Louie. Just tell him that I need two hundred and fifty dollars for the dog."

"Two hundred and fifty for the dog?" Maybelline asked, confused.

"Don't worry about it, Maybelline. Just tell him. He'll know."

"How nice, you're buying a dog," she said as she walked out, "but for two hundred and fifty dollars?"

"It's a seeing-eye dog."

"A seeing eye-dog? . . . How nice."

It wasn't ten minutes before she returned with her pay check for me to sign. "So you're buying a seeing eye dog?" she asked and I laughed.

"Get out of here," I said, "before that young guy comes over and steals you away."

She giggled her way out of the office. "Thanks," she said sticking her head into the office one last time before she left.

"Did you make your phone calls?"

"Yes, sir," she said and closed the door happily.

In the late afternoon while I was relaxing with a drink alone in the office, surrounded by my ghosts, Judge Masters called to inform me that earlier today the Houston Police had called a news conference to announce that the city was free of terror and that the mass murderer had been apprehended. He was securely in jail after having been caught in a high speed chase through the east side of town. It named the policemen that had done all the under cover work to get their man. Several gun shots had been exchanged but no one was hurt. He had put up quite a fight and the police had had to beat him in order to subdue him. His name, for my information, the judge said, was Alfredo Gomez-Leal. He was singing like a bird and the district attorney had a sure case. The grand jury would be returning the indictment in a matter of a day or so. Would I defend this creature? Then he said that the case had attracted so much publicity that the mayor had suggested at a dinner party last night that maybe Judge Medina, a fellow Hispanic, should hear the case.

"And why is that?" I asked. "Since when does the mayor have anything to do with appointing judges?"

"We all know she doesn't. It was just a political suggestion thrown out during a skull session. You see, the governor was there."

"The governor?"

"Yeah. He flew in from Austin."

"What did he have to say?"

"Well, you know him. He's forgotten his law."

"Not that he knew much to begin with."

"He's not the brightest person you'll ever meet. We all know that. He's been governor three years and that's a long time for him to be away from anything. He just doesn't remember. But he has his good qualities. We need people like him in office. He'll go along. He goes along with anything we say. He just says 'Sounds good to me. Sounds good to me.' "

"So he went along with all that was said?"

"Basically, yes."

"Why is the mayor so interested in having Judge Medina?"

The Judge thought for a while. "Well, Andy, like I said a while ago . . . so that there is not the slightest appearance of prejudice. They're going for murder one."

"Murder one?" I thought out loud, stunned, not believing what I had heard. "Judge, you and I and every lawyer and jurist in Texas knows that never has anyone, especially a Mexican, been given the death sentence for killing a Mexican. It has always been thought of in Texas, since the Texas Ranger days, as a misdemeanor murder. Why are we getting tough now?"

"Well, you know, Andy . . . the D.A., the mayor . . . Shit, let's face it . . . the governor . . . they're all very high on civil rights for everyone. They're trying to get Hispanics included. Everyone feels an injustice has been done all these years and they want to correct it. It's the spirit of the . . . Well, shit, you know . . . the Texas Sesquicentennial.

CHAPTER 18

It amazed me that so many people would want to see Alfredo Gomez die by lethal injection as a sacrifice for the Texas Sesquicentennial. In time the movement against Alfredo would grow throughout the state judiciary, fueled by the political shenanigans of the governor, the consolidated front of Texas Mayors for Civil Rights, the Longhorn Judicial Awareness Bureau and the Federation of Texas District Attorneys.

Furthermore, it amazed me that I could see the psychiatrist on the same day that Maybelline Garza's niece had called for an appointment.

This being her first day, Maybelline's niece, Josie, had been at the office early. I remarked how much like Maybelline she looked as she stood in the hallway waiting nervously for me to arrive.

She looked surprised at the amount of luggage that I carried with me: four suitcases, one in each hand and one under each arm. She ran to me when she saw that the suitcases under my arms were slipping and ready to fall. She grabbed the two suitcases from under my arms as they were about to slip and, when I told her I had more in the trunk of the car, she looked up to the ceiling and shook her head in an odd but precious way, almost like Clete. But the luggage in the car could wait. Those suitcases held mostly spring and summer clothes. She seemed relieved.

"Aunt Maybelline didn't want me to have the key to the office," she said, placing the suitcases by the door and then shrugging her shoulders. I could see that I was going to get along with Josie. She acted like everything that happened to her could be handled with a minimum of stress.

"Your Aunt, as usual, is right," I said unlocking the door. "It's better if you don't have the key."

"That's what she said. She didn't want me getting into any trouble."

We took the suitcases into the foyer past the chairs and Maybelline's desk and into the office and placed them in the large bathroom where Rene had hidden one afternoon to take off her clothes to show me the beautiful rear-view of her most intimate of parts. Josie was thrilled to be of help so early in her job. It gave her an advantage and confidence that she had not had before. When she was through she asked if there was anything else that I needed from her and I told her that during the days that she was there that she should take the clothes out of the suitcases and begin hanging them in the closet. But that was for later. For now she had done enough. "I don't want you to do too much," I said. "You're new on the job and this is temporary until your aunt comes back. So relax . . . . Answer the telephone, open the mail, unpack the suitcases when I'm not around."

"Thank you," she said. "You're so kind. Aunt Maybelline said you were kind."

She was a very attractive young lady, maybe twenty-five, maybe less, still going to college, and I was sure, permanently attached. "How did it go with your aunt?" I asked her as she was leaving the room.

She turned around and shrugged her shoulders as though she were not responsible for her aunt's sexual indiscretions, late in life as they were. "She's gone is all I know," she said. "The whole family is embarrassed."

"I understand," I said. "It's almost like owning a bitch in heat."

"That's exactly right. What if someone sees her in Las Vegas with this man? How is she ever going to live it down? My father is fit to be tied," she said. She walked out as I picked up the Yellow Pages and found a Hispanic-sounding psychiatrist and asked Josie to make an appointment as soon as possible. Maybe he would understand my problem. I had expected to see him in a couple of months.

Sol called and Josie answered the phone and came in and gave me the message, but I threw the message in the trash. He would never change. He just wanted to talk, for me to reassure him that what he was doing was the right thing. If he were in trouble, he would call back.

Josie then handed me a message and on it was written the time for the appointment in the afternoon.

"Three o'clock? When?" I asked her.

"Today," she informed me and the phone started to ring off the hook.

Louie called and so did Willie and so did Rene. Also the mysterious lady was calling as a go between for the gentlemen that had stolen the dog. I was sure that that was what Louie was calling about. Josie brought me a message from my father. At the bottom was the question: Why did you not come to see the burned garage? He was sure he had found something very important among the ashes. Josie repeated what he had told her: "He said for me to remind you of what your Aunt Victoria always says, that all good comes from some disaster or something like that. Also, he made me write this down." Josie read the message: "Your Aunt Victoria says that we should take into account that the honeysuckle is blooming in December."

I knew what Rene wanted. An Assistant DA called. I didn't know who he was. He left his name: Terry Thompson. I did not want to talk to him about the case. I was sure I knew more about it than he did and I would just be volunteering information. I wanted him to dig it out of Alfredo for himself, if he could. Judge Medina called about the trial. He would call me back.

My psychiatrist's office was above a Mexican record shop at the corner of Canal and South Wayside close to Navigation, where Clete had lost his dog. I walked up the enclosed steps on the outside of the building. Above the door at the street level before one entered the tunnel was the name Dr. Antonio Garcia-Sanchez, M.D., burned into a large piece of pine. I rang the buzzer as I was instructed by the small sign on the door jam and a woman's voice asked, "Who is it?"

"Mr. Garcia," I answered.

"Do you have an appointment?"

"Yes ma'am."

"Let's see . . . Garcia . . . Garcia . . . Garcia . . . Here it is . . . for three?"

"Yes ma'am."

"All right. Just push on the door."

I said, "Thank you," and walked into a small office. It reminded me of the small house with only one window where the naked fat lady lived in San Diego. The waiting area barely allowed a small desk and a two-person worn leather couch. The space between the desk and the couch was the length of my arm.

"The doctor always buys everything second-hand," the little secretary with the opalescent eyes explained when I tried to clean out some of the wrinkles on one of the cushions before sitting down. "You're an attorney," she said, peremptorily, more to herself than to me. I thought she was knitting, but she informed me later that it was crochet. "I meant it as a question," she said, writing on a legal pad. Although I was sitting on the opposite side of the room, I felt that I could have touched her white doughy skin from where I sat.

"Are you sure we're not in an elevator?" I joked and she laughed, good-naturedly.

"The doctor doesn't like to be too extravagant," she apologized in a whisper, her eyes darting toward the office door. "He thinks that the patients feel more secure in tight environments, like cats. Some of our patients even sit in cardboard boxes." She cocked an eye to see what kind of reaction that last statement would get as she chained and double-chained her yarn with her metal rod. I smiled, trying not to imagine what the inside of the doctor's office looked like. Her little opalescent eyes fixed me with a begging stare. "Was I a box person," she wanted to know, "or did I just sit on life as it came?"

"I don't care," I replied, "I'll sit on anything as long as I get helped."

"The Doctor believes in knitting and crocheting to soothe the nerves. He may ask you to take it up."

"I don't think I would like to knit," I said.

"Why not? Don't knock it until you try it. Some of our most important patients love to knit. They hated it at first, but now they won't go anywhere without their yarn . . . rose . . . shell . . . and chain . . . rose . . . shell . . . and . . . chain. See how pretty it looks?" She raised the large crocheted piece all the way up from her lap and held it in front of her body for me to admire. "You like that?" she asked, hidden behind the piece.

"It's very pretty," I murmured, not interested.

"What?"

"I said it's very pretty."

"You want to buy it for your wife . . . your girl friend?"

"No, thank you."

"Actually, this is not knitting. This is crochet. I'm doing an afghan. You and your wife or your girlfriend could wrap yourselves in this work of art and never feel the cold."

"No, thank you," I answered again to her persistence.

"It stretches so that both of you could do whatever you want inside it."

"I said no . . . thank you."

A patient was let out through the small thin door and he had to stand between me and the small desk, bending down and offensively pointing his glossy rear-end in my face. I turned my head to one side self-consciously and I slid onto the next cushion. And yet I remained within his range as he kept bending and unbending as he talked to the secretary, oblivious of me, writing only part of his name and straightening up only to bend again to finish his name. When he had his body and his next appointment straightened out, he left. I noticed that on his way out he picked up an umbrella and a bowler hat from the small hat-rack at the corner. "He thinks he's British," the thin secretary with the opalescent eyes said about him after he gently closed the door and we could hear him descending the wooden steps.

"Is he really?" I asked, the memory of his flaccid rear-end still an image in my mind.

"No," she replied, "but we don't discourage him. The doctor is a Spaniard and he likes his manners."

The door opened and with a flourish that would have been envied by old-time female movie stars, the small doctor strode toward me in long exaggerated theatrical steps. He had his hand extended for me to shake since crossing the door, a huge tooth-drying smile across his face. He walked as if on air. One couldn't help but notice that his shoes were cheap Italian with a sole so thin that he could feel the grain of the wood on the floor. As he shook my hand he called out my name over and over, as if he had not seen me in several years and we had been through some life-threatening experience together. He drew me closer to him in a European embrace and I could smell poultry and growing-mash on his clothes. He let go of my hand as he saw that he had offended me slightly by being so familiar with me in so short a time and probably by the knowledge that he knew that he smelled of fowl.

"Come . . . come . . . come . . ." he beseeched me, smiling seductively, holding the door open. The secretary was charmed with the little doctor. She sighed several times as she looked at him in adoration. She looked at me, wanting me to adore him also.

"Relax," she cooed. "Everything is going to be dipsy doodle."

"She's right you know," the doctor said as he led me into his office.

There was room for only the two of us and a couch and his desk and chair. On the middle of the floor was a thin throw rug made of straw that appeared to be half eaten by the Houston roaches.

"That is disposable," he said to me as he noticed that I was staring at the rug, "in case someone vomits on it. But sit down . . . . Please. I am Doctor Garcia-Sanchez. You are Mr. Garcia. Very pleased to meet you, Mr. Garcia." He stood up from his chair, handed me his business card and bent at the waist very formally. He gave out a childish giggle at the thought of what he had done.

"How do you do?" I said, sitting low on the couch, looking up at the little Doctor Garcia-Sanchez. I unconsciously felt the embossing on the business card with my thumb, and feeling a multitude of letters, curiously looked down to see what it said. It read, Juan Antonio Garcia-Sanchez, M.D., Ph.D. *Psiquiatra, Partero, Cirujano* y *Apostolico Romano*.

"It's a beautiful day outside," someone said in a shrill voice. It was not the doctor. The doctor had not moved his lips. The voice had come from a dark corner of the room. I could barely make out the parrot in his perch. He had a foot up to his mouth and in his foot he clasped an orange and he was peeling it with his beak. I realized then why the doctor smelled of bird and growing-mash. Then I caught a faint whiff of parrot throughout the whole room.

"Yes," I said, trying no to be rude, "it's a beautiful day outside."

The doctor laughed in fits that caused him to choke and cough. "It is not necessary to answer the parrot," he informed me, clearing his throat. "Of course, unless you want to. But I must caution you, he's very garrulous. Once you get him going you'll never shut him up."

"I thought he was kind of cute," I said.

"Ah, yes," the doctor agreed and went over and mocked the parrot, acting as if he was going to take the orange away from him, the parrot screeching in fright and flapping his wings, trying to get as far away as he could on his dirty perch. Little did I realize that this was their form of play and that what seemed to be fear and resentment by the parrot was actually the pleasure of the sport of taunts. Later, after he had eaten the orange during our hour of consultation, the parrot flew to the doctor's shoulder and nibbled lovingly on the doctor's ear, tiny crystalline pieces of orange, like tear-drops enclosed in their own membranes, dangling from the side of his powerful beak. After he tired of nibbling at the doctor's ear, he placed his head under the doctor's chin, begging him to rub it. The doctor rubbed the top of the parrot's head as unconsciouly as I had rubbed the embossing on the business card.

I had talked until I felt exhausted. "Anyway, that's it. My hour's up. A lot of people think I need your help."

"For the drinking?" the parrot asked. The little rascal had been listening all this time.

"Yes, for the drinking. That's mainly it."

"And what about you? What do you think?" the doctor asked. He had been rocking on his chair throughout, moving the parrot backward and forward.

"I suppose I do need to see you, to talk to you."

"Because you see ghosts? Ghosts of your antecendents?"

"Yes. Sometimes. When I'm alone . . . . I don't mean alone by myself. I may be in bed with my wife next to me and I can see them. But I'm alone with my thoughts."

"Which is frequently," the doctor said, not giving the parrot a chance to respond. The bird studied me from several angles.

"Yes," I said.

"Do you feel lonely? Out of place?"

"Yes, I do."

He fixed me with his best professional stare. "You're trying to see yourself justly in two cultures and you've lost your identity. Have you noticed that you don't have any personality?"

The parrot thought that was funny. He covered up a smirk with his four toes, two pointing forward and two backward. The doctor crossed his little leg under his long coat and smugly looked at me to see what I was going to reply. "I'm really from California and not Texas," he said, as if that explained everything. "That's why I know about these things. You have no personality and yet you appear successful. You are lost between two worlds that you cannot appease. The two worlds won't compromise, although you try. Everyone but you has a well defined personality: your parents, your brother Louie, your brother Willie, Becky, Connie, Dolores, Rene, John, Matt, Jim, Sue, Darrell, Bob, Ellie, Christie, Pete, Tom, Doyle, Pam, Becky, Peggy, Mary, Cathy, Allison, Father Rodriguez, Father Diaz, Thor, the fucking dog."

But that was not all. The doctor recited the names of everyone that I had talked about during the hour in a monotonal voice, each name seeming to pelt the green and red bird on his head, each name causing a deeper nod of his little cone-head until he fell asleep. The doctor carried the sleeping parrot in his hands and laid him in his bed, an old drawer full of underclothes. He was sure to cover the parrot to guard him against what the Mexicans called *masasuelos*, a sudden gust of cold air that could suddenly blow across the room and instantly kill a sleeping newborn child or a bird. As the doctor tip-toed back to his chair I could see the small bald spot at the top of the parrot's little cone head. "He worries so," the doctor whispered. "Did you see him? He was trying to memorize all the names from your antecedents up to now that I was reciting and it was too much for his little brain. He tries so hard to please. He's old, you know. Almost thirty-five. We've been together as a team for almost that long." He almost had to wipe a tear from his eye. "I was a gynecologist in California for several years, but I had to give it up when I began talking to the vaginas instead of the women. I could carry on complete conversations with them without ever looking up between the legs to the faces. This parrot I found as a baby without feathers between a woman's legs. She must have been trying to sneak him into the country and forgot about it. That was the day I quit . . . . When I got an answer."

"One does grow attached to the little animals," I agreed. The doctor gave a surprised look. "The pets, I mean," I said, feeling sorry for the doctor, who was imminently liable to lose his favorite pet and associate. "I know when we lost our cat that everyone cried, including myself. And now we have a dog."

"He cares for everyone," he said, looking morosely at his shoes. "But one does what one can do. Right?"

"Right," I said, straightening up in my couch.

"The chief reason for psychiatry," he continued, leaning toward me, his hands on his thighs, "is that the psychiatrist should appear to be in more need of help than the patient. This is where the parrot has been so valuable. Usually my patients will object to conversing with the parrot. They complain about the charges. 'One hundred dollars an hour to talk to a parrot?' they say. And what harm is there in that? 'You must think I'm crazy,' they say and then they laugh and leave, cured. You see, they think I'm crazier than they are and they say to themselves, if that's the case, if Garcia-Sanchez is crazier than I am and he is normal, then I must be more normal than normal. *Ipso facto*, the cure is rendered. The parrot has done the job. But poor him," he pouted, looking toward the little animal that was asleep and breathing deeply. "He's very tired. He used to be able to see ten patients a day. Look at him now. You're only number two."

"His eyes were starting to close right away when you started the litany of all the ghosts of my antecedents," I said, preoccupied with the little beast's health.

"His eyes," he said thoughtfuly. "They're giving him trouble." Then in a sudden change to anger, he said as if flustered, "But enough about the goddam parrot . . . . The diagnosis is self evident. Some day soon you will realize what your problem is. Just remember what I told you." He got up and extended his hand to me. I shook his hand and left. I could hear his breathing as I walked to the door.

The crocheting secretary looked at me with her opalescent eyes and winked knowingly, as if she realized the haunting disorientation I was in. I had been overwhelmed by the little doctor and his parrot. "You're probably wondering what that was all about. It takes time," she commiserated, taking only an instant away from her crocheting, enough so that she made a mistake. "Now look what you've made me do," she complained, unraveling about two yards of web-like material. She glanced at the empty day sheet and said, "Next week at the same time," and wrote in my name with one hand while continuing to crochet with the other. Inside I could hear that the parrot was awake from his nap and was arguing loudly, raising a squawk, with the doctor.

"Dummy, why didn't you ask him where the fat naked lady performed her act?" the parrot said.

"The lady is dead. Didn't you hear him tell me . . . . I was embarrassed for you. How many times must I tell you not to interrupt me."

"Many, many, many," the parrot squawked.

CHAPTER 19

As I slowly drove back through the neighborhood I passed a Catholic church where the children were leaving from their afternoon catechism class. I stopped to remember that in the old days in San Diego Father Procopio would lecture to the boys before the daily mass that it was wrong to fondle anyone, including yourself, until you got married. All the time Louie and Willie and Frankie and I would poke at each other, laughing silently, because we knew the truth and that, marriage or no marriage, we had played with ourselves with the help of the baker's son and had seen the baker playing with and making love to the flour girl and his own wife, all of this on the same day and no one had been punished. As a matter of fact, that had been the day that Willie and Louie had delivered the most bread for the year.

But Dolores could not understand where to draw the line of reason. She clung to her early teachings like a child to her mother, having been brought up in Houston by the same side of the Catholic church, the dreaded order of nuns known to us as the night-hawks, the same ones who had come to San Diego to open the parochial school and taught the little girls that even cleaning themselves was wrong. In the resulting confusion of what to do and what not to do and what to touch and what not to touch, the little girls that year in San Diego were endemically infected with yeasts that made their parts itch and swell like throbbing lips and caused them to be constantly sticking their little innocent hands inside their underclothes to scratch that which the nuns were trying so diligently for the girls to avoid.

Father Procupio had suspected the nuns were up to their old ways and, being wiser in those affairs, he was able to have the little doctor take the black-draped Mother Superior, a thin long lady with white skin as transparent as the shedded skin of the snake, and gently, speaking in euphemisms, he was able to convey to her that what they were telling the little girls was not right, that he had the right to declare the whole girl's catholic community an endemic area for vaginal yeasts. "That part must be washed and washed well . . . daily," the doctor and Father Procopio had demanded, speaking of the vagina as they would of their hair. The angered blade-like nun took her rolled up catechism roster and hit both the doctor and Father Procopio in the face with it. Father Procopio had threathened

Lionel G. Garcia

to send her and her group back to San Antonio where there was no room and she reluctantly complied and soon the girls were the picture of health.

And failing to keep the yeasty girls away from their intimate parts, the penguin-like nuns decreed that young women, desirable women—not the old hags—could not wear patent leather shoes because their little vaginas and underclothes would be reflected on the sheen and the shine of the shoe, to be seen by eager boys whose erotic preoccupation led them to go around on hands and knees gawking at the distorted vaginal images on the sheen and the shine of girls wearing immodestly reflective shoes. And furthermore, that the cut of the dress of the young virgin should include a full sleeve because sleeveless, the beginning of the breast, the part they considered the most stimulating, could be easily seen by just a slight tilt of the young girl's body. And everyone knew how erotically stimulating that was, that the beginning of the breast led to the fullness of it and therefore to one of the seats of eroticism—the dreaded orgasmic nipple.

What they had not understood was that they had made the little girls so desirable, so erotic, that the boys would badger them to death to tell them what the nuns had said, and the boys, with erections in full bloom, would fantasize what was and was not sexually important.

And when the few old ladies that gathered for the nightly Rosary and every Wednesday for the blessing of the Holy Sacrament asked Father Procopio that if they also should follow the decrees that the threatened children were bringing home from the nuns, the Priest bowed his little parrot-like head and mumbled that it was up to them. He had thought that surely the Mother Superior had excused them, since they were so old, but they insisted, giggling like young girls, that they had not gotten the word to that effect. To himself he said while shaving before the mass that there was no use in protecting old withered stinky cunts and loose dangling tits. And he promised later on in his daily evangelical anger of the morning, when he walked to and fro on the sidewalk from the Rectory to the Church studying the Scriptures, to tell them that all this Rosary business was a waste of time, since only four or five women ever gathered for the prayers and as far as he could figure with the collection plate as hungry as it was, he was not bringing in enough to pay the light bill. So Father Procupio ran them off to seek the solitude of prayer in their own homes.

So in reality what the nuns and the priest accomplished that year was to cause a series of infections among the children, some of the innocent boys also developing canker sores on their unwashed penises and testicles, plus an unjust dilemma among the mother's that had already bought patent leather shoes for their daughter's first communion. Lastly, the priest caused the formation of the first Holy Rosary Society where the four women met in their own homes, each alternately and self-importantly playing the role of the priest, exposing their large gold medallions to each other, the same ladies who had entrapped the mayor and the sheriff.

As I drove back it had started to get cold and the temperature according to the radio was to drop from the high eighties to the low forties in a few hours. Although we were two weeks away from 1986, the official sesquicentennial year, the station began a Sesquicentennial Minute describing how Travis had saved the rations for his men and had not eaten for a week before dying at the Alamo. My thoughts automatically drifted away from the radio and I felt that I should have asked the doctor if he knew about the pomegranate drench. A depression came over me and I felt like I did not know who I was. I looked to the heavens in that cold afternoon, through the paste-board sky, trying not to listen to the plight of Colonel Travis, and like Job several years before me, innocently, without trying to offend, mind you, asked the same God that gave us the reckless nuns, and the dogged priest, "Why me, God?" And I almost thought that he answered me.

In the minute removed from the Sesquicentennial Minute, in a mood to match the weather, feeling the dust of the bones of the ghosts of all my antecedents darkly covering me like the Shroud of Tamaulipas, I hurried back to my office and the uneasy comfort of my new home.

What I should have asked God that gray afternoon was what would become of the Texas Sesquicentennial? Was it possible to have more Sesquicentennial Minutes than there were minutes?

It took me longer to get back than I had anticipated. I made the mistake of taking the Gulf Freeway. It was again being worked on every half mile or so. In some cases the crews were building up the freeway by enlarging two lanes into ten and then, just as mysteriously, other crews were tearing down the freeway in large pieces of concrete and reducing ten lanes into two. The highway engineers were leaning against their pick-ups, spitting on the road and telling stories, laughing, adjusting their perspired underwear.

Josie was busy writing on a legal pad. She had a book on contract law opened and she was copying from it. She looked young and beautiful and she reminded me so much of Maybelline when Maybelline had been young. Who would have thought that at sixty-five Maybelline would once again come in heat? I didn't feel like worrying Josie about her aunt.

"What are you doing, Josie?" I asked as I heard the door close behind me.

She put the book away. "Oh, nothing. I was just studying. I like to study . . . especially when there's nothing for me to do." She gathered the messages that she had neatly stacked on her desk pad. "How did it go?" she asked as she followed me into the office.

"With the doctor?"

"Yes . . . with the doctor. What did he say?"

"He says that I don't know who I am."

"Now that's silly. Is that really what he said? Are you pulling my leg?"

I was taking off my coat. "It's getting cold out there."

"The weatherman says it will freeze in the north part of town over by Intercontinental Airport."

"That's okay by me," I said.

"That's sixty miles away from here. It could snow over there and be pleasant over here."

"You're funny," she said. Then, "Well, I tried to do my job. What more can I do?"

"What are you talking about?"

"About your appointment with the doctor . . . Aunt Maybelline wanted me to know everything that's going on while she's gone. I have to give her a report on what went on."

"Tell her everything went well. The guy is a little bit odd, but you know psychiatrists. They're all odd. This guy has a parrot that talks and assists him in his analysis."

She smiled as she stood in front of the desk. She cocked her head like the parrot. "You're kidding," she said.

"No, I'm not . . . but if you don't believe me, that's fine."

"It's not that I don't believe you, but it is hard to accept."

"I know. I was just kidding."

She smiled and said, "Here," as she placed the messages on my desk and started to walk away. "I knew you were kidding," she smiled. "I'll leave you alone now. You've been a popular man this afternoon. Look at all your phone calls."

Rene had called. My father had called. Louie had called. Willie had called. Donna Marie had called. Clete had called. Clete's wife had called. Alfredo Gomez had called. Connie had called and finally Dolores had called and I wondered why Dolores of all people would be wanting to call me?

Rene wanted me to come home. Why was I being such an ass-hole? She had a special way of showing her love. Junior was crying himself to sleep every night. Marie was back and in a very good mood now that she had gotten an abortion and the fight of that night had reinforced their love for one another. That was well and good for them, but I asked her if they didn't realize that other people lived around them, people that were acutely offended by that type of behavior.

"Oh, you know how Marie and I are," Rene said when I asked her if they had fought again. "You have to understand that that is the way mothers and daughters are. We call each other fucking whores and shit-heads and dirty cunts and things like that, but we don't really mean it. It's a hormone problem. It just shows we love each other. Didn't you realize that?"

"No, I don't realize that," I said. "I don't like to hear people talk like that to each other."

My father had called because I had yet to go see the garage. He thought that perhaps he had made a very important discovery. I promised him I would go see him today without fail. Louie wanted to know how much money we had agreed on to rescue Clete's dog and when I told him, he whistled into the telephone.

"Hell, that's a lot less than they wanted. You told them the dog was worth one-thousand dollars."

"I was just blowing air."

"They believed you. I talked them down to two-fifty."

"We can get the money, bro," he said.

We figured that if all went well, Clete could have the dog in a day or two, which would be a relief to everyone concerned, since Clete had not been out of the house since the kidnapping and the wife was running low on cash. Louie also wanted me to know that he and Donna Marie were again thinking of leaving Houston and going to Hollywood to see if Donna Marie could break into the movies. Willie wanted to know if we could form a family group to pitch in to rebuild the garage. He and Angie could be the directors of the enterprise. Donna Marie wanted to know when I was going to go see her. She repeated what Louie had said. She wanted a movie career in Hollywood. What did I think? It was important to her what I thought. She didn't mention Louie and when I asked her when she was going, she said "pretty soon. Texas sucks," she added. And when I asked her about her acting credentials, she answered, "I really don't need any. Not as good as I am at what I do."

Clete wanted to know if the kidnappers had called again and I told him they had not. He wanted to know if the deal was still on. I told him that as far as I knew that it was, but that I would let him know as soon as they called me. I asked him if he knew that his wife had called and he did not know, so he put his wife on the phone and she spoke to me cryptically about nothing, which led me to believe that she had wanted something from me that she did not want her husband to find out about.

Alfredo Gomez spoke in perfect English now that he was in jail. He had many confessions to make and needed to see me and a priest as soon as possible. He was being treated well and only hoped that his sheets would be changed daily. The food was tolerable but had no spices. He had taken to sitting in a corner and acting as if he were sick and so far none of the dreaded blacks had approached him. The district attorney had spoken with him, why had not I? I told him I had a very good idea that I had the case won if the district attorney insisted on trying him on first degree murder. I asked him what he thought about being a father some day and he replied, with what sounded over the telephone like tears in his eyes, that that was what every Mexican man lived for. "Good," I said. "You just keep thinking like that." My main concern was his testicles. Had anyone asked to see his testicles? And no one had. I felt relief. "Under no circumstances allow anyone to examine your testicles," I warned him. "If they do, refuse and call me immediately. And furthermore, under no circumstances should you speak excellent English, because the Texans will kill you for that sooner than for anything else."

I then called Father Rodriguez and asked him to please visit one Alfredo Gomez at city jail to administer the act of contrition. He would be glad to do it, he said, because it had been years, since Vatican II he thought, since any Mexican had gone to confession and he was anxious to review the process. He admonished me for not seeing my parents more often, especially now that the garage had burned down. "It's only been two days since the garage burned down," I pleaded. He and Father Diaz had gone to bless the ashes at my parent's insistence. He was the one that had made the discovery. No, he would not tell me what it was. It was up to my father to interpret those things. My interest piqued, I reassured him that I would be there today.

Connie wanted just to talk to see if we were still friends after her friend Ellie Barrera had shot the cavernous hole through our father's barbecue pit-washing machine. Never mind that he had been shooting at us. I told her to forget it and she put Ellie on the phone and he spoke in his favorite old army drunken low voice. He was real sorry, man. He didn't know what got into him. Nam, brother. Korea, brother. The big one, WW Two. Just jumped out of too many airplanes and landed on my head too many times, he supposed. He wanted to marry Connie and Connie wanted to marry him. What did I think? He wanted my approval. I was thinking that anything that the luckless Connie could do to bring happiness to herself would be welcomed by me. He promised not to drink anymore, although he was drunk then. Connie grabbed the phone from him and said she loved me and that everything would straighten out as soon as Ellie quit drinking. "He will, Andy. He's promised he will. What do you think?"

"I want what you want for yourself," I told her. "If you think you can make a go of it, fine."

"Thanks, Andy," she said. "I need some support from the family." I could hear Ellie shouting into the telephone. "We need support," he laughed.

Dolores had heard from my mother that I was under psychiatric care and she wanted me to know that she was saying rosaries and lighting a wellness-candle for me every night. Her husband did not know what she was doing and was very jealous, so in case the two of us should meet, would I please not mention it to him? She went on to say that she felt partially responsible for what had happened to me. It was her lack of physical love that had alienated us and if it had not been for the nuns, she would have been as gregarious and outgoing as a desperate-to-breed-before-death butterfly. Instead, she still felt that she could not undress in front of her husband and she still made love very silently, stealthily, as if robbing a store, under the cave that was her blanket and in the dark. She had still not seen a naked man, except for Michelangelo's David in the encyclopedia.

"But I don't scream anymore," she explained. "At least I haven't in a long time . . . Let's just say that I don't scream anymore. I really don't. I haven't screamed in . . . two year . . . five years . . . something like that . . . Anyway, I don't scream. Can you believe that?"

"It's hard to believe. I mean, the way you used to scream messed up my mind."

She laughed slightly over the telephone. "Yes, I know . . . How embarrassing. How did you ever put up with me for so long? How could you?"

"Love. That's it."

"Love. That's funny. I'm so embarrassed now! Oh, how could I?"

"That's the way you were."

"It's still no excuse . . . But tell me about the psychiatrist."

"The psychiatrist says I don't have a personality."

"They always say that. We have some friends that are psychiatrists. How many times have you seen him?"

"Just today. I just went this afternoon."

"Ohhhhhh. I thought your mother said that you'd been going for a while. This is your first visit?"

"Yeah. This afternoon. The guy is weird. He's got a parrot that you wouldn't believe. When did you talk to mother?"

"Earlier this afternoon. After you called her . . . Did I hear you say parrot?"

"Forget it," I said. "You heard wrong."

295

"I thought so," she answered, "but I could have sworn that you said parrot."

"I did. The guy has a parrot."

"What for?"

"Just as a topic of conversation, that's all."

"That's wierd."

"That's what I thought. But he's nice."

"I hope he treats you all right, Andy. What's his name?"

"Juan Antonio Garcia-Sanchez."

"Never heard of him . . . . Listen, I'm praying for you. Go on and get well soon. Maybe I'll talk to you again soon. Say hello to Rene. How is she, by the way?"

"I don't know. I'm not living with her anymore."

Dolores was silent for a moment. Finally she said, "I'm sorry to hear that, Andy. I really am. Your mom had said something about it, but I didn't think it was serious."

I called my father back and told him that I was on my way for a visit, to look at what remained of the burned garage and his discovery. We spoke for a while.

"I'll be in the back working when you come in," he said. "Don't even go to the house. Come on over to the garage. I'll be working there. Your mother and Aunt Victoria are trying to help me, but they are not as useful as I am. I have to show you what I found. It's unbelievable that such a thing should be found at this late date. I'm so excited . . . But what about you? I didn't have a chance to ask you. You were in such a hurry. Don't be in such a hurry. Did you go to the psychiatrist?"

"Yes . . . I went this afternoon."

"How did he make you feel? You don't sound very happy."

"I'm not. Did Mom tell you I left Rene?"

"Yes, son . . . I'm sorry for the both of you. She is a good woman."

"Well, I left her. I really don't want to live with her anymore. We are just not compatible. You were right all the time. We belong to two different worlds."

"Oh, don't put too much importance to those things. I said that when I was younger. Now that I look at life I don't know what's right and what's wrong. Your mother and I were never compatible and look at us now."

"Yes, but . . . what's done is done, as they say."

"You know what your Aunt Victoria says. She has a saying for everything . . . just like her father. 'No one knows what's in the caldron except the spoon that stirs it.' So it appeared to your mother and me that you and Rene were happy."

"It's just a front, Dad. That is why the spider never pees, as Aunt Victoria would say."

"That's probably right. Where are you staying?"

"Right now, at the office," I replied. He did not answer and I waited for a moment, a moment of painful desperation, before I asked him if it was possible for me to move in with them, use Frankie's old room, and he said yes, but we would first have to remove the pieces of the Shroud of Tamaulipas from the bed.

CHAPTER 20

Life's discoveries come not through persistent effort but by accident and it was an accident, the burning of the garage, that revealed to my father what appeared to be the remains of the Shroud of Tamaulipas.

My father was on his knees with a trowel in his hand, gently scraping the last pieces of a large cloth that had been burned into the garage floor. My mother and Aunt Victoria were standing together looking at him work, their arms folded to protect their frail chests from the strong north wind. Both had their heads and shoulders covered with their praying shawls, the special ones that the Altar Society had bought from Father Diaz. There was nothing left standing of the old garage. The barbecue pit-washing machine was charred black, the large hole that Ellie's shot had made pointing at me like a splintered deranged eye. The electric cord was burned with the copper wires exposed. The trunks that had been stacked against the wall were gone except for the metal-ware that Mother and Victoria had stacked at one of the corners of the floor. Likewise, the contents of the trunks had been rendered into a pile of ashes and debris that Mother and Victoria had swept up next to the pile of metal, the swirls of wind picking up the tops of the ashes, flying them off like a cloud of black gnats. The ice-house birds that had preferred the gables of the garage were now in the hackberry tree, making wild shrill sounds in their agitation. The honeysuckle planted as punishment for bad grades was gone, through blooming in December, burned to the roots; the disoriented bees were swarming around wondering what had happened to their food supply, gravitating slowly towards the honeysuckle by the house. "Get that bee off my back," I could hear my father say as I approached.

"There's two of them," Aunt Victoria said to my mother. "Do you see the other one? There . . . There . . . Clementina . . . can't you see the other one? . . . . Don't hit it. If you do, you'll make it sting."

"I've got them," my mother said.

"Are they gone?" Father asked, more intent on what he was doing than on the bees. They heard my footsteps on the loose gravel. "Well, look who's here . . . I told you to come earlier, Andres. Now I'm almost through," he said. "These two pieces and I think that's all."

I went to kiss my mother and Aunt Victoria. "How are you feeling, son?" Mom asked, concerned as only a Mexican mother can force herself to be.

"I'm all right. I feel fine," I said as I looked down at what Father was doing. With the exception of the two pieces he was working on, he had scraped the shroud off the floor.

"You look fine," Mom said.

Victoria kissed me and looked at me more lucidly and said, "That's Andres, right?"

"Yes," Mom told her, putting her arm around her to warm her up, "that's Andres."

"He's so handsome," Aunt Victoria said. "I remember when he was so tiny and dark. We used to worry about him, remember?"

"Who worried about him?" Mother asked.

Victoria said, "You. Don't you remember?"

"No I don't. I never worried about Andres. Now, I worried about Louie and Willie and Frankie and the girls . . ."

"Why did you worry about Frankie. He's so nice."

"I worried that he was too frail . . ."

"That he wouldn't live for long? . . ." Victoria asked.

"Yes."

"I wonder how he is," Victoria said, having forgotten that Frankie had died.

"God has him in heaven. He's dead . . . killed himself."

Victoria shook her head. "I wonder why? . . . How could I forget something like that?"

My father, intent on his work, said, "Sure, Andres is handsome. All my children are handsome and beautiful. They take after our family. The Garcias have always been handsome."

"Well" Mom said, faking hurt feelings, "how about the Barreras? Weren't we beautiful also?"

"Yes," Father said, mocking her, "I suppose so . . . but the Garcias are prettier."

"The Garcias were never pretty," Victoria contradicted, shaking her head in remembrance. "They all had a big jaw. I think he takes after his mother. The Barreras were a delicate family, almost feminine."

My father laughed. "Queers . . . that's it."

"No . . . I didn't mean it that way. I had a lot of lovers from the Barrera side," Victoria said.

"How's it going, Dad?" I asked. I was trying to look at what he was doing even though my mother was holding on to me.

"I'm doing fine . . . fine . . . fine," Dad said, each "fine" lower in volume than before. He had yet to take his eyes away from the burned cloth.

"I spoke to Father Rodriguez and he said that he had found the shroud."

"Humph!" he grunted. "Father Rodriquez and Father Diaz were both here to bless the ashes, but I can guarantee you that they did not find the Shroud. I found it. They're not about to get their hands dirty."

"Well maybe they helped a little," Mother said. "Just by being here."

"Remember that it takes more than one man to do a good job," Aunt Victoria said.

"All they did was look around and shake their heads. Father Diaz spent his time looking for a temporary piece of wood for his leg."

"He's getting his leg back. Did you know that, Andres?" Mom said.

"No. I hadn't heard. But I'm glad. It just doesn't look good for the priest to go around using a table leg. Why didn't the bishop give him some money?"

"That would be church money," Dad said, "and the bishop says that you can't use church money on the priests . . . It's all got to come from the bingo."

Mother looked at me suspiciously. "What were you doing talking to Father Rodriquez?"

"I have a man in jail that he needed to go see and I asked him if he would and he agreed. Are you satisfied?"

"I was just worried . . . Maybe you were in trouble and needed a priest."

"No . . . . I'm not in trouble."

"It's interesting," Mom said, looking down at the floor and thinking. "I mean, how many years has it been here and no one ever knew about it."

"Oh, how many times my father would talk about it. It was his dream that the shroud should go on forever." Aunt Victoria said.

"It doesn't look like it's going to," I said.

"You," my father said looking at Victoria angrily, picking up the last piece and putting it in a box, "you were the one that brought it to Houston from San Diego and didn't tell anyone."

Victoria looked at him and said, "Me?"

"Yes . . . you. You never told us. Your father gave it to you and you never told us."

Victoria looked at Mother, offended. "What is he saying? I never in my life saw the shroud."

Mother gave Dad a stern look. "Pick up the box and let's go inside," she told him. "Don't be accusing anyone of anything. If Victoria says she didn't bring it, she didn't bring it."

"Well then, who brought it?" my father asked. "That's what I want to know." He had picked up the box and was waiting for the women to begin walking toward the house. He was looking at where the leaning walls used to be. Reflectively, he said to me, "Andres, the shroud must have been in the roof joists for it to have fallen and spread where it did. It could not have fallen from the walls. In that case it would have fallen over something else. It would not have been this perfectly in place."

"Are you sure you got it all?" Mom asked him. "This has got to be all of it."

"That's all . . . I think," Dad replied. He sighed comfortably. "Now the task is to put it together. Come on Andres," he said grabbing me by the arm, "let's go inside . . . ."

Mom was walking ahead, guiding Aunt Victoria. She turned back to face me and asked, "Did you bring your clothes?"

Dad put his arm around me as he carried the box, "Sure, he brought his stuff with him . . . didn't you, Andres?"

"Yes, sir . . . I've got all my stuff. Let me go to the car and bring it in."

"No, Andres," Dad stopped me. "First things first. You've got to see how much I've done."

"Andres," Mom said, "how is poor Rene taking all of this? I'm sure she's very sad."

"I've talked to her every day. She wants me back."

"And little Andres?" she asked.

"Yes," Dad said, "how about little Andres?"

"I think he's taking it very hard. That's what Rene says. I haven't talked to him."

"You left without talking to him?" Aunt Victoria asked, feeling for the first step up to the kitchen door.

My father squeezed my arm and said, "You should have said something to him before you left . . . told him how much you loved him. He's feeling bad . . . I'm sure."

Mom looked back at me as she helped Victoria up the stairs. "I can imagine," she said. "Poor child. Tomorrow I'll call him and see if he can come over for some tortillas."

"If she wants you back, she'll get you back," Aunt Victoria said. "Remember that a woman thinks with her *panocha*."

The shroud was large, much larger than Frankie's bed and our father had placed the central pieces that he had meticulously scraped off the garage floor on the bed and the rest he had scattered throughout the floor. "What do you think?" he asked me as all of us stepped cautiously around the charred pieces. I stood at the foot of the bed and studied the center portion of the shroud. Although he had carefully moved it piece by piece into Frankie's room, he had failed to reproduce the true image on the Shroud: General Santa Anna on horseback, the image that our great-great-grandfather, Captain Agustin Garcia, had captured when he had wrapped the General with his white sheet to keep him warm. Astonished at what he had done, that the image not only of the general but of his great horse had been reproduced so perfectly on the white sheet, Captain Agustin Garcia vowed to keep the cloth forever in the family, as if keeping it intact would give the general, his mentor, everlasting life. The Shroud had become a rallying cry when Captain Agustin Garcia had unfurled it at the Battle of Tamaulipas as he led the victory charge against a superior American force. But here it was on Frankie's bed, the Shroud of Tamaulipas, its image distorted, looking more like an inverted open flower without a stem than the image of the famous general on horseback. Not even the much talked about but inexplicable halo surrounding the image was clear. Distraughtly, my father said, "To find a family treasure like this and not be able to make heads or tails out of it is very depressing."

"I told you," Aunt Victoria said, "that that is why the spider does not pee. You know things are not right when the honeysuckle blooms in December. Now just wait for the locusts to emerge, the locusts that do not sing."

"There are no locusts in Houston," our father informed her.

"Things just aren't right," my mother agreed.

Every day Father would ask Victoria about the shroud as he tried in vain to recreate its image, but it was useless to ask Aunt Victoria. Her recollection of things was becoming so distorted that she imagined herself as having been married six times and having had many lovers, despite her father's objections, and she came to believe that she had many illigitimate children scattered throughout Texas. She sat at the kitchen table wondering what her children's names had been, drinking coffee, eating saltines covered with white margarine and describing her life as she would have wanted it, not as she had lived it. As time went by, whenever the Shroud of Tamaulipas was mentioned to her, she smiled and said that it was not true, that the shroud did not exist.

"You say that, Victoria," my father would argue needlessly, "because you were told to say that by your father. He gave you the shroud so that my father would not have it. He trusted you with it more than he trusted your brothers."

"You'll never get me to admit anything," she said.

We removed the shroud from the bed by carefully picking up the woolen quilt underneath it. This was the way it was moved daily while I slept there in Frankie's old room. During the day my father would sit by the bed and try to re-arrange the image on the shroud in order to make some sense of it. Aunt Victoria would have nothing to do with it, although she may have had at one time the key to unlocking its mystery. As I lay in Frankie's bed at night trying desperately to sleep without the help of alcohol, I could still feel the presence of the inexplicable aura that the shroud would leave behind, saturating me to the bone, as the nuns had done to Dolores, with the feeling of remorse.

Several days after I had moved in, Louie and Donna Marie and Clete and his wife came for me and we drove to the drop point to pick up the hostaged dog.

We arrived at the east side address under a full moon and a cold night. Louie and I got out of the car and knocked on the door of the pre-arranged house. An illegal answered and eyed us suspiciously until he understood who we were. The dog was not there, but at another address, which he gave us after we paid him half the money. At the other address we could see through the door that the dog was asleep under the table, a bowl of dry dog food partially eaten in front of his nose. Louie handed over the rest of the money to the woman that had been calling and she sucked on her lips making a funny bird-like noise and the unfaithful dog came to her and kissed her hand.

I had never seen a more loving reunion as the one between Clete and his dog, not even the night that Willie came home from the war. When Thor saw Clete he remembered who Clete was and he began to cry and almost act out his recent dilemma. It would not have surprised me if he had talked. Clete, on the other hand was weeping and overcome with joy so much so that he embraced his dog in every conceivable way, starting from the head and kissing his way to the tail, showing so much emotion that his wife looked at us, embarrassed that he would love a dog more than his beautiful wife. At their house we went in for drinks to celebrate the return of the dog, who was now seemingly pasted to the side of his master and went with him everywhere his master went, even to the point of interfering with the blind man's walk rather than helping him.

"Thor's not very faithful," Louie said, trying to be unpleasant. "Hell, he was asleep under the table and when the woman called him, he went over and kissed her hand. Right Andy?"

"That's right. Louie's telling the truth."

Clete looked up to the ceiling, shaking his sightless head in disbelief. "Here boy," he said to the dog, taking out a biscuit from his pocket and letting the dog sniff it.

Pandora was adamant. "Clete," she scolded, "don't reward him. Look at all the trouble he's caused. He ain't worth the biscuit."

An angry and hurt Clete said, "I ain't rewarding him. I'm feeling for his head so I can kick him in the ass."

In the kitchen Pandora caught me alone and confessed that she had called me one day and thanked me for covering up for her when I had talked to Clete. She wanted to tell me how much she appreciated what I was doing for her husband. She only had fifty and needed two hunded dollars to pay Louie for the dog. Could I lend her the money? Before I could answer, Clete walked in with his punished dog and, as if to demean Clete, she grabbed me and kissed me for the longest time as the unsuspecting Clete stumbled over the dog, feeling his way for a cup and saucer.

"Goddamit, Thor," Clete shouted, shaking his head at the dog slowly like a turtle. "You've forgotten your training. Why are you so aggressive? You're acting like those Mexicans."

The dog seeing what Pandora had done to me, gave me an embarrassed glance, telling me that this was old hat, but still outside his sense of morals, and I took two bills out of my wallet and gave them to her.

She gleefully kissed me again, this time rolling her very long tongue inside my mouth and holding me very close while Clete burned his hand on the coffee pot and the dog howled at his master's pain.

CHAPTER 21

Aunt Victoria looked down at the cracker crumbs smeared with white margarine that had fallen on the table as mother combed her hair. She swept them off with her hand onto the floor. "There's something to this," she said, pursing her thin lips. "There's something to this sesquicentennial."

"What are you talking about?" my mother asked her, taking the long hair and beginning the tedious process of separating it into strands before braiding it. "We ought to cut your hair," mother said to her.

Victoria looked back at her and said, "You couldn't do it in a million years. In San Diego only the prostitutes wore their hair short."

Mother said, "But Victoria, that was so long ago. It's not true today. We live in different times. Lot's of good women wear their hair short."

Victoria said, "I'm astounded. Can you imagine, Clementina, that the honeysuckle bloomed in December and January and now February? It would have been worth the trip to San Diego to see the blooms. It would have been worth it to see if the locusts emerged and did not sing . . . Remember what's his name? The mayor and how important he thought he was? But that couldn't happen anymore, could it? Could it be this sesqui . . . thing?"

"We don't go back to San Diego anymore. There's no one there."

"And to see if Lothario is still alive after all these years. . . Remember that he fell off the roof while repairing it one afternoon and fell on top of the blooming pomegranates. He was never the same after that."

"Who was that?"

"Don Lothario. My lover."

"Lothario died."

"When?"

My father came in from Frankie's room having to rest his eyes. "Who was her lover?" he asked, looking for a cup and saucer.

"Don Lothario, she says," Mother replied. "She expects him to be Alive . . . How are you doing?"

My father shook his head and sat down wearily. "Nothing," he murmured as he blew on his coffee. "It is as if the Gods are laughing at me. Why have me find it if I can't put it together?"

"Remember that you found it burned," Mother said.

"And that the spider never pees," Victoria added.

The electrical shock sent through me was so explosively strong that I felt it heat the marrow of my bones. I was so repulsed that I felt like jumping off the table, but I couldn't. The doctor had strapped me down and he was happily explaining that it was not the voltage that was making me jump and twist my body, that it was the amperage. He stepped up the current as I watched him. I was trying to yell to him to stop, but I was gagged with a black rubber rod between my teeth. I wanted to scream that I would gladly suffer the mental problems associated with seeing the ghosts of my fore fathers than to go through another one of the shocks, when he yelled, "All clear!" and the parrot, who had been tightening one of the straps with his beak and four toes, jumped out of the way as my doctor hit me with the higher electrical force once more. My back sprung like a loaded bow, arching my rigid body between two points on the table, so that only the back of my head and my heels were touching for the longest time. "Now, now," he said, "it's not that bad. It's not going to kill you. I calibrate this little machine on the parrot every morning and look at him. Spry as a young chicken . . . . Relax. This is meant to rejuvenate you. We're only trying to make you realize what your problem is. And as long as you don't come up with the correct answer, we're going to have to continue our little frying game." And as he was saying that, he threw the switch and squirmed out the words that I could barely hear: "This is the last one . . . . I promise," he said.

He left me exhausted and breathing like a man with half a lung. The polarity of my mind had been changed so that I felt as though I had no mind at all, that I was in a vacuum with my memory lost. I felt nothing, knew nothing. Every single fact that had been stored in my mind was gone. It was only after I left the building and drove back and saw the airy ghosts of all my antecedents marching toward me on Travis Street that I realized who I was. I could see plainly my great-great-grandfather and my great-grandfather and my grandfather carrying with him the sack of meat when he died at the steps of the meat market. Along with them came the Generalisimo himself, and his trusted staff and commanders. Behind them limped the ever happy Colonel Fernandez still nursing the artillery wound and carrying the perfectly intact Shroud of Tamaulipas with its image and inexplicable halo as clear and circular as the eye of a hunting bird. And behind Fernandez was David Cruz, the former Davey Crockett, marching with his beloved children: Gumecindo, Gonzalo, Gabriel, Marta and Isabel. My mind exploded once again, an after-shock of the electrical impulse that had been stored somewhere in the recesses of both hemispheres and, just as easily as the group had appeared, they faded down the rained-on busy street, the sound of their drum and bugle growing more distant with every step. Slowly I regained my polarity; magnetic north was north once more and that was where my soul was pointing.

"You look like you've seen a ghost," Maybelline remarked as I staggered into the office. "Do you want a glass of water?"

I nodded that I did and barely made it into my office.

"Why do you torture yourself so?" Maybelline wanted to know, handing me the glass. "You've been through this ten times already. Stop it."

"You're right," I said as I drank the water and handed her the glass. "That's the end of that. He really let me have it today. He showed me no mercy. I won't go through that again."

"Good for you, Andy," she said, "you're not even a mental case. Who told you you were a mental case?"

"I just thought it was common knowledge."

"That's not true. No one I ever knew ever said that you needed shock treatments. Seeing the psychiatrist is all right. Dr. Finkelburg or whatever his name is said you needed a psychiatrist, but not shock. All these things are not for you, Andy. Even the parrot that you've told me about seems a little crazy. I mean, what psychiatrist would have a parrot as a consultant? It just doesn't stand to reason. Are you just trying to save money or what?"

I felt better already, having replenished the water that I had lost to the heat of the electrical charge. I was more lucid, ready to go to work.

Maybelline shook her head. "Just look at this," she said, handing over the telephone messages. "The judge says that he is going to set an early trial date to coincide with the Battle of San Jacinto. It could be because the district attorney is working very hard on a first degree murder conviction for the sesquicentennial. The judge denies the whole thing. But I bet you that's what they want."

"Did we get the toxicology report?"

"Yes, sir," she answered and sorted it out from among the many papers she held in her hand. I opened the envelope and read it.

"Has Alfredo called?" I asked her.

"Yes."

"Did Father Rodriguez ever get to see him? I mean, it's been at least two months."

"Yes, Father Rodriguez finally saw him yesterday. You know that the good Father doesn't know when one month changes into the next one. The Father apologized. He was lost. But Alfredo is very depressed. Father Rodriguez was so happy to see him and yet so confused with the act of contrition that he made Alfredo confess to things he didn't even do. Now Alfredo feels bad because he didn't do them and he's already been forgiven. The priest would not take a second confession because he says he doesn't know which one to believe, which one to pray for. Alfredo's still saying rosaries for his penance. He wants you to call him. He can receive a phone call from you. Here's the number . . . ."

"Rene called to tell you that she loves you more now than ever and that yesterday has been two months since you've left and everyday she misses you terribly. Junior is wetting the bed. They both need you very much. Oh, and Marie has moved out again, but they parted as friends . . . And oh, this is the psychiatrist. He called to let me know that you left in bad shape and to watch out for you, that if you were not here in one hour, to call back so that he could send the parrot flying out in the streets to locate you." That note she crumpled and threw away. "Louie called and said that he is almost sure that he and Donna Marie are going to Hollywood. Clete's wife, whoever that is, what's her name . . .?"

"Pandora," I answered quickly as my heart raced at the sound of her name.

"Well, she called to say how much she enjoyed having you over the other night and she knows of only one way that she can repay you . . . whatever that means."

"Is that all?"

"No. This sounds like trouble, but Dolores called and said she needed to talk to you desperately."

"Did she say what she wanted? Is she in trouble?"

"No. All she said was that she needed to see you. But if you ask me, I wouldn't go."

"Why?"

"Because I feel that you still love her very much and that she still loves you very much and nothing good is going to come of any meeting that you two are going to have. Why fan the flames?"

"Because it's there," I said, my heart continuing to race for Dolores now.

"That's not a good enough excuse, Andy. She's married. You could ruin her life, you know. What if her husband knew?"

"Since when are you giving advice to the love-lorn? Aren't you the one."

"I've never . . ."

"Never what? How about Las Vegas? Since Las Vegas you've been acting like a teenager. Your acting younger than Josie."

"Josie is not a teenager."

"Your acting younger than Josie anyway."

"I'm not married. You are. Dolores is. I have a right to have some fun."

"What about me?"

"Not like that you don't. You could ruin Dolores' marriage."

"Don't worry so much. I might not go."

"Good."

"Didn't Sol call?"

"Yes, sir. Here's the number," she said and walked out as I dialed Sol.

I had to go through all the formalities of a huge law practice before I spoke to Sol. I went through the switch-board, the general secretary, Sol's division's secretary and finally Sol's secretary and finally got to Sol.

"Just thought I would give you the latest," Sol told me.

"About the trial?"

"Yes. Have you heard?"

"No."

"Well, they've got some pretty big guns after you on this trial. The governor has personally donated one hundred dollars to the Federation of Texas District Attorneys for the demonstrations."

"There will be demonstrations, then . . . It's definite?"

"Yes. Just like I told you before. They're collecting money throughout the state to pay for the demonstrators. They'll have signs made and all that . . . sandwiches and cold drinks . . . . You know what's odd?"

"Tell me."

"Even the LULACS are donating money."

"I don't believe it."

"You'd better. I have it right here in front of me. I've got the list . . . State LULACS, twenty-five dollars."

"They don't know what they're doing. They just do what the governor tells them to do. It's sad to hear. Who else has donated?"

"Let's see . . . the mayor, of course."

"Of course."

"The district attorney and all his office, plus the county attorney and his office, the Association of Justices of the Peace, the Texas Rangers, the Highway Patrol, the Texas Association of Sheriffs, Texas Cattle Raisers Association, the King Ranch, Neiman Marcus . . . ."

"No churches?"

"No . . . not yet. But I hear that they're working on it. You know that the Methodists and the Baptists are going to jump on the bandwagon if someone is going to get punished."

"Well," I said, "thanks for calling and I appreciate the inside information. Keep me informed."

"Sure thing," he said.

Just thinking that Dolores had called and that she might love me was enough to revive the hopes that had been pacing my mind for the last months since I had left Rene. I had felt since the barbecue that Dolores was once again the woman for me, except that the serpentine nuns had saturated her with the expectations of painless hopes and false ideas. And now in her mature years she could still not undress in front of her husband as she had not been able to do in front of me and she had been destined like a burrowing animal to make love in the dark and in the cave-like hole made by the cover of the woolen blanket and without allowing a touch to her most private part.

But was there hope for her today? Had she called to let me know that finally she was liberated and wanted to make love in the sunlight on the sheet under the hackberry, that she was willing once more to show me out of her shorts the beautifully gleaming electrostatic pubic hairs, that she wanted to open her mysterious part wide to show me the inside as Rene had unashamedly done so many times?

I decided to take one last chance and to go see her.

"I don't know what to say," she blushed, keeping her legs crossed at her ankles as the nuns had taught her so many years ago, having been told before the mass that if she crossed her legs at the knee, she might show her panties and besides that, it was a sin to cross your legs in church. "I don't know why I called. It was an impulsive thing to do, I guess. Listen, you've got to forgive me. I just lost my mind. You see, I've been so worried about you. And anyway, I've done some checking of my own and your psychiatrist isn't even in the Yellow Pages. He's not even listed in the registry for the United States."

"He's in the Yellow Pages," I said. "Josie showed it to me."

"I couldn't find it."

"Well, you know our Yellow Pages. It all depends. Did you check the consumer book? The person to person book? The business to business book? The consumer to business book? The consumer to doctor book? . . . You know the goddam phone company. Which one?"

"I don't care, Andy. I couldn't find it with all the doctors names."

"It's there. His name is different when it's Anglicized."

"It's under Johnny Sanchez."

"I'd rather you didn't go to any psychiatrist, really. You know what I mean? It doesn't sound good and you really don't have all that many problems, do you?"

"Not really, not enough to fry for. I'm all right now. I don't think I need any more of those treatments. I'd rather be a little bit on the crazy side, anyway, like my brothers and sisters."

"Good! Now all you have to do is behave yourself and you'll be all right." She gave out a little triumphant laugh like a small teasing child that had convinced everyone to agree with her. "You've got to quit worrying me so much, Andy."

"Why should you care?"

She squirmed around her crossed ankles, moving her buttocks up to the edge of the sofa. "This is really hard for me to say. . . You know I still love you," she said. "I've always loved you . . . . Since you were a little kid."

"And your husband?"

"Oh, I love him too, but in a different way. I just love you that's all."

"I love you too, Dolores, but I don't want to play any parochial school games anymore." I had to talk in euphemisms to keep from offending her. "Do you love me sexually?"

She blushed again. "I don't know," she said. "That, I've never been able to figure out."

And with that I got up from my chair and walked to her and took her gently into my arms and kissed her passionately. I picked her up slowly, not wanting to disturb her thoughts and carried her into her darkened bedroom with the black walls and placed her in the middle of her bed. She lay motionless wishing for happiness this once, her eyes closed with her dark legs apart. I slid my hand up her thigh and at the same time tried to raise her skirt up to her panties, but she began to fight me and, when I finally was able to pull her panties down from under her skirt, she began to kick in earnest as she had done on our wedding night at the motel in Galveston. She pleaded for me to let her go, but it was too late for me. I had to find out once and for all if she had changed. As I touched her wet most intimate of parts, she screamed a scream that depolarized my hemispheres, made my soul point south once more and brought visions of parrots flying between my eyes and she ran down the hallway with her underwear around her knees as she had done in Galveston when all the old people from Minnesota had inquired if we were both doing all right, and she continued her delirious run through the darkened verandas as if she were being chased by the senior partner that had turned suddenly away at the sound of her scream and had jumped from the terrace of the Warwick Hotel taking his wife along with him in his fall, both landing on the pruned ligustrums.

That night the house burned down.

CHAPTER 22

The firemen were astonished that we had been able to save ourselves from the fire much less save the old woolen quilt which my father held onto as we saw the last bird fly off the fiery gables and the last flaming timber crash to the ground. My mother and Aunt Victoria wept as the old house fell. "What memories go with it," my mother cried as the firemen poured water unnecessarily on the long gone house. The memory of the day we all walked home crying when the school would not give Connie the award for being the smartest student in school because she was a Mexican greaser and the Anglo parents had made the principal cancel the award for that year or until an Anglo won. The day when Willie drove up weeping and beating on the walls to tell our parents that Chris, his son who had always wanted to be an attorney like his uncle Andy, had been killed in Vietnam. The night when our quietly tubercular brother Frankie, who never belonged anywhere in the family, killed himself in his bedroom because he could not stand the pain of living among diverging people. Our father's beer drinking friends throwing parts of his skull and brains onto the flaming barrel full of newspapers under the hackberry. Frankie dead in the same bedroom where I could still feel the prescence in my aching bones of the rambling ghosts of my antecedents. The college days when I had been ashamed to show my friends where I lived and what I ate and what my parents looked like and how they spoke and how they lived, not realizing it at the time, but when I joined them I saw that they shared equal shame, that the Anglos were also ashamed of who they were and who their parents were and how they lived and how they spoke. And realizing that I had lost in the two cultures the ability to be normal. And that a goddam crazy man and his parrot had been right.

1985 in Texas would be remembered as the year that the honey-suckle bloomed in December and the year that Christmas was almost forgotten because of the preoccupation with the upcoming Texas Sesquicentennial. Had it not been for the Jews, there would not have been Christmas. 1986, the Sesquicentennial Year, would be remembered as the year of the oil crisis, God's punishment of Texas for the excesses of the Sesquicentennial. For every Sesquicentennial Minute, for every Sesquicentennial Moment, for every barbecue in which the local Hispanics had to dress ashamedly in loose white clothing to lose again and again in the re-enactment of the battles of the revolution, there was a fall in the price of a barrel of oil. Never did the governor nor the legislature realize that the more they tried to fix things, the more God raised the ante. Everyone associated with the oil business lost two-thirds of his fortune. Oil-fed couples were jumping off the terrace of the Warwick Hotel in Houston and the Adolphus in Dallas and the Menger in San Antonio, without having heard the screams of nun-fed girls, landing on the freshly pruned ligustrums, hardly injuring themselves.

"You'll never believe what happened," Mother said, hurriedly leading Aunt Victoria inside as they returned from Sunday Mass. Mother took Victoria and sat her in the breakfast room. "It was something that couldn't be believed." Even the aged Victoria shook her head. They had been picked up and delivered by Imelda, the president of the Altar Society. We were living with Willie and Angie now that the house had burned down.

"What happened?" Father asked as we all sat around the table.

"Well," Mother said, wiping the perspiration from her brow and looking at Victoria, "Father Rodriguez was not to be believed this morning. The mass began as usual and then when he got to the sermon, he brought out the wire cage with the bingo balls and he plugged it in and the balls started to float in the air. 'For the sermon,' he said, 'we will have the last Bingo game of all time,' and he started to pick at the floating balls and he screamed the letters and the numbers . . . B . . . 3. I . . . 15. G . . . 42. N . . . 31 . . . ."

Aunt Victoria nodded her head as she listened to the numbers. "I won," she whispered so as not to interrupt our mother.

"That's nothing. Everyone won," mother said. "He went through all the numbers and everyone won. Then he said that he was leaving and he left us with one thought: That we should love God with all our heart and soul and forget about the church and the bingos and the rest. After that he walked out and forgot about the mass. Father Diaz came in, apologized, and finished the mass."

"That is hard to believe," Father said. "But in a way it's funny."

"Father Diaz looked good with his new leg," Victoria informed us.

"Oh, Victoria," Mother scolded her, "you would notice at a time like that. That's the old leg anyway. The one the bank took away from him."

Victoria challenged her. "No it's not. They say that this one has a spring at the knee to give him more of a boost when he walks."

"How would he know if he needs a boost or not?" Mother said. "He's only interested in money. Besides, he's so small."

"Now, Mother," Father said, "don't be so quick to condemn."

"To think," Mother said, "that Father Rodriquez would come to this."

"Don't condemn him," Father responded. "He's a good and honorable man that is sick. His mind has left him . . . poor man."

313

Lionel G. Garcia

Willie said, "A better man never walked this earth."

"Amen," my Father answered and we all nodded our head in agreement.

As Maybelline had predicted, the trial was set for April 21, the date of the Battle of San Jacinto. There was so much publicity that the District Attorney was trying the case himself with the help of two of his assistants. I was at the office early that morning and getting ready to walk the short distance to the courthouse. According to Maybelline, everything was set. And if Maybelline said that we were ready, that meant that we had done all the preparation that was needed. The veterinary pathologist had arrived from College Station the night before and had called again this morning to tell Maybelline that he was on his way from the hotel to eat breakfast before walking to the courthouse.

Outside the courthouse I encountered some fifty professional demonstrators, drinking coffee and eating donuts, all hired by the Federation of District Attorneys of the State of Texas, each carrying a professionally done sign that urged the court to "Kill the Mass Murderer" and "Murder the Mexican." One sign explained that "It Was About Time The Mexicans Were Killed For Killing Mexicans." "Gomez Has To Go," another sign read. There were several signs written in Spanish. I was able to read only two as I hurried past the angry threatening crowd. One said, "Alfredo No Vale Un Pedo." And finally the worst of all insults in the Spanish language, "Chingue Su Madre Alfredo." I doubted very seriously that the District Attorneys of Texas knew that this sign was being paraded up and down the sidewalks of downtown Houston. I looked up to the trees and the thousands of pigeons that normally inhabited the live-oaks and defecated on the side-walks had departed because there was enough chicken-shit on the side-walks already. The television crews were there to record the event. All of them tried for an interview, but I declined. They complained that the district attorney had given them five minutes. "But I'm not eternally running for office," I reminded them. "I can make a living practicing law."

Inside I recognized Dr. Nicely from the description he had given Maybelline. He was at the far corner of the hall next to the water fountain. He looked as amiable as he sounded over the telephone. I spoke briefly with him and told him to stay outside the courtroom. I would have him paged when I needed him, if indeed I would need him.

"Do we need to go over anything?" he asked.

"Not really," I told him. "If I call you, all I want you to do is to answer the questions truthfully, as we have done on the telephone, and everything will work out."

314

The trial lasted one day, since the District Attorney only had two witnesses: the policemen that had arrived at the scene of the crime. They were asked to describe it for the the jury. Gruesome pictures were shown all around. That took almost all morning long. After that testimony a confession was introduced as evidence and Judge Medina asked if I was going to object and I replied no. At first it surprised me that Alfredo had confessed to the murders and had signed the confession without telling me about it, but then I realized that, being a Mexican, he was going to admit that he had committed the crime. He was not going to use the law to his advantage. He was too much of a man for that. The prosecution rested its case.

Judge Medina looked down at me from behind his half-glasses and asked if the defense was ready. "Yes, your Honor," I replied. I stood up and asked Judge Medina if anyone had bothered to check the defendant's testicles. The judge and the district attorney were taken by surprise. The jury snickered, as did the crowded courtroom when the judge asked me and the district attorney to the bench. As we approached, Judge Medina rapped his gavel and sternly admonished the crowd that he would not tolerate any misbehavior in his courtroom. As I stood before the judge, he and the district attorney asked me in hushed tones what I had in mind. No one had checked the defendant's testicles and I demanded that they be checked, because the real reason behind this crime had been the cruelty shown toward Alfredo by his wife and her parents. I explained to the judge and the district attorney that, in their hatred for him, his wife and in-laws had systematically cuckolded him and then, to make sure that the wife did not get pregnant from him, had made him soak his testicles in the hot water drench made from the pomegranate root, and everyone that knew folk medicine knew that the extract from the pomegranate root was a sclerosing agent that sterilized the male and made his testicles indurated, as hard as concrete and as lifeless. The defendant was taken by the bailiff to be examined by the jail doctor and, further more, in the presence of the jail doctor he was to produce a semen sample. While we waited I called to the stand Dr. Nicely, the veterinary pathologist from Texas A&M University, renowned for his work with the Rockefeller Foundation in helping third world Latin American countries in fighting animal diseases.

"Dr. Nicely," I asked, "you have written extensively on the use of chemical castration among the Indians of Mexico, Peru, Brazil, et cetera?"

"Yes, I have," the good doctor replied.

"Did you write these articles and these toxicolgy reports?" I handed the papers to him and he examined them.

"Yes, I did," he replied.

"You're an expert on chemical castration?"

"Yes, I am. I didn't set out to be one, but in my work with the indigenous people of Latin America through the Rockefeller Foundation, I began to study the different forms of veterinary medicine that they practice."

"How long have you been a consultant to the Rockefeller Foundation?"

"Twenty-one years."

"I would like to enter these documents as evidence, your Honor," I said, and Judge Medina checked them out, as did the skeptical district attorney.

"What did you find about chemical castration, Dr. Nicely?"

"In all Indian cultures, the main form of chemical castration for animals and man is the use of hot water drenches made from the root of the pomegranate."

"Thank you for your time, doctor," I said. "I have no further questions."

The district attorney was dumbfounded. He had no questions. He asked for a short recess so that we could talk things over in the judge's chambers.

"What in the shit are you up to?" The district attorney wanted to know.

"I'm prepared to go to the Supreme Court again with this one," I said. "This is a case where a very proud man has been castrated by his wife and her parents. Do you two know," I said to him and the judge, "that the Muslims believe that if they don't take good testicles with them when they die, that they cannot be admitted into paradise? Do you know how much like the Muslims the Mexicans are? Do you understand that I am prepared to show that they mocked him by taking him to the Virgin of San Juan and had him go on his knees from the front steps to the altar, praying rosaries so that he could father a child, when they knew all the time that he had been castrated? . . . And that they stayed in the car drinking cokes while he prayed?"

Judge Medina looked at the district attorney. He asked, "What do you think, Joe?"

The district attorney looked at both of us and said, "Judge, you know that there's a lot riding on this one . . . We still haven't heard from the jail doctor, Andy. You may not have a case, after all. Why should I give in right now?"

"Because you and all your friends are trying the wrong case," I said. "How can you ask for murder one when there was no premeditation? He didn't plan to kill anyone. He goes to the beer joint to have a good time and he overhears some men talking. He recognizes himself as the one being laughed at. He runs home and kills his wife and his in-laws. That's it. Murder two at the most . . . You know that's the law, Judge Medina. You know very well that whatever is done here that doesn't satisfy me will be appealed and that I'll win the appeal. You'll be reversed and embarrassed."

Judge Medina fidgeted in his chair, but did not answer.

"We'll see, smart-ass," the district attorney answered.

In one hour the doctor was testifying under oath that Alfredo Gomez was sterile and his testicles were as hard and lumpy as walnuts. The district attorney argued that this could have been a pre-existing condition. I called Alfredo Gomez to the stand. Very carefully, using his affected stilted English, he was able to repeat the story as he had told it to me that morning in the traffic jam on the freeway. He was very embarrassed. He gleefully remembered, though, that he had fathered several children in Mexico and in Houston while his wife was in Mexico, prior to the pomegranate drench. The children could be produced, if the court wanted them. Judge Medina knew that all I had to do was tell Maybelline to call Louie and Willie and they could round up fifteen or twenty women and their illigitimate children that would testify that Alfredo Gomez was their father. The judge recessed the trial and we met in his office once more. I threatened to call the women to the stand that Maybelline had lined up. We reached a compromise. We got ninety-nine years for murder which in Texas meant that he could be free in two years under shock probation.

But things are not simple in this life. Alfredo Gomez commited suicide by hanging himself from his bed by a shoelace in Huntsville shortly after his arrival. Pandora and I had gone to see him that first week, to visit to make sure that he was comfortable. Instead we found him very depressed, bothered by every little thing—the sound of the emerging locusts at night, the uncommonly sweet smell of the honeysuckle, the errant bees that clung to the bars in his cell, the rush of the leaves outside his window, the noise of every breath that he took, the excessive rust on his suffocating bars. Even the oiliness of the worn boards of the floor of the central prison offended him, he said. And at night it frightened him because he could feel the white grass growing without sun under his cell. He pleaded with me not to let his parents know what had happened to him. For some reason he erroneously thought that a picture of his small rock-like testicles had been on the front page of the Houston papers and he believed that the whole world knew of his shameful impotency. After his death I sent Alfredo's money and a short letter to his parents explaining what had happened to him and where the body was buried. His father wrote to me to thank me for what I had done for his son. At the end he had written, "What a waste of a life."

Shortly afterwards I received a letter in my office addressed from a small motel in Tuscon, Arizona, the letter heavy with black ink and scribbled by an almost illegible hand. I was surprised that the letter, addressed as poorly as it was, had been able to reach me. I opened it last. It was from Dr. Juan Antonio Garcia-Sanchez, but I suspected that the handwriting was the parrot's. He excused himself for not telling me sooner, but he and the parrot had left Texas and were on their way to California with their little electrical machine. He had grown tired of the picayunish mental illnesses in Texas and wanted to die peacefully in the land of the great headache. All psychiatry is an illusion, he wrote, like making elephants disappear. He wished me health and asked me if I had arrived at my answer and, guessing that I had not, that I had been too self-conscious, he dictated to the parrot at the end these words: Bilateral cultural loss equals shame. And he signed the letter himself in his florid style, the name taking up a good deal of space. Underneath the signature was the four-toed print of his feathered associate.

We lived with Willie and Angie for a while, Louie and Donna Marie having gone to Hollywood, and then we moved in with Becky and Al. Connie still did not have a place of her own and Ellie was drinking again, so she was not getting married, not now, at least, that he carried a shotgun under the seat.

One day I decided that enough was enough and I announced that we were moving into my house. So we packed up and settled-in one afternoon when Rene wasn't there and surprised her. She was happy to see us all and junior was happy to have his grandparents living with him. He wanted to get fat on tortillas and Mother told him that she would make tortillas for him night and day. I had not realized how much I had missed them both.

The word from Rene was that Allison had given up her affair with Pete and had run off with the Presbyterian minister who was now selling cars. They were not divorced yet, but they were living together. The elders of the church were having trouble firing the minister and he had asked for sick leave because only a sick person would be doing what he was doing. Allison's husband, Bob, was broken-hearted over her affair and would not give her a divorce. Being Anglo, he wanted her back now more than ever. The minister's wife was suing the church for the minister's salary and for allowing Allison to do volunteer work at the church. John, the engineer, was divorcing Peggy and returning to Long Island. He had found out about Peggy and Matt, the dermatologist, and so had Christine, Matt's wife. Christine, as revenge, was having a series of affairs with several Houston Oilers because they were so gentle. Cathy left Pete because Pete had had an affair with Allison, although Cathy had had affairs for years with Tom and John and Darrell, the dentist. Cathy was now marrying the head of a large realty firm. She had hired Sue, who had quit teaching, and when Sue left Doyle, the stock-broker, in order to find herself, he tried to commit suicide by drinking lye. Doyle did not kill himself, but lost his esophagus and had to spend a long time in the hospital and now had to feed himself through a hole in his flank. Tom, the glue salesman, retired with Mary, his wife, to California. Darrell, the Canadian dentist, had also tried suicide when Cathy announced that she was getting married. The knot on the rope that he used came undone and he managed to tear down the ceiling in his office.

My father took to staying in his room reassembling the Shroud of Tamaulipas while my mother cooked for all of us. His passion for completing the image on the shroud consumed him more and more every day until there were times when he refused to come out to eat. Once, he burst through the door joyfully shouting that he had almost completed the figure of General Santa Anna on his horse, except that he had not been able to reconstruct the right foot. The next day he was back to his preoccupied self, making X's of his fingers. He could not find the pieces that made the foot, that must be stuck together to the pieces of God knows where, and in his melancholy he destroyed the image so that he could begin anew. He was to die without ever completing the image, not to even mention recreating the inexplicable aura surrounding it.

My Aunt Victoria continued to insist that she had been married six times, once to Pancho Villa. Despite that small inconvenience, she remained amazingly lucid through those times, much more so than my father and my mother. She traveled the day with a kerosene lantern, looking throughout the house for the hiding ghost of her irascible father. And to atone for the many heartaches that she had given him, she would cook at night for him, immense meals of boiled offal—intestines, feet, lungs, kidneys, liver, bile, heart, spleen, thymus, lymph glands, urinary bladders, crotch and skinned ears—that she later would fry in her own batter. It would send the family upstairs to seek refuge from the smell; In the morning I would have to cart it off to the city dumps to throw away, food that she delightedly thought her nocturnal father was secretly eating.

One day as she gummed her afternoon snack of coffee and saltines with white margarine, oozing of her smell of fried battered innards, I asked her about the mystery of the shroud and she stared at me unbelievingly and told me that there was no such thing, that there was no shroud except in the minds of the people who believed in it and that all histories are illusory, like mental illnesses and the images of parrots flying between the eyes, and that the inexplicable aura was the insatiable dreamings of a struggling people and that there would be no justice because the knowledge that there was in the world had already been confiscated and ripped inside out.

"As Don Andres said on the night of his death," she murmured, "there is an illusion of a shroud in every family."

12009086   32607

Gar   Garcia, Lionel G.
      A shroud in the
      family